Louis Fagan

The Life of Sir Anthony Panizzi, K. C. B.

Vol. II

Louis Fagan

The Life of Sir Anthony Panizzi, K. C. B.
Vol. II

ISBN/EAN: 9783337151287

Printed in Europe, USA, Canada, Australia, Japan

Cover: Foto ©Raphael Reischuk / pixelio.de

More available books at **www.hansebooks.com**

THE LIFE

OF

SIR ANTHONY PANIZZI, K.C.B.,

LATE PRINCIPAL LIBRARIAN OF THE BRITISH MUSEUM,
SENATOR OF ITALY,
&c., &c.

BY

LOUIS FAGAN,

OF THE DEPARTMENT OF PRINTS AND DRAWINGS, BRITISH MUSEUM.

With an Etching and other Illustrations by the Author.

TWO VOLUMES.

VOL. II.

SECOND EDITION.

London :
REMINGTON & CO., 133, NEW BOND STREET. W.

1880.

CONTENTS.

CHAPTER XVII.

CHAPTER XVIII.

CHAPTER XIX.

CHAPTER XX.

CHAPTER XXI.

CHAPTER XXII.

CHAPTER XXIII.

CHAPTER XXIV.

CHAPTER XXV.

CHAPTER XXVI.

CHAPTER XXVII.

CHAPTER XXVIII.

ILLUSTRATIONS TO VOL. II.

CHAPTER XIV.

Retirement of Sir H. Ellis—Selection of Principal Librarian—Securities—Mr. John Kenyon—Appointment—Proceedings in the House of Commons.

A MOST important phase in the life of Panizzi has now to be entered upon ; but, before reciting the facts of the case, we must premise that the high position then within his grasp was not obtained without some considerable personal pain and heartburning, owing to the ungenerous statements of the press, to which more particular allusion will presently be made.

In the year 1856, Sir Henry Ellis had attained his seventy-ninth year ; it is not, therefore, a matter of surprise that his failing energies were inadequate to the unceasing and important duties which of necessity were entailed upon him as the head of the British Museum ; indeed, he must himself have felt the necessity of withdrawing from so responsible a post. He was, however, anticipated (had such an idea ever seriously occurred to him) in his intention by a private request, delicately referred to him, and with the following liberal terms attached. The understanding was that he should voluntarily resign, and should receive the full amount of his salary and emoluments as a superannuation allowance. Complying with this offer, he accordingly tendered his resignation, and, on

B

the 9th of February, 1856, the Trustees passed a resolution thanking him for his long services. No
sooner had this decision been made public than a
certain newspaper, having received information of his
probable successor, was guilty of publishing the annexed ungenerous paragraph, eminently calculated to
wound, as it did, the susceptible feelings of Panizzi :—

"February 25th, 1856.

"We understand that Sir Henry Ellis has resigned the
situation of Principal Librarian. The majority of persons employed in that Institution, and of the public who frequent it,
would be delighted at an event that ought to have occurred
many years ago, if it were not that an extraordinary influence
is likely to obtain the appointment for a foreigner. It is of
the highest importance that this affront to British genius and
character be avoided, and that the right man be put in the
right place. When the Marquis of Lansdowne, from the best
motives, made the previous unfortunate selection, there was a
regulator that no longer exists ; the vigilant interference of
the lamented Joseph Hume often prevented official tyranny
and petty vexation."

In accordance with the Act of Parliament 26 Geo.
II. cap. 22, the Principal Librarian of the British
Museum is selected by the Sovereign from two persons recommended by the Archbishop of Canterbury,
the Lord Chancellor, and the Speaker of the House
of Commons, who are (as has already been remarked)
the "Principal Trustees."

Up to the year 1850, it will be remembered that the
offices of Principal Librarian and of Secretary were distinct appointments. The Secretary, whose duties and
position were at first simply clerical, gradually assumed such importance that, though still nominally

second to the Principal Librarian, he was practically the Chief Officer of the Museum, not always acting in unison with his superior in rank ; it was found, therefore, to be more desirable for the welfare of the Museum, as well as more economical that the two offices should be blended, and they were united in the person of Sir Henry Ellis.

In reference to this subject we invite the attention of our readers to the following letter from that gentleman :—

"British Museum,

February 14th, 1856.

"My dear Panizzi,

You seem to doubt whether, in the event of my resignation of office, you would be likely to succeed me in it. I cannot help thinking that you must be mistaken, although I have certainly heard that a candidate or two are either in the field, or intending to apply when the resignation becomes a reality. At the same time I must tell you I have heard no names.

I think it quite impossible that anybody who has not had experience in the Institution should be appointed.

Yours is, most unquestionably, the portion of the Museum which is not only the largest, but the most useful and extensive for public instruction ; the time of life, the toil, and the power of mind which you have brought to bear upon it and upon its improvement convince me that no stranger, especially without the knowledge which the experience of a quarter of a century has given you in the view of general management of the place, ought to be allowed to compete with you on this occasion.

I myself felt all which you now feel in 1827, at the time my predecessor was approaching his end. I had aided him with all my power for some years ; and I can show you various letters which are still precious to me, expressing his continuous gratitude.

B2

A week or two before he died he said to me, ' Well, Sir, I
shall soon depart, and you will be my successor.'   I said, ' O !
my dear Sir, I doubt.'   He raised his voice and said, ' Who
are they to have but you ? '

A stranger, you know, was put first, when the two names
were presented to Lord Lansdowne to lay before the King.
Mine was put second.   Lord Lansdowne, from his own
knowledge of the experience I had had in the Institution,
powerfully seconded by the then Earl Spencer's recommendation to the same effect, gave the palm to the second candidate;
stating in his subsequent letter to me, that without any de-
rogation to the *merits* of Mr. Clinton, His Majesty had been
pleased to appoint me ' Principal Librarian.'

I cannot help thinking your fears groundless.   I cannot believe that any stranger, did he know the toil of mind to be
encountered before experience can be obtained, would wish
for such an appointment.

Ever truly yours,

HENRY ELLIS."

Four days after the receipt of the above, Panizzi
addressed the Archbishop of Canterbury and the other
Principal Trustees, *mutatis mutandis*, as follows :—

"British Museum, February 18th, 1856.

" My Lord Archbishop,
                    Having just been informed by Sir Henry Ellis that
he has resigned his situation of Principal Librarian, I trust I
may be permitted to draw the attention of your Grace and of
the other Principal Trustees to my services, as giving me some
ground to hope that I may not be deemed unworthy of having
my name submitted to the Sovereign as being a fit person to
succeed Sir Henry.   The efficacy and importance of those
services have doubtless been noticed by the Trustees at large,
as they were by the Commissioners of Inquiry into the British
Museum, as expressed in their report.   I shall not, therefore,
presume to do more than refer with respectful confidence to

the opinion which both the Trustees and the Commissioner entertain of them.

I have the honour to be, my Lord Archbishop, &c.,

A. PANIZZI."

From the Lord-Chancellor he received the appended reply, which needs no comment, nor could Panizzi have expected his Lordship to act otherwise:—

"40, Upper Brook-street,
Feb. 18th, 1856.

"My dear Sir,

In answer to your application, I can say no more than that I feel it my bounden duty to consult exclusively the interests of the Museum.

You will, I am sure, feel that till I know who are the candidates for the office, I should do very wrong to say more.

Believe me, &c.,

CRANWORTH."

The Home Secretary, at that time Sir George Grey, received, without Panizzi's knowledge, several letters from eminent personages, strongly recommending him for the vacant post; to quote one of these will be sufficient evidence of their tendency:—

"Bridgewater House,
February 18th, 1856.

"My dear Sir George,

Having served as Chairman of the British Museum Commission, I have thought myself justified in writing to the Archbishop of Canterbury on the subject of the selection of a successor to Sir Henry Ellis. His Grace, who has received this intrusion with indulgence, seems to desire that I should repeat to you and Sir G. Lewis what I have ventured to state to him. Without troubling you at length, I may briefly state that, on the assumption that Mr. Panizzi's qualifications for the vacant post would not fail to receive His Grace's consideration, should that consideration be favourable, my voice would be at His Grace's disposal to defend, if need were, Mr. Panizzi's appointment, as, in my opinion, the best that could be made. I also adverted to some knowledge I happen to possess of the considerate and benevolent character of Mr. Panizzi's dealings with a very interesting class of men, his subordinates in the library. This feature in his merits being necessarily less under public notice than others which are too notorious to require my testimony, I considered it deserving of mention, co-existing, as I believe it does, with an assiduous exaction of duty, and an energetic exercise of authority.

Ever yours,

EGERTON ELLESMERE."

This letter was sent, together with others, to Panizzi on the 26th of February, 1870, by Sir George Grey himself:—

"37, Eaton Place.

"Dear Sir A. Panizzi,

I have been employing my leisure in looking over many letters and papers which accumulated during my tenure of the Home Office. Among them are some relating to your appointment as Principal Librarian to the Museum in 1856. I send you three letters which I think you may like to possess. When your life comes to be written, which I hope will not be for a long time, it is right that letters such as those should be among the papers which will form materials for it. Of the appointments with which I had anything to do while in office, there is none which I can look back upon with greater satisfaction than yours.

Believe me, very truly yours,

G. GREY."

Another letter, from Lord Ellesmere to Dr. Cureton, written whilst the appointment was pending, may be added:—

"Bridgewater House, February 19th, 1856.
" Dear Mr. Cureton,

If you know anything of Mr. Panizzi's prospects,
pray inform me.

I have written to Sir George Grey as well as to the Archbishop. Is there any formidable rival in the field ? I have
not heard of any, nor indeed have I heard anything on the
subject; and my only fear is that some of the Trustees may
dread the influence of knowledge and capacity, on Talleyrand's principle of avoiding zeal.

Ever faithfully yours,
EGERTON ELLESMERE."

Dr. Cureton again wrote as follows :—

"Cloisters, Feb. 19th, 1856.
" My dear Panizzi,

I have just seen the Archbishop, and I think there
can be no doubt that all is right in that quarter. He asked
me to let him have Parry's letter again, which I shall. I told
him that, as far as I knew, the Lord Chancellor and Speaker
were quite in your favour ; and he told me that, according to
the Act, they must send in *two* names, from which I certainly
conclude that he means yours for *one*. He was very kind. I
have also had a letter from Lord Ellesmere enquiring how
you get on, and wanting to know who else was spoken of.
He said that he had written to Sir George Grey on your behalf—should you not write a word of thanks to him ? He
seems, as you will see from his letter, much interested in your
success.

Yours always,
W. CURETON."

Other communications followed, amongst which
was one from Mr. Richard Ford :—

" February 26th, 1856 ; 123, Park-street.
" Dear Panizzi,

I shall be most anxious until I hear that you
have succeeded to the office in the B. M., for which of all

men you are *the best suited.* Indeed, if you take the place of
Sir Henry Ellis, it will be the most fortunate event for the
Museum that has ever happened. Pray, as soon as anything
definitively is known, give us the great pleasure of writing
me a line. I hear, also, that your bust is to be made by
Marocchetti ; he will model a fine thing from your *massy* forehead, into which so much brain and intelligence are stored
away. Is the subscription confined to the employés in the
Museum ? I should indeed delight in adding my name to a
memorial destined to do honour to so old and valued a friend.
The new Reading-Room would indeed be incomplete if the
effigy of him who projected the scheme, and who has carried
it out, did not occupy the niche of honour.

Ever yours truly,

RICH. FORD."

Before the announcement of the appointment
reached Panizzi, he received two epistles, one from
Lord Lansdowne, and the other from Sir George
Grey :—

" Dear Panizzi,

Though I believe your appointment to succeed
Sir H. Ellis at the Museum has been mentioned in the newspapers before it was made,—for it was only yesterday afternoon
that Sir George Grey brought it under the notice finally of
the Cabinet,—it is now certain, and [I] cannot refrain from
wishing you joy.

I had before felt it difficult to speak to you about it with
the confidence I felt, lest your expectations and mine might
not be realized by some untoward chance ; but I am sure you
will believe that there are none of the Trustees to whom it
gives greater pleasure than myself.

I remain,

Very faithfully yours,

LANSDOWNE."

Sunday morning,
    March 2nd."

"Home Office, March 5th, 1856."

"Dear Mr. Panizzi,

      I have much satisfaction in informing you that Her Majesty has been pleased to appoint you to the office of Principal Librarian of the Museum.

You will receive an official letter intimating to you your appointment, which, at the suggestion of the three Principal Trustees, in which Her Majesty's Government concur, will be made subject to any changes in the duties or emoluments of the Office which Parliament may think fit to make.

      Believe me, yours very faithfully,

G. GREY."

Close upon these followed the official letter from the Home Office :—

"Whitehall, March 5th, 1856.

"Sir,

      I am directed by Secretary Sir George Grey to inform you that the three Principal Trustees of the British Museum have recommended to Her Majesty two persons (of whom you are one) whom they judge fit to execute the office of Principal Librarian, and that Her Majesty has been pleased to appoint you to execute the said office of Principal Librarian of the British Museum.

I am to add that, in accordance with the suggestion of the three Principal Trustees, made with reference to various changes in the duties of this office, recommended by the Royal Commission in 1850, Her Majesty has been pleased to direct that your appointment shall be made subject to any change in the duties or emoluments of the office which Parliament may think fit to make.

      I am, Sir, your obedient servant,

H. WADDINGTON."

The actual appointment, under Her Majesty's sign manual, bears the date of the next day, viz., the 6th of March, 1856.

Panizzi had been privately informed of the intended resignation of Sir Henry Ellis at least a month before, for, on the 2nd of January, he wrote to Sir George Grey, recommending himself to H.R.H. the Prince Consort, under whose instructions the Hon. C. Grey wrote the following letter :—

                                          " Buckingham Palace,
                                                January 3rd, 1856.
" My dear Mr. Panizzi,
            Pray let me know what Act of Parliament it is that regulates your appointment. The Prince will not lose sight of this matter till a decision is come to, but he would wish to be thoroughly acquainted with all the circumstances of the case.
                          Yours very faithfully,
                                          C. GREY."

However, notwithstanding the tone of this letter, and whilst many others kept pouring in, there were not a few persons who tried their utmost to oppose the promotion which had been so well earned, and which, it may honestly be said, proved afterwards to have been so wise a step in the National interest.

The earliest protest is one which, though insignificant at first sight, is here placed before the reader, because it was sent to Panizzi by Lord Palmerston, who wrote on the 13th of March (1856) :—

" My dear Panizzi,
            The enclosed, which has been sent to me, will interest you.
                          Yours very sincerely,
                                          PALMERSTON."

                    ' THE BRITISH MUSEUM.
I protest against the advancement of Mr. Antonio Panizzi to the office of Principal Librarian of the British Museum, vacant by the retirement of Sir Henry Ellis, K.H.

1. Because the appointment, the said Antonio Panizzi being a foreigner, is an act of injustice towards English candidates ; a satire on the character of the Nation ; and a discouragement to the pursuit of its antiquities and literature.

2. Because as the office involves the chief "care and custody" of a National repository of objects of inestimable value, the appointment is a manifest incongruity, and a most inauspicious precedent.

3. Because the office confers the power of granting admission to the Reading-Room of the Museum, or of refusing it ; and it is not fit that National favours, or the refusal thereof, should be received at foreign hands.

4. Because the said Antonio Panizzi has had the audacity to propose the dismemberment of the Museum, in opposition to the express provision of the Act of the twenty-sixth year of George II.—a provision which received the approval of more than fifty members of various scientific societies in 1847.

5. Because the said Antonio Panizzi, on account of the failure of his engagements with regard to the Catalogue of printed books, and the fictions and absurdities of the only fragment thereof hitherto published, appears to have deserved reprehension rather than promotion.

6. Because it removes the said Antonio Panizzi from an office in which, under the guidance of common sense, his erudition, energy, and activity might have been serviceable, to a station for which he appears to be unfitted by his arrogance and irritability, as patent in certain blue books, and by the notorious verbosity of his composition.

&c., &c., &c.,

BOLTON CORNEY.

The Terrace, Barnes."

Can any protest be more short-sighted or ungenerous than this of " Bolton Corney's ?" The concise note of Lord Palmerston speaks volumes to the discerning mind as to his opinion of such vulgar and insulting trash. But for his Lordship's discriminating kindness in forwarding the document for Panizzi's reflection and information, the matter would be scarcely worth dwelling on for a single instant.

Again reference must be made to Mr. Francis Haywood, who, it will be remembered, was Panizzi's earliest friend at Liverpool, and who, it can well be imagined, was delighted to see his *quondam* Italian and penurious friend of 1824 now at the head of the greatest institution of its kind in the universe. Appended are Panizzi's letters previous to receiving his appointment as Principal Librarian:—

"B. M., February 20th, 1856.

"My dear Haywood,

All my friends have always laughed at my doubting to succeed; I alone have hitherto been mistrusting. If I am now to believe what I hear and see in writing, I cannot have any doubts. It seems, even to me, that the thing is as safe as it can be. The Archbishop is as sure as the Chancellor and the Speaker, and so is Sir G. Grey, from what I hear on authority that I cannot possibly doubt. But the thing is not done, and there is, therefore, the *possibility* of a miscarriage. What pleases me is that in this house *all*—excepting, of course, Madden and Hawkins, who looked to the promotion themselves—are strongly for me.

Yours ever,
A. PANIZZI."

"March 4th, 1856.

"My dear Haywood,

I have information on the perfect accuracy of which I may rely, that at Saturday's Cabinet my appointment was decided on. You may rest assured—there is no doubt.

Of course you must be one of my securities for £2,500, I believe ; I have informed Booth, who is now my other security for £750, of what is likely to happen. Ellice wishes to be my other security. The Master of the Rolls too offered, and so did Curcton, my old colleague, who *cried* when he learnt how the matter had been decided. You have no idea how many friends have spontaneously come to my assistance. But of the Government, Ellesmere has taken it up as a personal matter.

Yours ever,

A. Panizzi."

It is incumbent on the gentlemen holding higher appointments in the British Museum to name two securities; these, in Panizzi's case, were Mr. Francis Haywood and Mr. James Booth, both of whom, of course, were accepted. In order to commemorate the great event, the new Principal Librarian invited some of his intimate friends to dinner at Blackwall, amongst these should be mentioned Mr. John Kenyon, the philanthropist, philosopher, and poet. This gentleman died on the 3rd of December, 1856, and as a practical proof of the esteem in which he held Panizzi, left him a legacy of £500 and all his wines.

Lord Macaulay, who had been a Trustee of the British Museum since February, 1847 (an office which he highly esteemed, and to which he attended with much assiduity and greatly to the public advantage), showed, as we gather from his life by Trevelyan, no small anxiety as to the impending appointment. In writing (February, 1856) to Lord Lansdowne he said :—"I am glad of this, both on public and private grounds. Yet I fear that the appointment will be unpopular both within and without the walls of the Museum. There is a growing jealousy among men of science, which, between ourselves, appears even at the Board of Trustees. There is a notion that the Department of Natural History is neglected, and that the Library and Sculpture Gallery are unduly favoured. This feeling will certainly not be allayed by the appointment of Panizzi, whose great object, during many years, has been to make our Library the best in Europe, and who would at any time give three Mammoths for an Aldus."

With all due deference to Lord Macaulay's statement, we do not hesitate to say that the appointment was *not* unpopular, and shall, therefore, begin first by giving Panizzi's letters, addressed to the Keepers of the various Departments, some replies to these letters, and afterwards a selection of other correspondence from subordinate officers, summing up with sundry quotations from the numerous letters of congratulation from persons in various positions.

In relinquishing the Keepership of the Department of Printed Books, the new Principal Librarian thus wrote to Mr. Winter Jones, his successor :—

"British Museum, March 24th, 1856.

"My dear Jones,

I cannot quit the important Department, which for the last nineteen years I have had the honour to direct, without expressing to you and to those who have so much contributed to augmenting it and raising it to its present state, my heartfelt thanks for the zealous, intelligent, and unfailing assistance which I have received from all in the performance of my various duties.

It is not for me to say whether this Library can challenge comparison ; but this I can truly say, that having been so nobly seconded, it is not surprising if I have succeeded beyond what I ever ventured to hope in July, 1837.

I leave my old Department in your hands, confident that its future head will continue to receive from all my late fellow-labourers the support of which I feel so proud—that by your united efforts its usefulness will increase with its extent and its renown, and that you will all receive that meed of approbation which will be due to your untiring and intelligent exertions in the service of the public.

Please, my dear Jones, to make these sentiments of mine known to the whole Department, and believe me, ever yours truly, A. PANIZZI."

The answer ran thus :—

"British Museum,
March 24th, 1856.

"My Dear Sir,

I have communicated to this Department the most kind and flattering letter you have addressed to us, and I am desired to convey to you the expression of the pleasure all have experienced from its perusal. The gratification we feel in your promotion to the important post of Principal Librarian is much alloyed by our regret at your separation from us. All have been indebted to you for acts of kindness and consideration—not a few for substantial benefits. It is our pride that we have been enabled to take part in the labours of the Department ; but the *result* is due to the firm and able guidance those labours have at all times received from yourself. The approval and ready acknowledgment with which you have always met the exertions of others have proved no slight incentive to continued zeal and application.

The energy and enlarged views which have raised the Library to its present state of efficiency will now be employed in promoting the advancement of the Institution generally ; and supported and seconded as you doubtless will be by the

Trustees and Officers, we look forward with confidence to the time when the British Museum shall take its proper rank as one of the most powerful engines for the promotion of education and intelligence.

Believe me, my dear Sir, most truly yours,

J. WINTER JONES."

On the assumption of the office of Principal Librarian, Panizzi wrote a circular letter to the officers of the Museum, to which are appended a few of the answers received, in the order of dates.

" British Museum,

March 24th, 1856.

" Dear Sir,

Her Majesty having been graciously pleased to appoint me to the office of Principal Librarian, I beg to inform you that the Trustees, on Saturday last, put me in possession of that office.

I rely on receiving from you, and all those under you, that efficient assistance which is absolutely necessary for the good of the service, and which from your well known zeal and ability in the fulfilment of the duties of your office must prove eminently useful to this Institution.

You may reckon on your part on my endeavouring to do the utmost for the advantage of your Department, and of those employed in it, for the support of your authority, and for facilitating not only the execution of the orders of the Trustees, but a hearty compliance with their wishes.

I flatter myself that, by our united and harmonious exertions, by the utmost punctuality, and by steady attention in the performance of our duties, we shall eventually secure for the British Museum a still larger share of that ready support with which Parliament has hitherto generously encouraged our efforts.

I shall be highly gratified to learn that you concur in these views and sentiments, and

I remain, my dear Sir, yours faithfully,

A. PANIZZI."

"British Museum,
March 24th, 1856.

" My dear Sir,

I hasten to congratulate you on your appointment to the office of Principal Librarian, and to wish that you may long enjoy the honour so conferred on you.

Knowing the energy you have always evinced in the Department over which you have hitherto presided, the great attention you have paid to the interest of those confided to your care, I look forward with pleasure to the advantages we may all derive from the enlargement of your sphere of action.

I beg to assure you that it will be my earnest endeavour to assist you by every means in my power to carry out the orders of the Trustees, and to produce those united and harmonious exertions which cannot fail to be so beneficial to the interest, efficiency, and utility of the Institution, and so beneficial to the officers.

I remain, my dear Sir, yours very faithfully,
JOHN EDW. GRAY."

"British Museum,
March 25th, 1856.

" Dear Sir,

I have the greatest satisfaction in your appointment to the office of Principal Librarian, and offer you my warmest congratulations on the attainment of a post in which your abilities will be exercised so advantageously.

You cannot doubt that I concur most entirely in the sentiments of your letter—that I shall always consider it my first duty to devote myself to the interests of this Institution, and to satisfy the Trustees by punctuality, diligence, and general zeal in their service.

Without harmony of action and due subordination, all must be confusion in such an establishment as ours. I shall therefore be at all times eager to support your authority, and to follow your directions as the Principal Officer of the Trustees, and the proper interpreter of their wishes and instructions.

C

While endeavouring to satisfy you and them by my best personal exertions, I shall feel full assurance of your concern for the interests of the Department, and shall confide in your protection and assistance, as well as in your lenient consideration of such shortcomings as want of ability may render unavoidable.

Believe me, dear Sir, very faithfully yours,

EDWD. A. BOND."

" British Museum,
March 25th, 1856.

" My dear Sir,

I beg to acknowledge the receipt of your letter of the 24th inst., by which you acquaint me that the Trustees had, on Saturday last, put you in possession of the office of Principal Librarian, to which Her Majesty had been pleased to appoint you.

You do me but justice, and I speak with equal confidence of all those engaged with me in the Department of Printed Books, when you say that you rely on receiving from us that assistance which is absolutely necessary for the good of the service.

That I may reckon on your endeavouring to do the utmost for the advantage of this Department, and of those employed in it, for the support of authority and for facilitating the due execution of the orders, and a hearty compliance with the wishes of the Trustees, is no more than was to be expected from the vigour of your administration while at the head of this Department, and the generous earnestness with which you have at all times advocated the claims and supported the interests of all those placed under your orders.

I most fully concur in the views and sentiments enunciated in your letter, and particularly in the portion where you urge united and harmonious exertion and the utmost punctuality and steady attention in the performance of our duties ; and I beg to assure you that my best exertions shall be directed towards carrying out your views on these as well as on all other points.

Believe me, my dear Sir, most truly yours,

J. WINTER JONES."

Other letters, in the same congratulatory strain, were received from Dr. Birch, Mr. W. H. Carpenter, Mr. E. Hawkins, Mr. Robert Brown, Mr. G. R. Waterhouse, and Mr. J. J. Bennett.

Sir Frederick Madden, as it will be noticed, did not write at the time; but, after some correspondence between Panizzi and the Archbishop of Canterbury, he wrote on the 3rd of April.

Much interest will be attached, also, to the opinions of those not officially connected with the British Museum :—

" Orleans House, Mercredi soir,

5 Mars.

Je n'ai pas voulu vous offrir mes félicitations plus tôt, mon cher monsieur, parceque je voulais en même temps pouvoir vous dire que j'avais parlé à la Reine. Je savais que ma démarche arriverait comme la moutarde après dîner ; mais enfin je voulais l'avoir faite pour l'acquit de ma conscience et surtout pour la satisfaction de mon cœur. Or donc j'arrive de Buckingham Palace ; j'avais porté mon manuscript, et, tandis qu'on l'admirait, j'ai prononcé votre nom. 'Oh! a aussitôt dit Sa Majesté, Monsieur Panizzi, il remplace Sir Henry Ellis.' Cela m'a paru suffisant, et, bien que vous sachiez déjà à quoi vous en tenir, je n'ai pas voulu perdre un moment à vous le répéter, en y joignant mes plus vives félicitations et l'assurance, déjà vieille, de tous les sentiments avec lesquels je demeure,

Votre bien affectionné,

H. D'ORLEANS."

c2

" Stover, Newton Abbot,
Thursday, March 13th.

" Dear Mr. Panizzi,
           I congratulate you sincerely on your appointment,
and hope that you may have health long to enjoy this honourable position, and to devote to it the energy which you have
so efficiently devoted to the Department over which you
presided.

I shall come to Wimbledon directly after Easter, and shall
then, I hope, be there during the next five months, so that I
shall be able to attend at the Museum, whenever I can be of
use.

There are, no doubt, a great many improvements to be made
in the system and conduct of the British Museum; but they
still require much judgment for their introduction, that we
may carry with us, as far as possible, the co-operation of the
heads of Departments and the general concurrence of the
Establishment. The question of first appointments was, as I
remember, postponed, and requires to be clearly understood
and settled. I am not aware of any other point requiring
immediate attention, but shall come to the Museum as soon as
I come up to London.
                    Yours very faithfully,
                              SOMERSET."

" Hatchford, Cobham, Surrey, March 7th, 1856.
" Dear Mr. Panizzi,
           I am much relieved to find that your position is
secured, though I had not much ground for apprehension as to
the result. I shall not be in London, except casually, till after
Easter. I had intended to be there to-day for Lord Stanhope's
Motion, but am too lame. Perhaps before Easter is over you
may find a holiday or holinight to run down here, in which
case I should be glad to congratulate you in person, but I am
not *sure* that I could do so before the end of next week.
                    Ever yours, faithfully,
                              EGERTON ELLESMERE."

" March 10th, 1856 ; 58, Lincoln's Inn Fields.
" My dear Panizzi,
   I hope that this which I hear is true ; and that
you have obtained that which you have the best claim to, and
are the worthiest to hold. If this be so—as I trust heartily it
is—I beg to wish you long and happy years to enjoy what you
have so well earned.

Ever truly yours,

JOHN FOSTER."

To the foregoing, other distinguished personages
added their congratulatory expressions. Testimonials
signed by attendants—even the bookbinder might be
adduced—poured in, and might be put forward, did
space permit, to prove incontestably that the appointment was thoroughly stamped with public approval.

Our documentary evidence has been copious, in
order to establish, beyond doubt, the fact that Panizzi's
succession to the high trust to which he was appointed
met with general approval, and once for all to extin-
guish the croaking of his few detractors and calum-
niators.

So far everything was satisfactory. We cannot, however, conclude this chapter without referring, briefly,
to the proceedings in the House of Commons, on the
21st of April, 1856, when Lord John Russell, in Committee of Supply, moved the vote for the British
Museum ; confining ourselves to those parts of the proceedings which related to the appointment. Mr.
Monckton Milnes (now Lord Houghton) appeared to
object on the old ground of foreign birth ; yet, this
very objector had signed, with others, the Report of
1850, wherein it was stated that Panizzi's appointment
as Keeper of the Printed Books *did credit to the Prin-*

cipal Trustees of that day; that he had answered all accusations brought against him *with a success that they* (the Commissioners) *could hardly have antici-pated;* that it was owing to his Report of 1845 that the extensive grants for the purchase of books were pro-cured from Parliament; and that he had managed the affairs of the Library, for a long period, with *great ability and with universal approbation.*

Those who defended the appointment were there: first of all, the Speaker (the Right Hon. C. Shaw Lefevre, afterwards Lord Eversley), who stated:—

"For my own part, I am quite prepared, and so, I am sure, are all my colleagues, to accept the responsibility of selecting Mr. Panizzi, because I do not believe a better choice could have been made. The hon. gentleman has alluded to the fact of Mr. Panizzi being a foreigner, but that has been no unusual case in the British Museum."

Mr. (now Sir Austen H.) *Layard,* ". . . . . he was very much astonished to hear his honourable friend object to Mr. Panizzi on the ground of his being a foreigner, because that was an objection which ought not to come from that, the Liberal, side of the House."

Mr. Disraeli (now Lord Beaconsfield), ". . . . . had no hesitation in saying that, if the Trustees had not appointed Mr. Panizzi to the vacancy when it occurred, as the reward for his long and meritorious services, and of the intelligent qualities which he had displayed, they would have acted with great injustice, they would have inflicted a discouragement on the public service, and they would have been no longer entitled to the commendation and confidence of that House."

Lord John Russell, ". . . . . he really thought that we had become more liberal than that . . . . He thought that the appointment of Mr. Panizzi had been fully vindicated by the Speaker, and he trusted that there would be no further op-position to the vote."

Mr. Monckton Milnes said, in conclusion, "he should be glad to hear that the appointment was confirmed by public opinion, and justified by the conduct of Mr. Panizzi himself."

The documents already quoted, are, we trust, sufficient to fulfil the conditions required; but we surely ought to be more enlightened than to coincide with the opinions of the early Romans, who, as Cicero informs us, regarded the words *peregrinus* and *inimicus* as synonymous: (off. 1 xii. 38). *Hostis enim apud maiores nostros is dicebatur quem nunc 'peregrinum' dicimus.*

Be this as it may, it is pleasing to record that those who knew Panizzi best did not regard or treat him as *inimicus*.

This chapter may be fitly concluded with the subjoined copy of a testimonial as satisfactory and as well-merited as any man ever received. It is in the handwriting and signed by Mr. W. R. Hamilton, a Trustee of the British Museum.

" The Standing Committee of the Trustees of the British Museum think it their duty to address to the Government of Her Majesty, in the form of a minute to be communicated to the First Lord Commissioner of Her Majesty's Treasury, the following representation in favour of Mr. Antonio Panizzi, who for many years filled the office of Keeper of the Printed Books in this Institution, and was lately selected Principal Librarian in the same Establishment :—

' The Trustees are fully aware that the exemplary activity, zeal, and ability shewn by Mr. Panizzi, in the execution of his duties as Keeper of the Printed Books, are well known to the greater part, if not to all, the present members of Her Majesty's Government; but they wish, on the present occasion, to call the particular attention of Lord Palmerston to the very remarkable proofs which this gentleman has recently given of his devotion to the general service of the Museum, by the extension of its means of contributing to the instruction and accommodation of the public.

In the expression of their sentiments the Trustees are especially influenced by the deep sense they entertain of the obligation they are under to Mr. Panizzi for the suggestion of the building recently erected in the Interior Quadrangle of the Museum for supplying additional room for the books composing the Museum Library, and for the better accommodation for an increased and increasing number of visitors to the Reading-Room.

The success which has attended the erection of this Building, the universal admiration which it has excited among the thousands who have been admitted to view it since it was completed, the various excellent and simple arrangements for the supply of books to the readers, the ingenuity and invention displayed for the arrangement of a very large library within a very limited space, and the facilities which it may eventually afford for extending the available space for other departments, the novelty of the design and the comparatively small cost of the construction are all in a very great manner to be attributed to the energy and inventive powers of Mr. Panizzi whose views have been most efficiently carried out by the architect, Mr. Sydney Smirke, in the material construction of a building which, the Trustees believe, is without a rival on the Continent. All these facts are, however, too well known to Lord Palmerston for it to be necessary for the Trustees to dwell upon them further ; but they confidently hope that the circumstances of the case will be found sufficient to induce Her Majesty's Government to testify their appreciation of what Mr. Panizzi has thus done for the public benefit in such manner as may appear to them most expedient.'

(Signed) W. R. HAMILTON."

CHAPTER XV.

A FEW months only had elapsed since his official appointment, ere Panizzi was called upon to give practical proof of that energy which characterized him. Indeed it appears that he lost not one moment's time in setting to work to reform the Museum, not only as regarded the want of space—a general complaint—but as concerned improvement of the position of his subordinates. The successive Parliamentary papers will show the amount of correspondence, both private and official, through which he had to wade.

Still, however, anxiously maintaining chronological order, we shall, for the present, leave this important part of the Museum history, and descant upon what, at the time, was considered a valuable bequest of Sir William Temple, brother to Lord Palmerston, who died in London on the 24th of August, 1856, having for many years resided at Naples as Minister Plenipotentiary to that Court.

It was understood, previous to Sir William's death, that his collection of antiquities would come to the

British Museum. Although, perhaps, not a collection of the first order, it was of considerable intrinsic value, and looked upon by *connoisseurs* as a small Museum in itself.

On the 11th of September, 1856, Panizzi received the following private letter from Lord Palmerston:—

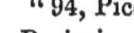
" 94, Piccadilly.

"My dear Panizzi,

My brother stated in his will, 'I desire that my collection of Antiquities be offered to the Trustees of the British Museum, to be preserved therein for the use and benefit of the public, and if within six calendar months after such offer shall have been made to the said Trustees, they shall signify their acceptance thereof, for the purpose aforesaid, then I give the said collection to them accordingly.'

Of course it will be understood by the Trustees that the Collection should be placed separately and kept altogether, and be described as my brother's gift, and the Infant Bacchus should be added to the collection of which it forms a part. As I cannot doubt that the Trustees will accept this bequest, I would beg to suggest that some proper person should be sent from the Museum to Naples, to pack up, properly and safely, the things of which the Collection consists. This would be more satisfactory than that the Collection should be packed up by persons on the spot without any responsible superintendence.

Fagan is returning to Naples in the middle of next week, and will take with him the list of articles, and the person sent to pack them up might go out with Fagan.* There are many

---

* The Biographer's Father of whom more particular mention will be made hereafter.

reasons why it is desirable that no time should be lost in
packing the Collection up. The way of sending it home may
be settled afterwards. It is possible that some ship-of-war
may be in the Bay of Naples which might bring the cases
home, if not too bulky, but otherwise the Museum will make
proper arrangements for their removal to England.

Yours sincerely,

PALMERSTON.

P.S.—On second thoughts, I send you the Catalogue, which
you will return to me before Wednesday. You had better have
a copy made of this Catalogue, and keep it in case any accident
should happen to the original.

P."

Panizzi immediately afterwards sent for Mr. Oldfield, then an Assistant in the Antiquity Department
of the British Museum, and directed him to proceed
at once to Naples, in order to report on the Collection,
and superintend its departure. His instructions ran
thus :—

"B. M., September 20th, 1856.

" Dear Sir,

After the full conversation which we have had on
the subject of the Sir William Temple's legacy of his collection
of antiquities to the Trustees of the British Museum, it is unnecessary for me to say more on that part of the subject, but
I have accordingly to request that you will take means for
leaving this country to repair to Naples without delay. There
the collection, I understand, is still in the house which Sir
William inhabited at Naples, and the objects will be delivered
up to you by George Fagan, Esq. (Attaché to H. M's Legation), who is in possession of a full and descriptive catalogue
of the said collection, and who is to act for Viscount Palmerston, the heir and sole executor of the Will of his late brother.
You will, of course, give an acknowledgment to Mr. Fagan
of what you receive.

The collection being speedily and carefully packed up, you will make it your duty, without loss of time, to enquire by what means it may be best transmitted to England. Acting for our Trustees, I have applied to the Lords Commissioners of the Admiralty, requesting them to order any of Her Majesty's ships that might be available, touching at Naples on its way to England, to receive on board the packages containing the said collection, the same being for public use and benefit, and should you be successful in obtaining such means of conveyance, you are requested to avail yourself of it in preference to any other, even if the arrival of the collection were to be thereby delayed. This delay would be of comparatively little importance ; what is really essential is that the collection should be carefully packed up and safely removed on board without loss of time.

If no such conveyance can be obtained, you will then forward the collection to England by the readiest and safest means available to the best of your judgment, and after having consulted with the gentleman in charge of Her Majesty's Legation, or with Her Majesty's Consul General at Naples.

As to the expenses you may have to incur for packing, packing-cases, transport of the objects from the Minister's House to the ship, on board of which they are to be placed, you are empowered to draw on me, either at a month *after date* or ten days *after sight*, for the amount, advising me of having so drawn, and carefully preserving the vouchers which justify the expense. Should you be obliged to remain at Naples more than is now contemplated, and find the sum of £50, which I have placed in your hands to meet your travelling and personal expense, insufficient, you are authorized to draw for £50 more on the same terms as above. On your return to England you will be so good as to transmit to me a statement of your expenses, accompanied by such vouchers as may be necessary, in order that they may be laid before the Standing Committee.

Immediately after the Collection is embarked you will be pleased to make the best of your way back to England.

Having the greatest reliance on your judgment, I concur with Mr. Hawkins in authorizing you to purchase, on account of the Trustees, any object or objects which you might think a very desirable addition for our Museum of Antiquities, to an amount not exceeding altogether £100, drawing for the same as above. Should any more important and peculiarly desirable purchase offer itself, please to make forthwith a special report on it, to be submitted to the Trustees, for their orders.

It may be superfluous to add that it will be desirable that, on your return, you should lay before the Trustees a report on any point that you may think of importance, respecting the public or private Collections which may fall under your notice, and the regulations under which the former are preserved, and made accessible to learned men and artists, as well as the public at large.

Be so good as to write to me fully and frequently for the information of the Trustees, and give me the earliest notice of the collection being on board the vessel which is to bring it to England.

Mr. Fagan will assist you as far as in his power with his advice and knowledge of men and things at Naples. I enclose, moreover, a letter for Mr. Petre, now in charge of Her Majesty's Mission, and another for Mr. Craven, one of its members.

Believe me, &c., &c.,"

A. PANIZZI."

On the 3rd of October, Mr. Oldfield wrote from Naples giving his private opinion of the collection, which he evidently did not consider of very great value. "The glass and the bronzes," he said, "are of considerable beauty and interest, but the sculpture as a whole unworthy of acceptance."

A notable incident should be here inserted. When certain R. Gargiulo was preparing the Catalogue of the Collection, it was discovered that four frescoes, of

not much importance, had upon them the stamp of the
Museo Borbonico. They had, in fact, been purloined
from that Museum by an agent, or ally, of the individual from whom Sir William bought them. Sir
William resolved to return them to their lawful
owners, but died before carrying out his intention.
Mr. Fagan, with Lord Palmerston's sanction, wrote to
the Neapolitan authorities immediately afterwards,
informing them of the discovery; stating also, of course,
how Sir William had unwittingly purchased objects
which he afterwards discovered had been abstracted
from Pompeii, and returning them in Lord Palmerston's name. After a few days, Signor d'Aloe called
on Mr. Fagan, and, stating that the matter had been
reported to the King, Ferdinand II., begged that Lord
Palmerston would retain the frescoes. Consequent
upon this, and upon the letter which communicated
the royal request, the frescoes were accepted.

The collection consists altogether of 1,571 pieces ;
of these the most interesting portions are the painted
vases, the bronzes, and the specimens of Greek and
Roman glasses. Special mention should also be made
of a magnificent *Krater*, with a painting of the death
of Hippolytus ; a very fine and rare globular vase, with
an ornamental cover, should be separately mentioned ;
and a *Lekythos* representing the judgment of Paris.
Amongst the bronzes, a small but fine bust of a faun,
and specimens of Greek armour from Ruvo, com-
prising a breast and back plate, and a very beautiful
bronze statue of the youthful Bacchus, deposited in
the Museum by Sir William during his life-time.

In the spring of 1857, Panizzi gave his serious attention to the cause of the staff of the Museum, and to the increase of their emoluments. Hitherto the servants of the Trustees, as it has been already observed, were not treated or paid in a commensurate manner by the Government, and no superannuation allowance was granted ; and it was properly remarked at the time that, to carry out any effectual measure of reform, it would be necessary to increase the value of the appointments—thus holding out an inducement for good men to remain, and giving the service of the Museum the tone of a *profession*.

It would relieve the Establishment from persons who were worn out or nearly so, and raise the general standard of activity ; and by clearing off an *arrear* of superannuation, would make room for the early introduction of a considerable number of officers and attendants of a superior class.

This step was ultimately carried out by Panizzi two years afterwards, much to the satisfaction of the whole Museum staff, as the following letter which they addressed to him testifies:—

" British Museum,
February 25th, 1861.

" Dear Sir,

We beg individually and collectively to offer to you in a more explicit manner than we were able to do on Saturday, our most sincere and grateful thanks for the highly gratifying intelligence which you so kindly conveyed to us on that day. We feel assured that the very important improvement in our position which you then announced to us, has not been obtained without the most persevering and energetic exertions on your part ; and we earnestly hope, by our zealous attention to the performance of our several duties, to merit the continued approbation of the Trustees, and thereby to justify this your crowning effort on our behalf."

It will be remembered that in 1845, Panizzi, after having obtained permission to visit his native town, was, when on the eve of reaching it, stopped by the Duke of Modena. Things had somewhat changed, perhaps, for the better; or at any rate the time was fast approaching when the foreign yoke was about, once for all, to disappear from Italy, and tyranny cease to exist in the land which had given birth to so many eminent men. On the 15th of June, 1857, Panizzi wrote to Lord Clarendon to obtain for him, through Count Apponyi, an Austrian passport; his Lordship at once set to work, and on the 17th of June communicated to Panizzi the welcome tidings that his Excellency, although he could not grant him the desired passport because *he had never been an Austrian*, still would not for an instant hesitate to affix his signature to his English passport. Accordingly he started by the end of August for Brescello, and actually reached that place without molestation. He thus wrote to Mr. Haywood from Milan :—

" September 9th.

" My reception has been all I could wish on the part of the Government, and beyond belief on that of my few remaining friends ; for I find the majority of them dead. But those who still live, and their families—I had left many of them children, and I find them now married with children of the same age that they themselves were when I left Italy—have received me with a cordiality and warmth of affection that has often and often moved me to tears. And then this country—and those monuments—and this sky! Oh my dear Haywood, what poor things are all those that are admired elsewhere! What nature has done and what the old generations did for Italy is unique; but I shall be very glad to be once more at the British Museum."

Whilst at Brescello, the biographer, who had the satisfaction of visiting that place in November, 1879, was told that Panizzi spent the entire day going from house to house seeing and embracing his relations and friends, making researches in the archives, and taking notes of all he saw; but nothing can be more touching than a letter which he wrote on the 22nd of October, 1857, to Dr. Minzi, and of which we place a translation intact before our readers :—

"British Museum,
October 22nd, 1857 (evening).

"My dear Minzi,
How many things have happened during the past thirty-five years! It was on this very day thirty-five years ago, that you accompanied me, with Zatti and Montani, to embark for Viadana.

It was then that my travels began. What changes! What fortune! How many sleepless nights! What follies! What ardent passion! What sufferings! What risks! But no more of this.

You know that I have been at Brescello, but you cannot conceive how dear such a visit was to me. Indeed it is impossible to describe my feelings. I can only say that no town, temple, or theatre, or palace afforded me such joy as I felt when I saw Brescello; the church of Brescello! the theatre of Brescello! and the Municipal Hall of Brescello! The very house where I was born, yours, Montani's house, and that of Francesco Panizzi. These sights almost brought tears to my eyes.

You complain of my silence . . . . You must know that weeks have passed without my being able to leave the house, and that I was reduced to such a state as not even to get sleep; my head felt giddy, and my heart beat so as to take away my breath; I had pains in my hands and feet, and nervousness, accompanied by continual noise in the ears. I went to Italy, and now I tell you what I achieved since we last parted.

D

From Keeper of the Printed Books, perhaps the most important Department in this Institution, I was appointed Director in Chief (Principal Librarian) of the Museum, about two years ago. It is a very high post, but when I came to take charge of the Museum, I found it so badly governed, such was the need of many reforms, that it required an iron resolution to replace order. I attempted it. Every one in the service great and small (about 230) soon learnt that they had to deal with one who was determined to make things go as they ought. I was already known in my Department, which was a model to all others, and every one knew the stuff I was made of. I found a collection of 220,000 printed books, and I left 530,000. I fought for years, defeated a squadron of ignorant men and enemies, who opposed a plan for a new Catalogue, which is now approaching completion, and which will be the finest Catalogue ever compiled. I made a plan for a Reading-Room to accommodate 300 readers, who are now more comfortably seated than at their own homes, and of a Library which will contain 1,400,000 volumes. The plan was approved by our best architect; the room is now finished and made use of. I am honoured by every one, and my enemies have disappeared. All this has naturally added strength and moral power to my new post. But, through hard work, I felt as if my brain would give way, and so I decided to visit Italy. There I slept very well, and the symptoms disappeared, but they returned slowly. My mode of living is moderate; I take medicine, but the pain on my left side has returned. How it will end I do not know, for work I must, and work hard too; and now that I have reached the summit of the mountain I feel as if I should like to descend, but I fear it is impossible. I am treated by every one like a Benjamin, amply paid and much honoured, and they will not listen to my retiring.

I have sent you a selfish letter, such a one as I should not have written to any one else, but only to a friend like you.

Your affectionate friend,

A. PANIZZI.

To continue the thread of our narrative, a trifling but pleasant incident occurred, two months before Panizzi left London for the Continent, which we cannot do better than narrate in his own words:—

"B. M., June 30th, 1857.

"My dear Haywood,

A week ago the Archduke Maximilian, who is going as Viceroy in Lombardy, after his marriage with the Princess Charlotte of Belgium, came to visit the Museum, and I received him. In the course of conversation it came out that I was an Italian, and that I intended going to Renaro at the beginning of August, returning in September. The Archduke then began to urge me that I should on my return (for he would not be there on my going) pay him a visit, that is, *to go and stay with him*. Of course I said *Domine non sum dignus*, but he pressed me repeatedly. I thought when he learnt who I was he would not press me again, but on Saturday last I unexpectedly received a despatch from the Austrian Minister here, Apponyi, sending me, in the Archduke's name, a very fine diamond ring with the Archduke's initials, and a reminder that he expects I will pay him a visit at Milan. Now this is very embarrassing. If I go to Milan, and he is there, I *must* present myself, and be his guest if he insists ; if I do so all the Italians who do not know me, more especially in Piedmont, will accuse me of treachery, of playing false to my country, and what not; and, on the other hand, if I had the moral courage to despise such an outcry I might do some little good—very little, if any, I know.

Yours, &c., &c.,

A. PANIZZI."

But to return to the Museum. The process of accumulation continued, and the influx of works of art and other antiquities was filling the National Institution to such an extent that it was deemed necessary to decide whether the Natural History Departments should be retained at Bloomsbury.

D2

The various heads of Departments were invited to send in their reports and opinions on the subject, and a few of their remarks may not appear superfluous :—

Mr. Hawkins, the Keeper of Antiquities, reported that he could find no room for the cases of Assyrian Sculptures which had arrived. Sir Charles Fellows complained that Ionic Trophy Monuments and other works of art found at Xanthus had been placed in an unbefitting position. Dr. Gray, of the Natural History Department, conveyed the pleasing intelligence that if the Zoological Collection in the basement were not speedily removed to a dryer place it would be utterly destroyed. Mr. Brown applied for additional room, as that occupied by the Botanical Department in the basement was quite inadequate to its demands. Professor Owen, in a report to the Trustees on the same subject, January, 1857, approved of all the statements of Dr. Gray, who, eight months later, came forward again with a demand for his gallery and series of glass cases, and the enlargement of the Insect-Room; and two months afterwards he laid before the Trustees a fuller statement. Many more examples might be adduced, but the reader who desires to push his investigations further should consult a lengthy Parliamentary paper on the subject, ordered by the House of Commons to be printed, 1st of July, 1858.

Panizzi also wrote two reports, one dated the 10th of November, 1857, and the other the 10th of June, 1858. In the first of these he fully discussed the means suggested for relieving two Departments, namely, those of Mineralogy and Geology, and then continued :—

" In the Department of Prints and Drawings the want of room, even to lodge the portfolios containing the collection, is sufficiently shown by the placing of presses in the narrow passage leading from the landing into the Print-Room. The display of some of the best prints and drawings has often been entertained by the Trustees, who felt how important it was that this should be done, but who never could carry their intention into effect for want of room. The Kouyunjik-Room, by the side of the North-Western portion of the Egyptian Saloon, had been built for the purpose of such an exhibition, when the influx of Assyrian antiquities forced the Trustees to devote that room to their display."

It appears that the Natural History Department will soon be removed. As there will, therefore, be more space for a smaller number of collections, we may hope that it will now be found possible to make good certain deficiencies which have long been fully recognised, especially in regard to the Exhibition of Prints and Drawings. Glass and China, too, will form a most attractive feature in the new arrangements.

The author himself has had ample opportunities during the last dozen years of visiting some of the most important Cabinets of Prints and Drawings in Europe, and he has no hesitation in saying that no single collection—not even a combination of two or three—could compare with that of which our National Institution can boast. Through the good taste of the present Principal Librarian, Mr. Bond, in placing so many screens in the King's Library, a step has been taken in the right direction, and no Englishman—nay, no Foreigner—visiting London should omit to inspect this wonderful assemblage of works of art.

It was Panizzi's own idea that, as well as rarities
from the Library, specimens of the handiwork of
Raphael, Michael Angelo, Dürer, Rembrandt—and,
indeed, his own *Francia*—should be framed and ex-
hibited to the public gaze.

Instruction, practicable and visible, is one of the
leading features of the age ; and it is our duty to
meet this increasing want by every means in our
power. It is not the feeling that in our hands are
the keys of knowledge which will impart instruction ;
it is the practical and sincere wish to utilize the means
within our grasp, to educate the masses, which will
alone work a result so eagerly sought for, and so
materially tending to the benefit of future generations.

The enormous pile of building which has just been
erected at South Kensington may, in a sense, be
said to owe its existence to the persistent efforts of
Panizzi, to secure more space for the collections he
loved so well.   The two following letters on the subject are, we consider, of great importance :—

"British Museum, October 8th, 1858. '

" My dear Sir George,

As neither you nor Lord John will come up
from Harpton Court to attend the meeting of the Standing
Committee at 12 o'clock to-morrow, I think it fair to ask you
both to give half-an-hour to the British Museum where you
are ; and this might be even more useful than if you were to
attend the meeting.

The Government are determined, it seems, to adopt the
principle of dividing the Museum ; and Professor Owen, in his
address to the British Association at Leeds, having read an
article in the last *Quarterly Review*, drops his objections to the
separation, and is indifferent about the *site* of the Natural
History Museum: he only demurs to there being Trustees.

Mr. D'Israeli says that the Government have evidence enough as to what is to be done, and that they want no more information. I believe he is egregiously mistaken, and that the evidence hitherto collected is sufficient to prove that things cannot remain in the present state, and that something must be done ; but there is no evidence or suggestion as to what that *something* must be (excepting only that the Superintendent of the Natural History, in the service of the Trustees, thinks that his present masters, or anything like them, are not desirable.) Now I have a great dread of these indefinite *somethings.* I fear that one or two members of the Government who have once walked through the Museum, or may have assisted at a meeting of Trustees, may think themselves quite competent to draw up a new constitution for this and other Museums, which pompously and plausibly proposed to the Houses of Parliament may be sanctioned, putting the British Museum and all its collections in a worse position than they are now; and rendering them less useful to the public. It seems, therefore, to me that you and Lord John should consider well the subject, and be prepared to advise the Government ; and, if necessary, resist any scheme that might be lightly or rashly introduced to Parliament.

I apprehend that, whatever be thought of Trustees, it will not be so easy to persuade the family Trustees of the Museum that they ought to be extinguished.

I do not think that the Government have yet considered which are the collections that ought not to be removed from the present British Museum, and which are those that ought to be removed elsewhere. We may agree as to removing the Natural History collections ; but is it quite clear we ought to keep ethnographical collections and works of mediæval or christian art ?

Has anyone thought how long it will be before what it may be decided upon to remove, can be removed, what is to be done in the meantime, and what alterations may be necessary in the present building to fit the space left empty by the removal of some collections for the reception of those which are to remain here ?

It seems to be generally considered desirable, if not necessary, that whenever the Museum or Museums are re-organised, lectures should be delivered by its officers. I humbly consider this a great mistake. No one can do more than one thing at a time well. A Keeper of collections will neglect them to prepare his lectures, and a lecturer will hurry through his lectures to attend to his collections ; and if not more inclined to one than to the other of his two trades, the same man may be both a bad lecturer and bad Keeper of collections. As the 'Jardin des Plantes' at Paris is so much talked of here, with its numerous lectures, I trust some evidence will be taken of its condition and of the working of its organisation before we adopt it here.

I should also think that before the extinction of the Museum Trust is decided upon, it would be well to consider whether it is desirable to allow Institutions like the Museum to be governed by learned and scientific men. I will not go so far as to say that the system of Trustees is the best that could be devised, but I am fully convinced, and ready to prove from experience that learned and scientific men are unfit to govern places like the Museum. Who then is to govern these establishments ?

There is a variety of minor points which are worth considering, besides those above mentioned. If you and Lord John were to agree to some general principles, I dare say Mr. Gladstone would probably agree with you on the whole ; and then you three might induce, and, if necessary, compel the Government to consent to adopting your views. I think it, however, requisite that, in some way or other, evidence should be taken from men whose opinion carries weight in these matters ; that the public and the Houses of Parliament should see that whatever be ultimately done is done on good grounds and after mature consideration. I think the information collected would be of great use in coming to a right determination, and I do not see how it can be possible to do so without.

The ' Supply' is coming home with a cargo of antiquities from Newton, and will call at Carthage for some fifty cases of antiquities from Davis. · It was to be at Malta on the 25th of last month, and will therefore soon be here. Where is all this enormous mass of things to be placed ?

Ever yours,
A. PANIZZI."

" Harpton, Radnor,
October 12th, 1858.

" My dear Panizzi,

I received your letter before Lord John went on to Liverpool, and had some conversation with him on the subject of it.

ı. There are, as it seems to me, two questions respecting the enlargement of the British Museum. The first may be called the legal question, which is ¦raised by Sir Philip Egerton and others—viz., whether Sir Hans Sloane made it a question of his gift that all his collections should be kept in one building, or whether, in dealing with these collections, there is a ' will of the founder,' which the legislature is bound to respect, and which is to be a law for all succeeding generations, whatever additions the different branches of the Museum may receive or require. If this view is to prevail, it is ¦clear that we are prevented from even˙entertaining any plan for the division of the collections, whatever its intrinsic advantages may be. But if this restriction upon the operations of the present generation is not admitted to exist, then we come to the second question—whether it is more expedient to enlarge the Museum by adding to the present building, or by detaching some branches of it, and providing them with a fit repository elsewhere.

I do not pretend to have mastered the subject sufficiently to have formed a confident opinion upon it; but so far as I am at present informed, the inclination of my mind is to believe that the Natural History branches would be provided for in a separate building, and to a certain extent under a separate management.

At the same time, if the scientific men are to take up the question as one of personal feeling and party struggle, and if the cause of stuffed beasts is to be argued against that of antiques, as if it was Whig against Tory, or Catholic against Protestant, I am not prepared to say what are the advantages, if separation are worth the strife and animosity, which its accomplishment would create.

A private gentleman, in arranging his expenditure, may say—I allot so much for my kitchen, so much for my cellar, so much for the education of my children, so much for my garden, so much for my shooting, hunting, &c., &c., and each of his servants must be satisfied with what they get. But what sort of life would he lead, and how long would he remain out of the Queen's Bench, if his gardeners wrote letters in the *Times* to complain that he starved his garden, and that his hot-houses were in a disgraceful state ; if his governess persuaded Roebuck to bring the state of his daughters' education before the House, and if his huntsman inserted articles in the *Sporting Magazine* in the style of Junius, displaying the scandalous defects in the management of his stables. Yet, with regard to luxuries, such as science and art, the Nation is practically in the same condition as a private individual. It must measure its expenditure by its means, and not, as in the case of the army and navy, consider its necessities first and its means afterwards. Yet the representative of each Department of Science and Art insists on having the largest possible building, in the best possible site, and each Department finds successively supporters and champions in Parliament.

I have no wish to volunteer advice where it is not asked ; if the Government think they can settle the question themselves, I have no wish to interfere. My only fear is that they may find it more difficult, on coming to close quarters, than it appears at a distance. If the Government refer it to the Trustees for their opinion, I shall be quite ready to take part in any Committee which may be appointed to consider and investigate the subject. At present I don't think the facts are well ascertained, nor do we know what are the precise objects which we should seek to obtain. I see, for example, a great difference between keeping a great exhibition of stuffed animals, &c., for all the nursery-maids and children to look at, and keeping a collection of Natural History for the use of men of science—like the Anatomical Collection at Surgeons' Hall in Lincoln's Inn Fields. I think that Lord John concurs generally in the view that I have expressed, as to the removal of the Natural History Collections.

There is much to be said in favour of the constitution of a governing body like the Museum Trustees. A body of scientific men might expect and demand too much; they would violate Talleyrand's caution about excess of zeal. On the other hand, it is desirable to relieve the executive Government from direct responsibility in such a matter.

Query—what is the oldest bilingual glossary of the Latin language ? What is the earliest vocabulary in which Latin is explained by some other tongue ? Is the earliest a Latin and Greek (not Greek and Latin) glossary, or a Latin and Gothic glossary, or a vocabulary in which Latin is rendered into the Lingua volgare ? If so, what is the date of the latter ? I hope you will not think this an unfair question to address to so distinguished a *bibliotecario* as yourself.

Yours, &c., &c.,
G. C. LEWIS."

That Panizzi was equally interested in other Departments of the Museum Mr. Newton could testify, if need were, for that of the antiquities, and the writer for his own.

Between Mr. Charles Thomas Newton, C.B., and Panizzi, there subsisted something more than an intimate friendship; a more proper term would be a warm attachment. We need no greater proof of Mr.

Newton's devotion to his friend than the fact that when in 1867 the latter was ill, and his life despaired of, the former devoted all his time to the care of his sometime colleague. The great number of letters before us, from the hand of Mr. Newton, would indeed fill a volume of most interesting matter, relating to his discoveries and travels in the Levant; for he was in the habit of communicating to his friend, it appears, all his adventures, whether at Rhodes, Mytilene, Budrum, or Rome. These letters make us wonder, by their freshness, how time and inclination could have been found to write them, and are certainly deserving of publication at some future time. So much important matter, from such a pen, would prove a treasure to future antiquarians and travellers.

Now Mr. Newton, who had been in the Museum since May, 1840, was, in February, 1852, appointed by Lord Granville to the Vice-Consulship of Mytilene.

Whilst there, he carried on various researches and excavations, sending home from time to time to the British Museum the fruit of his labours. In April, 1856, Mr. Newton received directions from the Foreign Office to proceed to Rome, to value the Campana collection then offered to the British Government. On his return from Rome to London he took this opportunity to submit his views as to further operations at Budrum ; these he naturally explained to Panizzi, and, through him, it was arranged that the two should one day go to Brocket Hall, Lord Palmerston's country seat, and there meet Lord Clarendon, to talk over the matter. Lord Palmerston, who was then Premier, with his usual *savoir-faire*, at once suggested that the Principal Librarian being present, and the two Ministers being both *ex-officio* Trustees of the British Museum, the meeting of this triad might be considered a quorum, for the settlement of a matter of so much consequence to the National Institution. It was then agreed that Mr. Newton should at once proceed to Budrum on special mission. Those were days when operations of this kind could be carried out with that secrecy and despatch which are necessary to insure success. In this particular case, there was the more reason for prompt action, because Ludwig Ross, a distinguished German explorer, had already visited Budrum, and noticed in his travels the Lions from the Mausoleum, then built into the walls of the Castle at Budrum.

Mr. Newton's demands were surely not exorbitant; he suggested that a firman authorizing the removal of the Lions should be obtained from the Porte, declaring that the sum of £2,000, and the services of a ship-of-war, for at least six months, would be necessary to insure the success of the expedition. These suggestions were, without loss of time, acted upon, and H.M.'s ship "Gorgon," commanded by Captain Towsey, was chartered, and she arrived at Budrum in the month of November, 1856.

It is unnecessary now to say that the finding of the ever famous tomb of Mausolus at Halicarnassus (Budrum) was an event of the first importance to Classical Archæology, or, what is better, that the recovery of part of the slabs of the frieze of this monument, along with other sculptures, was for the history of Greek sculpture in the age of Praxiteles and Scopas, of the same importance, as the marbles of the Parthenon for the history of sculpture in the time of Pheidias. Several of the slabs of the frieze from the Mausoleum had been obtained for the British Museum, through the late Lord Stratford de Redcliffe, some years previous to Mr. Newton's expedition; but a comparison of them with the newly-recovered fragments at once shows how admirably the skill of the artist, lost and obliterated in the older slabs, had been preserved in Mr. Newton's. It was not from the circumstances, perhaps, possible to affirm that this or that portion of the Sculptures was the work of Praxiteles, or of Scopas; but this at any rate could be said, that the Sculptures must be taken as works executed under the eyes of these artists, and, doubtless, greatly influenced by them. Here is what Mr. Newton says of them:—

"Budrum, 26th April, 1857.

"My dear Panizzi, '

Since I last wrote, we have made some brilliant discoveries. On the Eastern Side of the Mausoleum I have found a beautiful piece of frieze, three figures, an Amazon attacking a prostrate Greek, and a mounted figure.

This piece of frieze ranges with that now in the British Museum. It is in much finer condition, and is a most exquisite specimen of high relief. Being found in the Eastern Side, I think we may venture to consider it the work of Scopas, because a block of that size could not have been transported far without greater injury. On the North Side, digging on beyond the apparent boundary of the *temenos*, we came to a beautiful Hellenic wall about three feet behind the line cut out of the rock, which marks the boundaries of the quadrangle.

This wall, built of isodomous masonry, is evidently the boundary of the precinct (Pliny's *circuitus*) on this side. Digging beyond it to the North, I came to a magnificent colossal female head lying in the ground. The hair is arranged in regular curls on the forehead, and bound with a coif behind, like the head-dress on the contemporary silver coins of Syracuse. This head is one of the most interesting discoveries we have made. It is in fine condition; the nose and mouth have suffered a little. Following the wall Eastward from this point, we came to a mass of ruins lying as they had originally fallen. Near the surface was a Lion of the same size as those in the Castle, nearly entire and in magnificent condition. We have the two forelegs, and hope to find the paws. The face quite perfect, the inside of the mouth coloured red, the very roughness of the tongue rendered. This Lion, though perhaps inferior to the rest in style, and not finished throughout, is a most noble beast. I think the British public will admire him, because there is so little for the imagination to supply.

While we were getting him out, we discovered a [male (?) head in three pieces, but capable of being united without much loss. I think, an Apollo, exceedingly fine, on a smaller scale than the other; also part of a horse's head, on an enormous scale, bigger, I think, than the equestrian statue I first found. After getting these out, we came upon a most beautiful draped female figure in very fine condition, but headless; it is in two pieces, the first from the neck to the knees, the second from the knees to the feet. The drapery of this figure seems to me equal to any in the Elgin-Room. The statue must have been about ten feet long. As we were getting it out, we discovered another colossal figure lying a little to the North of it. This we had not time to get out yesterday, and to-day is Sunday, so it must remain till to-morrow. I forgot to mention that on the piece of the horse's head a portion of bronze bridle, with a circular ornament, was still fixed, but another piece of horse, with another piece of bronze bridle, was found close to it. You see that these discoveries promise well. My impression is that we are now, for the first time, exploring a part of the site where the ruins have not been disturbed since the building fell. Hence the completeness and fine condition of the sculpture. . . .

Yours very sincerely,
C. T. NEWTON."

On the 8th of June, of the same year, again Mr. Newton wrote to Panizzi ;—

"You will rejoice to hear that along the Eastern Side of the Mausoleum I found two more very fine slabs of frieze, one nearly six feet long, with an Amazon on horseback, sitting with her face to the tail, shooting at a foe behind her, after the Parthian fashion—a most bold and vigorous design; the other, a combat on foot. It is remarkable that these four slabs of frieze have been found in a line on the Eastern Side. This makes me think they are all from the hand of Scopas. Together they make up about 16 feet, which, with the slabs now in the British Museum, will make up a total length of about 80 feet. I hope you have secured the Genoa slab at any price.

On the North Side, I have found the other half of the head of the great horse. The bronze bit, in perfect preservation, was still in his mouth! The nostrils are distended, much in the manner of those in the horse's head from the Car of Night in the Elgin-Room, so that these two heads, the works of successive schools, will be an interesting subject of comparison. Besides this, I have found a face broken off from a colossal male head. I think this belongs to the figure in the chariot. It seems to be an ideal portrait, not unlike that of Alexander the Great on the coins of Lysimachus. It represents a man, perhaps Mausolus himself, in the prime of life, slightly bearded. It is in very fine condition, and is, altogether, the finest head I have ever seen, particularly interesting, because it seems to form the connecting link between the schools of Scopas and that of Lysippus. I have still got a good deal of ground to dig on the North Side, but the proprietors are very obstinate.

Yours ever sincerely,
C. T. NEWTON."

On the 17th of January, 1861, Mr. Newton was appointed Keeper of Greek and Roman Antiquities, then organized as a separate Department of the Museum. From that time to now he has been constantly occupied, with a success so well known that it is unnecessary to refer to it. In the enlargement and enriching of his Department, partly by the direction of excavations on classical soil—memorably those at Ephesus, which resulted in the discovery of the Temple of Diana—and partly by the purchase of celebrated collections of antiquities. Chief among his transactions of the latter kind was the purchase of the collection of the Duke de Blacas in 1866, which, as public opinion testified at the time, was a most important gain to the National Museum. The acquisition was not effected without difficulties, as may be seen from the following letter :—

"Hôtel des Deux Mondes, Paris,
November 25th, 1866.

"My dear Panizzi,

Jones tells me that after the meeting of the Trustees on Friday, Mr. D'Israeli had an interview with you about the Blacas purchase. I write, therefore, to thank you for having backed my recommendation, which I am quite sure you must have done strongly, or otherwise the Government would not have come to a decision so rapidly. I never was more astonished than when I received authority to treat on

E

Sunday morning last. While we were signing the contract poor DeWitte was at the Grand' Messe. ' If I had only known,' he said to me afterwards, ' two hours sooner what you were about, I would have telegraphed to the Emperor at Compiégne.' The French are greatly disgusted. From all I can learn, they meant to offer about £40,000, and keep the matter dragging on till they had found out our last offer. I am very much pleased at the result, because I know how greatly the value of our Museum, as a whole, will be increased by this purchase, which supplies exactly what we were most deficient in.

There will, I have no doubt, be a great outcry in England about the largeness of the sum; but I am perfectly ready to bear the brunt of all that. The public will find out in time what a prize they have got. I hear that Mérimée was very anxious that it should be secured for the Louvre. He was on the Commission, but was obliged to go South. Perhaps you may be writing to him; I should like very much to hear what he has to say about the purchase. There is no one who has done more to defend my purchases than he has, up to this date, so I hope he will now. I am going to see the collection of M. Thiers to-morrow morning, and shall be curious to hear what he says.

Yours ever sincerely,
C. T. NEWTON."

We trust that we shall not be held to have failed in our endeavour to do justice to the services rendered by Mr. Newton to the National Museum. Apart from the high attainments to which testimony should be offered, this gentleman was so intimately connected with the subject of the memoir, that the omission of such a record would have been a serious fault, considering the constant intercommunion which existed between the two, and the mutual assistance they rendered each other.

As a conclusion to our present chapter, it must be noted that on the 6th of July, 1859, Panizzi was admitted to the Honorary Degree of D.C.L. at the University of Oxford.

CHAPTER XVI.

DESIRE TO VISIT NAPLES—PIUS IX.—FERDINAND II.
— REVOLUTION, 1848 — POERIO AND SETTEMBRINI
— "GIOVINE ITALIA" — MR. GLADSTONE'S VISIT
TO NAPLES.

IT may be readily conceived that Panizzi, an interested
and enlightened observer, as well as a critic of foreign
and English politics, did not regard as matters of
secondary importance, or affection, the affairs of his
native Italy. In the summer of 1846, being desirous
of paying, for the first time, a visit to Naples, he applied, through Lord Palmerston, to the Government
of that State for the necessary permission. His
Lordship addressed a letter to Sir William Temple
on his friend's behalf, which ran as follows :—

"September 25th, 1846.

" Sir,
I have to inform you that Mr. Panizzi, a native of
Modena, who has been now for many years resident in Eng-
land, who holds the appointment of Keeper of the Printed
Books in the British Museum, wishes to go to Italy in the
course of this autumn, and to visit Naples.

Mr. Panizzi was many years ago connected with some persons who, on account of their political opinions, had incurred
the displeasure of the late Duke of Modena, but Mr. Panizzi
has long ceased to have anything to do with Italian politics,
and confines himself entirely to his official duties in England,
where he enjoys the friendship and esteem of distinguished
men of all parties.

Mr. Panizzi, however, would not like to enter the Neapolitan territory unless he were previously assured that he would be permitted to do so without hindrance, and that he would be free from molestation during the short time he might remain there, and as many members of H. M's Government have a great regard for Mr. Panizzi, and feel an interest in what concerns him, I have to desire that you will mention this to the Neapolitan Government, and that you will state H.M.'s Government would be much gratified if the requested assurance could be given.

I have, &c., &c.,　　PALMERSTON."

After some delay, in consequence, according to Sir William's account, of difficulties raised by the Minister of Police at Naples, the required permission was granted; but Panizzi did not think fit to avail himself of it upon this occasion. His visit, however, as will be seen, was only postponed. It will also be noticed that his influence was in course of time an important, if not the main instrument whereby the liberation of the unhappy victims of tyranny, then lying in the horrible dungeons of Naples, was effected.

In order to lay clearly before the reader the manner

in which such influence was exercised, it is best to give a brief account of the condition of Naples at and about the period of turmoil and revolution in Europe in the years 1847-9, and of the paternal treatment bestowed by the Government of Ferdinand

II., monarch of the Two Sicilies *(justly* entitled to
the appellation of *pater patriœ)* on many of his
ungrateful and recalcitrant subjects.

On the death (June 1st, 1846) of Gregory XVI.,
a pontiff with a true and earnest feeling of respect for things as they are, and a righteous
aversion to all unnecessary and gratuitous reforms,
great expectations were anticipated throughout all
Italy of good results from the rule of his successor,
Pius IX. The most sanguine hopes were entertained
that, through him, the rights of liberty would be
secured; and indeed, as Gioberti says, he was regarded as no less than the arbiter of peace in Europe.
Without casting the shadow of suspicion on the
genuineness of the new Pope's good intentions,
whereof he gave ample proof on his accession to the
Papal chair, it is nevertheless pretty evident that,
under the most favourable circumstances, these expectations stood but little chance of fulfilment. Even
had Pius IX. not been deceived in the first instance,
and by subsequent revolution frightened out of the
liberal principles to which he at first gave his adher-
ence, he was scarcely, himself, in a position to carry
them into practice. To preach reform and constitutionalism from the Vatican was to subvert the Papal
seat. External obstacles, again, would assuredly
stand in the way of him who should attempt to promote even moderate reforms in an Italian State of the
period. Many men who, in other places, and under
other circumstances, would have been regarded as
models of enlightenment and moderation, shamed by
the miserable history of their country, and exasper-

ated by long-continued oppression and misrule, had become somewhat blind to the wholesome doctrine that the art of construction is a chief constituent of political order. To another party, formidable in numbers if not conspicuous for wisdom, it was but labour lost to proffer anything in the shape of reform; these men would be content with nothing short of destruction. Of them and their adherents Panizzi has, as will be observed, expressed his fear and abhorrence in no measured terms. Hence his alienation from Mazzini, who, in his egregious selfishness, would have destroyed the elements of power that existed, but had never displayed the ability to provide a substitute.

Pius IX., whose intellectual powers were far from equal to the largeness of his heart, soon became involved in difficulties. His constant dread of acting prejudicially to the interests of the Church weighed him down; and the influence of Count Ludolf (Neapolitan Minister at Rome, well known for his retrogressive opinions) probably thwarted his good intentions in no small degree. From want of confidence in himself, as well as from despair at the impediments, subjective and objective, which perpetually obtruded themselves upon him, Pius had recourse for protection and direction to the counsel of others. Ill advisers were those whom he chose—Grasselini, Gizzi, and Antonelli. The results

of vacillation and evil communication were speedily
visible. Already, in November, 1846, a few short
months after his accession, in his address to the
Patriarchs and Archbishops, he roundly condemned
everything that bore the name of *Progress* as *seductive, false, deceitful, seditious, foolish, and destructive
of ties religious, political, and social.*

The first notable act of the reign of Pius IX. had
been to grant a general amnesty to all political
offenders. This act of clemency, though it gained
for him a certain amount of well-deserved popularity,
unhappily smothered in the heart of Ferdinand II.
all the veneration with which that monarch had been
wont to regard the occupants of St. Peter's chair.
The King even went so far, in his indignation, as to
stigmatise the Pope as the head of " Young Italy."
With his people it was different. The sensation
created at Naples by this amnesty was intense. The
inhabitants demanded that it should be placarded
throughout the city ; the King, however, not only set
his face against the proposal, but peremptorily forbade
all demonstrations in favour of His Holiness, sup-
pressed the sale of his portraits, and interdicted the
admission into the country of Roman newspapers.
Indeed, the very mention of the Pope's name was regarded as bordering on treason, and as calling for the
notice of the police.

It might possibly have come to pass, had foreign
powers possessed more satisfactory relations with one
another at this time, that better order would, under
the pressure of external suasion, have been maintained
in the Government of more than one Italian State,

The " Spanish Marriages " had created a coolness between France and England, and M. Guizot's foreign policy had thrown France, so far as regarded Italy, into the arms of Austria and the reactionary party. The prospect of establishing civil and religious liberty in the Peninsula looked extremely obscure. The clamouring for Reform, however, continued, intermittently throughout Italy. In Tuscany there appeared a speck of light in the surrounding darkness; for, urged by his people, the Grand Duke had shown himself nothing loth to grant reforms demanded of him. In Rome meetings and demonstrations were frequent. Amidst all this Ferdinand remained unmoved, notwithstanding the importunate entreaties of the emissaries of Louis-Philippe, the Duke d'Aumale, and Prince de Joinville. In fact his Majesty plainly and deliberately gave them to understand that their presence in his kingdom was undesirable.

Liberty of the Press being excluded from the King's Dominions, its place was filled by the usual substitute, the issue of anonymous pamphlets; amongst many others was one entitled *Protesta del Popolo delle due Sicilie*, from the pen of the celebrated Luigi Settembrini. This work, which was immediately seized, contained a long and detailed account of the cruelties inflicted during so many years by the Neapolitan Government on its hapless subjects. A copy of the pamphlet reached the hands of Ferdinand, who determined that no pains should be spared to discover its author. Suspicion fell on many of the leading Liberals, who were consequently imprisoned, amongst them Carlo Poerio, Mariano d'Ayala, Domenico

Mauro, and others. Banishment was the sentence of those who could not be seized, and amongst them was Settembrini, who escaping to Malta, no sooner found himself on safe ground, than he avowed himself as author of the pamphlet.

Meanwhile Calabria and Sicily were in a state of fermentation, and the King, perplexed by the general condition of affairs, was induced to grant a general amnesty.

The North of Italy was at this time in calmer and happier circumstances. Charles Albert, King of Sardinia, had consented to measures of Liberal Reform, and certain influential northern Italians, headed by Counts Mammiani and Balbo, Massimo d'Azeglio, Cavour and Silvio Pellico, had petitioned Ferdinand II. to make concessions similar to those they enjoyed in their kingdom, but without avail. Nor was England wanting in sympathy with the suffering, for Lord Minto, by direction of Lord Palmerston, had arrived from the north of Italy, at Naples, on an intercessory mission to the King in behalf of his people.

This interference of England caused much consternation in Austria. Prince Metternich warned Lord Palmerston that the Emperor was firmly resolved to keep his Empire intact. His Lordship's reply to the warning was characteristic; that, although he respected the rights of Austria, still he entertained a strong opinion that the people of Italy had a perfect right to use all legitimate means for their own amelioration. At Naples, notwithstanding Lord Minto's mission, troubles increased. The King remained as obdurate as ever, and was supported by the members of his family, with the single exception of the Count of Syracuse, who, for the expression of his views, was forthwith expelled from the kingdom.

Earnestly as England desired the promotion of liberty in Italy, she was not unmindful of the safety of Kings ; and, consequently, the then British Ambassador at Rome suggested that the English fleet should proceed to Naples to protect the King, and that Count Ludolf should be informed " that the encouragement of popular insurrection formed no part of the hearty support England was disposed to give to the progress of liberal reform in Italy, and at the same time strongly impressing on him the danger to which the King would be exposed, unless he made some advances to satisfy the just expectations of his subjects."

In December, 1847, a revolution of vast magnitude was impending at Palermo, and in the same month a final appeal was made to the King urging him to recognise the rights of his subjects.

The 12th of January, 1848, was fixed on as the day for the expiration of this ultimatum. As heretofore, the application was treated with contempt, and an armed force was dispatched, headed by the Duke Serra Capriola.

The first shots were fired on the 12th of January, the fête-day of the King, whereupon fresh troops were sent from Naples with orders to Désauget, the General commanding, that, in case of resistance, he should *make a garden of Palermo*. Désauget accordingly bombarded the town, but happily failed to make a *garden* or a desert of it, and was forced, after losing many men, to return to Naples. So matters went on

from bad to worse. No sooner had the King made
concessions than he withdrew them, continually fore-
swearing himself.

The subjugation of the Sicilians (in support of
whom Lord Minto, much disappointed by a pseudo-
constitution granted by the King, in which their rights
were simply disregarded, had set out for Palermo),
still remained as difficult of completion as ever. On
the 25th of March, the Sicilian Parliament met at the
last-named place, and declared the dethronement of
Ferdinand II. Thereupon ensued the bombardment
of Messina, whence arose the King's universally-
known nickname of *King Bomba.* The independence
of Sicily was now recognised by France and England.
In May the cry of " Religion in Danger !" was raised
by the Royalist clique, and the refusal of St.
Januarius to work his annual miracle infused much
terror into the superstitious minds of the lower orders.
Unfortunately, the means successfully employed in
times past by a certain French General to induce the
Saint to perform his duty were now impracticable.

By this time, a National Guard having been instituted, the King's position was really imperilled, and
he was in the act of preparing with his family to quit
Naples by sea, when the troops and the populace
came into collision. This, as usual, resulted in street
fighting ; also, as a natural consequence, the regulars
gained the mastery, and a sad massacre ensued ;
whilst to slaughter, the *Lazzaroni,* the natural adherents of the King, added the inevitable accompaniment
of pillage. Under such circumstances did Naples remain in a state of siege until the 15th of June.

Meantime the Sicilians had proclaimed the Duke of Genoa their future ruler; a division of 16,000 troops, under Filangieri, was dispatched for active service, and, after an obstinate resistance, landed at Messina.

In November the King proceeded to Gaeta, in order to meet there Pius IX., who, by this time having lost his popularity, had gained an equivalent by securing the friendship of Ferdinand. Whilst there, news of the Austrian victory at Novara reached the ears of the two confederates, and was the cause of great rejoicing to both; notwithstanding that, forced by popular pressure, Ferdinand had despatched 12,000 of his troops (he had promised 40,000) as a contingent to the Sardinian army. This great triumph of absolutism by no means disposed the King to alter, or even to moderate, his style of government. Arrests and acts of violence and brutality became continuous, and the unhappy Liberals were unduly rewarded for their attachment to the cause of freedom—Filippo Agresti, Carlo Poerio, and Luigi Settembrini being arrested and imprisoned in the dungeons of the "Vicaria," the most loathsome of the invariably loathsome Neapolitan prisons.

Thus much have we written to show the state of Naples at the time to which our biography appertains. Yet this brief sketch of the position would be incomplete did we altogether ignore the two patriots, Poerio and Settembrini, who, not merely on account of their notoriety as chiefs of the Liberal party, but as friends both of Panizzi and Mr. Gladstone, call for some especial notice in these pages.

Whoever has studied the history of Italy, more especially the history of the country in these latter times, will have learnt that Italian unity—the zeal for which had, during all the centuries between King Arduinus and Victor Emmanuel II., never become extinguished—was not accomplished by the efforts of any one individual. Amongst the number of those in the highest rank who devoted their lives to the achievement of the noble end, stand Poerio and Settembrini.

Their patriotism extended beyond the circumscription of their native town, province, or State; they felt that each subordinate nationality must blend with the others, to enable their common Italy to take her due place in the assembly of nations—to speak with undivided voice on the affairs of Europe; to be, in fact, the one Italy of their aspirations—strong because united. For this, while their individual designations were still Modenese, Neapolitans, Venetians, or what not, they must be, over and above all, Italians.

Poerio was born at Naples in 1803. He afterwards became a lawyer, and

for some time during the troubled reign of Ferdinand was, at least when at liberty, the leader of the "Left" in the Neapolitan Parliament. The term "a chequered life" might fairly be used as expressive of such a career; were it not that his undertakings, having all the same end in view, in which he was almost incessantly engaged, and the perpetual series of arrests and imprisonments which he suffered, imparted, as it were, a melancholy uniformity to his career. In 1831 the crown of Italy was offered by the patriots of the Romagna to Ferdinand II. That monarch, probably feeling an innate disability to govern constitutionally, or otherwise than according to the dictates of his own will, a condition doubtless affixed to the tender, declined the proffered gift. What he might have done had he accepted, must remain in the realm of conjecture ; his refusal to lend his aid to the settlement of the country's deplorably unsettled state caused plot upon plot to spring up on all sides. The name *Liberali* was now first given to the opponents of the King. These were unceasing in preaching to the people, according to their light, the blessings of Constitutional Government. If their skill in politics, as may reasonably be supposed, was small, their honesty and love of country were large ; and assuredly no form which they may have conceived, however crude, could have equalled in weakness and depravity the various petty tyrannies by which their country was distracted. Amongst these *Liberali*, the most active and beyond doubt the most able, was Carlo Poerio. It is worthy of remark that when, in 1847, Pius IX. had achieved his reputation as the first reformer of Italy, the only two men of note who disbelieved in him were Poerio and King Ferdinand II. After the breaking out of the Sicilian Revolution on the 12th of January, 1848, at the time he was a prisoner, Poerio's fortunes took a more favourable turn. Freed from his bondage, he was made Prime Minister, and subsequently Minister of Public Instruction. His aspirations, however, were too modest to assume such dignity—his aim was to be no more than a simple Member of Parliament, and in two months he had retired from all official life. But his days of freedom were destined to be but of short duration. On the 19th of July, 1849, he was again arrested, and confined in the Castel dell' Ovo, and from thence removed to the "Vicaria." From this he was on the 1st of February, 1850, taken in chains to the Arsenal, and with Michele Pironti sent as a common convict to Nisida.

Were we to relate *all* the adventures of Poerio, interesting and important as they are, it would be properly considered an interpolation in our biography. A great and melancholy portion of the story is best told in his own words. He was asked, on his way to the dungeons, how he was, and he answered *Fò questa cura di ferro da parecchi anni, e mi sento più forte (I have now been taking this iron remedy for several years, and feel much stronger)*. In a future chapter we shall have still more to say respecting this *martyr of liberty ;* but let us pass to those later years of his life, when tardy success 'hardly requited such loving patriotism, and barely compensated for his great misfortunes. In 1859, when he came out of prison, he was elected member for Arezzo, but steadily refused to accept a place in the Cabinet, although much pressed by Cavour. He died on the 28th of April, 1867.

Luigi Settembrini, though standing many rungs of the political ladder lower than Poerio, was nevertheless a hardy and enthusiastic patriot. Mr. Gladstone wrote of him in his letters to Lord Aberdeen (hereafter to be mentioned) as one *in a sphere by some degrees narrower, but with a character quite as pure and fair* as Poerio's. Settembrini was born at Naples, the 17th of April, 1813. His father was a lawyer, and, like his son, a patriot, and had fought for his country in the stirring days of 1820-1. Of Luigi's private life we may say that he was a teacher of Italian literature and an eminent classical scholar. In 1848 he, together with Poerio, was tried on the trumped-up charge of being member of a secret society. This charge was further supported by a letter concocted by the police, so gross and palpable a forgery that the very judges in the case considered it more prudent to reject it as evidence. With Poerio and forty more he was capitally convicted. The sentence was not executed, yet he was reserved for a fate as hard—perpetual imprisonment *upon a remote sea-girt rock.*

Although Settembrini was in the above case most unjustifiably, nay, iniquitously, convicted, and barbarously punished, it is well known that he was, as a matter of fact, an ardent supporter of the society

F

called "Giovine Italia," an association which, had the
sagacity of its directors been more, and the audacity
of its purposes less, might have given some trouble
to the then rulers of Italy. When the King of
Naples, as has been said, charged Pius IX. with being
at the head of *Young Italy*, he probably made use of
the most scurrilous phrase, by way of accusation,
which occurred to him. The "Giovine Italia," however, was an established fact, albeit the association
numbered not the Pope amongst its members, nor was
it under the special protection of the Church.
Tyranny has this superiority over luckless poverty
that it renders those on whom it presses dangerous as
well as ridiculous. This peculiar form of danger, the
Secret Society, which tyranny calls into existence, is
commonly less formidable to the powers against
which it is organised than to the causes which it is
intended to protect. Had the modest programme of
the "Giovine Italia" been carried into execution, a
despotism would have been created more unbearable
than the yoke of Austria, the Vatican, and King
Bomba united. The prime object of this society was
to abolish all Princes then reigning in Italy—including, of course, the Pope—and not only to drive the
Austrians out of the country, but the French from
Corsica and the English from Malta. When these
laudable ends had been accomplished, a great Military Republic was to be established under a supreme
Dictator, residing at Rome, with ten consuls to govern
the ten divisions into which the whole of Italy was to
be parcelled out. Each province or division was to
be under a colonel, its Municipal Government being

administered by a captain. To each division, subject to the officers thereof, was to belong a treasurer, him self also a military man. In addition to these officers an order was to be instituted entitled "Apostoles," whose duty it should be to act as dictatorial or consular agents, and to settle and arrange matters in general.

The regulations for the internal conduct of the Society show a certain skill of organization, coupled with a good deal of the childishness of bugbear solemnity usually appertaining to such associations. The following will serve as specimens of some of the more important of these regulations :—"No meetings of members to be allowed, and no conversation between members more than two in number at any one time. Oaths to be sworn on a skull and dagger. The Republican flag to be a white skull on a black field, and the motto *Unità, Libertà, Indipendenza.* The dress to be black, and the arms a musket and bayonet, with a side dagger. Drilling to form a principal and constant duty."

Although a Secret Society of this description is a standing monument of folly and wickedness, yet it is hardly possible, considering the state of things in Italy at the time of which we write, not to feel some compassion and make some allowance for the conspirators of "Giovine Italia." Their great idea—the Unity of Italy—had been set forth by Dante according to a poet's conception. Macchiavelli had planned its execution as a statesman. The love of country was extended by the patriotic subject of the kingdom of the Two Sicilies to every corner of his native land.

F2

The dream—if dream it may be called—has found its accomplishment in reality within our own time, but happily not by the agency nor after the ideas and programme of " Young Italy."

In the early part of 1851 Mr. Gladstone made his

memorable visit to Naples; *Si natura negat facit indig-*

natio versum. The great statesman possessed a nature particularly averse to revolutionary sentiments or prejudices, and a more impartial judge betwixt King and People never existed. Shortly after his arrival he had "supped full of horrors," and he longed to express his inward feelings on the palpable absence of justice in the actions of the Neapolitan Government, and the cruelties practised on the persons of hapless political offenders, many wrongfully condemned—cruelties of which he was an unwilling and shocked witness. His observations resulted in the two celebrated letters to Lord Aberdeen. The general character of the administration is well summed up in a pithy sentence quoted in the first, *E la negazione di Dio eretta a sistema di governo.* (This is the negation of God erected into a system of government.)

Mr. Gladstone, with his usual moderation and desire of accuracy, declines, in these letters, to decide, and shows himself willing to give Ferdinand the benefit of all doubt on the subject. He even records an instance of "a direct and unceremonious appeal to the King's humanity, which met with a response on his part evidently sincere." His account of the prisons of Naples inclines us to refer our readers to this correspondence rather than to transfer his description to our own pages. Suffice it to say, that he calls them "the extreme of filth and horror," the Vicaria "that charnel-house," in which, amongst other iniquities, even proper medical assistance was withheld from the sick prisoners.

It was not long ere an answer to these statements was attempted by the Neapolitan Government, under the title *Rassegna degli Errori e delle Fallacie pubblicate dal Sig. Gladstone*, &c., &c. This brochure evinced an ingenuity of sophistical argument, to say the least of it, only worthy of such a cause. Before any authorized reply to it appeared, it had been skilfully and sufficiently answered by an anonymous author in a pamphlet entitled :—*A Detailed Exposure of the Apology put forth by the Neapolitan Government, in reply to the Charges of Mr. Gladstone, under the title of Rassegna, &c., &c. (1852). London.* Mr. Gladstone's own answer, entitled, *An Examination of the Official Reply of the Neapolitan Government*, was published soon afterwards. In this the writer grants the utmost limits of concession to his opponents ; whatever rests not on manifestly sufficient evidence, nay, on moral certainty, he retracts : whatever even seems to require modification, he unhesitatingly modifies ; but, modification and retraction notwithstanding, it must be acknowledged that the case stands much as it was. To quote the author's own words :—" I believe that, for my own vindication, I might without any new publication have relied in perfect safety upon the verdict already given by the public opinion and announced by the press of Europe. The arrow has shot deep into the mark, and cannot be dislodged."

Judging from a letter of Mr. Gladstone's to Panizzi, it may be concluded that the latter had much to do with the publication of these famous letters :—

"October 6th, 1849.

" My dear Panizzi,

" . . . . You and I have, I think, been looking with much the same feeling at what has been passing in Rome. I am no great revolutionist elsewhere; but I am persuaded that the civil Government of three millions of people ought not to be carried on only by priests, and a real representative system giving the community the power of the purse, is the best, and, so far as I can see, ought to be accepted or endured.

Always very sincerely yours,

W. E. GLADSTONE."

CHAPTER XVII.

Cardinal Alberoni—Panizzi and Lord Shrewsbury — Correspondence arising from Mr. Gladstone's Visit to Naples.

There now arose, mainly out of the great subject treated by the Gladstone letters, a correspondence of even more importance to this biography. This was between Panizzi and Lord Shrewsbury, who died at Naples, 9th of November, 1852. In 1850 he went to reside on the continent, where it was his greatest pleasure to live in quiet retirement at his villa near Palermo. From thence he visited Switzerland, but returned to Sicily in October, 1852. The autumn of that year he spent at Rome. In politics he was a Whig. In the Catholic Directory we read " that the angelic purity of Lord Shrewsbury was the theme of every one's admiration, and never did he allow a light or indelicate word, or the slightest allusion contrary to modesty to be made before him."

In order that the reader may rightly understand the first few lines of this chapter, it must be stated *en passant*, that Panizzi had written in the " British and Foreign Review " for October, 1844, an article on the Republic of San Marino, and in it had attempted a vindication of that brilliant example of a self-made man and dexterous (we may say unscrupulous) politician, Cardinal Alberoni.

Let it also be said that the dark as well as the bright side of Alberoni's character is therein treated with perfect impartiality. His intention was to write a full biography of the eminent Cardinal, and had requested Lord Shrewsbury to procure him some documents at Rome, as material for the work.

The commencement of Lord Shrewsbury's first letter contains the answer to this commission :—

"Palermo, April 5th, 1851.

"Dear Mr. Panizzi,

As a private opportunity offers for England, I take advantage of it to say that I have by no means neglected your commission, yet I can only say in general terms that I have not succeeded in all your desire, for just now I cannot lay my hand on the correspondence, but the papers are where no one can get at them without a great deal of fuss, and without the intervention of some influential person on the spot, and who will undertake to examine them at the same time; and now that Cardinal Wiseman has, to our great surprise, left the position he was destined for, and taken up another where we did not expect to see him, the scheme you had so honourably intended for the vindication of an injured Prelate, and calumniated diplomatist and statesman, must fall to the ground for the present. Of course you have "Istoria del Cardinale Alberoni, Seconda Edizione, &c., &c., Amsterdam, 1720." This appears, by the notice of it, to be an authentic and able defence of the Cardinal, containing four letters written by *himself* from Sestri, *in reply to the accusations brought against him.* If you can suggest anything I shall be happy to attend to it, but things at Rome are so perplexed and troublesome that it is difficult to get anyone to take an interest in matters that do not immediately concern their own duties. Had our friend Cardinal Wiseman remained, the thing could have been done no doubt, but he too has other questions to occupy him just at present. . . ."

The following brilliant passage in the same letter commences the controversy between the correspondents on the affairs of the Neapolitan Government—
Risum teneatis?

" We enjoy the peace and quiet—*both civil and religious*—of this place amazingly: and begin to feel that we are safer and happier under the absolutism of Ferdinand II., and the Martial Law of our Good Prince Satriano, than under the boasted sway of the ' Glorious Principles ! !' For, under your good friend Ferdinand, and his worthy representative, we are sure of safety and protection, as long as we observe the law, as becomes a peaceful member of society. But, under the ' Glorious Principles ' we violate no law, and fancy ourselves safe, when, lo and behold, we are arraigned as criminals, and condemned to be mulct to the last farthing by an *ex post facto* arrangement of the collective wisdom (?) of the freest and most enlightened nation under the sun! But I shall shock your sensitive nerves, and scandalize your constitutional orthodoxy, so I must bid you good-bye, and beg of you to believe me, dear Mr. Panizzi, your very obedient and obliged friend and servant,

SHREWSBURY."

Thus Panizzi replied to the first of these passages:—

" British Museum, April 24th, 1851.

" My dear Lord,

I have had the honour to receive, a few days ago, your Lordship's letter of the fifth inst., than which no letter could have given me greater pleasure. I should have acknowledged this honour ere this, had not the malady and subsequent death of Lord Langdale, one of the best friends I have ever had, taken from me the power of fulfilling even the most agreeable duty of thanking your Lordship for the kindness in remembering my request in reference to Alberoni, and still more for that of addressing to me so excellent a letter as you have been pleased to do. I cannot give your Lordship better proof of the value I set on your communication than by respectfully and frankly laying before your Lordship my views on the various topics to which your letter draws my attention, even when those views do not unfortunately coincide with your Lordship's. Before coming to that, however, I wish to say a few words respecting Alberoni. From Prince Castelcicala I had already received a message, for which I begged him to thank your Lordship, showing that you had not forgotten the favour I had been encouraged by your kindness to ask your Lordship. I now beg to enclose a memorandum in Italian, stating in a few words what I want from Rome, and why I want it, and if a a further attempt could be made I should feel obliged; if not, we must have patience. The Emperor of Russia has actually graciously condescended to order the copies of certain documents in his Imperial Archives to be made out and sent to me, and at Rome one cannot, even through the powerful interest of your Lordship, find means of knowing whether certain papers contain any charge against a Cardinal, who was certainly innocent, who is calumniated in history, and whose innocence, it is expected, would be fully established were the contents of the papers in question known. These are mortifying comparisons, my Lord, for us both as Catholics, and for me, moreover, as an Italian. The schismatic Emperor more ready to assist in proving the innocence of a Cardinal than Rome! ! ! Whatever has been printed and published respecting Alberoni I have procured, and the letters mentioned by your Lordship were the documents which led me first to suppose him innocent and calumniated, a supposition which further researches have amply confirmed.

I sincerely wish Cardinal Wiseman had remained at Rome, not so much on account of the assistance which, I do not doubt, his Eminence would have lent me in the Alberoni affair, as, on account of the irreparable mischief that his coming back to England has produced. . . ."

The reader need hardly to be reminded that the
last sentence refers to the celebrated " Papal aggression" of 1851. Panizzi's answer to Lord Shrewsbury's curious laudation of the Government of Naples
is direct and incisive :—

"I am grieved, my Lord, more than I can express, at the
praises your Lordship bestows on the Government of his
Sicilian Majesty. I am grieved, because the countenance of
such a Government by so high an authority as your Lordship's encourages tyranny and despotism, to which two
abominations all the miseries of mankind are to be attributed. I say *all* advisedly ; for all the follies, the wickedness, the crimes of the extreme Republicans, whom I detest
as cordially as the Neapolitan Government can do, are *all*
owing to the detestable Governments under which people
live, and by which they are driven to madness. Nations are,
to a very great extent (I am almost inclined to say altogether)
what their spiritual and temporal rulers make them ; and in
the same manner that we attribute much of the unfortunate
state of Ireland to the English misgovernment of old, we must
be just and attribute the miseries of Sicily, her dissatisfaction,
her rebellious spirit, her crimes, and her cruelties to misgovernment. It is misgovernment that makes repealers,
socialists, red republicans, &c. I wish I could say that
things have improved of late in the Neapolitan Government ;
but, my Lord, Europe has heard with horror of the iniquitous, cruel, and worse than heathenish trials and condem-
nations that have lately taken place against men whose innocence is as well known and clear as daylight. I should not speak
so positively were it not that Mr. Gladstone, the member for the
Oxford University, whose talents, whose honesty, and whose sober
political principles need no praise, has just come from Naples
in such a state of indignation against the Government as I
should never have expected to see in such a man. He has
made it his business to enquire into the truth of the charges,

into the 'proofs brought forward to support them, into the character of the accusers, witnesses, and judges, into the conduct of the Government, into the treatment of the accused, both before and after condemnation, and he has come to the conclusion, which he has expressed to me and to others in these precise words, deliberately weighed and then repeated, *the Government of Naples is the Government of Hell upon earth.* These expressions from an English gentleman, uttered in English, with the accent of deep religious conviction, need no comment. Mr. Gladstone has shown me documents in support of his conviction, and they bear him out most abundantly. As a strong Conservative, and because he is a Conservative, as a Christian and as a gentleman, Mr. Gladstone (I use his own words) feels himself bound in conscience to expose iniquities which I am horrified in thinking of. He will do so in the House of Commons, as far as he can, but the details are so horrible, so revolting, so indecent that he will not be able to tell before an assembly of gentlemen the whole truth. But what he will and can say will produce the proper effect in Europe, not on Republicans only, but on statesmen of Conservative principles, who feel these principles disgraced and compromised by such abominations. No Government can be formed in England, should the present one be forced to make way, without Mr. Gladstone, who, in office as out of office, will not spare the guilty. Another man of unimpeachable character, of remarkable talents, of opposite political principles, Sir William Molesworth, fully agrees with Mr. Gladstone, and both say openly that they rejoice at the majority of the House of Commons that kept Palmerston in office last summer, when they both voted in the minority.

Your Lordship is at perfect liberty to state all this; neither Mr. Gladstone nor Sir William Molesworth shrink from the responsibility of their statements; on the contrary, they make them openly and unreservedly. I pledge my honour that I do not overstate what they say; in fact, it is IMPOSSIBLE to do so. If your Lordship, however, has any doubt, just please to write to either or both of them, and ask if I exaggerate.

And now, my Lord, allow me for the sake of humanity, whose cause I know no one has more at heart than your Lordship, for the sake of good government and religion, allow me to beseech you heartily to refrain from praising a government like that of Naples, or rather let me entreat your Lordship to use the powerful influence you must possess to open the eyes of the authorities, and induce them, for their own sake, for the sake of humanity, to behave like Christians."

The reply to this contained in the following extract is both in form and substance a wonderful specimen of logical reasoning. We abstain from further comment on it and at once insert it, lest we detract from the enjoyment the reader must derive from its perusal:—

"Palermo, May 21st, 1851.

" Dear Mr. Panizzi,

I am very thankful for your kind, interesting, though melancholy letter of the 24th ult., but which only reached me yesterday evening, and as our post goes to-morrow, I have but little time to say anything. But the main question you have treated is so important and big with all sorts of consequences, that I cannot refrain from immediately touching on it. I translated that portion relating to Naples, and took it to the Lord Lieutenant, who will forthwith send it to Naples, and ask for some official document in return. He at once, as I was sure he could with a safe conscience, denied the truth of the main charges. That the prisons are in a very unsatisfactory state, cannot be denied, and is sadly to be lamented. But reforms are almost always tedious and difficult. In what condition were the prisons in England some fifty years ago? Yet the King is by no means unmindful of them, and the female prisons have been thoroughly amended. They are now in the hands of the Jesuits and the Sisters of Charity. . . . But the iniquities of the Judicial system, as applied to State prisoners, is the great offence. Now, from what I had heard from Sir William Temple myself and from others, and what I hear now from the good Prince who rules this island, I am thoroughly convinced that Mr. Gladstone has been deceived by false testimony. The King's government is the least vindictive it is possible to conceive; before 1848 there was not one State prisoner in Naples, and before the Revolution here, there had not been one single capital execution for six years. So much the worse you will say, and so say I. It was this mistaken leniency that wrought out half of the social mischief. Remember the trials are all public, the witnesses are examined in public, the proceedings are published in the public papers, and out of the thousands who have offended, very few are arrested and tried. The proceedings are slow for the purpose of giving, not violating justice, ... Sir W. Temple told me all that you have now asserted on the authority of Mr. Gladstone and Sir W. Molesworth, and he added that of all the liberal side of the late Chamber of Deputies there was not one who was not either an exile or a prisoner. I was horrified at the statement, and went forthwith to a most respectable English *Resident*, who knew Naples well: he immediately said, 'That is false, to my own knowledge, for I am acquainted with several who are neither one nor the other.' But the truth is that Sir W. Temple is mystified, and thus mystifies others. He and Lord Napier, and all the Consuls, and all the travelling Ministers (such as Lord Minto) are, and have been ever in the hands of the Revolutionary Party, and are duped by them, and I am confident that Mr. Gladstone's evidence will turn out of the same quality. After all, who were the liberals' deputies?—who the men who infuriated the people on the 15th of May, and overturned the Constitution? They were Red Republicans, sworn to dethrone the Sovereign. Would they have been better treated in Ireland than in Naples? . . . . The Revolution here was nothing but a history of atrocious

crime and atrocious tyranny—regular mob-law exercised by
a mob of armed banditti.   There is no more honourable or
humane or upright a man than Filangieri, nor a more
humane and upright and honourable a Prince than his
Sovereign; but, as M. Fortunato told Baillie Cochrane, ' the
characters of the Sovereign and his servants are sacrificed to
the calumnies spread abroad in Naples,' by those who ought
to know better.   No man reverences Liberty more than I
do, or sees, and hates the evils of despotism; but mob-law is
the greatest evil of all, and this, so far, has been the only
blessing which so-called Constitutional liberty has hitherto
brought to poor ill-fated Italy. . . . .

Very truly and sincerely yours,

SHREWSBURY."

And, at the risk of exceeding our limits of space,
Panizzi's reply must be given in full:—

" British Museum, June 4th, 1851.

" My dear Lord,

The day before yesterday I had the honour to
receive your Lordship's letter of the 21st of last month.   I
need not add that I am very much obliged to your Lordship
for it.   As your Lordship observes, the points now the chief
subjects of our correspondence are so very important that I hope
you will forgive me if I take the liberty of freely expressing
my opinion when I am so unfortunate as to differ from your
Lordship; for on such subjects flattery, and even over-defer-
ence, are a crime.   It is the more necessary that I should,
with ! due respect, but freely, express my dissent, when
requisite, from your Lordship's conclusions, as the opinion of
your Lordship, and a correct knowledge of the facts on your
part may lead to very important consequences.

I need not state it especially and prominently, perhaps,
but *ad abundantiam* I wish it to be well understood, that in
what I am going to say I mean nothing disrespectful towards
His Sicilian Majesty, whom I supposed to be moved only by

a sincere desire of performing the duties of his high station as a Christian Prince. I give him, therefore, credit for the very best intentions, and I trust I am not wrong in supposing that far from feeling offended with those who, like myself, strive to open his eyes to the real state of his Government (supposing the opinions and statements of so humble a person like myself were to be known to his Majesty), he would feel thankful. As to the Prince of Satriano, I cannot figure to myself a Filangieri otherwise than humane, high-minded, and a lover of truth and justice. It is a name of which an Italian must be proud. . . . .

Your Lordship's letter refers to three very distinct topics. First, the conduct of the Liberals ; second, that of the King and his Government ; third, that of the Courts of Law.

With respect to the first point, I shall not trouble your Lordship with many observations. If it be true that the people had no reason to be dissatisfied ; if it be true that in Sicily, for instance, they were guilty of the atrocities laid at their door ; if the chambers of representatives were formed out of needy lawyers and brawling demagogues, how is it, my Lord, that the Government which has always been strong and despotic has not produced better results ? Whose fault is it that people don't know when they ought to be satisfied, that when they can they are cruel, ferocious, and all that, that needy lawyers and demagogues carry the day ? . .

I hope, my dear Lord, that a passage in your letter is mis-understood by me. Your Lordship seems to think that it was owing to the leniency of the Government that the Liberals did all the alleged mischief, and that, by shedding of blood, better results would have been obtained. If so, I beg to differ entirely from your Lordship. I am not one of those squeamish sort of persons who faint at the mention of punishment of death, even for political crimes; but assuredly the Neapolitan Government has never been accused of weak-ness on that score. I believe there have been more people put to death in the two Sicilies for political crimes since the

G

French Revolution in 1789 began than in any other country in the world, France excepted. In Spain civil war has raged for so many years that it is impossible to draw a comparison. But in no part of Germany or of the North, of course not in England, nor even in other parts of Italy, has blood been shed more recklessly, more cruelly, or more remorselessly than in the kingdom of the two Sicilies. And what is the result, I ask once more? Oh, my Lord, that blood letting is a terrible and dangerous remedy! . . . It is a game at which two may play, and if Kings are too ready to put to death, they may teach republicans the same readiness. . . . .

As to the conduct of the King's Government, I can only say that, if there be no aristocracy in either Sicily or Naples, it is only because it has been destroyed by the King's Government—that it is owing to the Government that the French law of succession has been introduced in the kingdom of Naples, and then in Sicily, that in those kingdoms the scandal has been often seen repeated of the Sovereign swearing to statutes and fundamental laws, and then breaking his oath without fear of God or man. . . . . This may be kingcraft of some sort, but it is not either religion or morality. . . . . I hear it often said, 'Oh, the people are deceived and misled by demagogues, on whom they ought not to place confidence.' Why, on whom are they to place confidence? The poor people, when what passes before their eyes shows to them that those who govern them hold nothing sacred, and that the more solemn the oath, the more explicit the promises, the more earnest the appeals to loyalty, the more easy the perjury, the more barefaced the quibbling, the more gross the deception of those who relied on oaths, on promises, and on fair words?

After the 15th of May, 1848, a proclamation was published at Naples, signed by the King only; weigh well his words as an English gentleman, and recollect there are not two principles of morals—one for Kings and the other for other persons, or one for England, and one for Naples. . . . . Well, then, what has been done, and *with what success*—for I am a man of facts, and not of theories—to establish that good Government that is to be the forerunner of the Guarantees for it ? And if the Constitutional system is impossible, why did the King give a Constitution ? . . . .

I now come to the third point. Your Lordship tells me that Mr. Gladstone has been deceived. . . . . You say distinctly not only that Sir W. Temple and Sir W. Molesworth are mistaken and have been deceived, but you hold as undoubted that Sicilian liberals, as well as foreign Diplomatists and Consuls, and Captains, and Admirals, and Ministers, &c., &c., all are either knaves or fools, who either wilfully or stupidly misrepresent the truth. Well, if I had no other data to judge of the validity of this sweeping exception than that the bulk of the persons here mentioned are Englishmen, I should not assent to your views. And not only many of them are Englishmen, that is belonging to a nation, as a whole, the most veracious on earth, but both English and Foreigners are persons of standing, &c. . . . . On what ground is your Lordship induced to doubt their trustworthiness ? Of your own knowledge you cannot know much. You collect your information from persons belonging to one side only, &c., &c. . . . . It is not said of all the Deputies on the liberal side of the late Chamber "there is not one who is not either an exile or a prisoner." What is said is what follows : 'Of the whole number of deputies (160), only 140 attended when the Chamber sat, of these 140 there are 24 in prison and 52 in exile, that is to say, more than half.' Let the names of those 140 who attended be looked after, and let the Government say where are 76 of them. If the Government do not do so, it may be, my Lord, I shall have the painful duty of sending a list to your Lordship myself for the Government's information. And in looking after deputies, I · wish you would inquire after one who was assassinated, and also ask for a certain Peluso, a priest, who enjoys a pension from the Government. . . . . With respect to

G2

the evidence of Mr. Gladstone individually, I beg to submit the following facts. Mr. Gladstone is a political opponent of the Ministers, and just before leaving London for Naples last summer, voted against Lord Palmerston on the Greek question. He went from here as strongly impressed as your Lordship can now be that Lord Palmerston's policy was wrong at Naples, and that Sir W. Temple was greatly to blame for calumniating the Neapolitan Government. Such were Mr. Gladstone's feelings on arriving at Naples. To say that he is a most scrupulously honourable man as well as one of the most acute living Statesmen, is to say what everybody knows. What must be stated in addition, as it is important to the point now in discussion, is that Mr. Gladstone is a thorough Italian Scholar, and reads as well as speaks the language as fluently and correctly as a well educated Italian. . . . .

" Now, my Lord, I defy those who tell you that Mr. Gladstone has been deceived to show that they have taken one-tenth of the trouble he has taken. . . . And I beg also to add that in Europe a statement of facts by Mr. Gladstone, even unsupported, which it is far from being, will outweigh the statements of all the judges and other officials of the Neapolitan Court. My blood boils to have to call such people *judges*, and such a den a Court! . . . I shall not apologise for the length of this letter. It was due to Mr. Gladstone to show that he is not likely to have been deceived, and it was due to your Lordship to show that you must have been deceived. I hope and trust you will not countenance by your praises, or by an extenuation of its faults, a Government which is a disgrace to humanity and to Christianity. . . .

Believe me, with great respect and truth,

Yours, &c., &c.,

A. PANIZZI."

Nothing daunted by such strong and keen weapons of argument, Lord Shrewsbury returns to the charge with a supply of counter-ammunition in the shape of a worthless pamphlet, written by one Mr. Macfarlane, and termed, in unconscious irony, the "Cause of Order."

"Palermo, June 12th, 1851.

"Dear Mr. Panizzi,

I send you an interesting little *brochure*, which, I trust, will serve to show that Mr. Gladstone has been mystified. Rely upon it, the Government of Naples, whatever imperfections it may have (and what Government is without them?) is by no means deserving of the censures which have been so liberally and so unjustly cast upon it by a certain class of writers, and still more, and with far greater effect, by a certain class of speakers and talkers.

Macfarlane's statements, in his 'Glance at Revolutionized Italy,' and in his appendix, I am convinced, are by no means too favourable. The absurd, ridiculous, superficial, and *notoriously false* facts and figures of Mr. Whiteside will never counteract the solid truth of the rival, and more experienced, and far more talented tourist. . . ."

The remainder of this letter is hardly worth quoting. Arguments, or assertions, are repeated, and there is much discussion on "the havoc, crime, and plunder" of the "Glorious Revolution," on the previous fulness of municipal coffers and general prosperity of the country; on the progress of all works of commerce and agriculture, the making of new roads and harbours, the lightness of taxation, &c. There was "no grievance except old Maio's slack hand over the demagogues. Had there been a Satriano or a Pronio there had been no Revolution, nor even a serious thought of it."

The statements of the English Blue Books are stigmatised as a mass of error and bad faith.

The extreme prolixity of Lord Shrewsbury's letters, and the weariness of the "damnable iteration" in which they abound, render it difficult, and indeed unnecessary, to present them in their entirety. In fact, so much of Panizzi's portion of the correspondence, as is set out in full, gives all that is wanted of his opponent's argument and of the answer to it. Lord Shrewsbury harps much on Sicily (out of which he comparatively rarely ventures) in his defence of the Government of King Ferdinand. Slightly oblivious of the fact that it is despotism that has reduced the Southern Italians to the state in which he finds them, he decides that such despotism should be perpetuated as the only form of Government which suits those it has created. To attempt to improve by absurd and iniquitous revolution, to interfere with the well-settled and satisfactory state of things here described by Lord Shrewsbury, and with the benevolent régime which had so ordered matters, would be reprehensible in the last degree. Meanwhile nothing can exceed the contempt with which the writer speaks of the almost too happy people of this too happily governed Kingdom; prefacing his notice by advising those who have rashly maligned the King and his Government to come over, and see and judge for themselves :—

" Let any one come here and read the official documents, and hear and see the lamentable history of a period which will ever be a blot upon our national honour and honesty, (for we violated every principle of international law,) he will imbibe very different notions of both the King and the Government which too many of us have been so unjustly and inveterately maligning. The people of these countries are no more fit for liberty than cats and dogs. They know not what it is, or how to use it, nor are there materials to guarantee its due exercise even if they understood it better. Large and free municipal privileges, *such as they really have*, with a good Governmental administration, and a strong hand to repress crime, is all that they are suited for, and all that they ought or do desire. . . . In the meanwhile, read Macfarlane, and sip in wisdom and instruction from his sprightly stream. . . . *You* look to his facts and assertions and the authorities upon which they rest, and believe that both you and Mr. Gladstone and Sir W. Molesworth have all been mystified, even more so than the readers of the Blue Books."

No apology, we feel sure, is needed for the introduction in this correspondence of such letters from Mr. Gladstone as reached Panizzi during its continuance, and bear on the subject matter. A passage in the following epistle will remind the reader of the contrast between revolutions in more than one foreign country, and the manner in which such movements have happily been hitherto dealt with in England:—

"June 21st, 1851.

"My dear Panizzi,

You speak of the scanty justice done here to the cause of Italy. No doubt it is true, but something must be allowed for the imperfection of all organs contrived by men. Parliament fails, sometimes egregiously, in its duty to England. I have often thought it impenetrably hardened in injustice when the question has been about some acts of our own to Foreign Powers or countries. I am then the less surprised that it has little time or thought for Italy, not having enough for its own immediate duties, and of course preferring, not perhaps without a tinge of selfishness, what lies nearest home. I do, however, *most deeply* grieve over the silence of Parliament about the expedition to Rome in 1849. That was a great opportunity and should not have been missed. It was missed, out of a misplaced regard to democracy, the sham democracy of France.

I am, however, certain as matter of *fact* that the Italian habit of preaching unity and nationality in preference to showing grievance, produces a revulsion here; for if there are two things on earth that John Bull hates, they are an abstract proposition or idea and the Pope. . . . .

Most sincerely yours,
W. E. GLADSTONE."

To speak of Lord Shrewsbury as an honourable, high-minded man—a gentleman in the strictest sense of the term, who honestly espoused the worse, inasmuch as he conscientiously believed it to be the better cause—would be almost offering an insult to his memory. An English Roman Catholic of the older sort, he was religiously (though perhaps unconsciously) rather than politically biassed in favour of the peculiar manner of Government obtaining in the Kingdom of the Two Sicilies. Many members of that great Church to which he belonged will not hold her disparaged by the assertion that, in her relations to man, there are two great points which she chiefly regards. First, that men shall always be kept in due subjection to the powers that be in both Church and State, and secondly that they shall, while in that state of subjection, be rendered by their rulers as comfortable and contented as possible under the circumstances. A third object, which Christians are apt to look on as of some little importance —that men should be in mind so developed as to deem themselves of some account, both as individuals and as members of the State—she regards but distantly, if at all. Considering Lord Shrewsbury's

mental constitution, his view of the matters around
him is in no wise surprising; but let the first well-
authenticated case of anything approaching to
tyranny and oppression reach his ears, and his
humanity and indignation are at once apparent. Of
this he shall be his own witness. Nor is his feeling
of generosity lessened by the fact that, in protesting
against the treatment awarded to the unhappy
Poerio by the best of all possible governments, he ac-
cuses the sufferer of political crimes of the deepest
dye, and brings accusations against him, the falsehood
of which the most superficial enquiry would have
demonstrated. Lord Shrewsbury confined himself
not to expressions of sympathy only ; he forthwith
set himself heartily to bring what personal influence
he possessed to bear towards procuring alleviation of
the sufferings of the hapless criminal :—

"Palermo, June 26th, 1851.
  " It was this day's post that brought me your favour of the
4th. I cannot say how distressed I am at what you tell me
of the fate of poor Poerio, for however guilty the man may
be, his punishment is barbarous, inhuman, and unchristian.
I cannot doubt what Mr. Gladstone saw. I really had no idea
that, in these times, old habits and ways of thinking in these
matters had still prevailed in Naples, to the exclusion of those
more becoming, polite, and enlightened methods of dealing
with State criminals. Our worthy Chief Governor is not yet
returned from his tour, but I hope to see him before our next
post leaves, and shall not fail to press this point upon him ;
and too happy shall I be to be able to report that the rigors
of Poerio's confinement have been already mitigated. Though
I know full well that no man is more capable of discriminating
between truth and falsehood than Mr. Gladstone, still I have

heard so much of Poerio's criminality as to leave no reasonable doubt upon my mind that, whatever defects there may have been in the evidence upon which he was convicted, there is no question of his guilt. He was, I think, an exile for his conduct in '30, lived at Paris on terms of intimacy with Mazzini, and there published several Revolutionary Pamphlets, in fine, the whole Ministry, of which he formed a part, Dragonetti's, perhaps, excepted, were noted and proved Republicans, such as Pepe and Saliceti. How, then, can any one doubt their determination to dethrone the King by means of the *Constituent* Assembly into which they were determined to transform the new Chamber, in May, '48 ? No one at Naples doubted it . . . .

" June 29th.

" . . . . I have just seen our good Prince. I shall copy those portions of your letter relating to Poerio, and will send them to old Fortunato. But, fearing they might never reach the King, I will also send them to our friend the Marquis del Vasto, who has constant opportunities of seeing his Majesty. . . . Rely upon it, I shall do all I can . . . what a pity Mr. Gladstone had not himself gone to the King ; but now I hope he will wait to see if any good comes from this before naming the subject in Parliament. The Prince of Satriano says you may make what use you will of the enclosed MS.; he wishes it to be known, and would not object even to its publication ; though, as he is preparing an elaborate work in detail, it would perhaps be better only to show it privately, certainly to Mr. Gladstone. I have left both open for the Prince of Castelcicala. . . ."

In a letter from Mr. Gladstone to Panizzi a fair estimate is given of Lord Shrewsbury's letters, and the general line of argument pursued by him.

" July 7th, 1851.

" Lord Shrewsbury's letter really comes to nothing, so far as the issues raised by me are concerned. Meanwhile, the time is nearly exhausted, and next week I must absolutely print unless I learn that something good has been *done*, which may be an effective premise of more. It is an ugly and painful controversy, but I cannot help it. . . ."

To Lord Shrewsbury's advice contained in his letter of the 12th of June, asking Panizzi *to come and see, and judge* for himself, he replied, at once accepting the invitation :—

"July 14th, 1851.

". . . Now I am ready. I have *scraped* together £100 for the purpose. I am ready to start on the 1st of September, and to go with your Lordship, in your presence and with your concurrence, verify all the statements made by Mr. Gladstone. If your Lordship and I find that they are unfounded, I shall publish the fact to the world; if they are well grounded, I shall respectfully beg of your Lordship to endeavour to convince the Neapolitan Government of the injustice of their proceedings. It is superfluous to say that this is to be kept between your Lordship and myself entirely at present, or else the enquiry would be nugatory, and our end, that of discovering the truth, in justice to the Government as well as to the victims—defeated. I wish nothing but the truth to come out. Let us, therefore, do our best to find it out. It is worth the trouble. I can dedicate to this the above sum and two months—September and October. . ."

To this Lord Shrewsbury replied, giving his opinion and advice as to the most effective way of carrying out the proposed plan, and excusing himself from personal participation :—

"July 25, 1851.

"I think your best plan will be to ask an audience of the King at once, and speak to him frankly on the matter. He will, I doubt not, listen to you, and give you the facilities you desire; but the *object* of your audience must not be known beforehand, or it may be thwarted. I have only *one* acquaintance at Naples—the Marquis del Vasto . . . through him I think I could ensure you an audience of the King, but neither must know the precise object. I never was presented to the King in my life, though he has been extremely kind to us. I could not meet you at Naples for several reasons—that it always disagrees with me, &c., &c. You might open your audience with the King as the bearer of Mr. Gladstone's statement, which, I should think, he would never otherwise see. I hear it has been sent to Naples; but if only to the Minister, the King will probably never see it. He listened most patiently to Baillie Cochrane, and is, I have good reason to believe, most anxious to learn the truth, which others may be as anxious to conceal from him."

The letters of Mr. Gladstone on Panizzi's proposed journey must be given here :—

"August 2nd, 1851.

"The Prince Castelcicala has sent a letter to Lord Aberdeen; it is not much to the purpose, but calls me a detractor and a calumniator. I could almost wish I were."

"August 5th, 1851.

"It would indeed be greatly for my interest that you should go to Naples; your journey would lighten my responsibility, and afford me incomparable means of self-defence against the bold assertions with which I expect to be met. .

Yet I can hardly in conscience recommend it to you, without conditions—your 'going would attract notice—your antecedents would be learned, and your steps watched. I cannot think you would ever be allowed to see the interior aspect of things with the sanction of the Government, whatever introductions you might have and whatever influence might be used in your favour. Certainly the case would be different if Lord Shrewsbury were to be the examining party, and you his unobserved, and therefore independent companion, and, I think, that in your place I should so put it to Lord Shrewsbury himself. . . . . I am reading with some spice of dissatisfaction Petruccelli's 'Rivoluzione di

Napoli.' It certainly appears from this book that there were a party determined that the Constitution should not work. But the question always comes back, *how* such a party ought to be encountered.

Yours, &c., &c.,
W. E. GLADSTONE."

Lord Shrewsbury's application, which he duly made on Panizzi's behalf to the Marquis del Vasto, unhappily failed of success; the Marquis being represented by his Lordship as a *good, honest courtier, and will not meddle.*

Respecting the Gladstone Pamphlet, Lord Shrewsbury wrote:

"I see that Lord Palmerston has noticed Gladstone's Pamphlet, in very fine and honourable terms; still I hope the 20,000 is a misprint for 2,000. Is it not so? If not, I am glad the letter has been published, and sent to all the Courts; for it is the common cause of humanity and good Government, and even touches the honour of all crowned heads. I have always thought Lord Palmerston an honest, well-meaning, straightforward man—though too quick, credulous, and domineering. . . . . I wish Mr. Gladstone all the credit and all the success he deserves."

It would have been of much importance to Panizzi to obtain the countenance and influence of Lord Shrewsbury, both for his proposed interview with the King and during the whole of his visit in Naples; but his Lordship's arrangements were incompatible with those which the traveller was under the necessity of making for his journey. He thus wrote :—

"B. M., August 25th, 1851.
I am firmly of opinion that the King does not know of all the iniquities now exposed by Mr. Gladstone, nor the cruelties

of the prisons, and I start from this as a fact in my plans and dreams. . . . . If your Lordship can manage to meet me—which I repeat ought not to be a very difficult matter for the Earl of Shrewsbury—we might under Providence be instrumental in alleviating an amount of human misery unparalleled in the world. . . . I shall be obliged for an early answer, as I am kept in London only by this business, and will take no holidays till I hear that I cannot employ the time allowed for them in a more useful manner than running from house to house in the country here. . . . Gladstone's letters have gone through *ten* editions, and are the theme of every conversation. *All* the press, including that part opposed to the Minister and to Gladstone, as, for instance, the *Morning Herald*, have all taken Gladstone's side; and in *The Times* of last Friday there was a letter from " our correspondent" from Naples supporting Gladstone. . . . ."

Panizzi now applied, in view of his long proposed visit, for permission to enter the Kingdom of Naples, and received the following answer:—

" Foreign Office,
August 26th, 1851.

" Sir,
. . . . Lord Palmerston apprehends that you have been naturalized by Act of Parliament, and, if so, you are fully entitled to be considered as a British subject in every country but that of your birth, which his Lordship believes was the Duchy of Modena, and as a British subject you have a right to British protection in the Kingdom of Naples.
I am, &c., &c.,
H. U. ADDINGTON."

Early in October Panizzi set forth on his journey.

Previous to his departure, Mr. Gladstone, who, it need hardly be said, took the deepest interest in his self-imposed mission, supplied him with the names of men of influence at Naples who were likely to be of the greatest service to him in attaining the object he had in view ; these were Mr. Fagan and Signor Lacaita, mentioned in the subjoined letters :—

"Fasque, September 24th, 1851.

". . . . I have just seen yesterday's *Times*, and it seems the Neapolitan *reply* is ready and printed. I shall trust very much to you to aid me with matter for correcting it according to your inquiries in Naples. The persons on whose *accuracy* I am most disposed to rely are Mr. Fagan, at the Mission, and Signor Lacaita. . . . By this day's post I have certain news of Poerio, from one who has seen him within a month ; he was *in hospital* and allowed to walk for an hour or two detached from any other criminal, and carrying chains on him which my informant tells me weigh 20 or 25 pounds. . . ."

Another letter, also from Mr. Gladstone, may be given, written four days before the last :—

"September 20th.

"I return Lord Shrewsbury's letter. It is, I think, all things considered, very honourable to his candour, and I would hope you may do good through his means. . . I earnestly hope the vindication and confutation will fall into your hands while you are *on the spot*. *Here* I shall be almost powerless to deal with the falsified details which it will probably produce. . . . I have had a good deal of interesting correspondence about my letters. Not the most pleasant of it is a letter from Mons. Guizot, very frank and kind, condemning outright my publication, and fully accepting the King of Naples, and all about him as a choice of evils. I have replied in terms which I hope will likewise be intelligible.

"In Naples be sure to see and converse with Mr. Fagan of the Legation. Signor Lacaita, No. 3, Vico Tre Campane, a most excellent man, hunted by the Government . . . ."

And October 3rd, 1851 :—

"I most earnestly hope you will see the Neapolitan answer to me while you are in Italy, and, if possible, on the spot, for you will have facilities there, to verify or expose, such as cannot easily be attained.

The Neapolitan Government have written to ask Lord Palmerston whether he sanctioned my publication, to which he has replied by referring to my statement that I was alone responsible. . . . .

Yours, &c., &c.,

W. E. GLADSTONE."

We shall, in our next chapter, follow Panizzi on his important mission, and give an abstract, as faithful and accurate as possible, of his doings whilst at Naples.

To the many who followed the course and knew the issue of the exertions then made, even this may appear unnecessary; but unless the name of the chief actor is to be passed over in the annals of humanity, our imperfect record will not be useless.

CHAPTER XVIII.

PANIZZI being, as Lord Palmerston stated, a British
subject, would have been perfectly safe anywhere on
European soil, saving that portion of it occupied by
the diminutive but to him important State of Modena,
yet with such extensive range he found it impossible
to suppress a patriotic yearning for his native town,
and determined to visit it on his way southwards.

The reader must now bear in mind that we have,
in order to avoid confusion, gone back to the year
1851; whereas, in a former chapter, treating of the
British Museum and other matters, Panizzi has been
described as being at Brescello in 1857.

The fact that Francis V., in 1848, the second year
of his reign, had granted an amnesty to all political
offenders, encouraged Panizzi in his resolve. As, in
such a case, it was advisable to be perfectly certain
before carrying his design into execution, he made
application to the proper authorities for information
whether his name was mentioned in this Act of
Amnesty, from which it was not altogether unreasonable to imagine it might perchance have been excluded. To this application the answer was in the

H

affirmative, but it was penned, not, as in common courtesy it should have been, by the Minister himself, but
by his secretary.

This example of official disrespect filled the recipient
with "righteous indignation," and he wrote (18th of
August, 1851) to a near relative of his at Modena in
these words :—"His Excellency! ! ! does not condescend to write himself; perhaps he has more to do
than Lord Russell or Lord Palmerston, both of whom
always find time to write to me on the very same
day." Thus, notwithstanding all the assurances of
the Modenese Government he continued his journey,
not caring even to pass through his native country,
if he were likely to incur the risk of becoming an
object of displeasure and suspicion; conscious, too, that
either he himself or the authorities must have very
much changed if he were not so.

On reaching Genoa he received news of a sad loss
that had befallen him in the death of his sister;
and how deeply he was affected by the intelligence
may be gleaned from the annexed letter :—

Rome, 28th October, 1851.

"My dear Haywood,

I have not had the courage even to write to
you, owing to the great distress of mind that I have been
suffering under since I arrived at Genoa, where I found letters
informing me incidentally, and supposing I was aware of it,
of the death of my sister, whom I hoped to see a few days
after the letters themselves reached me. The news of her
death was addressed to London, and has reached it since I
left. I felt strongly inclined to give up my journey, and return to England at once. I could not, however, do so, for
reasons I need not trouble you with, and so here I am, very

melancholy, and not enjoying this most wonderful place as I otherwise should. I arrived here the night before last, and have, of course, seen little ; but I have seen St. Peter's, and what more could I have seen, or can I hope to see one-tenth as magnificent ? Lord Shrewsbury is here, and had made arrangements to present me to the Pope before I arrived. . . .

Yours, &c., &c.,

A. Panizzi."

At Rome, Dr. Minzi, who was engaged in ascertaining the origin, and devising the remedy for the fever then prevailing there, encountered his friend Panizzi. The latter, during his stay, was perpetually beset by spies. On leaving, he took the precaution of engaging the company of Minzi, and to him he imparted the following directions:—That, were he carried off at the frontier by police agents, he (Minzi) was to write three letters—one to Sir William Temple, at Naples; a second to Lord Holland, also at Naples ; and a third to Lord Shrewsbury. As a matter of fact, he was stopped at the Neapolitan frontier; but, after careful examination of the passport, and much unnecessary delay, was allowed to cross. His name, however, appeared in the so-called *Libro Nero.*

On his arrival at Naples he proceeded to Lord Holland's house, at the Palazzo Roccella, where he remained during his sojourn in the place ; he now brought all his energies to bear on the acquisition of every possible scrap of information which might further him in his mission. Before long he received help, and this was from Mr. Fagan,* who, having

* He knew the people and country well. In 1849 he was named Commissioner for the settlement of British claims at Naples, and at Messina in 1851. In 1856 he was appointed Secretary of Legation to the Argentine Confederation, and after arriving at a satisfactory conclusion with respect

H2

been Attaché at Naples since June, 1837, was, indeed, the only person who was able to assist Panizzi. The help received from him was in the shape of a letter of introduction to the Signora Parilli, which must be allowed to tell its own story:—

"Dear Mr. Panizzi,

I send you word, through a friend of mine that the Signora Parilli expects you to-morrow morning. She does not know who you are, but introduce yourself as the "friend of Fagan." An aunt of Poerio is a nun, and knows all about him.

Yours, &c., &c.,

GEORGE FAGAN."

Shortly afterwards, Panizzi's interview with Ferdinand II. took place, on which occasion he was accompanied by Mr. Fagan. The day fixed was a Sunday, the hour twelve at noon. At ten minutes to twelve they arrived at the palace, " We are before our time," said Panizzi, " Now the first question the King will ask, will be " Have you been to Church?" So they at once hastened into the Church opposite (San Francesco di Paolo), and remaining but a couple of minutes, came forth prepared to stand before the King and answer, with clear consciences, this expected question, which in fact was the first the King put to them.

It was quite clear that His Majesty was fully aware, through information obtained from spies, of all Panizzi's movements. He received him, however, with the greatest courtesy, and almost before he him-

to the settlement of British claims in Buenos Ayres in 1858, was appointed Chargé d'Affaires to the Republic of Ecuador, and afterwards Minister to Venezuela in 1865, where he died at Caracas, of yellow fever, in 1869.

self had uttered a word, allowed him to talk on the subject of Poerio and Settembrini, and the prisons of Naples. On this theme Panizzi descanted uninterruptedly for full twenty minutes, when the King rose closing the interview with the remarkable words: *Addio, terribile Panizzi.*

During his stay at Lord Holland's, the Neapolitan Government, in order that he should take his walks abroad with greater safety, kindly furnished him with constant attendance, in the shape of a pair of trusty followers or spies. It is painful to relate that Panizzi treated their delicate and unobtrusive attention with extremely bad taste, not to say ingratitude. He was never weary of playing tricks on his faithful attendants, of mischievously imposing on them; ably supported in this evil practice by his friend, and notably by Mr. Fagan, he made them deviate from the path in which it was their combined duty and pleasure to walk. Panizzi and his companions would get in and out of cabs, in the manner of a late well-known actor, though not with the intention of bilking the cab-driver. On one occasion, in trying to walk down their pursuers, they became involved in a cul-de-sac, and turning to come out, met their suite face to face. Pursuers and pursued burst into a hearty reciprocal laugh, the latter passed on, and the former fell to their place in the rear, and continued the chase.

Panizzi himself even allowed others to personate him. For example, in one instance he gave out, for the information of his retinue, that he was going on a shooting excursion in the neighbourhood of

Naples. The person really bent on this errand was Lord Holland's physician, Dr. Chepmell, who, in the character of Panizzi, was duly followed about the whole day. Let us hope that these honest members of the Police witnessed, though they had little chance of enjoying, a good day's sport.

Like all truly great men, and in particular Henry the Great, of France and Navarre, Panizzi, when in the company of his friends, was devoid of all feeling of unofficial personal dignity, and delighted, when not seriously engaged, in little diversions as free, if not as innocent and touching, as those indulged in by that great monarch.

On one occasion—he was by nature so physically sensitive as (to use a common phrase) to be excessively ticklish—Dr. Chepmell, and another intimate friend, Signor Carafa, had got him on the floor and were subjecting him to the titillating operation. They were rolling him in the fire-place—his face was black with charcoal, his clothes white with ashes—when suddenly a servant announced the Duca di X . . . . who had come to pay his respects to the "Great Pan." All the astounded Duke could do was to stand in the middle of the room and gaze, speechless, hat in hand, on the unexpected and inexplicable spectacle.

Meantime, leave had been obtained for Panizzi to visit the famous *Vicaria*. Of this he received information from Lord Feilding, who was to accompany him over the prison :—

"November 18th, 1851.

"My dear Panizzi,

Will you hold yourself in readiness to accompany me over the 'Vicaria' to-morrow. in case it can be managed to obtain permission ?

Yours, &c., &c.,   FEILDING."

" November 19th.

" All is arranged for to-day.

FEILDING."

Before visiting the " Vicaria," he was careful to draw up a most elaborate précis of all the questions to be asked of officials, all portions of the prison worthy of note, and all such points of information as should render his inspection as thorough as possible.

To give, in our own words, an account of this visit would be too long for these pages, but Panizzi, on the following day that he inspected the prison, wrote down a few brief observations, in conjunction with Lord Feilding (November 20th, 1851) :—

" The general impression on our minds was most unfavourable. The mixing together of criminals of every description (homicide excepted) without distinction, the total want of occupation for the prisoners, with the exception of about thirty shoemakers who worked in two cells apart, and the fact that prisoners before trial and prisoners after trial are huddled indiscriminately together, are facts which speak for themselves, as to the total unfitness of the Neapolitan prison discipline for the reformation of the offender. A criminal, when he has undergone his term of imprisonment here, must come out infinitely more savage and demoralized than when he went in. Humanity, policy, and religion call loudly for a reform in these sinks of horror."

The following is Panizzi's report :—" Yesterday, Wednesday, the 19th of November, 1851, I accompanied Lord Feilding to see the prisons of the " Vicaria." We got permission through Father Costa, a Jesuit, who came with us, with another father whose name I never heard ; the Chief Gaoler and the Inspector of the Police went with us through the gaol. We entered it at a quarter past two o'clock, and left it at three minutes past four by my watch.

" Near the stairs by which we entered there are prisons looking into the quadrangle of the " Vicaria." As two of the judges, as we were told they were, came downstairs to get into their carriage, the shutters of the prison nearest the bottom of the stairs were closed, and opened immediately after the carriage had driven off.

" Having got upstairs, we entered a small room in which a person sat keeping some register or other, and were immediately ushered into a smaller room, where an inspector sat. On the table we found three different sorts of bread—*i.e.*, common bread, bread for the sick, and bread which is given to the prisoners in the evening. The whole of this bread was good of its kind ; the only objection to the evening bread might be its being heavy.

" We entered the first *Camerone dei Nobili*, which has only one window at the end of it. It is a long, vaulted, low room, very dull, and the atmosphere of which I should call very bad, had we not experienced worse. Off this room, on the left, are six smaller rooms, communicating with the Camerone by doors, some of them closing with railings, and others with oak shutters. In these rooms are kept such prisoners as can afford to pay for better accommodation—that is a small bed, instead of the common beds of the " Camerone." The air of these rooms was better, because, by leaving the windows open, a thorough draft was created through them. But the air was cold and damp; there was no means of excluding the air and cold. Except in one or two of these rooms there was a *paper* window instead of glass; in the other there was nothing. So that you must either have the cold from without, or close the enormous oak shutters, and exclude both air and light, not only from each of these rooms themselves, but from the Camerone, which, to a certain extent, receives both, particularly air, from them. The atmosphere at night, when all those windows are closed, must be intolerable; and I am firmly persuaded that, were it not that the shutters are opened to try the soundness of the double row of iron bars by which each window is secured, the inmates would be smothered. These bars are tried five times during the night. Of course, every time this operation takes place, the inmates are roused from their sleep or slumber, and whilst the shutters are open a chilling draft must be created.

" In the Camerone sleep 120 persons.

" We saw no *kitchen* or *infirmary*, both being removed to San Francesco ; but in the room which was the infirmary, and which is better than the others, we saw a poor fellow lying down asleep, but he seemed to me very ill, and looked like a dead person."

Of this celebrated prison the writer of these " memoirs" is enabled, from personal observation and knowledge, to give some account.

The *Vicaria*, or Castel Capuano, was originally situated outside, but is now enclosed within the city

of Naples.   The first building was erected by William,·
the Norman, for a Royal Palace, and surrounded by
fortifications.   Here the Kings of Naples successively
resided, until Ferdinand of Arragon demolished the
fortifications, thereby rendering it useless as a strong-
hold.

In the year 1540 the Viceroy, Pedro de Toledo, rebuilt
it in its present form, and gave it the name of "Vicaria."
The magnificent chambers (stained with many a crime)
were converted into Law Courts, the smaller rooms
were utilized as dungeons.   For 310 years it remained
a so-called "Palazzo di Giustizia."   Of the peculiar
species of Justice and Law administered it is hardly
necessary to speak, except perhaps to call them by their
proper names of cruelty, chicanery, and oppression.
Nor is it surprising that during these centuries, ecclesiastical and civil tyranny should have had equal sway
within the walls of the " Vicaria."

In 1848 this vast and gloomy edifice, which stands
at the end of the Strada dei Tribunali, bore, carved in
stone, in bold relief, over its one heavily barred en-
trance, that badge of Italian servitude, the Austrian
double headed eagle.   Near the dungeons were sta-
tioned Swiss guards.   Inside the gate, and arranged
around a circular court-yard, were the houses inhabited by the guardians of the courts, and, in addition to these, the residence of the executioner, whose
implements, the scaffold and gallows, and all their
appurtenances were displayed outside.   Three broad
staircases led respectively to the Civil and Criminal
Courts and to the cells.   As regards these, one door
afforded access to the prison reserved for nobility,

another to that set apart for the lower orders. Over the last was a picture of the Virgin and Child.

With the *Vicaria Vecchia* had disappeared many a secret chamber and loathsome living tomb, the remains of Spanish barbarity. According to Celano, 4,000 human beings were at one time immured in these dens, but in the building as it now stands there would not be room for more than 1,500.

Many famous productions have cheered the solitude of these sombre walls. In one of these cells Antonio Sella wrote his first essay on political economy; in another Mattia Prete, the famous Calabrese painter, 1613—1699, was a prisoner and condemned to death. Him, however, the Viceroy reprieved in these graceful words: *Vita excellens in arte non debet mori.*

Even so late as 1859 the present writer has himself seen the eleven wire cages, swinging between the windows of the buildings, each containing human heads.

The horrors of the *Vicaria* have been fully dwelt upon here and elsewhere; but we may mention that, on the 22nd of November, Panizzi paid a second visit to the prison, with the view of more fully examining certain matters which had either been omitted or superficially surveyed during his first inspection. We forbear, however, from entering further into the horrible details connected with the place, which deserved no better appellation than the one given to it by Mr. Gladstone—a very *hell upon earth.*

In December Panizzi took his departure for England. He was accompanied to the last by his never failing followers, the spies, who had come to do him the final kind office of seeing him on board. Signor

Lacaita, who was also present to bid him adieu, took the liberty of asking them what they wanted and whom they were watching? *Quel pezzo grosso* (that big fellow), replied they, "and to see that he is safely off."

In conclusion, an extract from a letter of Lord Shrewsbury's, after Panizzi's return, may possibly be read with interest:—

"Palermo, December 28th, 1851.

"Dear Mr. Panizzi,

. . . . What a blessed thing it is that the *Coup d'Etat* answered so beautifully, and did not place you in the dilemma of either making an immense detour, or of journeying in the midst of those robbers and assassins, the Socialists and *Rouges* Republicans. One sees *now* why it was that Kossuth was so anxious to return in the Spring, and what sort of connection our friend Palmerston has made in his chivalrous efforts *in endeavouring to promote the cause of national freedom in those nations that stood in need of it!* Lamartine did not use a more revolutionary phraseology in his first address to the French Republic, when he announced that the Treaties of 1815 had ceased to exist, and that France "proclaimed herself the intellectual and cordial ally of every right, of every progress, of every legitimate developement of the institutions of nations *which wish to live on the same principle as herself.*"

Verily those two letters of Esterhazy and Battyani came most seasonably to blow out the Kossuth Bubble, and scatter it to the winds, shewing what an empty notion it was that Kossuth was working for the regeneration of Hungary! I never questioned the honesty or patriotic intentions of our illustrious Foreign Secretary, or that he ever fancied he was not pursuing the best and wisest policy. But it is now clear that he and Lamartine are men of the same school, and that *their* principles, when attempted to be carried into action under untoward circumstances, and at unseasonable times, will end in disappointment to those who profess them, and in infinite mischief to those in whose favour they are evoked. To no country will this apply more aptly than to that beauteous region from which you are just returned. Her hour is not yet come. She is wholly unfit for the change from Absolute to Constitutional liberty. She has no materials within herself for the new edifice. The Law of 19 in Sicily, and the Code Napoléon in her Continental States, have so utterly deranged the mechanism of her old feudal construction, and uprooted the foundations on which any solid structure could be raised, that it is as clear as it is in France that Socialism and Red Republicanism would turn up instead of a Limited Monarchy the moment you had set the elements at work. Nor had Louis Napoléon a better cause to shew for dissolving the National Assembly than had Ferdinand for sending *his* Chamber to their homes, and stopping them in the same wild and unprincipled career. One can only, therefore, *now* legitimately work for her social, not for her political regeneration. Municipal privileges are the only liberties, a good administration of the Law is the only phase of which she is susceptible. Any efforts you may make in these directions may tend to good, and if you and Palmerston will steadily pursue that object *only*, *and by means suitable to their end*, you may effect much for the happiness of the people, as well as for the security of the Throne.

Very truly yours, &c.,

SHREWSBURY.

CHAPTER XIX.

LEGION OF HONOUR, &C.—ECCLESIASTICAL TITLES BILL —SERJEANT SHEE'S BILL—CONCORDAT OF 1855.

IT was remarked of Panizzi, when in Italy as a proof of his general unobtrusiveness and lack of desire for distinction, that his visiting card bore only the simple inscription "Mr. Panizzi." There were certainly a few countries in the world, and one especially, where, although he never laid claim to the gift of prophecy, he was by no means likely to have honour thrust upon him. As in early years his soul had been vexed by the mild constitutionalism of Parma and Modena, so in riper age he showed himself perversely antagonistic, not only to the sway of the King of Naples, but to every Government of Europe which bore in his eyes the slightest tinge of that especial object of his hatred—*absolutism*. Yet there were some, and amongst them one which would hardly have been accepted by Panizzi as the most disinterested supporter of liberty, that deemed this would-be liberator of the oppressed, this ex-Carbonaro, this revolutionary firebrand, worthy of notice, and even of some outward and visible sign of distinction and esteem. It was a real shock to his modesty when he was presented with the cross of the "Legion of Honour" by the President of the French Republic. *

---

* The presentation was confirmed on the 24th of December, 1851.

Letters to Lord Rutherfurd and to Mr. Haywood, which are subjoined, clearly show how surprised Panizzi was at this unexpected honour:—

"British Museum, Tuesday.

"My dear Rutherfurd,

. . . . I am in good health and happy, but for one thing that happened to me at Paris, where I dined at the President's last Saturday, and who suddenly presented me with the Cross of Officer of the Legion of Honour! This makes me miserable. Keep this to yourself. At Naples things are worse than described by Mr. Gladstone.

Yours, &c., &c., A. PANIZZI.

"My dear Haywood,

I arrived here last evening in perfect health, and very happy to be back again. I dined on Saturday at the President's at Paris, who (I must tell you how annoyed I am at it—it makes me miserable) suddenly presented me with the Cross of Officer of the Legion of Honour! Of course I could not say no, but hope to be forbidden accepting it. Meanwhile it makes me unhappy.

Yours, &c., &c., A. PANIZZI.

A second decoration, the Royal order of "Saint Maurice and Lazarus" of Sardinia, was presented to him a few years later, in December, 1855, in which year Victor Emmanuel visited London with Cavour. Of this last honour, considering by whom it was conferred, Panizzi may possibly have been prouder than of his first, but, with innate modesty, he forbore to ask the requisite permission to accept either, and preferred to remain almost to the end of an honourable life undecorated;—despising medals, orders, and unreal designations which, he well knew, could not add to his reputation.

In the year 1851, shortly after his return to England, there landed on these shores the bugbear of
Popery in its most appalling form, which scared the
natives of the island into a state of mind bordering on
temporary imbecility. Those who remember the Papal
Aggression* will also, with shame, remember the
foolish fanaticism that burst forth in every quarter,
the undignified terror of many who should have known
better than to put so little confidence in their own
cause, and the extravagant and senseless rumours with
which the air was filled. To this unseemly panic Lord
John Russell's notorious *Durham Letter* materially
contributed ; but although there was no ground for
alarm, there was, it cannot be denied, abundance of
room for indignation. Many men of the most tried
judgment and unquestionable moderation (albeit their
voices were well nigh drowned in the general cla-
mour), who treated the abrogation of the ancient sees
by the Pope, and all other his *bruta fulmina* with
the contempt they deserved, were, nevertheless, not
disposed to sit down calmly under an insult to the
Church and people of England, aggravated by the
studied offensiveness with which it was offered.
Such as these were the last, however, to see the
necessity for, and did their best to oppose, the

* In a Consistory holden in Rome, 30th September, 1850, Pius IX. named
fourteen new cardinals, of whom four only were Italians. Amongst the ten
foreigners was Dr. Wiseman, at the time Vicar-Apostolic of the London dis-
trict, who was at the same time nominated Lord Archbishop of Westminster.
On the 27th of October following, Dr. Ullathorne was enthroned as Roman
Catholic Bishop of Birmingham, in St. Chad's Cathedral in that town. The
same day a pastoral letter from Dr. Wiseman was read in all the Roman
Catholic chapels of his See, and on its becoming generally known that all
England had been parcelled out into Romish dioceses, the strongest indig-
nation was expressed throughout the empire.

construction of such a steam-engine to crack a cockchafer as the notorious " Ecclesiastical Titles Bill." Happily, this clumsy machine has been rarely, if ever, set in motion, and after some years of useless existence has, as all know, been finally broken up. It was impossible that Panizzi, as a moderate Roman Catholic, should have joined in the general outburst, or lent himself to swell the ranks of the crew around him. But he had been brought up in a country where the power of the priesthood has something of reality, and wherein the behests of the Pope are of a little more importance than they ever have been, or ever will be, in this realm. He was thoroughly imbued with that dislike and horror of clericalism which those of the Latin branch of the Church, when once they have broken free, yea, but a little, from the more rigorous bonds of their religion, seldom fail to show. It would be hard, then, to judge Panizzi severely, if he seems to have shared the alarm prevalent at the time, and to have betrayed some dread of the consequences of the Pope's invasion of England. Let it be remembered, too, that he was an Italian before he was an English man ; and that nothing could more effectually have roused his ire, than the insensate conduct of Pius IX., " the most foolish man," as some one has well said of him, " that ever sat in the Papal chair."

With this apology for any seeming weakness, or extravagance, in Panizzi's judgment of the *Papal Aggression*, the following letter on the subject is laid before the reader :—

I

" British Museum,
February 18th, 1851.
" My dear Haywood,
            I have written Kings and Popes, and I don't
see why what is there said does not apply to England.   You
say it is a Protestant country.   The United Kingdom was
Protestant before 1829, but I don't see now how you can say
it is Protestant.   As to the Church of England, I am not sure
that in point of numbers it exceeds much the Catholics, and
as the latter are eligible to all offices and places, with one or
two exceptions, as well as Protestants, I cannot understand
why the events which have happened in other countries are
not considered a precedent here.   Suppose you had a Catholic
Minister here—or, indeed, suppose a Catholic Peer or Member of Parliament was to be treated as Santa Rosa was in
Piedmont, would not that be interfering in temporal affairs?
And why should not, in the time and when the opportunity
offer, an English Catholic be treated as the Piedmontese was
for his conduct in political affairs.   Of course, neither you nor
I mind being refused the Sacrament or a burial in a conse-
crated place; but is it nothing that the family of a man who
is himself indifferent to it should be harassed or distressed in
this way?   Is not the conduct of the Bishops at Thurles a
serious interference with the power of the State?   You seem
to me to be of Roebuck's opinion that nothing should be done,
which astonishes me in a man of practical sense as you are.
Show me a country where the interference of the Popes has
not had to be checked, except the United States of America,
and I do not suppose you are prepared, like Roebuck, to
take all the consequences of such an exceptional precedent.
Moreover, show me a country where the Pope has dared, of
his own accord alone, to upset the old diocesan partition, and
establish a new one, and appoint at once thirteen Bishops.
The agitation shown at this moment is proof enough that
the Pope and his supporters have an enormous power in this
country.

Is England to depend on the *bon plaisir* of the Pope whether he will use or abuse that power ? Do you think the Pope has acted against the wish of Austria and France in this business ? Do you not see Austria giving up all the old principles of the Emperors to the Pope, in order to propitiate the support of the Church of Rome ? Do you not see Montalembert supporting the French President who re-instated the Pope ? Do you not see a war preparing against the Protestant cantons in Switzerland ? Do you think that the conduct of the Pope against the King of Sardinia is wholly from religious motives ? Did Wiseman come back from Rome by Vienna as the most direct way ? I told you before the Catholic Emancipation that you would regret your trusting the priests, and you laughed then ; that you should laugh now is astonishing. Depend upon it, you will find that the storm will not soon be over, and that your philo-sophers will learn at their own *dear* cost what the Papal Power is.

It is not such milk and water measures that will stop the torrent as those contemplated. England must prepare for a struggle of greater moment and importance than any in which she has been hitherto embarked. Keep this well in mind ; it will not be over either in your time or mine.

Yours ever,

A. PANIZZI."

Probably, Panizzi, before the day of his death, learnt to understand why the events in other countries should not be considered a precedent in this, and how the case of Santa Rosa would be hardly likely to occur in the British Parliament. His underestimate in this letter of the numerical superiority of the Anglican body to the Roman Catholics in England is manifestly due to his mixing up the three kingdoms together; a confusion especially misleading in any consideration

12

of the Papal Aggression, inasmuch as that movement
was not extended to Scotland (where, however, it has
a short time since been carried out peaceably and
quietly enough), and in Ireland the titles of the Romish
prelates have been always the same with those borne
by their rivals of what may be called, without offence,
the Colonial Church.

More interesting, perhaps, than this letter, is another
document put forth by Panizzi on the same matter ;
its length, we regret, must prevent us from offering it
to our readers ; however, he recommends a curious if
not altogether original prophylactic against ecclesiastical invasion from abroad.   His remarks on the
foreign character assumed by an Englishman who
takes Roman orders, and of the allegiance (it can
hardly be called divided) by which he thereby becomes
bound are remarkable.   The remedy which he proposes for ecclesiastical defection from patriotism would
be, if carried thoroughly into effect, a little too drastic;
and, if used short of thoroughly, might work a little
more to the disadvantage of those who applied it than
of those on whom it should be inflicted.

It has been thought best, at the risk of interrupt-
ing the proper sequence in order of time of this history,
to continue and finish in this place the account of
Panizzi's connection with and views on the Ecclesiastical questions which sprang up at home and abroad
in his time.   For this purpose a few years must be
skipped, and the reader referred to the year 1854.
Perhaps some apology should be offered for the introduction here of a correspondence in that year on
Serjeant (afterwards Justice) Shee's Bill on the

Temporalities of the Irish Church, inasmuch as that Bill obtained but little notoriety at the time, and the Serjeant's proposed reforms were never carried into effect by legislation. But the following letters bear witness to the variety of questions on which Panizzi was habitually consulted, and the frequency with which his opinions were sought by his friends and acquaintances, and it may be interesting to some to know what judgment he may have formed upon a point relating to the much vexed question of Irish Church property, a question which even yet remains to be thoroughly solved. Moreover, to those who knew Justice Shee, the tone of the letter first quoted may serve to recall the unaffected modesty and simplicity which distinguished the character of him who may truly be called one of the best of men :—

"Serjeants' Inn, May 31st, 1854.

" Dear Mr. Panizzi,

Our conversation yesterday made me think that I might be, what I have always wished to be, useful in mitigating the evils which we regretted.

I have on the Order Book a Notice of a Motion for leave to bring in 'A Bill to alter and amend the laws relating to the Temporalities of the Irish Church, and to increase the means of religious instruction and Church accommodation for Her Majesty's subjects in Ireland.'

If I had not good grounds for knowing that it would give satisfaction to those whose just discontent at the existing state of things in Ireland is a material element in the weakness and the difficulty of all liberal Government, I would not propose it.

But I believe it would not only be acceptable to the Irish Catholic Church and people, but a durable and easily defensible, because a just and reasonable, settlement.

My notion of doing good with it is—by influencing public opinion in its favour—and my object would be in a great degree gained if, after a temperate explanation of my Bill from me, the Government would allow it to be read a first time as a thing not unworthy of consideration.

Will you oblige me by reading it ?

And if you think it is of a nature to induce any friend of yours to change his opinion as to the unreasonableness of parties and persons on the question, you are quite at liberty to communicate it to him.

Believe me, faithfully yours,
WILLIAM SHEE."

To this Panizzi answered thus :—

"British Museum,
June 1st, 1854.

" My dear Sir,

I have read with the utmost attention the draft of Bill which accompanied your letter of yesterday.   The subject is as important as it is difficult, and it is with the utmost diffidence that I venture to express an opinion on the practicability of your suggestions.   I am afraid that any equitable proposal like yours would be resolutely resisted by the Church of England, not so much for what you propose doing now, but for the sake of the precedent you would establish.   On the other hand, that section of the Catholics which is the most violent and noisy, and, therefore, I fear, the most influential in Ireland, would not be satisfied with the arrangement you propose, but would look upon it as the thin edge of the wedge, and an instalment only of what they think due to them.

I am afraid that the question of the Temporalities of the Church of Ireland is of such a nature that no moderate man can hope to settle it to the satisfaction of both parties, so long as either possesses any thing.   The only way of settling it would be to take every farthing of property from them all, and paying them all alike ; but this is what can never be done without a revolution.

There is a friend of mine to whom I should like to show your draft of Bill, and beg, therefore, to keep it two or three days for the purpose.

In the present state of public affairs, even if the Government were disposed to entertain the principle of your Bill (and this is supposing a great deal), I am afraid the Ministers will not consent to its being introduced during this session. Of this, however, I am even a worse judge than of the rest.

Believe me, &c.,

A. PANIZZI."

Lord John Russell's opinion of the Bill was expressed no less decidedly, though a little more curtly than Panizzi's :—

"June 10th, 1854.

"I think, as you do, that the Serjeant's Bill would have no chance in Parliament.

Yours, &c., &c.,

J. RUSSELL."

On the 18th of August, 1855, a Concordat between the Courts of Austria and Rome was signed. This compact, by which a great deal of the liberty of the Austrian Church was given up to the Papacy, caused much dissatisfaction. In 1868, it was virtually abolished by the Legislatures of Austria and Hungary. To none was it more distasteful than to Panizzi, in whom, as will have been already seen, there was a wholesome dread of the Roman Church (a dread not altogether unreasonable, when certain countries and Governments had to be taken into account), and this was strongly expressed in two letters from him to Mr. Gladstone and to Mr. Haywood respectively. In the last of these, it must be granted that Panizzi very accurately estimates the opposition likely to be offered by disunited Sceptics and Freethinkers, void of combativeness and enthusiasm, to the disciplined forces of the Pope and the Curia.

"B. M., June 1st, 1855.
"My dear Sir,
. . . . First of all, any Government agreeing to a Concordat on the ground discussed, the Civil Power is not paramount, but subject to the superior power of Rome. When Napoleon became King of Italy, he thought it right to ask the approval and confirmation of the sale of the Church property, by the Pope. It was at once granted ; but when afterwards the State was going to dispose of one hundred millions of francs more of that property, the Pope protested, and argued that Napoleon himself, by asking the Papal sanction for past sales, acknowledged that no sale could be lawful without the consent of Rome.

In the second place, the Court of Rome makes a great distinction between a Treaty and a Concordat. The latter she looks upon, properly speaking, as a boon granted by the Head of the Church, to any inferior Civil Power who humbly sues for the favour.

I enclose you the first article of one of the most recent acts of this kind—the very one, in fact, which the Papal Court complains to have been broken by the Sardinian Government, by the Siccardi Law. In the third place, the Court of Rome does not consider herself bound to observe Concordats on her side.

First of all the general maxim of the Comitia is alleged, that 'non juramenta sed perjuria potius dicenda sunt quæ contra utilitatem Ecclesiasticam attentantur.'

As the Church is the judge of the *utility*, being the highest power, they say, no oath or promise can be binding if against Ecclesiastical utility. Next in the matter of Concordats, the doctrine is explicitly taught that the Pope has the power to derogate to them.

I give you extracts from the works of a great Canonist, who states the pretensions of Rome to confute them; that, however, is another point: the point is what they at Rome affirm.

Now for the extracts. The first Article of the Convention between Gregory XVI. and Charles Albert, dated March 27th, 1841, runs thus :—'Avuto riguardo alle circostanze de'Tempi, alle necessità delle private amministrazione della guistizia, ed alla mancanza de'mezzi corrispondenti dei Tribunali Vescovili, la Santa Sede non farà difficoltà che i magistrati laici giudichino gli Ecclesiastici per tutti i reati che hanno la qualificazione di crimini.' *Ergo*, the Santa Sede 'può fare difficoltà' if she chooses, and the Civil power by asking to be allowed to try a priest guilty of murder, for instance, acknowledges the right of the Holy See: *Ergo, in altre circostanze*, that same Santa Sede can make *difficoltà*. You need not my saying more. The Canonist who stated the doctrines of Rome on Concordat to refute them, is Schmidt (Anton), Professor of Canon Law at Heidelberg, in the last century, whose words are as follows :—

'I.—Summum Pontificem Concordatis cum Natione germ. initis, derogare posse contendunt præter Authores Pontificios Branden.

'II.—S. Pontifex, ajunt, summus Christi Vicarius, & jure divino habet dispensationem, ac plenissimam administrationem omnium bonorum ad quascunque Ecclesias pertinentium, consequenter ex plenitudine potestatis potest vel in totum, vel pro parte Concordata tollere.

'III.—Concordata ceu Indulta ordinaria in favorem Germanorum admissa continent meram gratiam, non tam vim pacti, quàm privilegii, & sicuti privilegium revocari potest, ita in libera S. Pontificis remanet facultate, an iisdem stare, vel ab eis recedere velit.

'IV.—Licèt coram Puteo dec. 47, dicantur habere vim contractûs, intelligendum hoc ex parte Germanorum, quòd videlicet illi non solum ex jure divino sint obligati ut Christiani ad parendum Rom. Pontifici, sed etiam ex speciali Concordia quasi in vim contractæ pacificationis inita, ut in omni judicio Germani sedi Apostolicæ rebelles minus forent excusabiles; si obedientiæ suavi jugo excusso, etiam pacta firmata violare præsumant, adeoque Concordata dicunt saltem negotium ex pacto, & privilegio mixtum.

'V.—Id quod confirmatur etiam ex eo, quod S. Pontifex suam summam, & absolutam potestatem, quam a Christo accepit, de rebus Ecclesiæ, officiis, & beneficiis Ecclesiasticis disponendi a se abdicare non possit, quin semper penes se majorem adhuc retineat.

' VI.—Successores succedunt jure singulari non universali, nempe jure Electionis, novo titulo, novo jure, & sic Nicolaus V. non potuit suis successoribus taliter legem imponere, quam ipsi de omnimoda necessitate tenerentur servare.'

(Thesaurus Juris Ecclesiastici sive Dissertationes Selectæ, &c., vol. 1, p. 339).   Such doctrines ought to be known. Many Canonists, Catholics, have differed from them.   I have never heard them condemned or disavowed at Rome; on the contrary, taught in the Universities in the Papal States.

Yours, &c., &c.,

A. PANIZZI.

" B. M., Nov. 29th, 1855.

" My dear Haywood,

And so you are not afraid of the influence of the Church because Scepticism and Infidelity prevail? It is because they prevail that I fear the Concordat.   If the Protestants were animated by religious fanaticism, as they were some centuries ago, they would resist and prefer martyrdom to submitting to Rome ; but Philosophy, and Scepticism, and Infidelity, and all that, are all negative qualities.   They do not give strength and courage.

Do you think all the Sceptics and Infidels in the world would fight like the Waldenses, the Hussites, and the Germans under the King of Sweden?

Moreover, the number of Infidels and Sceptics is limited to the upper classes generally. What hold can they have on the ignorant masses, who have only in view the gallows in this world and hell in the next?

There were Infidels and Sceptics enough in Spain and Italy in the sixteenth century, and the united tyranny of the temporal and spiritual power kept Italy obedient to Rome.

It was towards the end of the reign of Louis XIV. that the French Protestants were obliged to submit.

Yours, &c., &c.,
A. PANIZZI."

Having now completed this ecclesiastical episode of Panizzi's life, it behoves us to return to our interrupted narrative and to the relation of the results of his expedition to Italy, as well as his further action in the liberation of his suffering friends and countrymen.

CHAPTER XX.

No sooner had Panizzi arrived in London than he set about devising some means of escape from the dungeons of the Neapolitan Government for his unhappy friends. For the present he was forced to confine his efforts to the deliverance of Settembrini, then in captivity on the small island of San Stefano; the relief of Poerio, who was in stricter bondage in another prison, inland, and more closely watched, being a case of secondary consideration to that of his fellow sufferer. That the work was both arduous and dangerous hazard may be easily conceived, and that as yet no very palpable improvement in the state of Naples had resulted, notwithstanding Panizzi's laudable exertions during his visit, may be gathered from the following extract from a letter addressed to him at this time by Sir William Temple:—

"Naples, January 15th, 1852.

" There is no appearance of any change in the police here, as the trial for the affair of the 15th of May is conducted in a more illegal way than that of Poerio. The judge puts words into the witnesses' mouths, or, at least, reads them their former depositions, and threatens them with punishment if they do not adhere to them."

On the subject of poor Settembrini and his family, Panizzi wrote in these terms to Mr. Haywood:—

"B. M., March 20th, 1852.

"You may recollect the name of Settembrini among those of the persons condemned to death, and then to an *Ergastolo* for life, of whom Gladstone spoke in his publications, and I myself more at length in my article in the *Edinburgh Review*, in which I inserted the letter which he (Settembrini) wrote to his wife whilst the judges were deliberating on his fate. When at Naples, I became acquainted with Settembrini's wife and his two children—a boy and a girl. The persecut ons to which that poor woman and those children have been subjected are incredible. Among other things, no teacher dared give instruction to the boy for fear of losing the permission which every teacher must obtain from the Government to be allowed to follow his profession."

On February 21st, 1852, Lord Shrewsbury wrote to Panizzi:—"We were glad to hear of your safe return, and sincerely trust your visit to Italy will not pass without its fruit, both at home and abroad, by removing some English prejudices in favour of the Revolutionary party, and by aiding in the expected re-form of the Prison discipline and Police Government at Naples." On both these points, and more especially the first, his Lordship may be pardoned for having been somewhat sanguine.

There was but little need for Panizzi to seek the aid and support of Mr. Gladstone in his present plans. On his co-operation he could ever count, even without asking ; nor was the continued main-tenance of that tyranny and injustice, which he had so distinguished himself by denouncing, likely to diminish the great statesman's sympathy for its victims.

"Liverpool, November 5th, 1853.

"My dear Panizzi,

Be assurred that if anything like an opportunity shall offer, I will not be slack in seizing it on behalf of the poor Neapolitans. Were I inclined to halt, the recollection of your journey, undertaken for the love of them and of truth, would shame me into activity. I will not fail to communicate with Clarendon.

Yours, &c., &c.,

W. E. GLADSTONE."

"Hagley, December 14th, 1853.

"My dear Panizzi,

I have read Poerio's letter with horror, but also with admiration. The last, however does not lessen, it enhances, the first ; and though I do not well see what can be done hopefully, yet a man does not come readily to the conclusion that one can do nothing under such circumstances. But first of all can your judgment suggest anything? I am coming to town at latest on Friday. Will you either come to me on Saturday morning or write (if not before). I am sure Lord Clarendon would do anything that he may think gives a chance, and I will strain any point. Think the whole matter over before we meet.

Yours, &c., &c.,

W. E. GLADSTONE.

Do not be afraid of proposing to me anything that may strike you. I return the letter."

From the year 1852 to 1858, inclusive, many letters, notwithstanding the numerous difficulties in transmission, had passed between Settembrini and Panizzi. The former's letters were consigned through his wife to Sir W. Temple, and by him forwarded to England. Of the replies, unfortunately none have reached us. They were directed to Mr. Fagan, who delivered them to Madame Settembrini. She had them copied in very small characters, in invisible ink expressly prepared for the purpose. Various devices were resorted to for introducing these letters into the prison. At one time they would be hidden in linen or hemp, sent to the prisoners, that they might occupy their time in weaving ; at others they would be sewn into the soles of the sailors' shoes, and a multitude of other modes of concealment was resorted to. It is satisfactory to relate that the ingenuity bestowed on their safe delivery was amply repaid by success, and that the officials of this contraband post-office escaped discovery.

Settembrini's portion of this correspondence is in itself so interesting, and contains so much matter of value affecting this narrative, that it has been thought fit to give somewhat copious extracts from it. By the following it would appear that the prison of S. Stefano was no very desirable exchange for the dungeons of the " Vicaria," and, moreover, afforded no great encouragement to any hope or plot for escape :—

" S. S., November 27th, 1852.
" . . . I am at present in a *real* dungeon. Neither I nor any of the prisoners are permitted to descend from the floor to which each of them is assigned. I remain as much as possible in my own cell, or rather den, to avoid coming in contact with desperate characters. I never see a human face, and can only at times catch a glimpse of the sky that is over the prison yard. Only when the marine courier arrives, am I allowed to come down and see him, assist at the examination of my effects, and receive my letters, returning immediately to my cell. Under these circumstances, you can understand how every plan becomes impossible. Time and my own sense of honour may guide me, under altered circumstances, but for the present I can do naught else but suffer, and suffer in

silence. Meanwhile, I trust God will have mercy on me, for
at times I feel my spirits dying within me, and fear, if ever I
leave this place alive, I shall come out mentally and morally
degraded."

The extract next in order shows that, however close
his prison, he was fortunate enough to be able to
avail himself, notwithstanding great obstacles, of the
advantages of that scholarship for which he was so
distinguished. His selection of his author also
deserves a word of praise. After speaking of his son
Raffaele, he says :—

"S. S., Feb. 16th 1854.

" I present you with another production of mine, in the shape
of a small volume containing some of Lucian's dialogues, which I
have translated into Italian. Whenever you have time, I
would beg you to glance at my work, and give me frankly and
honestly your opinion of it. Should this attempt not prove
wholly unworthy, I shall hope to complete the work, leaving
out all passages that might now be considered objectionable,
and when it may please God to restore me to mankind, I propose publishing it with an introductory preface, in which I
should like to mention the benefactors of my family, Lord and
Lady Holland, Sir William Temple, and you, my dear Sir.
Should it not please you, I shall simply destroy it. Labouring
under immense difficulties, without books or assistance of any
kind ; writing in a room of Cyclopean horrors, on the deal
boards of my bed, distracted by the hammering of a cobbler
next to me, I am indeed unable to offer anything of genuine
worth, such genius as I may have possessed being dead within
me ; but as an Italian, and a man of letters, you will judge my
work, understand my intentions, and tell me truly whether you
deem it worthy of presentation to my noble friends and yourself. Do not be surprised at my coming forward, in this age
of noise and turmoil, with a translation from the Greek. In
my present state I am so far removed from this actual world

that, in order to bear my life, I take my thoughts back to antiquity, where, with my Lucian, I can smile at mankind and at all things past and present. Be indulgent, I pray, and believe only in the sincerity of my intentions."

In the middle of the year 1855 Panizzi had sufficiently matured his plan of action to be able to enter definitely on the execution of his great design. He had been hitherto much hampered by the difficulties of obtaining sufficient money to make a beginning of the enterprise. If this could be accomplished in time, he arranged to start for Italy himself in July of the same year. Although the main purpose of his journey was undoubtedly the deliverance of Settembrini and his fellow-captives, he thought it best to keep this purpose as far as possible concealed. An opportunity, however, had occurred, whereby he might probably combine the business of his office with the pleasure of succouring his unfortunate friends. On the 25th of July he applied to the Trustees of the British Museum for an extra month's leave of absence, at the same time informing them that a circumstance had lately come to his knowledge whereof advantage might be taken to render a portion of his vacation useful to the Library; this referred to the then impending sale of books belonging to Filippo Senesi of Perugia. An extract from a letter to Sir James Lacaita, shows something of the embarrassments under which Panizzi was labouring for want of sufficient funds for his undertaking:—

"B. M., 26th July.

". . . . The escape seems most feasible in company with an English friend. I shall direct it myself in person. No

K

danger for us. What I require is money. I have £300 of
L——; to this I shall add £100 of my own, which I shall
borrow. I want £800 at least. I must see Gladstone to-day.
I know not what he means to do. Do all you can at Edinbro'
to find me money."

This obstacle, however, was happily overcome, and
on the 3rd of August, he thus wrote to Lacaita :—

" The affair promises well, and the difficulties are enormous,
but as I have found money beyond what I had hoped, I am of
good courage. There is no danger of being defrauded, for I
pay no one now; but there is a possibility of being betrayed.
The sum needed is enormous, and is required for the charter-
ing of a steamer, which is to be found. Time presses. Mr.
Gladstone has behaved wonderfully, or properly speaking
Mrs. Gladstone, who has given me £100 of her own, and
found £200 more amongst her friends."

Panizzi being now well on his way southward, it is
necessary to leave him for the present, in order to
give a short account of an incident at Naples, most
conspicuous perhaps for its effect on European politics,
or on the relations between England and the kingdom of the Two Sicilies, in which it created a passing
disturbance. It appears to have been about this time
a deeply-rooted idea in the Neapolitan official mind,
that the real and actual disasters, mostly self-inflicted,
which the English had suffered in the Crimea, joined
to the ill-success which the lively Neapolitan imagination represented as continuously occurring to the
British arms, had reduced England almost to the level
of Naples. The time, it was thought, had come when
this once great Power, the abettor of contumacious
subjects against their rightful sovereigns, the upholder
of sedition and rebellion against legitimate authority,

might be insulted with impunity, and a long-standing grudge might be satisfied. Nor was the opportunity for indulging this patriotic feeling wanting. In August 1855, Mad^{mo.} Parepa, a singer, who had married a Maltese gentleman, and thereby become a British subject, was very anxious to obtain a benefit-night at the *San Carlo*, at Naples. She had been recommended to Sir William Temple, who had a short time before obtained a promise in her favour from the Duke Satriano, Tito, " Superintendent of the Theatres." Of this promise Sir William requested his Attaché, Mr. Fagan, to remind the Duke; he accordingly called one evening on his Grace at his box in the theatre, so-termed *Il Fondo*, and delivered the message. As he was leaving he became aware of the presence of an agent of police, apparently on duty, with evil intentions, as was indeed the fact. This man was one Vignati, who had been sent by the Minister of Police, Mazza, with a message threatening the Duke with imprisonment and other dire consequences for having received a member of the British Legation with so much civility. The message delivered by the man was overheard by some one in the theatre; Mazza himself was also heard saying, in a loud voice, " I shall not allow myself to be imposed upon by England, now a fourth-class Power !"

This Caligula, still living and well-known to the biographer, was as notable in his younger days for the energy with which he exercised his office as for the suavity of his manner in executing his intentions. It is recorded of him that, amongst other arbitrary proceedings, he, on one occasion, sent for Signor Nicco-

K2

lini (now of the National Museum, Naples) and loaded
him with abuse for presuming to wear a beard.   Dis-
regarding the advice to hold his tongue, given him by
a bystander, Niccolini boldly answered the Minister
that if the growing of beards was illegal he ought at
least to publish an order prohibiting it.   *No, no,* said
Mazza, *no publishing of orders for me, to be held up
to ridicule by Piedmontese newspapers.   You go and
cut off your beard, and see you keep clear of conspira-
cies!*   On another occasion at Catanzaro, in an excess
of temper, he went so far as to break his cook's
arm.

The occurrence at the theatre was communicated
that same evening to Sir William Temple, who lost
no time in sending a note of remonstrance to the
Minister for Foreign Affairs.   That functionary,
however, seemed in no hurry, either to make apology
or give redress for the insult that had been offered to
the British Mission.   However insignificant and
unworthy of resentment Naples might be, however
small in comparison with England, the insolence was
too great to be passed over.   The matter was at once
reported to the Government at home, and communicated by Mr. Fagan to Panizzi, who answered as
follows.—(August 22nd, 1855.)—" I am delighted to
hear directly from you what I have already heard
and considered incredible.   Lord Palmerston will
not, I presume, overlook this affair. . . . . "
Nor was Panizzi mistaken.   Lord Palmerston's action
in the matter was, as might be supposed, prompt and
decisive :—

"Piccadilly, August 25th, 1855.
"My dear William,
. . . King Bomba's insult to England, through the British Mission at Naples, must be properly atoned for. Clarendon being at Paris, nothing can be decided till he returns, and the Cabinet can be assembled. But I have written to Clarendon to say that my opinion is that we ought to insist upon the immediate dismissal of Mazza, and upon a promise that he shall never again be employed in any public capacity. I would not make this demand till our reserve squadron, now in attendance on the Queen, but which will return with her on Tuesday, and which consists of three line-of-battle ships, shall have anchored in the Bay of Naples, opposite the King's Palace, and shall have taken on board the Mission and the Consul, and then I would have a boat sent on shore, with a demand that in two hours an answer should be sent by the King, saying that Mazza was dismissed, allowing half an hour for the letter to go, half an hour for the answer to come back, and a whole hour for writing the answer. If the time passed without a satisfactory reply, the palace should share the fate of Sweaborg* *(e poi dopo)*, if that should not be sufficient. However, we shall see what resolution may be come to when the Cabinet meets on the question.

Yours affectionately,

PALMERSTON."

That Ferdinand II. was extremely loth to dismiss Mazza may be gathered from his delay in making up his mind to do so. The case, however, was urgent, and, pressed by his son Francis to hesitate no longer, inasmuch as the Minister was aware of his impending fate, the King removed Mazza from his office, and issued a decree† stating that he had been called to *another office.*

---

* Bombarded 9th of August, 1855.
† September 14th, 1855.

Amid all this turmoil and confusion in the Government of Naples—this system of continuous oppression—there was one person who, notwithstanding all his misdeeds, may fairly claim some little share of our commiseration—the King himself. On the evidence of Mr. Gladstone and others, it is clear that Ferdinand was not wholly without his good traits of character. He was not devoid of a certain amount of intelligence.

Tyranny and slavery, however, exercise a doubly evil influence, and harm the despot as much as the victim, the owner as the slave. At the time of the Mazza case, his Majesty, taught by experience, had arrived at that wholesome judgment of persons and things which trusts nobody and nothing. He had long ceased to put confidence even in his own Ministers; political matters he directed himself, and himself wrote all the more important political despatches, many of which display considerable acumen. It would not, indeed, be unfair to impute a portion of his faults to the peculiar character of his subjects, of whom he was wont to say that they differed so much from, and were so greatly inferior to, any other people of the Peninsula, that he alone could govern them.

Meanwhile, Panizzi's arrangements for the deliverance of the prisoners of San Stefano had been gradually and surely progressing, and to all appearance hopefully. He had communicated to Settembrini the manner in which he proposed to make the attempt, and from him received the following letter:—

"Santo Stefano,
August 31st, 1855.

"As a precaution I write this letter with invisible ink, which will be made legible before it is forwarded to you. For the same reason, and in the same way, your letters of the 30th and 31st July have been sent to me. I cannot tell you what I felt on reading them. You are a man who surpasses every expectation. We dared not hope for a steamer; now you offer us one, it is all that we could desire. From your letter it appears that the steamer will not start from Naples, as I had expected. This matters little to us, but it is most important that it should be known in Naples not less than twelve days before. Communication with this place is neither easy nor frequent, and we must know the date fixed upon at least four days in advance, as there are certain indispensable preparations to be made. Now the time it will necessarily take for this letter to reach you, and for you to come to a determination and give Madame Louison (Settembrini), through some person, twelve days' notice, will bring us to the month of October, which will be more suitable, as the cold weather and rains will then have set in, moreover the nights will be longer.

In short we are ready, only requiring four days' notice, but the date fixed upon must be known in Naples twelve days before. In deciding upon the day, however, care should be taken that there be little or no moon during the early hours of the night, and, therefore, it seems to me that we ought to choose some time between the 6th and 18th of October, and, if it could be the night preceding a holiday, so much the better.

We shall, therefore, wait to be informed on what day the steamer will pass, and what will be the signals. We are on the upper floor of the building where there are some small windows which look to westward; in the remainder of the building there are only small apertures and loop-holes which are almost invisible. The third window, commencing from the north, is ours; and from this window we have a view of the whole space between Ponza and Capo Circello. The steamer should carry a conspicuous signal as our telescopes are not very good. She ought to find herself at 4.30 or 5 o'clock two miles from the northern extremity of Ventotene, and then, if it is thought necessary, unfurl a sail to enable us to see and recognize her. Then, if she passes to the east, there will be sufficient time and light to see the wall with an archway; almost immediately below which, on the shore, is a small creek where the boat will have to wait, and where we intend to be at 2 o'clock a.m. When the steamer has lost sight of the small windows she will proceed eastward, bearing to the south, as if making for Messina. During the night she can return from S.S.E. as I have written in another letter, but must not come too near Santo Stefano, and thence she would put out the boat. When we reach the archway, we will make a signal with a lantern, which we will repeat on reaching the sea. If a password is necessary, we might say, *God help us*, and may God truly help us, and lead me with my companions to a place of safety ; I trust I shall not have to write to you again. Keep well.

P.S.—If it should be stormy on the day fixed, the steamer could come, without any signals, on the following day or the first fine one, for we shall commence operations the moment we know the date, and complete them on seeing the steamer; and if a storm should rise while the boat is waiting in the above-mentioned creek, obliging it to put off from the shore, it must make a great effort to return, and throw us a rope which we can lay hold of. It is necessary to foresee what is likely to take place."

Not long after the date of this letter, Panizzi sent to Mr. Fagan a summary of his plan of rescue, containing all the details of the work, and the mode in which he proposed to carry it out. This ran as follows:—

"Genoa, 31st August, 1855.

" 1.—In the last days of September and beginning of October, a steamer will pass to the eastward of the Convent (*i.e.*, the prison), where are the birds (prisoners), having one white streamer flying from each mast, or from one mast, which streamer will be hauled down for some moments, and then hoisted again when it is at its nearest point to the island.

" 2.—The steamer will proceed on her course and run out of sight.

" 3.—On the night of that day she will return, and approach the Convent as nearly as she can with safety, without chance of discovery.

" 4.—At midnight she will send her boats to the island, and they will proceed towards the place already fixed upon in the plan.

" 5.—The boats will not touch the shore, but will wait off till a light is shown from the beach, when they will approach within hail.

" 6.—The password from the Nuns is the name of the friend of Louison *(i.e., Panizzi)*.

" 7.—The password from the boat will be the name of Louison's father (*i.e., Luigi*).

" 8.—If the Nuns be prevented coming to the beach between twelve and four o'clock that night, the steamer will put to sea, and return again at the same hour, and the same process will be repeated.

" 9.—If the second attempt fails, the matter must be deferred.

" 10.—If the steamer does not appear, it is because difficulties have prevented it.

" Now if Madame Settembrini has a short memory, it will be best to commit these points to writing, and enclose them in a wax pill covered with gutta-percha (a piece of which is enclosed), and which she will put in her mouth and swallow, if examined closely at the Convent.   But better still if there be nothing in writing."

The plan set forth met with the fullest approbation from Mr. Fagan ; he, however, wrote to Panizzi " to be most cautious, for although Mazza had left the Police, *they*, the English, were watched night and day, and were hated by the King's partisans."

The great difficulty in the undertaking turned out to be the obtaining of a vessel.   Owing to the exigencies of the Crimean War, Panizzi, up to the 31st of August, had been unable either to charter or buy a craft suitable for his purpose.   At length the desired object was attained in the shape of the screw steamer " Isle of Thanet."   But now comes the melancholy part of the story ; failure of skilfully and anxiously concerted plans, waste of money collected with so much pain, arduous and continuous labour miserably thrown away ; bitter disappointment to Panizzi, and prolonged incarceration of the wretched inmates of S. Stefano.   The ill-fated vessel charged with the restoration to freedom of Settembrini and his companions was but laden, after all, with the destruction of the hopes of all concerned in the attempted liberation. Scarcely had she started from Hull, when she met with a disabling accident which forced her to put back for repairs.   These being completed, she set forth a second time, and had proceeded no further than Yarmouth when she was caught in a storm on the 25th of October and totally lost. So ended by no default of skill, but by the merest caprice of fortune, an enterprise which, if we consider the persons engaged, the means within their reach, and the purity of its purpose, must ever be reckoned as a most brilliant attempt; and so did not end, at least with all true lovers of freedom and humanity, the glory of those that had embarked upon it.

Amongst others who felt the disappointment of the failure almost as keenly as Panizzi himself was Mr. Gladstone, who lost no time in writing a letter of condolence on the ill-success of the expedition:—

"Hawarden, Chester, November 6th, 1855.

"My dear Panizzi,

I cannot help writing you a line, however barren of condolence. I had hoped it might please God that your benevolent plan should succeed. It seems usually so hopeless to do good in this world, on a large scale, that one desires to become intensely concentrated on what lies within a small compass. For myself, too, I feel that with respect to the Italians I have had a great deal more credit than I have fairly earned; and I wished to have a hand in *doing* something by way of a step towards rectifying the account. I am so little informed of the reasons and particulars of your mode of proceeding, that I will at present go no further; but whenever the opportunity offers, I shall be most desirous to converse with you. I hope to hear more in the interval if you have more that can be usefully said.

I have resumed, during this recess, some old studies on Homer, and have also gone back for collateral illustration to that field of which I am very fond—the Italian romance. So for the first time I have been reading you on Ariosto and Bojardo, and on the romance in general; let me add, with great interest and pleasure, and with profit too, unless it be

my own fault. But I am curious to know whether you still
hold all the opinions that you had when you gave these books
to the world. Are you still willing to have it thought to be
probably your opinion that Berni is better than Bojardo?
I am inclined to like Domenichi better than Berni, because
he is so much nearer Bojardo. Mr. Hallam speaks of him
with contempt. I doubt if he had paid much attention to
either.

I have also been reading the 'Orlandino' and the 'Ricciar-
detto.' All these poems have an interest attaching to them as
parts of a great chapter of literature. The last of them, at
least the first half of it, though far from unexceptionable,
seems to me better and not worse than Ariosto, in the one
point for which he is justly censured.

Yours, &c., &c.,
W. E. GLADSTONE."

A few graceful words to the same effect were also
received by Panizzi from Sir W. Temple:—" Should
the aid of friends be necessary, I hope you will reckon
me among the number."

The following letter, with which the present
chapter concludes, distinctly proves of what stuff
Settembrini was composed, and the same commendation may, without presumption, be extended to his
companions :—

" Santo Stefano, December 3rd, 1855.

" To think that you and your generous friends should have
spent so much time and money, and should have undertaken
a long journey all in vain, grieves me beyond measure, for I
can imagine all you must have done and hoped to achieve,
and how disappointed you must have been at the unfortunate results. Do not, however, think of me ; I am inured to
suffering, and am not worth so much trouble. I grieve on
your account, the more as my own ill-luck seems to pursue
those who interest themselves on my behalf. Should you be

forced to give this matter up, do not let it vex or trouble you. . . . Do not distress yourself about me and my companions; we have lost but one hope more, and we have lost so many already, the greater loss is his who has laboured and spent, and done so much in vain. If the matter is still delayed, and if, nevertheless, you and your friends are still willing to conduct it to an issue, you will be guided by your generous and noble hearts rather than by our merits. In such case give me timely advice, in order that I may inform you if it is still possible for us to do anything to second your efforts, and also whether any unforeseen obstacle may not render it necessary to change the original plan. . ."

CHAPTER XXI.

BIANCHINI'S APPOINTMENT — SETTEMBRINI FUND — CONVENTION WITH ARGENTINE REPUBLIC—CORRESPONDENCE—ORSINI—NAPOLEON III.

AFTER the suppression of Mazza, a marked change for the better took place in the general conduct of the Neapolitan Police; Bianchini, the new Minister, presented in every way a favourable contrast to his predecessor in office. Under his gentle rule, not only was the normal system of molestation and oppression as far as possible relaxed, but the strongest front faced those dangers, arising from revolutionary incendiarism, which not only the ill-governed State, but, through its Government, the cause of Liberty in general, was perpetually incurring. "There is a lull," wrote Sir William Temple to Panizzi (January 17th, 1856), "in the proceedings of the Police; Campagna has been kept in order, and there are no longer attacks upon *hats* and *beards;* and people breathe more freely."

Although, however, the ardour for the *chasse aux rouges* had sensibly diminished, and the King's subjects were enjoying their liberty—quite a novelty to them—of being able to walk abroad in comparative security, it must not be supposed that the benefits arising from the improved state of things had extended to those political adversaries who were

already in durance. Of carrying out his schemes
for the rescue of Settembrini and his companions at
San Stefano, Panizzi, notwithstanding his former
failure, had by no means abandoned hope or intention. In framing his future projects to this end, he
had met at Genoa, where he now was, with valuable
assistance, in the shape of the counsel and co-operation of Dr. Bertani. After deducting the loss
sustained by the wreck of the "Isle of Thanet," for
it was not fully insured, there remained still in hand
a considerable sum of money, a portion of the fund
lately set on foot for the liberation of the prisoners.
This sum, until some further design for accomplishing
the rescue had been definitely determined upon,
Panizzi felt some scruple in retaining ; and accordingly wrote to the respective donors of the money
offering to return the contributions.

They, however, with one or two exceptions, preferred to leave the whole of their subscriptions in his
possession, to be applied by him either to the main
purpose, or to such uses as, in his judgment, might
seem best for the benefit of Settembrini and his
family, who were at this time in a state of the deepest
distress. The letters of Lord Overstone and Lord
Zetland seem worthy of reproduction :—

"February 25th, 1856.
" My dear Panizzi,
        " I regret to learn you have not been able to apply the
money to the purpose originally contemplated. I am sure,
however, it will be destined, under your superintendence, to
very useful and benevolent purposes, and I beg you to con-

sider yourself as vested with full and unrestricted authority so far as regards,

Yours, &c., &c.,

OVERSTONE."

_____

" October 8, 1856.

" My dear Panizzi,

" As one of the contributors to the fund which you raised, I will beg you to retain my contribution, to be appropriated in the manner you think best for Settembrini and his family. The first object would, of course, be his liberation; but if that cannot be effected, I am quite satisfied to leave it to your judgment how to appropriate it to the best advantage for him and his family.

Yours, &c., &c.,

ZETLAND."

Here we may pause for an instant to reflect on the steadiness of Panizzi's character. With an aim in view he was never faint-hearted or desponding, even when the victim of constantly repeated rebuffs; it is well to note this ever-recurring trait in his character, for the recollection may serve as an encouragement to others who might be inclined to despair instead of imitating his example.

The "Settembrini Fund," amounting to about £1,000, was finally entrusted to the charge and management of Mr. Gladstone, and by him securely invested in England.

Meantime, a new influence had been brought to bear at Naples on the fortunes of Settembrini and the rest. The King had concluded with the Government of the Argentine Republic a Convention, whereby he was to be at liberty to deport to that State such political offenders (including, as it would appear, others of a different and more criminal caste) detained at this time in the Neapolitan prisons, as should choose to avail themselves of the commutation for exile proffered them. It is not clear whether this alternative was actually offered to Settembrini, Poerio, and their immediate companions ; but it is evident, not only that they would have been at perfect liberty to avail themselves of it, but that the King would have been delighted to rid himself of them by the means proposed. The question whether or not they would be adopting a judicious course of action in agreeing to the terms offered by the Convention, and accepting the modicum of liberty they could purchase at the price of expatriation, divided their friends and benefactors into two factions.

On one side, Panizzi himself was strongly opposed to their taking such steps, and vehemently supported a different course, viz., that they should petition the King directly for their pardon and release. He appears, and, to judge from his own words, not unreasonably, to have suspected something latent in the Convention which might prove an insurmountable obstacle to the voluntary return of the exiles from their new country to the old, or, indeed, to Europe in general. In a letter to Lacaita (February 17th, 1857) he thus expressed himself strongly on the subject:—

" I wish you would try to dissuade any Neapolitan prisoners to accept the alternative of going to the Argentine Republic. They have no güarantee or protection whatever that the conditions under which they consent to go will be observed. *They will be made slaves.* I know very well the agent who has set this going : he is a most clever Alsatian Jew, who has several times put together enormous fortunes by schemes and

L

speculations of an adventurer, and who has been as many times reduced to beggary. I know that some of the prisoners, among others Poerio and Settembrini, have been offered by the Neapolitan Government a free pardon, if they will petition the King, and they have refused! This is not firmness, but fool-hardiness. There is nothing disparaging for a man who is bound hand and foot, and has a dagger put to his throat, to ask to be released. Any man, however brave, will run away from a mad dog. If they were asked to acknowledge them-selves guilty, they would be right to refuse, and rather die in prison ; but it is sheer folly to refuse to ask to be let out. This is the opinion of *all* their friends here. It seems that Fagan urges them to go to America.

Ever yours,
A. PANIZZI."

The position of matters at this time, as regards carrying out the terms of the Convention, was re-ported to Lord Shelburne, who had been requested to consult Lord Clarendon on the subject. This, however, he appears not to have considered of any very great importance. Mr. Gladstone seems equally to have oscillated between the two alternatives of exile to La Plata and a petition for a not dishonour-able pardon :—

"February 5th, 1857.

" My dear Panizzi,

The paper on the Argentine Colonization reads well, but everything depends on the good faith of the parties. What are the guarantees for the fulfilment of the terms? I see them not. On the other hand, I agree with you that if a petition could be framed, praying in terms of due respect for liberation, without directly or indirectly confessing guilt, there could be no dishonour in presenting it.

Yours, &c., &c.,
W. E. GLADSTONE."

On the other hand, Lord Palmerston, though he expresses no belief one way or other, yet perceives in the possible want of *bona fides* in carrying out the Convention on either side, not in the proposal of emigration, the chance that the prisoners might have to submit to that deprivation of future liberty, so much feared by Panizzi :—

           " 11th February, 1857.
" My dear Panizzi,

   " . . . As to Settembrini, I doubt whether he and any of his fellow-prisoners would not do well to agree *to go* to South America. They would not be bound to *stay* there ; and it would be for them to decide whether their liberty is worth purchasing by two voyages across the Atlantic.

        Yours, &c., &c.,
          PALMERSTON."

Settembrini, meanwhile, distracted by the diversity of opinion among his friends, and perplexed by the strenuous opposition displayed by Panizzi to the emigration scheme, applied to Mr. Fagan for explanation of this apparently uncalled for opposition, and for further advice as to his own action. As regards the alternative of petitioning the King for pardon, we confess that, on the point of honour, we coincide more strongly in Settembrini's opinions, stated in the following letter, than in the views expressed in Panizzi's letter to Lacaita. What the former wrote to Mr. Fagan is so well worth reading, and so characteristic of the writer, that we make no apology for presenting long extracts.

L2

"Santo Stefano, March 2nd, 1857.

"My dear Mr. Fagan,—

The kindness which you have at all times shown me emboldens me to write and explain to you a plan of mine which appears to me reasonable, and to beg you to let me know through my wife (who will be the bearer of this letter) whether there is anything on which I might be misinformed. Mr. Panizzi, in the name of his friends and himself, advises me to ask for a pardon. He evidently sees no other way, and I myself have given up hope. He tells me on no account to accept an offer to go to the Argentine Republic, but for what reason I am unable to discover, though I have mused over it for days. Mr. Panizzi is to me such an authority, I respect, love, and owe him so much, in fact, that I am really grieved to find myself differing from him. I feel sure that he has either been misinformed as to my intentions, or that he knows more than I do. As in his letter he seems to have expressed his settled conviction, I will not write to him, for it would seem discourteous to contradict him. For this reason I beg you will tell me whether you know what has induced Mr. Panizzi to give me this advice, or, at least, to explain to him my motives, if you approve of them. You, my dear Sir, having lived amongst us for so many years, and knowing so well both the intentions and opinions of the Government and the Liberal party, can understand how, under present circumstances, a request for pardon is not merely a personal matter, is not only the sacrifice of one's dignity, and of that legitimate pride which every honest man ought to feel; it is not merely coming to terms with a robber or highwayman, and begging him to spare your life, but it is a matter of public interest, and means the recantation of political creed, and the recognition as right and legal of all the enormous injustice committed during the last nine years. It would be telling the nation we have all been in the wrong; it would be giving the lie to England and France (who have solemnly condemned the conduct of the Neapolitan Government; it would be saying to the public opinion of Europe, you have been deceived. The Neapolitan Government well knows the value of such requests, and, while using all manner of insinuations and suggestions to extort them, will not take them into consideration unless they are of the most abject character, wishing not only to humiliate, but to degrade the applicants. I would sooner remain here than leave my prison through such a door. I know that many others have asked for mercy, and I do not blame them, but I trust no one will blame me for my irrevocable resolve. . . . Such pardon as the Government offers is contemptible, and death or the galleys would be preferable. My honour and conscience are my own, no power in the world can rob me of these my last possessions. I am thoroughly convinced that in asking for a reprieve I should injure both myself and our common cause, therefore I have decided not to make an application on any terms. There still remains one honourable way of leaving my prison. By going to America my personal dignity would not suffer, for it is the Government who offers, not I who ask. It will do no harm to the common cause; for though it may appear that in leaving I show a want of confidence in the country, yet I shall give no grounds for suspicion that in remaining I wish to ask or accept pardon. Oh, my dear sir, in this prison I am daily losing intelligence, conscience, and all human feeling, and the thought that for the last seven years I have lived on other people's charity breaks my heart and aggravates my troubles. This state of things is insupportable. To escape from it a year ago I ran great risk, and now I would go not only to the Argentine Republic or Patagonia, but even to Victoria or the Pole. I never had any intention of settling abroad, but would remain there as short a time as possible, returning to Europe and Piedmont, there to meet my poor wife and beloved son, and live on the fruits of my own labour. It would merely be banishment to Piedmont with the preliminary conditions of twice crossing the ocean, even for those who could not return so soon to Europe, the journey would not be altogether an evil, for either our country would remain as it is (and the Argentine Republic would be preferable to a prison), or matters will change for the better, and then they could at any time return home.   This opinion seems reasonable to me ; but on perusing Mr. Panizzi's letter, I am so impressed by his authority that I have hesitated.   I have racked my brains to find reasons for the contrary, and have found none to satisfy me.   The Convention has not met with favour in this country, for I believe two reasons—prejudice against a Government which, being hated, cannot please in what it does, and also from sheer ignorance, which associates the ideas of a disastrous and interminable journey to a country haunted by yellow fever and infested with savages and all sorts of horrors.   None but the ignorant multitude would attach importance to such rumours.   Many have tried to persuade me that once despatched to those regions we should never be allowed to return, and that the Convention has been artfully drawn up to lead us into a trap.   Abiding, however, by the first and trustworthy information which you, Sir, most kindly imparted to my wife, I still believe that the man who does not accept the conditions of a colonist (and who lets the Government know that he wants nothing from it, but will live at his own expense) could not be compelled to submit to any restrictions, but might remain or return at his own pleasure.   It is quite just that a colonist who contracts a debt should be watched, and not allowed to depart without satisfying all claims ; but he who accepts nothing owes nothing. It would be an enormity of a novel kind should the Argentine Republic consent to act as the police of the Bourbons, and become the jailers of their political prisoners.   It would be a pretty sort of recommendation to Europe, a fine inducement to strangers to settle in Argentina, if they were to act thus in total opposition to the spirit and letter of their constitution, which, thanks to your kindness, I have read.   I therefore repeat my belief that there would be no difficulty in leaving the place, and that no secret conventions exist in that respect ; but if you, dear Sir, should now think differently, or even suspect anything of the kind, I beg you let me know frankly ; I earnestly entreat this, as it is to me a matter of the greatest importance. In consequence of your assurance that it would be possible to return to Europe (and from what I have myself read in the Convention) I am firmly persuaded that it will be the most reasonable course to go. Mr. Panizzi now advises me not to do so, without, however, stating his reasons, and I beg you to relieve me of my doubts as soon as possible. My future intentions would be (if allowed to return) to embark immediately in any merchant vessel at hand, and sail for Genoa or Marseilles. Three years ago my son Raffaele went to Monte Video in a trading vessel, and made the voyage out and back in less than ten months, including the time of his stay there, which was not short. The voyage from La Plata to Genoa could be accomplished in two months, or even less. Now I cannot discover any injury to either the public cause or myself in all this. If others see harm I would beg them to indicate clearly in what it is, in order that I may alter my opinion and do nothing painful to myself or displeasing to those who love me and whom I both love and respect. To your courtesy, my dear Sir, I look for the answer which will either change my opinion or confirm me in the intention which at present seems reasonable to me. In conclusion I must inform you that all political prisoners, including those confined at Ponza and Ventotene, have been asked whether or not they are willing to go to the Argentine Republic (we galley slaves alone excepted). I cannot assign any reason for this exception. I do not know whether the Government are unwilling to send us out, whether they have reserved us for a second expedition, or have abandoned the whole matter from irritation at the refusal of almost all the prisoners. But I believe that, in spite of the delay, the matter will still be carried into effect, even for us " forzati " who are kept here as so much refuse from the gallows.

Yours, &c., &c.,   LUIGI SETTEMBRINI."

Whether the Convention had already turned out a "complete failure" or not, the pace at which the whole business was progressing must have given ample time to Settembrini to make up his own mind, as well as to collect and digest all the advice worth following as to the line of action best for him to adopt. The parties to the Convention, and notably the King himself, seem certainly to have been in no hurry to bring the affair to a climax. "Nothing is known," wrote Mr. Fagan again to Panizzi (April 25th, 1857,) "with certainty respecting the affair of the political prisoners. The two frigates which are now being fitted out will not be ready for sea before the end of next month. The general impression appears to be that about 250 persons will be sent, but they are all men belonging to the lower class, and not all condemned for political offences."

In this stage of delay and uncertainty we will take the liberty to leave the proceedings for the present, in order to bring on the scene another character, afterwards a somewhat intimate acquaintance of Panizzi's

—it would be scarcely warrantable to call him a friend—in notoriety, more than equal to Poerio or Settembrini, but not as they were, of honourable and untarnished celebrity. Few are living but

have heard or read of Felice Orsini; equally few
are they who do not hold both the man and his
criminal intentions in deep execration. He was
born at Meldole, in the States of the Church, in
1819. From his youth upwards, his fixed idea
his sole purpose of life was Revolution; conspiracy was to him as the breath of his nostrils.
It cannot in strict truth be alleged that he absolutely
and deliberately set his mind on murder, as the
surest or most desirable means to accomplish his
object, but neither can it be denied that if
murder became a most necessary ingredient in his
plans, if it showed him the easiest way, he was
ready, without scruple even, to adopt such fell
measures. Orsini's first imprisonment for political
crime was in 1844. In February, 1845, he was again
convicted before the Supreme Tribunal of Rome, and
condemned to the galleys for life, for a plot against the
Government. Fortunately for himself, he was com-
prised in the general amnesty of the 16th of July,
1846, published by Pius IX. on his accession to the
Papal chair, and released, or perhaps it ought to be
said let loose, in the same year. In May, 1847, he
was expelled from Tuscany for his political intrigues.
Two years afterwards he was elected a Deputy in the
Roman Constituent Assembly; but, in 1853, was
forced to quit Roman territory. He first sought
refuge in London, which, however, in a short time,
he left, and for a period was busied in roaming
through Piedmont, Switzerland, and Lombardy,
continually, wherever he went, plotting and scheming
under the assumed name of Tito Celci. He was next

heard of under the name of Hernof, at Vienna, in 1855, when he was arrested and sent to the fortress of Mantua. Thence, by energy and skill, no less by good fortune, he made his escape in the night of 28th-29th March, of the same year. He next visited Marseilles and Genoa, whence he returned to London. At this period he was on most intimate terms with Mazzini. Their friendship, however, was not of life-long duration : it ended in a quarrel.

By Mazzini, it appears, Orsini was first introduced to Panizzi; but the introduction must have been merely formal, as there is no record of any inter-course between the two arising therefrom, and Panizzi seems to have lost sight of him very soon afterwards. However on the 14th of August, 1856, he was recom-mended by Mr. John Craufurd as a proper person to become a reader in the Library of the British Museum. The letter of introduction was delivered by Orsini himself, on the 18th of the same month, when he met with Panizzi, and a strong mutual liking for one another sprang up. In fact, as we know from the best of sources, this sympathetic feeling very nearly assumed the proportions of friendship ; for Panizzi expressed himself as never having been so much cap-tivated by any one as by Orsini. The familiarity thus quickly established, showed early signs of endurance ; and the following letter, which throws a good deal of light as well on the character as on the history of the writer, may be read with interest :—

"14, Cambridge Terrace, Hyde Park,
" My dear Sir,   27th August, 1856.
       I have examined the Catalogue of the Library respecting the Art and Science of Warfare. It is but poorly

furnished with the most instructive works published during and after the wars of Napoleon. It is the same with the United Service Institution, where I was admitted for the purpose of consulting the books which I required for the composition of the military work that I have in hand, and I have in consequence had to order various books from France at my own expense ; but, however, I shall soon have to study the work of which I send you the title : " La grande Tactique du Marquis de Ternay," Colonel of the Staff. These works, especially that of Martray, I could not procure on account of the expense, but should you think it desirable for the Library to acquire them, it would be of great assistance to me. The Paris edition of Ternay's work ought not to cost more than 25 francs, and that of Brussels much less. The work which I am engaged upon will be in English, and contain all the information required by officers in the field, from the Sub-Lieutenants of the three branches of which an army is composed, up to the Chief Staff Officer inclusive. It is a serious undertaking as it must be restricted to a portable volume, and include, with clearness and conciseness, the *omne scibile* of military affairs. With diligence and assiduity, assisted by the studies of my youthful days, I promise myself I shall succeed; still it is a work I shall not be able to finish in less than six or eight months. While thus engaged, I could devote some hours a day to other occupations, and I should like, if possible, to give lessons in the Italian language, literature, and in military art and science. Having been myself major of the staff, I can give good lessons in the latter, and am tolerably conversant with the former. Up to the present time my life has been unusually eventful, and passed mostly amidst dangers—a constant source of anxiety to my family, who have suffered no slight losses on my account. As I am a little more quiet just now, I wish to derive advantage from my acquirements, while awaiting the longed-for moment when I may once again take up arms for our independence. I have been advised to

advertise in the *Times* that I am willing to give lessons; I
should not like to do this, it would seem as if I wished to
turn my good name to profit, although, instead of such an expedient, I think, if you would, you might greatly assist me
amongst your acquaintances, and in any case I am quite ready
to follow your advice. With my private life you are not,
however, acquainted; but on this I give you full liberty to
apply even to my adversaries, whether in opinion, or party,
or otherwise, for we all have such. Of languages, I know
French well, and for private lessons can make myself understood in English. I have written this to avoid troubling
you, and if you will kindly let me know, I can
call upon you at any time for better advice as
to what I have said here. On political affairs I know
nothing positive, but keep myself (as I told you) independent
of every one, and should the Sardinian Government deem my
slender services available for any enterprise, however daring,
I am, and always shall be,.ready, I mean, of course, for the independence of my native land ; for that, since I could understand the idea, I have ever been restless, and have sacrificed
all. In saying I am ready to lend a hand to the Sardinian
Government, I am influenced solely by the love of my country
and by the conviction that at the present time, if it will, it is
the only Government that can render Italy *independent, united*,
and *great;* and I shall think myself happy if, by devoting all
my energies in an important act, fraught with *serious consequences* to the oppressors of Italy, I can at the same time put
an end to a life which has so far been for me but sad, passion-
ate, and melancholy. Pardon this expression of my feelings.
From what I hear, it appears that my little book has met with
some success, even in Piedmont and with all parties ; certainly
I have in no way exaggerated, but endeavoured to impress the
necessity of sacrificing all political principle to the National
Independence. I have done so myself since my first imprisonment in 1844. Nothing remains for me now but to beg you

to excuse this long letter, and with every respect to assure you
that I am,

Dear Sir, your very humble and devoted servant,

FELICE ORSINI."

In another letter, dated "Glastonbury, 7th February, 1857," he says in further development of his political dreams :—

"The book, with the documents, &c. . . . . is now finished. . . . In an introduction I insist on this point, that all our efforts should be directed towards the national independence. While thus engaged, every thought of political theories must rest in peace ; we are bound to be on the side of that Italian Government which, excluding the Pope and any foreign dynasty, will furnish us with the means of making war on Austria. All this I say with the frankness that has been natural to me throughout life, with the patriotic ardour that ever burns within me, and with the firm *conviction* that by such conduct alone can the Italians work their redemption."

To refer to the hideous, and, it may be said with justice, the vulgar crime of which Orsini and his accomplices were guilty, is not here necessary, further than will suffice to refresh the memory of the reader. The attempt took place on the evening of the 14th of January, 1858, at the moment when the Emperor Napoleon III. and the Empress arrived at the Opera. The details are too well known to need repetition. On March 13th following Orsini was guillotined.

That the crime had been long premeditated, and that Orsini had not been impelled to it by any sudden frenzied impulse, is clear from a passage in his

defence of himself, if defence it could be called, on
his trial:—"From my youth," said he, "I have only
had one object, and one fixed idea, the deliverance of
my country, and vengeance against the Austrians, and
I have constantly conspired against them up to 1848.
.   .   .   .   When in England, I was imbued with a
mania of being useful to my country. I witnessed
ridiculous attempts being made by Mazzini, who sent
15 or 20 men to Italy, where they lost their lives. I
tried loyal means; I went over to England, and in all
the meetings which I addressed, advocated the principle of non-intervention.   .   .   .   .   After the fall
of Rome, I felt convinced that Napoleon would no
longer assist us: and I said to myself, that man must
be killed.   .   .   .   .   I am very sorry that so many
people were wounded, and if my blood could repair
this misfortune, I am quite ready to give it for the
people. Here it is!" These words were described
by the French newspapers at the time as bombastic—
an epithet singularly out of place. Terrible they
might well be called, and full of ghastly meaning:
witnesses not only to the atrocity of the crime itself,
but to the length of time—two whole years—during
which the plot to commit it had been in process of
elaboration.

On the eve of his execution, Orsini addressed a
letter to the Emperor, in which he said:—"Near the
close of my career, I yet wish to make a last effort,
for the sake of Italy. Her independence has hitherto
prompted me to defy all dangers, to court all sacrifices. *Italy has been the constant object of my affec-*
tions, and this is the last thought that I wish to record
in the words which I address to your Majesty."

Let the reader compare the passage with Orsini's letters to Panizzi. The death of Napoleon, considered

 so necessary to the cause of Italian Union by Orsini, might possibly not have promoted that good end. But could it have been that the alarm caused to the Emperor by the assassin's attempt was one of the chief reasons that led him to take arms against Austria in 1859?

It has been told the writer of this memoir, on various occasions in the course of conversation, that, when the news appeared in the second edition of the *Times* of Saturday, January 16th, 1858, that "Orsini or Corsini" had attempted the murder of the Emperor, Panizzi, who was in the habit of visiting Brooks's every afternoon, was at once, and on that very Saturday, questioned by other members of the Club whether the assassin was his friend. Panizzi replied that he doubted it very much, seeing that he himself had an appointment with Orsini for the following day, when they were both to call on Lord Palmerston together. This was thought at the time to be a deep but futile scheme for establishing an *alibi*. Of the truth of the story we have no evidence beyond what we have mentioned. So far as we have been able to ascertain, there is nothing to show that Orsini was in London at all in this month of January. It is a matter of regret that we cannot help the reader further to judge of the truth or falsehood of the anecdote.

As we would not ourselves be held to have painted
the would-be assassin in too dark a colour, so would
we willingly grant all indulgence to any who, from
merely reading the facts of his history, should be inclined to depict him in the deepest of hues. That, by
many ordinary Englishmen, such a man, who scrupled
not to attack and destroy all, known or unknown, who
stood in his way, might aptly be called the mad dog
of society, is perfectly conceivable. But, granting all
that can be brought against him, and in no wise seeking to justify his actions, we nevertheless submit that
the character of Orsini is rather deserving of careful
study, and even of allowance, if that study be made
fully and without prejudice, than of hasty condemnation. A fanatic of fanatics, he was undoubtedly, both
to friends and foes, the most dangerous of men ; but
he had also the good points of a fanatic—he was un-
selfish, and of necessity disinterested. If, to use the
mildest of terms, he little more than undervalued his
neighbour's life, he at least threw his own into the
balance. Nor can it be denied, from what has been
said and quoted above, that patriotism (unenlightened
it might be, carried to a crime as it assuredly was,
yet earnest and sincere, and having no taint of self-
seeking, though much of self-imposture), was the
man's one inspiration throughout his life. That
personally he was not of a vulgarly brutal cast of
mind is evident if only from his letters to Panizzi.
His learning and ability were more than common
place; as a soldier his skill and courage were un-
questioned. We would be content to speak of him,
however, in no higher terms than were employed by

his advocate at his trial. "He was not there," said M. Jules Favre, " either to justify or to save his client, but he came there with the wish to endeavour to cast on his immortal soul some rays of that truth which he trusted would protect his memory against the execration of posterity."

CHAPTER XXII

DEPARTURE OF NEAPOLITAN PRISONERS—AT CADIZ—
CORK—" CAPTAIN JAMES "—POERIO'S LETTER—
FERDINAND II.

THE scheme for getting rid of the political offenders, the charge of whom was probably day by day increasing in weight upon the Neapolitan authorities in the same ratio as captivity itself to their victims, was coming near its accomplishment. On the 27th of December, 1858, a decree was issued by the King, offering to the prisoners, in accordance with the tenor of the Argentine Convention, choice between emigration and continuation of durance. This decree commenced as follows, in words possibly not intended to be ironical:—" By the Grace of God, &c., &c., &c. Having given proofs of our sovereign clemency to the greater part of those condemned for offences against the security of the State during the events of 1848-9, &c., &c., &c." It was read in the presence of the prisoners, who, with one exception, accepted the conditions therein offered. The single voice, however, which constituted the minority, overbalanced a majority rather of numbers than importance. Poerio utterly refused to accept any of this qualified liberty.

" Better," said he, " death on the gallows than this futile and costly journey to a far off land, there to meet a death more obscure and less honoured." This refusal of the leading criminal to accept his freedom under the Convention was of such importance that the idea of any treaty was abandoned, and the whole plan for the deportation of the prisoners fell to the ground. Nor was his resolution to bide his time in captivity fruitless. On the 6th of January, 1859, a second decree, in substitution of the former, was promulgated, the main point of which was that certain of the prisoners, in number sixty-six, including Poerio and Settembrini, should be at liberty to leave the galleys on condition of going to New York.

This was readily accepted by the select number, and on the 16th of January, Poerio arrived at Pozzuoli, where, on the same day, he embarked on board the " Stromboli," a vessel which had been fitted up as a prison. Pironti, eminent amongst those oppressed by the Neapolitan Government, had been attacked by paralysis, and was left behind in safe custody.

Poerio, on his embarkation, was still in chains, and little provision had been made for the comforts of the party on starting for their voyage across the Atlantic. No adequate or suitable clothing was provided for them, and, as a matter of fact, they were literally in rags.

Meanwhile, in London Panizzi was alert for the safety and protection of the exiles in case they reached New York. The United States Government, about that time, had repeatedly protested against some of the European Goverments deporting their paupers, jail-birds and prisoners to America, and threatened

M2

not only to prevent their landing, but to compel the captains who brought them to take them back. Of course no serious apprehensions were entertained for those Italians, if they fell into the right hands at first. Panizzi consulted Mr. Henry Stevens, who recommended that correct information and supplies should be sent direct to the Collector of Customs in New York, and in such manner arouse his personal interest in the patriots. Accordingly the following letter was written by Mr. Stevens to Mr. Schell, who not only took a lively interest in the affair himself, but encouraged others to the same purpose. A steamer was kept for many days in readiness to go down the Bay to meet Poerio and his companions and welcome them to New York. It was, therefore, no slight disappointment when the news was received that they had found their way to England.

"Morley's Hotel,
London, January 28th, 1859.

" My dear Sir,

You are doubtless familiar with the story of the Italians whom the King of Naples, since his amnesty at the end of December last, has sent to New York. There are sixty or seventy of them, and it is expected that they will reach America towards the end of February. They go from Naples to Cadiz by steamer, and will probably be transhipped there to a merchant vessel about the 22nd of January.

Much interest is felt and expressed for them here, and I have no doubt, as they are all exiles for political offences, they will receive a cordial welcome on our shores.

I take the liberty not only to call your attention to them, but to request that you will be so good as to deliver, as early as possible after their arrival, the enclosed letter to one of them, Mr. Luigi Settembrini. The letter is from Mr. Panizzi, the Chief

Officer of the British Museum, who takes a deep interest in them all, but more especially in Mr. Luigi Settembrini and Baron Carlo Poerio, both gentlemen of distinction, the latter formerly a Minister of State.

The letter to Mr. Settembrini contains matters of importance, and will direct him and others to Messrs. Brown Brothers & Co., where they will find *something to their advantage.*

I will only add that some little apprehension has been expressed lest the *manner* in which the King of Naples has sent these unfortunates to our shores might bring trouble upon them ; but their misfortunes are too well known to warrant the belief that exiles for political opinions will be opposed on their landing in the *Land of Freedom.*

They will not be destitute, thank God, when they land. Besides the sum of fifty dollars given by the King to each one, they will be provided for by private hands.

I remain, &c., &c.,

HENRY STEVENS

(Of Vermont)."

It was on board the "Stromboli" that Poerio and Settembrini met for the first time since their captivity. Little opportunity was, however, afforded for the moment of renewing their acquaintance with each other, for the former, shortly after his arrival on board, was seized with severe illness, and compelled to keep his bed.

It is pleasing to relate an instance of true kindness and humanity on the part of at least one officer connected with the Neapolitan Government, and to record that Ferdinando Cafiero, Commander of the "Stromboli," directed that his illustrious prisoner should be placed in his own (the captain's) cabin.

They set sail, escorted by the "Ettore Fieramosca," man-of-war ; and the writer of this "Memoir," as an eye-witness of their departure, well recollects the enthusiasm displayed on the occasion. On their way to Gibraltar they fell in with a Sardinian vessel, flying the national tricolour. This was a signal for the exiles to run on deck, and, with deep emotion, salute the flag, the symbol of liberty and good government in Italy. On the 26th of January, they reached Cadiz, where another ship was to be chartered to take them to the United States.

One morning, while at Cadiz, Settembrini was sent for on board the "Ettore Fieramosca," a message reaching him that an English officer wished to speak to him. Here a great and most agreeable surprise awaited him. His astonishment can scarcely be conceived when he recognized in the English officer his own son Raffaele.* At this time Raffaele was but a youth in the merchant service. Having been at school in England, he spoke English fluently, and in language and general appearance was well fitted for the character he had assumed. He had taken the name of James, and represented himself as the captain of a merchantman trading between London and Madeira.

Anything like friendly converse between father and son at this meeting was, of course, out of the question, but the latter managed to transmit the whispered words, *You shall not go to America.* Captain "James," it should be mentioned, had reached Cadiz by means of a plan carried out through the agency of the Neapolitan consul at that port, and concerted in London by

---

* Now a distinguished officer in the Italian Navy.

Panizzi.   All things being thus happily arranged, the party embarked in the American ship, " David Stewart," commanded by Captain Prentiss.   The " David Stewart" was very well found, and comfortable accommodation seems to have been provided *for her passengers.*

Two days afterwards, she started in tow of the " Stromboli," and escorted by the " Ettore Fieramosca," which had orders to see her well out to sea. Having established a good offing, the two Neapolitan men-of-war returned.   Captain "James," meantime, had shown himself equal to the occasion.   He had changed his character of master of a merchant vessel for that of steward on board the American vessel.   On the night of the Neapolitan's departure, he communicated to his father a design which he had formed for compelling the Captain to return to Lisbon, adding that, in case resistance was offered, he was provided with arms to enforce compliance.

Settembrini, as might be expected, listened eagerly to his son's proposal ; but, in accordance with his general demeanour, strongly objected to violence of any sort.

The design was forthwith imparted to the exiles, who were sufficiently numerous to carry the point without resort to force.   By an accident, they were driven to act a little prematurely, but, as it happened, in no way detrimentally to their ultimate success.   A seaman trod on a percussion cap, and the explosion gave the alarm to the captain.   On this the passengers at once took action, and, presenting to him a protest against being taken to New York, demanded

that he should make for the first port he could reach
in England.   The captain, one-third of whose freight
had been retained as a guarantee for the performance
of his contract, remonstrated, and the demand was
for the moment not pressed.   On the following
morning, however, it was repeated in a more decided
manner.   The exiles drew attention to their numbers,
being 66 as against 17 of the ship's hands; they
represented that, having suffered much from their
confinement, and many of them being of advanced
age, they were not in a state to undergo with safety a
long voyage, and added that one of their number,
being well skilled in navigation, would manœuvre the
ship, in case the captain and crew should refuse their
assistance.   This skilled seaman was none other than
Raffaele, who had appeared in yet a new *rôle*, and
came on deck in a mate's uniform of the Galway line
of steamers.   The passengers, of course, met with
little further opposition.   They quietly took possession of the vessel, setting watches, and taking all
precautions to ensure due execution by the captain
of their orders, which were to make for Cork.   The
weather proved obstructive, and the voyage tedious,
but in the course of a fortnight, they were safely landed
at Queenstown.

Great was the excitement caused here by the
arrival of the distinguished visitors, with whom heartfelt sympathy had for so long been expressed in every
part of the United Kingdom.   Lively as was the
pleasure expressed at their safety in these countries,
the disappointment felt by the inhabitants of New
York, who had prepared for Poërio and his com-

panions the warmest reception, was equally keen. The Italian residents had appointed a Committee to supply funds for the emigrants to return to Sardinia, which was understood to be their destination after America. All was in readiness to give them a cordial welcome. From Mr. Dallas, the American Minister, Panizzi received the following short note:—

"Legation, U.S., London,
March 9th, 1859.

"My dear Mr. Panizzi,

   You will see by the enclosed newspaper slips how much my countrymen will be disappointed by the revolt of your friends, and their safe arrival at Queenstown.

Always, &c., &c.,

G. M. DALLAS."

It may be mentioned here that Panizzi, with the concurrence of Mr. and Mrs. Gladstone, placed £100 at the disposal of Settembrini and Poerio, to be delivered to them at Gibraltar, which sum, however, they never received, not having landed there. This loss was soon compensated by the good fortune which, as we have narrated, had now befallen them. Not that the enthusiasm shown in their behalf throughout the country was likely to allow forgetfulness of the necessity for material assistance. One of the first to propose a mode of benefitting them was Charles Dickens:—

"Tavistock House,
March 14th, 1859.

"My dear Panizzi,

   If you should feel no delicacy in mentioning, or see no objection to mentioning, to Signor Poerio, or any of the wronged Neapolitan gentlemen to whom it is your happiness and honour to be a friend, on their arrival in this country, an idea that has occurred to me, I should regard it as a great kindness in you if you would be my exponent. I think you will have no difficulty in believing that I would not, on any consideration, obtrude my name or projects upon any one of those noble souls, if there were any reason of the slightest kind against it. And if you see any such reason, I pray you instantly to banish my letter from your thoughts.

It seems to me probable that some narrative of their ten years' suffering will, somehow or other, sooner or later, be by some of them laid before the English people. The just interest and indignation alive here, will, I suppose, elicit it. False narratives and garbled stories will, in any case, of a certainty get about. If the true history of the matter is to be told, I have that sympathy with them and respect for them which would, all other considerations apart, render it unspeakably gratifying to me to be the means of its diffusion. What I desire to lay before them is simply this. If for my successor to *Household Words* a narrative of their ten years' trial could be written, I would take any conceivable pains to have it rendered into English, and presented in the sincerest and best way to a very large and comprehensive audience. It should be published exactly as you might think best for them, and remunerated in any way that you might think generous and right. They want no mouth piece and no introducer ; but perhaps they might have no objection to be associated with an English writer, possibly not unknown to them by some general reputation, and who certainly would be animated by a strong public and private respect for their honour, spirit, and unmerited misfortunes. This is the whole matter. Assuming that such a thing is to be done, I long for the privilege of helping to do it. These gentlemen might consider it an independent means of making money, and I should be delighted to pay the money.

In my absence from town, my friend and sub-editor, Mr. Wills (to whom I had expressed my feeling on the subject), has seen, I think, three of the gentlemen together. But as I hear, returning home to-night, that they are in your good hands, and as nobody can be a better judge than you of anything that concerns them, I at once decide to write to you and to take no other step whatever.   Forgive me for the trouble I have occasioned you in the reading of this letter, and never think of it again if you think that by pursuing it you would cause them an instant's uneasiness.

Believe me, &c.,
CHARLES DICKENS."

In London a Committee for the relief of the exiles was formed, and large sums were received.

The first letter Panizzi received from Poerio was dated from Cork, 27th of March, 1859.   In this there was, however, little beyond an acknowledgment of a letter received, and expression of gratitude for the trouble taken on his behalf.   Although Poerio, starting from Cork on the 29th of March, soon joined his friends in London, they had but little uninterrupted enjoyment of each other's company for some time.   Invitations poured in for the great exile from every quarter.   Amongst his entertainers may be mentioned Lord Granville, the Duke of Sutherland, the Marquis of Lansdowne, and the Duke of Argyll.

The following note of invitation from Lord Palmerston must not be omitted :—

" 94, Piccadilly,
April 1st, 1859.

" My dear Panizzi,

Come and dine here to-morrow at eight, and bring Baron Poerio and Settembrini if he likes to come ; and don't mind the date of this note.

Yours sincerely,
PALMERSTON."

And Mr. Gladstone wrote on Poerio's behalf as follows:—

"April 12th.

"My dear Panizzi,

Lady Charlotte Egerton asks, through me, Baron Poerio and any one of his friends to her party to-night. Pray let them appear if possible. They will find me there at 10.15.

Yours, &c., &c.,

W. E. GLADSTONE."

This continued dissipation, and the cold of the English climate, from which he suffered intensely, began to weigh heavily on Poerio. He was forced by his state of health to refuse many invitations, and the only other amusement of which we have any record is a visit to the House of Commons on the 18th of April, under the auspices of Lord Shaftesbury.

It would be too much to expect that amongst the large number of sixty-six prisoners, however exalted the political creed which they might profess, there should not be at least one or two black sheep. There were certainly some amongst the lower order of these exiles, with whom Panizzi had a good deal of trouble. Notwithstanding all his rigid justice in apportioning the money of which he had the charge, they vexed him much by claiming more than their share, by accusations of unfairness, and, in some cases, even by the vilest ingratitude and abuse. Nor did they confine their annoyance to him alone. Poerio, writing subsequently (3rd of June, 1859,) from Turin, gives anything but a pleasing account of these gentry who had accompanied him to Italy:—"I have had a great deal of trouble here on account of the English subscription in favour of the exiles. One of them who was

destined to receive 250 francs told a great many in
secret that this terrible injustice of classification was
all my work," with a good deal more to the same
effect, on which it is needless to expend time and
space.

But the calls of patriotism were altogether too
urgent on Poerio to allow him to spend very much
of his time in London society. About the middle
of May he left for Turin, where he entered on a long
correspondence with Panizzi. Here, for the first time
in these volumes, we are able to present the reader with
a comprehensive letter from Poerio, although short extracts from others have been given above. His letters
are, both in language and style, the acme of combined
nervousness and elegance, and we can only express our
regret that, to meet the exigencies of the general reader,
we are compelled to give this in English, feeling that
by translation the beauty and force of the original must
materially suffer. Most interesting in themselves, but
of still greater value as throwing light on contemporary history, are the accounts of the sad continuance
of disorder and misgovernment in the administration
of Naples; of the various other complications in the
affairs of the Peninsula; the course of action adopted
by the French Emperor in connection with the attitude
of the Sardinian Government, (which last, Poerio
seems to consider occasionally as somewhat hesitating
and undecided); and the dawn of the first possibility of
effecting the union of distracted Italy, in the achievement of which, however, a thousand difficulties seemed
yet to be overcome. Some few necessary excisions of
matter of little importance have been made, but this

has not materially reduced the bulk of the correspondence. Of Panizzi's share we unfortunately possess
nothing. A good notion, however, of his opinions on
Italian, and (as connected with Italian) of European
politics, as well as of his unwearying efforts in the
cause, and the confidence that his compatriots rested
in his exertions and influence here, may be gathered
from the communications which he received from his
friend and others who had suffered from or witnessed
the revolting cruelties committed for so many years in
Naples and elsewhere ; but there is no querulousness,
no recalling of the past ; every energy, every aspira-
tion, is devoted to the one glorious object—the unity
and independence of Italy :—

> "Turin, 21st of August, 1859.

" My dearest Panizzi,
            I send you my ideas respecting your project,
which would be excellent if it were only practicable.

Your programme, if I mistake not, may be summed up as
follows :—The formation of a single Assembly of representatives from the four States of Central Italy, such assembly to
proceed immediately—To confirm in common the separate
decisions arrived at with regard to the deposition of the Princes
and the annexation to Piedmont; to publish a manifesto to
Europe, short, but solemn, energetic, and rich in facts which
justify this severe but unavoidable determination ; to
nominate a Regent, who shall assume in its entirety and in the
name of the Sardinian Government the exercise of executive
power, commencing with the appointment of a commander-in-
chief to all the forces now under arms, such forces to be con-
bined and formed into a single army. After this the Assembly
would adjourn, leaving the Regent full power to have himself
represented at the European Congress called for by this Assembly, in order to obtain a decision in conformity with the solemn

vote of the country, and to repel any aggression on the part of *anybody* who might intend forcibly to reinstate the deposed Princes.

First of all I must take exception in *law* to the *judicial* validity of the nomination of a Regent.

A popular Assembly, legitimately elected, has most certainly the right of declaring that the people represented by it intends to choose for its Prince the monarch of another State, and intends to identify itself with that State. But after this decision has been arrived at, the logical and legal order of things would be to address that Prince, in order to ascertain whether he is willing to accept this free and spontaneous surrender. If he accept, he alone can and in fact must nominate an authority to govern the annexed provinces provisionally in his name. The Assembly cannot do this, because, in proclaiming a new Prince, it invests him with the sovereign power. Victor Emmanuel proceeded in this way with the Lombards, who submitted to him of their own free will—that is to say, he nominated a Governor to rule in his name, neither did he act otherwise towards the people from whom he accepted the dictatorship. The only exception to this rule is when it is *physically* impossible for the Prince who has been proclaimed to speak his mind. It is not so in our case, because the King of Piedmont reigns both by right and in deed, and is personally free. He is, moreover, at the head of an army, and has made himself a champion of the war of independence. It is, therefore, necessary to address him. He is not only able, but is bound to declare himself openly, and in accepting he will be obliged to provide a government for those provinces until an European Congress recognizes the fact as accomplished, and includes him in the new public statute. Most assuredly no one will ever assert that the Congress ought to *compel* Victor Emmanuel to accept the submission of Central Italy, unless he had openly acceded at the proper time, and acted frankly in conformity with his utterances. Silence in this case might be termed prudent; but it

certainly would not be very generous, particularly if it be considered that these people are determined to fight to the last
against anybody who would wish to prevent them from *belonging to him.*

According to your plan, I conclude that King Victor
Emmanuel must not only accept the surrender and nominate a
Vicegerent or Lieutenant who will govern under his guidance, but must also prepare himself to protect and sustain the
annexed provinces to the utmost of his power, and at the
same time declare himself ready manfully to repel any aggression. It would, in truth, not only be strange, but indecorous,
in a King invoked and proclaimed if he were to act negli-
gently and look on with indifference at the cruel sacrifice of
his new people, who are ready to shed the last drop of their
blood to preserve their fidelity to him.

But this sacred duty will not be performed, and it is vain
to hope for it, because just now a timid rather than a spirited
policy prevails in the Piedmontese Cabinet.

I do not wish utterly to condemn it, because I know but
too well the gravity of affairs generally, and the difficulties of
such a perilous situation. Possibly the requisite boldness
would amount to temerity, but it is none the less true that
when a man cannot, or does not wish to, run any risk or
leave anything to chance, he has no right to look for
brilliant or glorious results, neither can he expect to add
four millions of people to his own proper subjects without incurring any risk, and merely by remaining a careless spectator
of the dangers to which others are exposed. . . .

Let us suppose that the Piedmontese Government can do
nothing to display a large amount of energy and tenacity
of purpose; let us suppose that, notwithstanding the safe re-
mission, the amalgamation of the four States, the single
Assembly, and the unanimous declaration, are matters of
supreme importance to the future of Italy, but how can one ever
hope for this fusion in the midst of such discordant elements?
It is true that the four States have formed a military confed-

eration for mutual defence, but this fact of itself clearly shows that there is no intention of proceeding further, and of forming a single State. . . .

Everybody *apparently* wishes for the fusion with Piedmont, but a great many object to the idea of a single State. Nor do the Romans and the Tuscans, who are so different in character, in customs, and in aspirations, intend to hold together. The Duchies alone really wish for the union with Piedmont. The Romans would in reality like a separate government, and the Tuscans who reason closely, know that in the actual condition of affairs the fusion with Piedmont is impossible, but they pretend to want it (and voted *unanimously* for it only yesterday), because it is for the present the only straightforward way of avoiding a relapse into the clutches of the Grand Duke and his myrmidons. In fact, when they had a chance of accomplishing the fusion, although they were advised to take advantage of it, they neither did so nor even desired it. Their own Ambassadors in Paris and London (Peruzzi and Lajatico) put it on one side, advancing instead a number of *schemes* and solutions, commencing with a Prince of the House of Savoy and finishing with Prince Leuchtenberg. The *Times* published the document, the *Augsburg Gazzette* has repeated it with evident satisfaction, and they have not denied it.

Lajatico (as you tell me) now writes in the same way as Marliani—that is, for the formation of a single Assembly which is to repeat the vote for annexation to Piedmont, forgetting that Parma has no Assembly, and on account of the unfortunate dissensions and paltry points of honour between the two rival cities of that nutshell, poor Manfredi has been obliged to have recourse to a *Plebiscite;* that, moreover, to escape from the machinations of an Armelonghi, who wanted to supplant him, he has been compelled to call upon Farini to act as Dictator. For my own part, I think that henceforth neither Marliani, nor Peruzzi, nor Lajatico, nor Linati will be able to persuade the people or obtain the one single Assembly as proposed by you. But even conceding that our respective friends fully approve,

N

and supposing that everybody consents, also that there is an
unanimous declaration of the desire to become Piedmontese,
that Europe is called to witness it, and that a *sole* Regent is
appointed (a matter of considerable difficulty in view of the
passions, and ambition, and rivalry, and suspicion aroused),
and conceding, moreover, that everything should go on according to a preconceived idea, let us see what would in all
probability occur in actual *practice.*

Your dilemma is this : by such an arrangement you either
succeed in convening an European Congress, which will deli-
berate upon the present *abnormal* and disturbed condition of
central Italy, or the failure will at least be glorious. In the
first case, therefore, you only rest upon a hope, and a hope
that is evaporating daily, since France at heart does not *so far*
wish for the Congress, and I do not see who is to force it on
her.

I must say that Lord John Russell's noble declaration to the
effect that England does not intend to take part in any Congress, unless the bases of peace and rearrangement of Italy are
different from those defined in the preliminaries at Villafranca,
so that room may be left for discussion, does great honour to
his high political capacity ; but his declaration does not in the
smallest degree further the possibility of this European Congress, particularly if it be borne in mind that those preliminaries are now being reduced at Zurich, to a definitive peace
upon still more onerous conditions, and with the intervention
of Sardinia.

The first part of the dilemma being disposed of, the second
remains. I fully agree that in fighting manfully the fall will
be glorious, but this glory will belong solely to the com-
batants, and will redound to the perpetual ignominy of Piedmont, which is condemned by some of its antecedents, and is
perhaps obliged by dire necessity to remain a quiet though
armed spectator of the struggle. The same Piedmont that has
nevertheless assumed the magnanimous task of the redemption
of Italy: that Piedmont which is the only State possessing the

backbone of national strength; that Piedmont which contains
in itself the fortunes of the Italy of the future, and to which we
must all at least give our moral support, so that it may not
utterly lose its reputation by too openly showing either its present impotence or the paltriness of its policy of partial aggrandizement—a policy which is, perhaps, a supreme necessity of
the novel *situation* wherein an imprudent peace has
placed it.

But let us see whether there is not a third hypothesis besides
these two, and perhaps something even more probable, because
I consider it certain that Central Italy cannot *all* be annexed to
Piedmont, and likewise certain that France will not consent to
the forcible restorations.

I maintain, in fact, that there will be no restorations at all,
and my opinion is not shaken either by Reiset's journey or by
the mission of Poniatowski, nor even by the reception of one of
the fugitive Princes at the Tuileries. I hold that the Emperor will permit the convocation of the Assembly devised by
you, exactly as he has allowed the gathering of the local Assem-
blies and the record of their votes in favour of Piedmont.

But will this fact create any necessity for a Congress?
Herein lies the essential part of it. You dare not make the
assertion, and I tell you most distinctly that the Congress will
never take place. But what will occur instead? Precisely
that which Napoleon is now preparing with so many twists and
turns—namely, the formation of a Central Italian State, of
which his cousin will be the monarch—a State that will be
located upon the two seas, and that will cut Italy in halves,
putting an end to all communication between the Sardo-Lom-
bardian States and that of the Two Sicilies, and excluding for
ever any hope of future aggrandizement.

The means for arriving at this end are simple. He will
praise the high-minded proposal, but will lament its imprac-
ticability. He will recall to mind the preliminaries of Villafranca, and the consent that was given for the restorations, and
he will make it appear that those conditions can be modified in

N2

the Zurich negotiations (which depend solely upon him for their continuance), but never in the sense of annexation to Piedmont. He will have it whispered in the ears of those in power that in order to elude the ravenous claws of eaglets they will have to confide themselves to the care of the Imperial Eagle   Montanelli and his set (who did not abstain from voting for Piedmont without a reason) will then come forward.

They will have a long train of people prepared for the purpose, and the Prince will be trumpeted forth from all corners. They will demand universal suffrage, and Napoleon, son of Jérome, will be hailed King of Etruria. . . . .

Now, what am I to do in such a deplorable state of affairs ? Exiles in general are not treated with much consideration, particularly when they want to give gratuitous advice. Everyone naturally says, here is a man who was not able to preserve his own country wanting, forsooth, to teach others how to save theirs ; and there are certain people going about those provinces (especially some of my compatriots with whom I should not like on any account to be confused.) Altogether (take note of this) I am suspicious of the very persons that I ought to see, and I cannot trust the sincerity of their assurances. Besides Farini, Minghetti, and Ricasoli (the three men upon whom things entirely depend) have been already advised from your place, and have received their instructions from Marliani and Lajatico.

My journey would create a heap of absurd rumours without resulting in any advantage, seeing that I shall certainly not succeed in persuading them, if they will not be persuaded, and if, after all, they are already convinced, the trouble would go for nothing.

But to what conclusion does all this lead us ?

In Italy itself you will never be able to combat Napoleon's policy as long as Italy remains in its present condition—that is to say, while he keeps Piedmont subject to continual pressure, occupies Lombardy with eighty thousand men, is the sole arbiter of affairs in Zurich, holds the Pope with vain hopes in a state of uncertainty, and caresses the Bourbons of Naples, lending them courage to resist the representations of England.

It was perhaps a great error to have invoked his aid at all, and I do not intend to disguise the fact; but the error of the Tory Cabinet in allowing him to come alone was certainly greater. It is not now a question of expelling him, because this could not be brought about without war, and everybody has either had enough or is averse to it.

It is merely a question of limiting his influence, in the same way that the war was localized. We must give him a fragment in order to save the remainder, strengthening this Subalpine Kingdom and perhaps the Southern Kingdom too, at the expense of the territory of the Pope, whose temporal dominion cannot last any longer. But this Southern Kingdom must cease to be the prey of a party that is so infamously reactionary, and the civil government must be restored upon the basis of true liberty. This particular change, which will infuse new spirit into the life of Italy, is not difficult of attainment *now* that the true Mayor of the Palace and virtual King is Filangieri, a man of large and tractable conscience, if those metallic wires which actuate it are properly manipulated.

But all this cannot be originated in Italy. In order to obtain such a result we must work elsewhere, and work with all our might.

A plan will be submitted to Lord John Russell by a person who is exceedingly well versed in Italian affairs, and whose political instincts are of the highest. This plan is admirable in its simplicity, and not difficult to carry out, if there be hearty goodwill towards the work, and it be taken in hand at once. . . . .

Yours most affectionately,

CARLO POERIO."

On the 22nd of May, 1859, Ferdinand II., King of the Two Sicilies, died. The news of his death was not received with that universal burst of lamentation which follows when the world at large has suffered an irreparable loss.   Indeed, it is painful to relate that throughout a considerable portion of the Christian and civilized world the sad tidings were even welcomed, and with an unseemly manifestation of rejoicing; not a few seeming even to be of opinion that a great obstacle of Christianity and civilization had at length been mercifully removed.

CHAPTER XXIII.

ITALIAN UNITY—VICTOR EMMANUEL II.—WAR OF 1859
—FARINI— CAVOUR — CORRESPONDENCE— POERIO
ON SOUTHERN ITALY—SIR JAMES LACAITA—VISIT
TO TURIN—THE BIOGRAPHER.

PERHAPS only when Italy shall have given indubitable proofs of her fitness to hold her own amongst the highest Powers of Europe will the remarkable chain of events which has led to the accomplishment of Italian Unity be fully appreciated. True that these events are of somewhat recent occurrence, and require the mellowness of time to impart to them their due historical importance. As time progresses, however, the story of United Italy will arrive at its proper significance, and there is reasonable hope that the new kingdom, hitherto not too harshly tried, will attain that healthy maturity of which its youth has given so fair a promise. To form the links which were to bind the mass of separate and discordant States into one, war and still war, external or internal, succeeded each other; but, whilst assigning all due weight to fortune from without, it would be to the last degree ungracious to stint of their just meed of praise the workers from within, whether we regard the mild wisdom of the school of patriots, whereof Poerio, Settembrini, and Panizzi were examples, or the reckless valour of more ardent revolutionists—

valour which, it must be granted, was not without its uses when occasion demanded, and which in its excess was skilfully controlled by one of whom it were but faint commendation to say that amongst all the records of eminent statesmen, his superior could not easily be found.

Our observations have shown that Panizzi did not confine his love of country to that part of Italy wherewith he himself was most intimately connected. Having achieved his mission in favour of liberty in the South, we now (1859) find him turning his attention to the North of the Peninsula. By way of introduction to our account of his proceedings in this quarter, it may be well to give a short epitome of the events of the year in question, when the first foundations of Italian unity may be said to have been laid.

Victor Emmanuel, on succeeding to the throne in consequence of his father's abdication, enjoyed the reputation of an experienced and intrepid soldier, yet was not in other respects a general favourite with his people. Nor was unpopularity at home the only difficulty in his way. When, after the fatal day of Novara, he received the crown from Charles Albert, who resigned it not until he had vainly sought honourable death in battle, he swore to avenge the wrongs of Italy, and to uphold the free institutions of his own realm. For this he had to reckon both with Austria and Naples, who, with unparalleled effrontery, called upon him to govern his kingdom in such a manner as should be in conformity with the mode of government in the other States of the Peninsula. To such a de-

mand the King did not deign to listen, and his opponents were forced to be content with denouncing
Sardinia as a hot-bed of sedition and revolutionary
agitation. In the beginning of 1859 Victor Emmanuel,
who, in his speech to Parliament, had remarked on the
threatening appearance of the political horizon, commenced preparations for war against Austria. The
circumstances which precipitated the war are too fresh
in the recollection of our readers to be dwelt on here
to any length. Cavour, on the part of Sardinia, was
under promise to England to make no hostile demon-
stration against Austria. France had declared that
she would aid Sardinia only in the case of the latter
being attacked. The preliminaries to an European
Congress were actually under discussion, when the
Emperor of Austria suddenly broke off all negotiations,
and demanded of Sardinia an immediate disarmament,
a summons which was treated by Cavour with contempt. At this juncture, Austria, with that peculiar
aptitude for blundering which has so characterised her
action, sent, in the night of April 28-29, 1859, her
armies across the Ticino, thus affording an occasion of
action whereof the two allies were not slow to avail
themselves. The French troops hastened to cross the
Alps. Battle followed battle with uniform success to the
allied arms, when, like a thunderbolt, news of the Peace
of Villafranca fell on Europe. Unexplained at the time,
the reasons for it soon came within the range of tolerably
accurate conjecture. In the first place the eagerness
with which people of the other States in Italy prepared to unite themselves with Sardinia (which Cavour
had foreseen, but which had failed to strike Louis

Napoleon,) was hardly to the taste of the French Emperor. Whatever were his objects in the war, the unity of Italy was certainly not one of them. He had employed his army, and thereby diverted his people ; he had gained a satisfactory amount of glory, though perhaps not so much as his ambition led him to hope for. In his victories, (though it were hard to apply to them the epithet *Pyrrhic*,) he had undoubtedly sustained greater loss than his adversary ; and he possibly thought it as well to refrain from following the Austrians to the strong position to which they had retired, and from whence not all the armies of Italy, Sardinia, and France united could in all probability have succeeded in dislodging them. His fortitude and forbearance were, however, as all know, not without their substantial reward.

It is ours, not to write history, but simply to supply aid to its study ; and these may, we hope, be afforded to the reader by the somewhat varied correspondence of which this chapter will mainly consist. The several writers quoted are at any rate worth listening to, and not least among them Luigi Carlo Farini, the Dictator, well-known as the friend of Mr. Gladstone, a letter from whom (dated March 18th, 1859) comes first in order on our list :—

"   .   .   . Times are so serious that my mind is filled with anxious thoughts. Yesterday the Austrians blew up the bridge at Buffalora. It is all very well for our friend Hudson to say they will not attack us, but surely they strike us in our honour by violating our property with their treaties.

" I should like to see what John Bull would do if
they attempted to mine his house. Even yesterday
they expelled from Milan one of our most esteemed
staff-officers, Cav. Incisa. Such acts are committed
daily, but we must console ourselves by seeing how
the whole of Italy is giving a new and great example
of unity and strength. Ten thousand volunteers are
coming from all parts of Italy; it is a crusade; *your*
Modena has sent more than all the other States, considering its extent (a thing which cannot be seen
without emotion). The stupefied Governments have
lost strength. National rights reign supreme in
public opinion. My dear friend, awful events are at
hand. We count much upon your advocating our
cause in England."

" The noble Neapolitan exiles, for whom the English
people so justly feel, may prove the means of advancing the common cause. Let them only say that Neapolitan tyranny is not of native, but of foreign growth,
and in order to chastise Bomba, it will be necessary to
chastise Vienna. Let us hope they may say so, for it
is the unvarnished truth."

That Panizzi rated the strength of Austria and the
Quadrilateral at its proper value, and considered that
the Italians were about this time *in trepidis rebus*, is
plain from the following letter to Mr. Haywood. It
bears no date, but evidently must have been written
(from the British Museum) just before the conclusion
of the war :—

" These Italian affairs have, as you may suppose,
made me feverish. First of all, I think the Austrians
are not quite done for yet, although I think they will

be. Even in these times of wonder I don't believe
they can have lost Vicenza and Mantua, and if the
whole country is not really up, the King of Piedmont
will find these two very hard bits. That they are yet
in the Austrians' hands I argue from the fact of
Radetzky's troops retiring in two columns towards
them—what is more, taking with him political prisoners, which shows he is not quite defeated. Even
when Mantua and Piacenza are taken, there is the
pass of Caldiero, fortified in an awful manner, as I
have seen myself, and such fortresses as Legnano,
Peschiera, and Verona, in which fifty thousand men
can defy three times the number."

"If the Tyrolese are up to the whole of the Vene-
tian territory, the Austrians may find it awkward, as
they are out of favour here, and they may not have
either time or the means of victualling their forces.
But between us I do not very much like the peasants
to take up arms in earnest, even if they join in a
popular movement at first. They must enrol themselves, and that I do not think they will do. I foresee, therefore, great difficulties, and at all events great
fighting. Yes, and depend upon it the French, if
they last as a republic, or even have a Bonaparte, will
interfere. As to myself, what can I do? I am more
than fifty, and not a soldier, and what they want now
are young men ready to shoulder a musket or to
command."

"In the second place, I am almost certain that the
Italians will differ among themselves (not as to the
Austrians, or us to being dismayed, but as to the form
of Government.) The King of Sardinia had no chance

to keep his crown but by acting as he has done, as they would have proclaimed a republic in Lombardy with the help of the Swiss, and he would have had a revolution in the same sense at home. But the spirit of the 'Giovine Italia' is at work there, and I think there will be yet a great deal of trouble before the form of government is settled. My views you know, and I fear I should have no one listening to me, and the utmost I could expect would be to be looked upon as a crazy Angloman. In the third place, I have hardly any friend alive who would care for me, or on whom I could have influence. I am a greater stranger in Italy than here."

Towards the middle of the year, Panizzi himself visited the scene of action, whence he wrote a graphic account of affairs in the North of Italy to Mr. Gladstone, in a far more cheerful tone than that of the last letter quoted :—

"San Maurizio, near Reggio,
September 4th, 1859.

"My dear Sir,—

. . . . I went to Bologna to see the opening of the Assembly last Thursday, and I hope to give them some good advice as to the wording of the resolutions which are to be proposed to-morrow, proclaiming the independence of Romagna. On Thursday I shall go to Parma again to assist at the opening of their Assembly. I am now staying with some distant cousins at a villa which Ariosto, who lived here, had celebrated.

I cannot tell you how gratified I am at what I have seen ever since I came to this part of Italy, on Monday last. The order and quiet which prevail everywhere are only equalled by the unanimity with which every man, woman, and child is determined not to submit again to the fallen Government. I

am happy to see that the determination is supported by large
numbers of volunteers who flock to enlist: they come not only
from the towns but from the country; and at night, since I
have been here, I have heard a variety of songs in dialect in
praise of Garibaldi and his soldiers, ridiculing the Austrians
and the late Duke of Modena, in very expressive although in
not very polite terms.   I have seen persons who are well
affected to the Duke—the cousins at whose house I am staying,
and to whose family the Archbishop of Modena belongs,
amongst them—and one and all say that a restoration of the
fallen dynasty would be a great calamity.   Here, in fact—at
Parma as well as Bologna—the universal wish is to be united
to Piedmont.   The organization of the recruits proceeds with
the greatest rapidity, and the instructors (old soldiers) are
struck by the military qualities displayed by the population.
The Republican and Mazzinian agents are secreted everywhere;
still I think that the only danger to be feared is that if things
were to continue long in this state of suspense, with hardly any
Government in fact, anarchists might cause mischief, although
not triumph ultimately.

Yours, &c., &c.,

A. PANIZZI."

" I have just heard that
the Austrians, most of them
dressed in the uniform of
the Duke of Modena, are
gathering their forces to
cross the Po, and come to
the right of it."

Amongst the nume-
rous letters in our pos-
session, written by Count
Cavour to Panizzi, the
most important and in-
teresting, and at the

same time the most truly characteristic, both in form and substance, of the great Statesman, is one dated the 24th of October, 1859. It was written from Leri, Cavour's country seat. Thither he had, immediately after the war, retired for a time from public life, and with a heavy heart; for the obscurity in terms and apparent treachery of the Peace of Villafranca, had affected him with a torturing suspicion that he had been betrayed. It is something of a tribute to Cavour's greatness that Rattazzi, who succeeded him, was fain, in his embarrassment in carrying on the Government, to seek the counsel of his predecessor, the flame of whose patriotism (however deeply wounded his own feelings may have been) burnt as brightly in his retirement as in office, as it needs but the following letter to show :—

"Leri, October 24th, 1859.

"My dear Panizzi,

Your letter of the 17th inst. was only delivered to me yesterday, too late for me to answer it then. I hasten to do so this morning, though I fear that my reply can hardly reach London before the question of the Congress shall have been decided.

In the present state of affairs, considering the engagements entered into at Villafranca and to a certain extent confirmed at Zurich by the Emperor, it appears evident to me that an European Congress is indispensable. Were there to be no Congress, and were France to prevent the egress of Central Italy from the provisional condition by opposing the stipulated fusions, those countries would be exposed to serious dangers. The eminent men in the Romagna—and there are many such there—might incite Garibaldi to attempt an enterprise in the

Marches and perhaps even in the Abruzzi; at Modena the occupation of the trans-Padan Mantuan territory by Austria— an inevitable consequence of the treaty—might give rise to lamentable collisions ; Tuscany perhaps might be more patient of an uncertain condition, but even there the intrigues of the reactionaries supported by the priests would probably be the cause of serious perturbations. Hence the interests of Italy absolutely require a Congress, and, if this is plain, England should participate therein both for her own honour and for our benefit. Austria will not oppose her intervention, but will accept her reservations when it is stipulated that nothing is to be said about the provinces retained under Austrian dominion. It is hard for us to renounce a plea in favour of unhappy Venice ; still we must repress our deep sympathies for fear of sacrificing the possible for the desirable.

Austria, relieved of apprehension respecting Venice, ought to concur in the English maxim that the wishes of the Italians should be respected. To put this in more diplomatic form it would be sufficient to say that the Powers undertake not to impose by force of arms any form of Government on the people of Central Italy. This is the principle of non-intervention already proclaimed by the Emperor in his writings and in his speeches. Supported by France and by England, and perhaps by Russia too, it will soon be admitted by Austria and accepted by Prussia.

Passing on to the constitution of the Congress, I do not hesitate to declare for the exclusion of the minor Powers. If only the Duchies and Tuscany were concerned their intervention would be advantageous ; but as the most difficult—I will say too the most important question—is that of the Romagna provinces, I fear the Pope would find vehement defenders in Spain and in Portugal.

The Congress once assembled, there can be no doubt as to the course of England. She would first of all propose that the wish of the people legally expressed should receive the sanction of Europe. Supposing this proposition to be rejected, the next would be that the people be consulted by means of universal suffrage, to be verified by the members of the Congress. This proposal would find support in France, and would probably be accepted. If it were not, England would have to enter into a negative phase, and to withstand the proposals of Austria and that of France too. The Duke of Modena being abandoned by every one, even his own relations, there will be nothing to oppose but the restoration of the House of Lorraine in Tuscany, the installation of the Duchess of Parma at Modena, and the re-establishment of the Papal dominion in the Romagna provinces.

Such resolutions as these may be resisted, not only on the ground of the popular rights, but also, and still more efficaciously, in the interest of the monarchical principle, and with reference to ideas of order and stability. Unless we wish to see the now stifled revolution revive, menacing and powerful, it must not be confronted by feeble Governments without root in the soil, destitute of both physical and moral force. If we wish to see thrones respected, we ought not to fill them with despised and despicable princes, whose very names are in irritating antagonism to the sentiment—the national sentiment—now dominating in Italy. If the Grand Duke or his son return to Florence, then, in less than a month, Tuscany will be the head quarters of Mazzini and of the belligerent revolution. Perhaps it will be said that the Duchess or Parma is a strong-minded woman, and is not unappreciated. However this may be, the so hateful remembrances of the father could not be effaced, nor could confidence be inspired in the son. Besides, the system of compensations which some would wish to apply in favour of this branch of the Bourbon family is in direct collision with the sentiments and the ideas which now prevail in Europe. The Modenese would be smitten in their dignity if they found themselves allotted by way of jointure to the widow of that rascal, the petty Duke of Parma. Better for them the restoration of their former Sovereign. In that case they would be victims of a false principle; but they would

O

not be treated as a flock of sheep, disposed of as a counter-
balance for conditions deemed onerous by one of the contract-
ing parties.

The Treaty of Vienna is odious enough in many parts; but
it is not so odious as that of Campoformio.

With regard to the Romagna provinces, it will be easy for
England to get the idea of papal reforms scouted. To entertain such an idea is worse than hateful—it is ridiculous. There
is no need to be either a great statesman or a great theologian
to feel convinced that the Pope not only does not wish but
really cannot consent to serious reforms. So long as he is
Pope and King he must in conscience employ the powers of
the King to enforce the decrees of the Pontiff. The separation of the two authorities is impossible. The Pope cannot
consent to the freedom of instruction, nor to the freedom of
public worship, nor to the freedom of the press. He cannot
tolerate municipal freedom unless this be understood as an
authority of the Town Councils to regulate at will the public
roads and the manner of paving them. The Pope as Pope will
more easily submit to the loss of a province than to the pro-
mulgation of the Napoleonic Civil Code in his States. The
Papal restoration ought to be prevented at every cost : it is
not only an Italian question, but one of European interest.
It concerns us, but it also concerns England, Prussia, even
Russia, and all countries where the development of civilization
is an object, for this requires as an essential condition the absolute separation of the two Powers. If the Pope should obtain
a victory in Italy, the presumption and the pride of the Cullens
and the McHales would swell beyond bounds, and Europe
would be menaced before very long with the danger of religious struggles similar to those of past ages. Let everything
be given up rather than sacrifice the Romagna provinces.
Their cause is, I say again, the cause of civilization.

If England should succeed in warding off the Austro-French
proposals, let her reproduce those which she originally brought
forward : and if these do not prevail, let her propose the im-

mediate union of Parma and Carrara with Piedmont, and the establishment of a Government, provisional but strongly constituted, to rule over Florence, Modena, and Bologna.

These are my views: take them for what they are worth. Far away from the turmoil of affairs, and having but slight relations with the Ministers, I am probably unaware of many things which might modify my opinion. Still, judging the question of Central Italy from the data which history in some way impresses upon our minds, I am strongly of opinion that if England were to follow the part which I have traced, she would succeed in the object of assuring the destinies of Central Italy to our advantage and her own glory. Farewell, my dear friend. Continue the advocacy of our cause before the noble English nation, and your efforts will not be fruitless. I say again now what I said to the Chamber and to Italy in February—the statesmen who have ennobled their career by accomplishing the emancipation of the negroes will not bear the condemnation of Italy to eternal slavery.*

Most truly yours,

C. CAVOUR."

The next letter to Mr. Ellice (to whom, as there was no one whom Panizzi so much loved and respected, he never lost an opportunity of communicating both the intelligence he received and his own comments and opinions thereon) is lively and amusing, and contains much matter within a small compass. The observations on the Rattazzi Government probably in no wise exaggerate its defects :—

"B. M., October 29th, 1859.

". . . I can tell you for certain there will be a Congress about Italy in which England will take

---

* These memorable words were uttered in the sitting of the 9th of February, 1859, during the discussion on the loan contracted to prepare for war against Austria.

o2

part. The Emperor of the French feels he is in a
scrape, and urges England to help him out of it, and
our Government are inclined to help him under
certain conditions, England wanting him in return on
some other account. He has accepted as explicitly
as possible England's terms, and hitherto he has kept
his word to her; if he does not break it, the Government are quite satisfied that all will go well for Italy.
Indeed, if England and France act together, there is
no doubt their policy must prevail."

"As to the Italians themselves, there is too much
softness in Piedmont on the part of the Government;
the King is the only man who dares; his Ministers
are miserable little bureaucrats. We must have a
change there, and Cavour must come back; and this
is what our Ministers wish. The people of central
Italy, who have given themselves up so heartily to
Piedmont, are tired of the prudence of the King's
Government, which does nothing for them, and there
is great fear that they may break loose, and, taking
the matter in their hands, rush on the Pope's soldiers
or the Rubicon, whom they will rout to a certainty.
The whole of the Umbria and the Marches will rise
at once; they have been quite ready to do so for two
months past, and it is with difficulty they are kept
quiet. If they rise, and the soldiers of central Italy
(Garibaldi is to lead them) rush in, you may be
certain that the kingdom of Naples will be in a
flame. Garibaldi with ten thousand men, Roma-
gnuoli, will conquer the whole kingdom down to Reggio.
The proclamations of Garibaldi, which you will have
seen two days ago in the papers, are ominous. In

Italy I did my best to keep him quiet, and so did other friends; but I now see he is taking the *mord aux dents*, and no wonder. The King of Sardinia has sent for him, but as he is no longer in his service it is thought he may, under some pretext or other, respectfully decline the summons. A revolution at Naples, or its invasion by Garibaldi, would just now be very disagreeable to the English Government, as the question of change of government, both in the kingdom of Naples proper and in Sicily, might be brought on the tapis, and then you easily foresee a great imbroglio—greater than any that has hitherto taken place, as far as English interests are concerned."

"I understand the ministers are quite united with each other, and all pleased with Lord Palmerston, of whom Mr. Gibson has spoken to a friend of mine not long ago. Lord Palmerston and Lord John are particularly united together; this I know from the latter. Gladstone, I am also told, runs quite straight. The Court is quite Austrian, and, were it not for fear of this trio, would probably try the Tories again. There is a conspiracy of crinolines in favour of the Duchess of Parma, the Empress of the French, and the Queen of Spain. The latter wanted to send ten thousand men to assist the Pope, but France and England have put a veto on that."

This may be fitly succeeded by two more letters from Panizzi to Mr. Ellice. To each reader's judgment and discretion may fairly be left the decision whether the historical parallel in the second of these is thoroughly correct, and whether either Elizabeth or Cromwell had much notion of religious liberalism, or defended Protestantism on the ground of its being the liberal religion.

"B. M., January 4th, 1860.

". . . All the diplomacy in the world will not bring back either those d—d Dukes or the Pope, and the provinces whence they have been expelled. If Napoleon sticks to the point of not allowing any *armed* intervention in their favour, the legitimate Sovereigns are dished. But, it is said, he has some interested motive if he act so. I suppose he has; so much the better if his interests coincide with the interests and wishes of Italy. It is a pity no one else has the same interest; but, if no one will do the trick, even he is welcome. I see that after all he is the only one who does something for that country. If the Pope and Austrian influence are done for, what is to come after it is of less importance. If the European powers will aid and abet Austria in keeping Venice, and in preventing a united kingdom of North Italy being formed under Victor Emmanuel, I am sorry for it, but they cannot complain if Plonplon is preferred by the Italians to the Austrian and priestly tyranny. Better Austria than the Pope, but better Plonplon than either. That is the scale."

"B. M., April 21st, 1860.

" . . . How could you suppose that I ever could have said that Elizabeth and Cromwell interfered to support *Catholicism?* My answer was, and is, this:

"Europe is now in about the same state with respect to politics as it was in Elizabeth's and Cromwell's times as to religion. These two personages did not follow the policy which is now so much praised of taking no side with either party, but showing the greatest indifference to right or wrong. England, I think, has not reached the lofty station it now occupies, by adopting this policy; nor will she keep that position by such means.

" In the same manner that Elizabeth and Cromwell took the side of liberalism in religion (Protestantism) England ought now to take the side of liberty in politics, and she would thus rise still higher.

" In 1848 England allowed liberty to be crushed everywhere; she even allowed Russia to lend an army to Austria to crush an old and constitutional kingdom. See how the Protestants are now treated all over the Austrian Empire; how the Jesuitical party is rampant in Germany and in Ireland; how Europe is crouching to Napoleon. Is this to the advantage of free Protestant England?

" Now, suppose, instead of proclaiming her determination to keep aloof (which neither Elizabeth nor Cromwell would have approved) the Government of Queen Victoria has told Russia and Austria that if Despots were to join to crush liberty, free governments would support those who tried to recover their freedom, do you think England would now be worse off?

" If, instead of cheering Austria on to crush little Piedmont, whose great crime was to support the principles of civil and religious liberty, England had stood by those principles as she ought, do you think Napoleon would now stand as high as he does?

" Austria would never have dared to act as she did, had she not been encouraged by the then English Government; and the war which has given Savoy and Nice to France would never have taken place if England had done something for the cause of freedom. That position which now Napoleon occupies would have been occupied by England to her manifest advantage, and to that of mankind.

" When the Protestants were hard pushed at La Rochelle, Elizabeth did not stand by looking on, nor did her Parliament talk so much as ours does.   When the poor Vaudois were persecuted by the Duke of Savoy, Cromwell was not so, squeamish about non-intervention, but sent word to Mazarin to make the Duke understand that the persecution *must* cease— and it did cease.

" Compare those times with ours, and then laugh, if you can, at my political notions. When do you return ?"

Two months after the date of the last-quoted letter, Panizzi received an interesting account of Southern Italy from Poerio, which is subjoined :—

" Turin, June 1st, 1860.

" My dearest Friend,

While I have been waiting for an answer to the letter which I wrote to you from Florence, new and unexpected events and new complications have arisen, demanding the prompt and energetic co-operation of everybody who is devoted to our cause.

Therefore I am forced to have recourse to you as one of those few who, to a fixed determination of aiding their country, add by their own personal importance the capacity of doing good upon an extensive scale.

Palermo has fallen, and the National idea is triumphant throughout the island.

Of course there are many obstacles to be overcome. Nevertheless before long that noble region will be irrevocably lost to the Bourbons, and regained for Italy. But what will become of the seven millions of Italians who still groan beneath the detestable tyranny of the Bourbons? It is now said that the Government, in order to gain time (as it did in 1848) intends putting on the mask of liberalism, and retains the Count of Syracuse as the principal actor in this impudent farce. He has a few adherents, and is not wanting in desire to represent a Louis-Philippe in miniature.

In the meantime the Mazzini set are agitating because they know that of the whole Italian territory the Southern Provinces of the peninsula are best adapted to their designs.

Neither are the partisans of Murat standing idle, but are working effectually in the army with the most seductive promises.

Finally, there is the Subversive (Sanfedista) Party, of the purest race, who would like to reserve for Naples the fate of Palermo, and who have decided to put the whole country to fire and pillage You see, therefore, that there are four parties, all fairly strong, and all hostile to the true National Party, which solely desires the unity of Italy under the constitutional sceptre of King Victor Emmanuel. Any one who has any experience in political matters will easily understand that for this National Party to engage in the struggle with any hope of success it must be provided with ready means, otherwise the remaining divisions will pre-occupy the field, and the country, after going through twelve years of the most cruel despotism, will fall into civil war, and thence into the most frightful state of anarchy. The danger is imminent, and the remedy must be prompt. The numbers who have decided to undertake the enterprise amount to several thousands; but the pecuniary resources are most limited. Besides, it must be borne in mind that if delay is disastrous, to enter upon the task with insufficient means would be still more so, since a failure would lend strength to a detested Government, which is now tottering under the weight of its crimes, and which could never stand against a well-supported effort. In this state of affairs your political friends, of whom you have so many in that noble country, ought not to let slip this favourable occasion for assisting us—an opportunity which cannot again present itself, and of which others will avail themselves, to the eternal prejudice of Italy, unless steps be taken in time to prevent it. Nor do I think that they ought to be influenced by certain restricted views which several of them wish to put forward.

The only solution of the question is really the *Italy of the Italians*, which, far from compromising the peace of Europe, would serve to consolidate it by removing a continued incentive to foreign ambition. Once decide upon a policy of non-intervention, and the struggle between the two principles in Italy can neither be long nor sanguinary.

The liberal party in Europe will then count one more truly independent state, which will make its principles respected, and will certainly contribute both to their triumph and to the general development of civilization.

The Bourbons will be crushed, and to the great benefit of every one, since their detestable Government is incompatible with Italian independence. The most disastrous error of the times would be that of wishing to maintain them on the throne at any cost, because it would outrage the moral sense of the whole of Italy. Neither do I see the necessity of supporting and bolstering up a race which is the very incarnation of perjury. If the Bourbons were to remain in Naples, even with a fictitious constitution, they would sooner or later be supplanted by a Napoleonic régime.

Enthusiasm evaporates in time; but if we now follow up this terrible current which urges the main stream, Italy can be rendered free and united. If, however, the opportunity is allowed to pass, dualism, with all its terrible consequences, will be the result.

A thousand greetings to our friends! I embrace you heartily, and am ever

Your most affectionate friend,

CARLO POERIO."

While on the subject of Southern Italy we may remind our readers that there has been frequent mention made above of a gentleman, who, as a constant friend and correspondent of Panizzi, and as a prominent personage in Neapolitan matters, demands some further notice. Mr., afterwards Sir James Lacaita, was, previously to the year 1850, legal adviser to the British Legation at Naples. In this position, by his great official capacity, and by his well-proved exemplary character, he succeeded in gaining the friendship of Sir William Temple. He had the further good fortune to make the acquaintance of Mr. Gladstone, at the house of Lord Leven, who was spending a winter at Naples. This acquaintance soon ripened into intimacy, a consequence which was almost a matter of course, for Lacaita was well fitted to win the confidence and attract the liking of those who, themselves possessed of merit, could discover and value merit in others. Endowed with distinguished abilities, and a master of the English language; in political matters of sound and matured judgment, and (as will hereafter be seen) of unassailable honour and integrity; such very exceptional characteristics soon marked him out for invidious distinction by the partisans of King Bomba. On the 26th of December, 1850, he was arrested in the street as a dangerous person and thrown into prison. All his papers were ordered to be examined in his presence;

but, Sir William Temple having requested the
"Attaché " of the Legation, Mr. Fagan, to claim as
many of these as possible in the name of Her Bri-
tannic Majesty's Government, a large proportion was
thereby saved.

A certain note, however, which originated in a
mere joke, was detained, and turned out to be the
innocent cause of serious trouble. Previously to his
arrest, Lacaita, in conjunction with Lord and Lady
Leven and their three daughters, had planned a tour
for eight days to La Cava, Salerno and Amalfi. In
sportive mood it was laid down by the " tourists " that
no authority of one over the other was to be recognised
amongst the members of this party, and to distinguish
nominally the perfect freedom and equality of the
society, they dubbed themselves the " Republic." It
must have been with mingled feelings of indignation
and gratification that the police discovered amongst
the confiscated papers a note written by Lady Anne
Melville, after the return from the tour, containing
the words, *Will you come to tea, and talk over the
grand Republican days?* In vain was it explained to
the authorities that the note had no political significance, but the suspicious adjective was merely playful
reference to the little temporary republic of " tourists,"
and to no dangerous revolutionary organisation.

Either lacking a natural sense of humour, or holding jocosity to be impossible in so grave a matter as
anything *Republican* in the then state of Italian
politics, they altogether rejected this, to them, fanciful
interpretation. The letter was registered (it is still in
the archives of the Criminal Court of Naples), and

formed one of the chief grounds for the charge of sedition and conspiracy brought against Lacaita.

In the summer of 1860, Cavour, well aware of the negotiations that were being carried on between England, France and Naples, and desirous of obtaining some trustworthy person to watch his interests, and supply him with information—and being, moreover, unable, for reasons which may be easily understood, to charge his own Minister, the Marquis d'Azeglio, with the mission—applied to Lacaita, who, on receiving the message, although laid up with severe illness, immediately rose from his bed and went straight to Lord Russell's house. His Lordship, having an engagement with the Neapolitan Minister, had given direction that no person whatever should be admitted. Sir James, however, being intimate with the family, managed to see his Lordship, and was able there and then to turn the current of affairs in a totally different direction, and to prevent the French Ambassador Count Persigny, and his Neapolitan colleague the Marquis La Greca, from carrying out their plans. Had it not been for Sir James Lacaita's prompt and skilful intervention, England would doubtless have been remitted to the position she had held in 1848.

Nothing now remained to those whom Lacaita had thus thwarted but to win him over to the side of Francis II., and this it was thought might be effected by offering him the post of Minister at the Court of St. James's, in the room of Count Ludolf. The chief instrument employed for the conversion of this dangerous opponent was Signor Giovanni Manna, the Neapolitan Minister of Finance, who was now at Paris,

whither he had been sent to negotiate a loan.   Manna,
who was a personal friend of Lacaita's, started from
Paris in August with the sole object of persuading
him to accept the offer; holding out as a further inducement to a change of opinion a considerable bonus,
besides a not insignificant salary and the title of
Marquis, which might well be regarded as superseding
the inferior rank of knighthood which had already
been conferred upon him.

The unification of Italy was regarded by most politicians of the time, Lacaita included, as, to say the least
of it, a remote possibility.   To the King's offer, and the
numerous advantages accompanying it, Lacaita simply
replied, *This is bribery.*   In this conclusion he was supported by the advice of two distinguished statesmen,
Lord Lansdowne and Mr. Gladstone, and by a letter
from Panizzi (dated Homburg, 23rd of August, 1860),
which did not reach him until a few days after his
refusal of the post :—

" . . . . I willingly comply with your request, and
frankly give you the advice which you ask on the point
which you truly describe as delicate and knotty—that
is, whether you ought to accept the appointment as
Minister of His Sicilian Majesty at the Court of St.
James's.

" As Minister of that King you must first of all
oppose the enterprise of Garibaldi, who wishes to
unite the whole of Italy under one sole head, and if
that head should be Victor Emmanuel, you, Sir James
Lacaita, would have to support an abominable and
cruel scion of an execrated race against the only
Sovereign who has shown that he is an Italian ; in

fact, you would have to help in cutting up Italy. I do not presume to judge those gentlemen who have undertaken to serve his said Neapolitan Majesty; but they were on the spot, had served—at least some of them—the dynasty, and perhaps had not duly considered before they accepted their posts. But are you, who are free, and in your sober senses, to serve a Bourbon like him of Naples? Are you to stand by the side of those who proclaimed martial law?—you to join a Government which now shoots down the noblest Italians who have liberated Sicily from a detested yoke? No one *cui sanum sinciput* can believe that the King of Naples is to be trusted, when he gives utterance to the sentiments which he now pretends to profess, and every one who is not bereft of sense knows and feels that the man is still the faithful and true ally of Austria, the tool of the harsh stepmother, the blind and abject slave of the priesthood which has made Rome a sewer. And would you give your honoured name, your influence, your talents to a man without affection and without faith like that King? My dear Lacaita, that name, that influence, those talents belong to Italy and to an honourable King, not to a schismatic party—not to a perfidious and treacherous perjurer.

"I use strong expressions: the case justifies them. You may show this letter of mine to any one you please, and tell what I think without any reserve whatever! . . . ."

In September, 1860, Panizzi paid another visit to Italy, of which, and of the condition of affairs in that country, he gave an account in the two following extracts from letters to Mr. Ellice, written after his return.

Some remarks on the evil which Garibaldi's mistaken zeal was likely to produce on the state of Rome and on the French Emperor are well worth reading. The " confabulation " with the King at Turin, mentioned in the first letter, at which Cavour was present, was held in a stable with great secrecy. Only such passages are given as bear most directly on the history of the time :—

" B. M., Oct. 5, 1860.

" . . . I have seen and had long confabulations with the King at Turin, and with the Emperor at Paris. I can tell you that Garibaldi, who seemed to have lost his senses, and who was surrounded by a set of scamps who made a fool and tool of him, honest fellow! will by this time have made an *amende honorable*, and submitted to the King, or be put down.

" Be assured that Cavour and the rational party in Italy (that is ninety-nine per cent. of the population) are not such fools as to attack Austria. It is owing to the threats of Garibaldi, the French Emperor having undertaken to preserve from injury or insult the person of the Pope, that the French garrison at Rome has been increased. But that garrison will not defend any part of the Papal territory except what it actually occupies ; and should the Pope leave Rome, as he was on the point of doing ten days ago, the French will withdraw, and the Sardinian army occupy Rome.

" The note or letter of Lord John to Cavour has *disgusted* many and surprised all. I think it was written of his own accord, and perhaps without the knowledge of his colleagues. He who has been so long a consistent friend of Italy write such a letter, when the Government of the King of Sardinia was supposed to be in difficulties, and was in fact so! Those are the acts which make even the French Emperor popular, and which, by encouraging the despotic party in Germany, may kindle a war. . . . There will be no anarchy in Italy, and the Emperor Napoleon *may be relied on*.

"Nothing serves more in France than English abuse. Of this I am certain, and I have most curious proofs. I am also positive that he is personally a firm friend of England, and that he has more to do than people suppose to quiet the *Anglophobia* of the French. . . . I had the pleasure of seeing prisoner of war at Turin, that worthy companion in arms of Monsignor Lamoricière, Monsignor Schmidt, he who butchered people at Perugia where he was obliged to surrender at last. It was delightful to see the provoking indifference with which the Piedmontese looked at him. . . . . Cavour wanted to make a present of several hundred Irishmen taken prisoners to the English Government, but the present was respectfully declined. . . . ."

"B. M., Oct. 11th, 1860.

" . . . . I am astonished to see the Paris correspondent of *The Times* allowed to write as he does about the King of Sardinia and his Minister. His misrepresentations are all directed to disparage them all and so far favourable to Austria. In to-day's number that correspondent, in order to throw discredit on Cavour's statement, said that he was not

P

to be believed, as he had asked *Savoy* although he had promised not to give up any part of the Piedmontese territory. The King is represented as *swearing* and *mad* with rage whenever the cession of Savoy is mentioned. Now I have spoken to the King about this transaction, and have most respectfully said things which were, from their nature, calculated to irritate. The King was not irritated, he was not in a rage, and did not swear; he spoke with great moderation, and with great feeling. I was struck with it . . . . . ."

Our budget of correspondence, which has been resorted to more copiously than was at first intended, may be closed, so far as this chapter is concerned, by a letter from Panizzi to Mr. Gladstone, which is given in its integrity :—

"British Museum,
November 27th, 1860.

"My dear Sir,
Your letter has filled me with apprehension for poor Italy, and with gratitude for your warm interest in her cause. I felt reason daily to mistrust the conduct of my Paris interlocutor, and I am the more afraid, seeing that you, too, feel there is reason for mistrust. When the conduct of the fleet at Gaeta was first known, I wrote to say that it was suspicious, and at variance with recent professions. My letter went through the Minister to St. Cloud, and I received from my friend with whom the correspondence was carried on the enclosed answer, which please return. Lord P. has seen it, but no one else. I was not satisfied, and I wrote again to my friend to say so, but he is not in Paris, and he had to send my last letter from the country to Paris. He has since written that the Minister would be glad to correspond chiefly with me; but now he is out, and my communications are stopped.

Nor do I know how I could reach St. Cloud without it being known to many who ought not to know it. The appointment of Walewski and that of Flahaut portend no good to Italy and to the English alliance. If this interference by sea and by land continue, it is evident that it is intended to allow a civil war to kindle in Italy, to have a pretext for interfering, not certainly for the good of the country. Is it possible that the three Emperors and the supporters of the Pope and of despotism in Germany have agreed to settle matters to their own advantage, leaving Prussia, England, and Italy out? Allowing Russia to act as she thinks best in the East, France on the Rhine and in Italy, and Austria in the outer provinces of the Turkish Empire, close to Hungary! It is an extravagant supposition, but the conduct of France is still more so.

Believe me always,

Yours most sincerely obliged,

A. PANIZZI."

The author is well aware that nothing short of his long-standing intimacy with the subject of this "Memoir" could justify the introduction into the work of anything approaching egotism, unless it were to illustrate an essential point in the character of which he is treating; but in writing of the year 1860, recollections crowd upon the memory which he trusts his readers will excuse him for committing to paper. In that same year he (then a boy of thirteen) was sent, under the charge of a Queen's Messenger, from Naples to a school in England. Arriving in London, he was most kindly received by Panizzi, and well remembers his first interview with one who was thenceforth to be his staunchest friend. Not that this was the first time that the latter had bestowed his good offices upon the

P2

family of the writer, whose eldest brother, now Major Fagan, owes and acknowledges a debt of gratitude for the kindness received at his hands in youthful days, and up to the time of receiving his Commission and starting for India in 1859.

But pleasant and important as it would be, for some reasons, to dwell upon many happy reminiscences of uninterrupted intercourse with a pre-eminent man, the task which is here undertaken leads us to more serious matters relating to that period, and that yet remain to occupy the space which should be devoted rather to the information of our readers than to a recital of personal recollections.

CHAPTER XXIV.

ENGLAND IN 1859 — RELATIONS WITH FRANCE—FIRST
VISIT TO BIARRITZ — NAPOLEON III.—LETTERS
FROM MR. GLADSTONE, M. MERIMEE, M. FOULD,
AND MR. E. ELLICE.

As might have been expected, the formation of a
new and extensive kingdom was a question of too
deep moment not to exercise an important, though
possibly an indirect, influence on England's relations
with States at once more powerful and nearer to her
own shores than Italy.

It is purposed in the present chapter to deal with
events more immediately affecting this country than
Italian politics. In and previously to the year 1859,
England, it must be confessed, did not occupy her
former stable and exalted position amongst the
nations of Europe. Her late struggle with Russia—
a struggle from which though she had arisen Phœnix-
like—had taught her a lesson which had not been
neglected; she had gained strength it is true, but not in
such a degree as to render altogether unwarrantable
the disparaging taunts in which certain foreign Statesmen indulged at her expense. "Of a truth," says
the prince of comic writers (may the quotation be
pardoned?), "wise folk learn a good many things from
their enemies" (Aristophanes, The Birds 1, 387), and
well do the words apply to England, who then learnt

wisdom from her foes. Bitter experiences in the
Crimea taught us the miserable insufficiency of our
military system, and already action had commenced
for future improvement. Regarding, not unreasonably, with some feeling of alarm the threatening
aspect of Continental affairs, we had at last opened
our eyes to the knowledge that the dispersion of the
troops retained in the country over all parts of the
United Kingdom (and of these, many in the sister
isle, employed on what may be considered as little
better than police duty) was not the policy most
adapted to secure home defence, or to maintain that
army in the fittest condition for service abroad. It
was in the year 1859 that the Volunteer force of
Great Britain, which, with the exception of one
solitary battalion, had been extinct since the beginning of the century, was revived, or, to speak more
accurately, sprang up into a fresh existence: indeed,
in the succeeding year the movement acquired strength
so rapidly as to appear before the nation as an army,
imperfect naturally and undeveloped, but giving such
promises of efficiency as have since been so fully and
amply ratified.

It is not our intention to enter on the subject of
reforms in the regular army which ensued, nor is
there any necessity to detail all the circumstances
which led England to turn her attention to her own
safety, and in the interests of this to set her house in
order. The causes for apprehension may have been
exaggerated, but that they were altogether without
foundation is incredible. It is indisputable that after
the cession of Nice and Savoy to the Emperor of the

French, disquieting rumours as to his further intentions were afloat. His next project, it was said, was the annexation of Geneva, and among other means of aggrandisement which he contemplated, one was an advance of the French frontier to the Ebro, in exchange for which Spain was to receive aid and support in the subjugation of Portugal. These designs of the Emperor were not only freely discussed in society, but set forth in pamphlets apparently stamped with Imperial authority. Lord Palmerston watched with much misgiving the great additional military and naval preparations on the part of France, and to him they were a source of grave anxiety; nor must these rumours, magnified and distorted as they may have been, be regarded by us with contempt, when it is known that such keen observers, and acute politicians, as the Prime Minister, Mr. Gladstone, and Panizzi himself, viewed them with perturbed reflections.

In this year (1860), Panizzi, for the first time, had been invited by His Majesty Napoleon III. to spend his holidays at Biarritz, in company with his old friend Prosper Mérimée. Correspondence of much importance is here adduced, and is given in full, as bearing upon the suspicions and presages of evil already referred to. The first letter in order is from the pen of Panizzi to Mérimée, and from it may be gathered all that is needful of the dreaded omens which threatened to disturb the peaceful relations existing between England and France, whose alliance involved the peace of the whole civilized world, whilst its rupture would throw broadcast the seeds of dissension and of war. The letters themselves indicate the close relations between the two correspondents, and their intimacy, will be reverted to hereafter :—

> "British Museum,
>
> Sept. 30 (Sunday), 1860.

"My dear Mérimée,

. . . . . I have been so fortunate as to have an opportunity of at once communicating to a very influential personage the chief points of the conversation I had the honour of holding with the Emperor respecting the want of cordiality, not to say coolness, now unhappily prevailing between France and England, my object being humbly to contribute, as far as might be in my power, to the growth of better feelings. I have dwelt on the earnestness with which His Majesty had expressed himself with respect to the English alliance, and on the warmth with which he had spoken of his affection for this nation.   I did not fail to repeat what His Majesty had said of his consciousness of never having done a single act which could be construed as injurious or even unfriendly to England; of his feeling that he had most scrupulously fulfilled his duties as an ally ; of his having nothing so much at heart as to be on the most intimate terms with this country, feeling confident that that would be for the advantage of both France and England, whilst it gave him, personally, heartfelt satisfaction.

What I said was extremely well received, and the same wish was expressed as that which had been expressed by His Majesty, that the two countries should always act cordially together ; that His Majesty would find England most desirous to cultivate an alliance so eminently advantageous to both nations, provided that could be done without sacrifice to England's honour and interests, and that on this side of the channel they were not aware of ever having given France any just cause of complaint.   But that many things created the impression that France, not satisfied with the eminent position in which she was placed, was striving to extend her influence and possession beyond what was just and fair towards her neighbours. In support of this impression a great many facts were alleged. It was stated that Savoy and Nice were an‑ nexed not only against the most explicit professions to the contrary, but on pretence that would justify any other annex‑ ation of territories that France might covet. I was, moreover, told that France, knowing how injurious it might be to English interests to alter the territorial arrangements on the coast of Barbary with reference to Gibraltar, had nevertheless encouraged an unjust attack on the part of Spain or Morocco; that France was favourable to the fall and partition of the Turkish Empire, well-knowing that England would oppose this consummation with all her might; that agents were traced to Belgium and other parts, endeavouring to create a party in those populations favourable to the annexation of territories now belonging to other States, to France ; that agents had even been found at work in Ireland, that the num‑ ber of pamphlets published in France directed to prepare the world for extensive territorial alterations in favour of an en‑ largement of the French Empire, and the belief that many of such pamphlets were published with the approbation, if not at the instigation of the French Government, rendered them ap‑ parently an indication of the intentions of that Government. It is only necessary, in conclusion, to advert to the great, con‑ stant, and progressive armaments of France, both by land and by sea. As to the latter, Englishmen are convinced they cannot be directed to any other end but eventually to offen‑ sive warfare, especially against England. France, they say, cannot want for any defensive purpose so large a navy as she has, to which she is steadily adding; and it is obviously for aggressive purposes that she drills her sailors and troops to em‑ bark and disembark with rapidity and precision, and that she builds vessels intended for the transport and landing of large bodies of soldiers. It depends on France, I was told, to be on the very best and most intimate terms with this country, that is, by not acting in a manner which excites well-grounded suspicions of her intentions. There is every disposition on

the part of England to meet her more than half way, but if
the acts of the Imperial Government are not calculated to
inspire confidence, it will be impossible for England not to be
on her guard, and prepare herself for any contingencies. As
to the accusation that England encourages other powers to
coalesce to attack France, I am told it is utterly unfounded.
It is positively denied, moreover, that there is any intention
of forming any coalition, or even of coming to an understanding for the purpose of injuring France. It is, however, admitted that nations who watch the conduct of France are un-
easy for their own security, and that they will probably come
to some understanding should it ever come to pass that France
becomes aggressive.

In conclusion, I was told, the peace of the world as well as
the happiness of mankind, is in the hands of France. If she
will not attempt to injure others, no one will think of injuring
her; and so far as England is concerned, if France will be
satisfied with what is fair and honourable, she may rely on the
sincere desire of this country of being on the best terms with
her, and of her acting accordingly.

You are at liberty to show this letter to the Minister, and
even to place it in his hands should he wish to show it to his
august master, who ought to know exactly by what feelings
and motives political men are moved in this country towards
France.

A good understanding with England must be of some value
to France. She has raised the storm ; she must do her best
to allay it if she have at heart the English alliance.

I hope you will be authorised to answer this letter in a
manner that will prepare the way to a lasting return of cordiality on both sides.

Yours, &c., &c.,

A. PANIZZI."

M. Mérimée's reply partakes much of the style of
the special pleader. Whilst he strongly disclaims
his belief in the Emperor's bad faith, as suggested by

Panizzi, his defence of Louis Napoleon seems hardly inconsistent with the truth of certain of the allegations. He himself appears to have considered his criticism of English policy the strongest point in his letter :—

"Paris, Samedi 6 Octobre, 1860.

"Mon cher Panizzi, ...

En attendant, vous saurez que je ne suis revenu de voyage que hier soir, où j'ai trouvé votre lettre. Je l'ai portée ce matin chez Son Excellence. Je vois que les dispositions de Lord Palmerston sont telles que je me les représentais, c'est-à-dire le contraire de bienveillantes, mais je ne me doutais pas qu'il *dit* la moitié des choses extraordinaires qu'il vous a dites. Dans l'exposé de ses griefs il y a une bonne partie de faussetés complètes auxquelles il n'y a qu'un démenti formel à donner. Puis il y a des niaiseries que je ne me serais jamais attendu à entendre dans la bouche d'un homme d'Etat ou soit-disant tel. Par exemple, cette bonne bêtise que la France médite une invasion en Angleterre, parce que dans des ports de mer on exerce les soldats à embarquer et débarquer promptement. Il me semble que, lorsque dans l'espace de deux ans on a eu cent cinquante mille hommes à débarquer en Italie, douze mille à débarquer en Chine, six mille à débarquer en Syrie ; quand, de plus, la plus importante de nos colonies, l'Algérie a une armée de cinquante mille hommes qui ne communique avec la France que par mer, il me semble, dis-je, qu'il n'est pas inutile d'apprendre aux soldats à entrer dans un vaisseau et à en sortir. Quant aux armements, vous pouvez dire hardiment qu'il ne s'en fait point. On donne des congés de semestre dans tous les régiments, et, à mon avis, *on a tort*, attendu l'état des choses en Italie. Les armements maritimes sont aussi faux que les préparatifs de l'armée de terre. Si vous voulez lire la brochure que je vous ai portée, vous verrez la vérité sur tout cela. Le pauvre Louis-Philippe avait laissé dépérir la flotte. De plus on est dans une époque de rénovation et il est nécessaire de transformer les bâtiments à voiles. Je conçois que l'Angleterre veuille avoir le monopole de la mer, et qu'elle y tienne, mais elle l'aura toujours, attendu qu'elle dispose d'un bien plus grand nombre de marins que toute autre puissance. Nous avons eu des escadres d'élite qui, sous les ordres d'un chef excellent comme l'Amiral Lalande, auraient peut-être battu une escadre Anglaise, mais si, en gagnant ·une bataille, nous perdions mille matelots et les Anglais dix mille, nous ne pourrions réparer notre perte, tandis qu'en un mois l'Angleterre trouverait dix mille autres matelots aussi bons. Il me paraît par trop bouffon de la part de Lord Palmerston de dire que l'Angleterre ne cherche pas et ne cherchera pas à former une coalition contre la France, et d'ajouter aussitôt que les puissances inquiètes *will probably come to some understanding!* Une autre assertion non moins extravagante, c'est de nous accuser d'avoir encouragé l'Espagne à faire la guerre au Maroc. J'étais en Espagne au moment où cette guerre s'est faite, et s'il y a à Madrid un ministre anglais avec des yeux et des oreilles, il aurait pu dire que la guerre a été faite par l'explosion du sentiment national, et que les lettres de Lord John Russell ont eu pour résultat d'exalter ce sentiment et d'exciter à la haine contre l'Angleterre. Il n'est pas moins étrange de prétendre que la France qui a aidé l'Angleterre à retarder la destruction de l'empire Ottoman, pousse maintenant à sa ruine. Vos ministres sont comme les malades qui ne veulent pas que leur médecin leur dise que leur état est grave. Ressusciter ou même faire vivre longtemps la Turquie est impossible, et il serait insensé de se quereller sur les remèdes à lui donner, lorsqu'il faudrait au contraire s'entendre sur la manière de l'enterrer. Que la France ait de l'ambition, je ne le nie pas. C'est une idée ou plutôt un préjugé national, qu'elle s'est amoindrie en perdant une partie des conquêtes de la révolution. Je crois que l'Empereur ne partage pas ce préjugé, mais, en tout cas, dans l'hypothèse qu'il l'aurait, vous ne le supposez pas assez dépourvu de bon sens pour risquer d'avoir toute l'Europe sur les bras, sur la chance d'ôter cent cinquante

mille âmes à la Bavière et autant à la Prusse? Ce que la
France gagnerait en étendue, elle le perdrait en homogénéité,
et, tout considéré, elle s'affaiblirait au lieu de prendre
des forces. Ce qui me frappe surtout dans la politique
anglaise de notre temps, c'est sa petitesse. Elle n'agit ni
pour des idées grandes, ni même pour des intérêts. Elle
n'a que des jalousies et se borne à prendre le contrepied
des puissances qui excitent ses sentiments de jalousie. Le
résultat est de diminuer son importance en Europe et de la réduire au rôle de puissance de second ordre. En ménageant la
chèvre et le chou comme elle a fait, en observant la neutralité
peu impartiale entre l'Autriche et la France, elle n'a obtenu
l'amitié ni de l'une ni de l'autre. Y a-t-il quelque chose de
plus misérable que sa politique à Naples et en Vénétie? Comment M. de Rechberg peut-il avoir la moindre confiance en
des gens qui encouragent Garibaldi et Kossuth et qui ne
veulent pas l'affranchissement de la Vénétie? Tout se fait en
Angleterre en vue de conserver des portefeuilles. On fait
toutes les fautes possibles pour conserver une trentaine de voix
douteuses. On ne s'inquiète que du présent et on ne songe
pas à l'avenir. Il est certain qu'il y a dans ce moment en
Europe un malaise général qui amènera une catastrophe et une
grande modification de la carte. Des hommes vraiment politiques, voyant le mal, chercheraient le remède. Vos ministres
ne pensent pas à la guérison du malade. Ils veulent conserver
la maladie. Cela est digne de vieillards qui n'ont que quelques
années devant eux; mais je doute que les grands ministres du
commencement de ce siècle eussent pensé et agi de la sorte.

Je viens d'un pays où l'on est très dévot et où la catastrophe
de Lamoricière a fait une grande sensation. J'ai vu des gens
fort piteux et fort découragés, mais nullement dangereux. Je
vois que Garibaldi se soumet et va reprendre sa charrue. Il
fait bien. Son affaire est de se battre, et il n'entend rien à
organiser. Il parait que le gâchis est grand en Sicile et à
Naples, et qu'il est parvenu à faire regretter le gouvernement
déchu. Cependant il parait que tous les gens sensés sont

unanimes pour croire que l'annexion est le seul moyen de ré-
tablir un peu d'ordre pour le moment. Je trouve qu'il y a de
l'habileté dans les ménagements de M. de Cavour pour Garibaldi, mais j'aurais voulu le voir un peu plus énergique au
sujet de Mazzini. Je crains que les reproches de Lord Palmerston, qui, entre nous, me semblent dénoter peu de bonne
foi, ne produisent pas un très bon effet sur l'Empereur. M.
Fould, que je n'ai pas rencontré ce matin, en sera, je pense,
très irrité. Je lui ai laissé un mot en le priant de ne faire
aucun usage de cette lettre avant d'en avoir causé avec moi.
Vous pouvez, quand vous en trouverez l'occasion, assurer
hautement que s'il y a eu en Irlande quelques menées con-
traires au Gouvernement Anglais, elles sont l'œuvre de nos
Catholiques et que le Gouvernement de l'Empereur n'y est pour
rien absolument.

Adieu, mon cher Panizzi, portez-vous bien et ne m'oubliez
pas auprès de nos amis. . . . . . . J'espère encore que le pape
s'en ira un de ces jours.

Tout à vous.

P. MERIMEE."

We next offer Mr. Gladstone's opinion of England's
relations with France, and would draw attention to
the sense of security pervading his expressions in a
letter to Panizzi. How these sentiments were modified at a later date will be shown further on :—

"11, Downing Street,
Whitehall,
October 16th, 1860.

" My dear Panizzi,
I return all; but I have not, I think, completely
deciphered M. Mérimée's important letter. If there is a flavour
of bitterness in it, I cannot deny that it may be in some
degree due to us. Instead of saying anything akin to what
is complained of, I will merely point to topics of consolation,
such as follow. In my opinion, under the present Ministry,

no coalition will be formed against France. The English
nation is really Italian in feeling ; and in proportion as
France is the same will there be a broader and firmer ground
for concord and co-operation. The foolish alarms which have
been unhappily prevalent in this country are abating by
degrees. They implied a most extravagant compliment to
France, and a compliment that I for one grudged her not a
little. Lastly, the Commercial Treaty, if the work be completed by the French Government in the spirit of courage,
sagacity, and good faith with which it has been begun, will,
by processes all the more safe because they are quiet and
gradual, lay the most solid foundations of active goodwill
between the two countries. How much I desire that goodwill I can hardly tell you. France and England are the two
really great Powers of Europe ; and two such forces, if they
move in severance from one another, cannot but disturb the
political system. The case of Savoy and Nice was, as I think,
an unhappy one; but if on the one side it may be said that it
was exceptional, and if on the other calm reflection must admit
that it has been made too much of, then every day that passes
over our heads will have its healing power. On the whole,
unless we have new faults and follies, we ought to do well in
this all important matter.

Yours most sincerely,

W. E. GLADSTONE."

" I shall look anxiously for your next. In answer to a question which you reported about me, you might have said with
truth that I am now denounced as one of the most dangerous
and revolutionary characters in England."

Panizzi's letter of September 30, above-quoted, was
forwarded by Mérimée to M. Achille Fould, and in due
course he replied, commenting on it. As the correspondence would be incomplete without this, it is
inserted, but the contents scarcely call for any special
remarks on our part.

(For "Ferdinand," *infra*, read "François.")

"4 Novembre, 1860.

"Mon cher collègue,

En vérité notre ami Panizzi, ou ses honorables interlocuteurs ont une singulière idée du caractère de l'Empereur. S'il fallait attacher de l'importance aux propos que vous transmet M. Panizzi, Machiavel ne serait qu'un enfant naïf auprès de Napoléon III. Pendant que nous faisons des efforts pour calmer l'irritation de l'Espagne, et arrêter son zèle pour la cause de Rome, c'est l'Empereur qu'on accuse d'avoir sous mains provoqué le rappel de la Légation Espagnole de Turin, et je le sais de la meilleure source, rien n'est plus faux que cette dernière supposition. Ce qui est vrai, c'est que nous avons essayé d'agir dans un sens tout à fait opposé à celui allégué. Voilà pour l'affaire d'Espagne.

Quant à l'envoi de notre flotte à Gaeta je conviens qu'il y a une sorte de contradiction dans notre conduite ; mais elle est bien plus apparente que réelle. Les explications diplomatiques ont déjà été données sur ce point. L'envoi de la flotte a été purement une affaire de sentiment et d'humanité. Si cette mesure manque de logique elle ne peut pas être taxée de parjure. La meilleure preuve de notre sincérité, c'est que nous avons immédiatement désillusionné le Roi de Naples, à qui la présence de nos vaisseaux avait donné des espérances mal fondées, en lui refusant de faire avancer un corps de troupes à Terracina, comme il nous le demandait. Je crois savoir que Ferdinand (François) II., s'apprête à profiter de notre flotte pour quitter Gaeta. On ne pourrait vraiment pas reprocher à l'Empereur de s'être laissé toucher par le malheur de ce jeune souverain et la situation de la famille dont il est entouré.

Quant à la question d'alliance entre la France et l'Angleterre pour régler le sort de l'Italie je ne sais que vous dire. Cela me parait pour le moment prématuré.

Mille bonnes amitiés,

ACHILLE FOULD."

Now follows the exposition of Mr. Gladstone's modified views, set forth in two letters. From these we gather that, on further observation, he had come to regard the conduct of the Emperor of the French, both in Italy and elsewhere, as somewhat more than equivocal, and as calculated to engender strife, and threaten the existing peaceful relations of the two countries :—

"Nov. 26, 1860.

"My dear Panizzi,

You know, and therefore I need not describe, the spirit in which I received your recent communications respecting certain conversations which you held in Paris, and in which I have looked upon the acts of your interlocutor. But since I saw you his conduct has really become so equivocal that I do not see how it is possible for one who pursues it to expect that he should retain confidence, much less that he should remove mistrust.

The seizure of Terracina is defended, if at all, by a plea which seems little short of ridiculous—I mean strategic necessity for the defence of Rome.

But there is a construction for the act alike obvious and rational—namely this, that disturbance is to be prolonged in Southern Italy, under the notion that the establishment there of a nation and a kingdom is an evil, and that every chance is to be kept open of averting it.

It seems intended to facilitate the escape of the soldiers of King Francis into the mountain districts of the Regno, and to make those districts the focus of resistance to Victor Emmanuel.

This construction is supported by the incomprehensible conduct of France with respect to Gaeta.

If Victor Emmanuel could be conceived anxious to get hold of Francis and his family, then we could also conceive the duty or the policy of baffling him ; but it is impossible that the French Government can entertain such an idea

Q

To keep open Gaeta on the side of the sea is to prolong suffering and bloodshed for the present—fear and insecurity for the future.   Such a policy, if it be a policy, appears inhuman. I admit that, notwithstanding the unhappy affair of Savoy, and especially of Nice, the great acts done by France for Italy last year have rendered to that country an inestimable service.   I do not enter into any comparative question as between the path pursued by France and that taken by England.   I assume no right to be her judge.   I merely write in the interest of peace, and of a fervent desire that there should be constant and cordial goodwill between France and England. Whatever susceptibility my countrymen may have shown, a consistent course on the part of the French Emperor with regard to Italy would have been acknowledged by them. They were utterly thrown abroad by the terms of Villafranca; but they, perhaps, did not then make sufficient allowance for difficulties, and they were pleased to see that Zurich was an amendment upon the prior proceeding.   But what is it possible to say or think or urge when the Sardinian force is only permitted to conduct one-half a siege, and when (as I am told) the French have either secured the passage, or themselves actually carried provisions into Gaeta?

Before these unhappy proceedings, the English mind was getting rapidly clear of its prepossessions.   The publication of the Treaty, in which the Emperor has behaved so admirably, will do an infinity of good—or will, at any rate, lay the ground for it—and this will grow as the terms of it are better understood.   Why is an opportunity to be made for the light-minded and the evil-minded to point to other ambiguities of conduct on questions in which it is of such vast importance that France and England should have a common feeling?

Believe me,

Sincerely yours,

W. E. GLADSTONE."

"11, Downing Street,
Whitehall,
Nov. 27, 1860.

"My dear Panizzi,

I return the letter you sent me. It was, I think, quite capable of a good construction on Nov. 4, when it was written; and the writer tells us he had then learned that Ferdinand, evidently meaning Francis, was about to use the French Fleet as a means of escape. By this time he must have pretty well unlearned that piece of knowledge, and the character of the act, I think, stands out such as I described it yesterday. I impute no Machiavelism, or ism of any other kind. What I have been saying to every one all this year has been, *Give the Emperor's acts a fair construction ;* but a fair construction of *these* acts unhappily lends to them a rather foul aspect. I entirely withhold even now my belief from any such notions as those which you describe in your last page, and I do not take these false strokes of policy as indications of a plot extending far beyond them. They may be due to uncertainty, and to apprehensions of the future Italy; such as are, however, quite unworthy of a country so able and so certain to hold its own as France. But they are alike deductions from the glory it has won, evils in themselves, menaces to the general peace, and sources of mistrust *here*, such that as far as they go make it impossible to deny that the feeling is legitimate.

As to my interest in Italy, I wish it could be one-tenth part as useful as it is true. She has been to me for the last eighteen months a principal cause, not only of joy and satisfaction, but even of the desire for political existence.

Yours sincerely,

W. E. GLADSTONE."

The substance of these two letters was forthwith communicated as follows by Panizzi to Mérimée :—

"B. M., 29th November, 1860.

" . . . . Shortly after my return I informed Mr. Gladstone of my having had the honour of conversing with His Majesty, and told Mr. Gladstone of the great interest with which the Emperor spoke of him. This gentleman was much pleased with what I told him, but was of opinion that certain actions had been unjustly judged, and felt confident of the loyalty of the Emperor; and, notwithstanding the conduct of General Goyon at Viterbo, and of Admiral Barbier de Tinan at Gaeta, he still adheres to his former opinions.

"But yesterday Mr. Gladstone sent me a long letter, in which he tells me how he deplores the conduct of the Imperial Government at Gaeta, at Viterbo, at Terracina, and, in fact, everywhere; and which almost confirms what he has constantly tried to make people disbelieve. He is much mortified. I answered him, but from a second letter received this morning, I feel I cannot conceal the sudden change in Mr. Gladstone's convictions. And if so firm a partisan of the Emperor has changed, think what the effect must be on those who have always suspected the Emperor.

" As His Majesty placed so much confidence, and justly so, in the sentiments of Mr. Gladstone, I have thought it right to inform him (H.M.) of this change and its cause, and this I do entirely at my own risk, hoping that something will be done, in order to restore to His Majesty the confidence of those who, here, are his real friends. As for myself, I am at your disposal."

The following letter to Count Cavour, the only one in our possession, will serve to show Panizzi's opinions of the real intent of the policy of Louis Napoleon towards Italy—an opinion not, in our own judgment, destitute of considerable support from facts :—

"British Museum,
7th of December,
1860.

"My dear and distinguished Friend,

You are already aware that I wrote to let the Emperor know of the bad impression which his conduct was producing here, and that Mr. Gladstone, who had always defended him, was beginning to feel it impossible to trust in him, especially after what he did at Gaeta.

The Emperor has read my letter, and has given me to understand, in answer, that his feelings are the same as they were two years ago : that he still wishes to promote the independence of the Italian nation, and ever so many fine things of that sort, which amount to nothing. But there is in the answer a passage of considerable importance, which I copy:—
'The Emperor replied to me that all that has been done was done in concert with the King's Government, and that it would be wrong to hold him alone responsible for what has happened. The King is quite aware of the Emperor's ideas on all that has taken place ; and he knows, moreover, what the Emperor ardently desires above all.' I know not what to think of this. Neither the King nor his Government can have approved either the conduct of Guyon or that of Barbier de Tinan, of which I specially complained. How is all this going on? I don't know, and cannot stomach it.

My rejoinder was that if the matter stood as thus reported to me, I could not but confess that the King's Government was involved in the responsibility, but that I was unable to comprehend why such a King should be patronized as he of Gaeta, sprung of a generation of ruthless tyrants; that we should never have expected to see the wings of the Imperial eagle extended over the lawless people of Naples, red with human blood, and that we were completely at sea. I said too that the most influential persons here believed the Emperor was favourable to a certain measure of Italian independence, but not to Italian unity; and to this is attributed the protection accorded to the King of Gaeta; that it was held for certain too that H.M. would go to war next spring, but not for the unity of Italy.

I ought perhaps to have said more, but did not wish to go beyond certain limits. There are some here who think that the Emperor has an understanding with you over there to go to war next spring, but I do not know what good it would do us to have Francis at Gaeta. In short we understand nothing at all.

Yours, &c., &c.,
A. PANIZZI."

"P.S.—Please tell Hudson what I am writing. I have let Palmerston and Gladstone read the answer which I got from Paris: they have both formed the same opinion of it."

What schemes and intentions the Emperor may have secretly entertained at this period (if, indeed, such a creature of circumstances can be supposed to have been capable of possessing fixed intentions beyond the exigencies of the hour) will probably remain hidden from human ken until records now in obscure recesses shall come out into the light of publicity. That ambitious ideas floated through his brain, and that, if it had been possible to carry out his projects, he would have hesitated but little about the means of executing them, there is little doubt; but that, for some reason, he did not see the way to their fulfilment seems equally certain. Happily—and probably owing to the firm attitude of England—the cloud passed over, and no rupture occurred between the two great powers. In a little more than two years after the date of the letter last quoted, Panizzi received from the Emperor a second invitation to Biarritz. What led to this invitation we find him thus explaining to his friend Ellice :—

> " Paris, 52, Rue de Lille,
> " Monday, Aug. 11th, 1862.

. . . .

" . . . It is perfectly true that Her Majesty, on hearing from Mérimée himself that I was to pass through Paris, did me the honour of inviting me to dine at St. Cloud last Wednesday, which of course I did. I am not, however, so conceited as to suppose that Her Majesty, who knows me very little, asked me in consequence of that slight knowledge of me ; no doubt she asked me out of kindness to Mérimée. We had a most agreeable party on that day. The Empress was kind, more than I can express, both at dinner and after, when the ladies and gentlemen who had dined, accompanied by several carriages (she driving her mother) went to see a new contrivance to run carriages on a railway (of which I understood nothing). We returned to St. Cloud about 11 o'clock by bye-lanes without any escort whatever, and in the most private manner. The Emperor, who was to arrive on that day, not having come, the Empress most gracefully said that Mérimée and I must wait for him, and dine again yesterday, which we did. He was uncommonly gracious and friendly; owing to a mistake, we arrived long before the dinner hour; we walked in the garden, Her Majesty, and Mérimée, as well as myself, till dinner time; then, after dinner, he called me to a private room and we had a long conversation, during which he encouraged me to speak out, and I did so. The conclusion was an invitation to Biarritz. I was most struck with the Prince Imperial. He is a handsome, intelligent, charming boy; he speaks English just as well as you do. . . . ."

This chapter may close with part of a letter from Panizzi to Mr. Gladstone, wherein he appears to give the result of his visit to Biarritz, and of his conversations with the Emperor Napoleon. Much of the provocation stated by the writer to have been given to His Majesty it is difficult to deny; but those who have studied the subject, or retain any memory of the circumstances of the time, will agree that the conduct of the Emperor himself was the chief source of all those accusations, true or false, which were brought against him.

" British Museum,
November 3rd, 1862.

" . . . As to the conduct of Napoleon respecting Italy, of course you know I am completely with you; but I must say that some of our friends have acted as if they wished to furnish him with a pretext for behaving as he has hitherto done. He has been told that no confidence can be placed in his word (if even true he cannot like to be told), he has been *bullied* and threatened, those who have treated him with insolence and have grossly insulted him, not only as Emperor, but as if he were the vilest of mortals, have been made most of by some public men in England (I will tell you what I allude to when we meet), all this has greatly, and not unnaturally, vexed him, and indisposed him to listen to the advice of statesmen whom he no longer considered as his friends. One of the very few Frenchmen who looks upon the English alliance as the best for France, as well as for the good of Europe generally, and who has long been doing his utmost to smooth difficulties and soften asperities has often said to me:—'On se croit réciproquement plus mauvais qu'on n'est en réalité, il n'y a pas moyen de s'entendre.' I have found by experience the perfect truth of this."

Here we abandon this subject : leaving at the same time material for much thought as to the instability of all human events, either private or public, and as to the uncertainty of individual character. How inconspicuous may be the turning-point upon which hangs the good or evil of the future, and with what jealous care the actions of the powerful and ambitious should be watched ; how a thought or a word may lead to the misery and destruction of thousands ; and how soon all that was fair, prosperous, and peaceful may be turned into hideous bloodshed, dissension, and misery ! Like the Cæsars of old, the Napoleonic dynasty was ever craving for increased dominion ; and although we, who live in these later days, have seen the last hopes of Imperial power in France seemingly extinguished, as we look back to the time when such haughty spirits had to be kept in check, we cannot but feel a certain amount of gratitude that such contingencies are unlikely ever again to inspire us with apprehension from so formidable a quarter.

CHAPTER XXV.

ILL HEALTH—EXTRA LEAVE—DEPUTY PRINCIPAL LI-
BRARIAN — DEPARTURE FOR NAPLES — STORM —
NAPLES—EXCURSIONS—LA CAVA—MONTE CASSINO
—MONASTIC SOCIETIES—RETURN TO ENGLAND.

AFTER his return from Biarritz the strain to which
the constitution of Panizzi had been subjected by his
laborious life gave him decided warning of failing
powers. Amongst other disagreeable symptoms he
suffered much from *insomnia*. On several occasions
he informed the author of these memoirs that he
feared he should be compelled to relinquish his position at the British Museum; nevertheless he continued
to carry on his work with unabated ardour. He rose
every morning at 8 o'clock, and set the example of
punctuality to his subordinates by appearing at his
post by 10. Struggling manfully against his threatening infirmities, and using every possible means to refit
himself for the due performance of his duties, he
applied, in the beginning of December, 1862, to the
Trustees for leave of absence from the 15th of that
month to the 1st of May following. It need not be
said that his request was freely granted. As Principal
Librarian it was incumbent on him before leaving to
fix upon some competent officer to discharge his important duties; and this substitute he very soon found
in the person of his longwhile colleague Mr. J.

Winter Jones, at that time Keeper of the Printed Book Department. This gentleman he nominated as his deputy in accordance with the rules of the Institution set forth in the 2nd Chap., §§ 2 and 3 of the statutes. The document, which gave legal force to this temporary transfer of office, was signed by the Archbishop of Canterbury, and the Speaker of the House of Commons, on the 9th of December, 1862. Soon afterwards Panizzi received a kind and sympathizing letter from Sir G. Cornewall Lewis, dated December 16, 1862 :—

" Some of your friends are apprehensive that your labours at the Museum have been detrimental to your health, and are of opinion that you would derive some benefit from a short interval of rest. I was not aware, when I had the pleasure of seeing you yesterday, that you had been unwell ; but pray let me know whether you are desirous of leaving London for a time for the sake of your health. If you are, the matter might doubtless be represented to the Trustees.

" I have read your report upon the present state of accommodation at the Museum.

" After the recess, I intend to move for a Committee on the National Gallery question, to which the papers relating to the deficient space at the Museum may be referred."

On the 18th of December Panizzi, accompanied by the author, who had been sent from school, started for Naples. So far as Marseilles the journey was satisfactorily accomplished, the travellers occupying a special carriage, provided by order of the Emperor. Panizzi had called on His Majesty on his way through

Paris, and thus this accommodation had been afforded him. Arriving at Marseilles, the travellers embarked on board one of the *Messageries* steamers, trusting to reach Naples by Christmas Day. A terrific storm, however, which burst upon them shortly after starting, delayed their progress ; so severe was it that at one moment they were in jeopardy of their lives. At last, after a most tedious passage, Civita-Vecchia was sighted. Here they landed, and, leaving it on the following day, reached Naples on the 26th.

As in 1852, Panizzi went to Lady Holland's residence at the Palazzo Roccella, whence he sent Mr. Ellice (January 13, 1863) his first observations on the changes which had taken place at Naples :—

" . . . This country, after centuries of misgovernment, will take many years before it derives from the new state of things the advantages which we all wish ; there is, however, an undeniable improvement, in spite of the priests, the brigands, and the Emperor of the French, in everything. The dislike of the Bourbons is general, and there is no Muratist party ; but the late Italian Ministry has done everything in its power to create dissatisfaction by the pedantry of its regulations, the total disregard of the habits, feelings, and prejudices of this ignorant population, and the incredible want of tact in its agents."

Just at the time of the arrival at Naples, an English gentleman had been arrested there on the charge of being the bearer of treasonable letters from Rome. He happened to be a friend of Panizzi's, and consequently no little anxiety and apprehension arose in the mind of the latter regarding his future destiny.

On an early day in January therefore, Panizzi,
Lord Henry Lennox, and the writer set out to visit
the prisoner ; the necessary permission to do so was
not, however, obtained without considerable difficulty.
By an extract from a letter on this case, written by
the first-named to a friend, it seems that since the
disappearance of the old *régime* some considerable
improvement in the treatment of political offenders
had been introduced :—

"Jan. 13th.

"I have just been to see Mr. X——, and I must
say that a better prison I never saw. He has a magnificent view, good food, books, and is allowed to see
friends. The Governor, who is a worthy man, retired the moment we entered the room. There was
some difficulty in allowing young Fagan to enter the
prison, so we made use of him by telling him to take
note of all he saw. The sentence passed on our
friend is certainly severe, but he fully deserves it.
Still, I am doing my best to get him off as lightly as
is possible."

Panizzi took a sensible view of the way of enjoying
and availing himself of the advantages of a vacation.
To his active mind, perfect quiescence was not for a
moment to be tolerated ; and he resolved upon that
wholesome and necessary recreation and diversion,
which have so great a tendency to restore relaxed
vigour. Delightful were the excursions made in and
around Naples. One of these was to the celebrated
Benedictine Monastery of La Trinità della Cava,
founded in 1011 by Alferius Pappacarboni, its first
Abbot. Here the library, with its rare and priceless

contents, was, as may be imagined, the chief point of attraction. The visitors were to have been accompanied by the then abbot, Pappalettere, who, as well as Padre Tosti, of Monte Cassino, was a much esteemed friend of both Mr. Gladstone and Panizzi. Unfortunately Pappalettere had lately got himself into bad odour with the Pope, having rashly expressed himself respecting the Italian cause in terms too favourable to suit the taste of his Holiness, and had, in consequence, been summoned to Rome to give an account of his conduct. Panizzi, consulted as to the course he would recommend him to adopt, at once advised him to disregard the invitation, and to remain quietly where he was—sound advice, and, as the sequel shows, wise, had it been acted on. There are individuals, however, who, asking for advice, disregard it, and adopt the contrary course ; and in this instance one of this class was Pappalettere. Obeying the Pope, he went to Rome, and, as a reward for his obedience, underwent what can be expressed by no other words than some years of close confinement. On one expedition to La Cava the travellers had a narrow escape from a sudden termination to their earthly career. In proceeding along a portion of the road, bordering on a deep precipice, either from the overladen state of the carriage or from the bad condition of the road, a wheel came off. The promptitude and agility of the driver, saved the party from inevitable destruction. Jumping down, he at once pulled the horses from the threatening precipice ; but for his presence of mind the writer would not have been here to record the mishap nor to present the world with this memoir.

Another visit in the neighbourhood was to Monte
Cassino, founded by St. Benedict A.D. 529, on the
site of a temple of Apollo. It is situated on a mountain from which it derives its name, near the ruins of
the ancient Casinum, and approached by a well-paved
and winding road, the ascent of which occupies about
two hours. The Abbey in the eleventh and twelfth
centuries was the seat of science, particularly of medicine, the celebrated School of Salerno having been
founded by the monks of Monte Cassino.

Of this monastery, Dante thus speaks in Canto XXII.
of the " Paradiso," line 37 :—

> Quel monte, a cui Cassino è nella costa,
> Fu frequentato già in sulla cima
> Dalla gente ingannata e mal disposta.
> Ed io son quel che su vi portai prima
> Lo nome di Colui che in terra addusse
> La verità che tanto ci sublima ;
> E tanta grazia sovra me rilusse,
> Ch' io ritrassi le ville circostanti
> Dall' empio culto che il mondo sedusse.

> . . . . . In old days,
> That mountain, at whose side Cassino rests,
> Was, on its height, frequented by a race
> Deceived and ill-disposed; and I it was,
> Who thither carried first the name of Him,
> Who brought the soul-subliming truth to man.
> And such a speeding grace shone over me,
> That from their impious worship I reclaim'd
> The dwellers round about, who with the world
> Were in delusion lost. . . . .
>   —(*Cary's Translation.*)

At the time of this visit the founder's tomb was in
course of restoration, and amongst those who contributed to the good work was Mr. Gladstone, who re-

quested Panizzi to pay, in his name, to the restoration fund the sum of 100 ducats, equivalent to about £16 of English money.

One of the first acts of the newly-established Government of Italy was the suppression of the religious houses. Although it cannot be denied by the candid student of history that, in mediæval times, Monastic Societies were of the utmost benefit, and, indeed, in many respects, actually necessary to civilization, and to many other important ends; and although the debt we owe them for the preservation of literature and art, which, but for their fostering care, would have eternally perished, can never be duly estimated; yet it must be admitted by the most determined lover of antiquity that, in the state of modern society, the monastery is at the present day somewhat out of place. The ends such Institutions formerly subserved, and their power to subserve such ends, have alike become extinct. In our times they appear to exist simply to perpetuate the vicious and unreasonable principle that a man may live in the world, yet not be of it, that he may cast aside his duties as a citizen and every feeling which binds him to his country, sacrificing such sacred obligations to the devout (and selfish) care of his own soul.

At the time of which we write, Italy, above all nations, abounded to superfluity in these establishments; and suspicions, not ill-founded nor unreasonable, were entertained of the loyalty of some of their members, from the perpetual drain made by them on the able-bodied population.

It is, however, to be regretted that the officials to

R

whom was entrusted the dissolution of the convents
of Italy did not set about their far from pleasant
duties in such a manner as to contrast more favour-
ably with the conduct of Henry VIII. under similar
circumstances, whereas they displayed an amount of
harshness and brutality—nay, cruelty—calculated to
throw discredit not only on themselves, but on the
country by which they were employed, and, what is
more serious still, on the character of Italians in
general.

Panizzi, ever alive to injustice and cruelty, and
jealous of the fair fame of his country, with an equal
abhorrence of the wrongs committed in the name of
freedom and of a liberal constitution, though weighed
with the tyrannies of King Bomba, was especially in-
dignant at the conduct of the Commission.   On this
painful subject he gave free vent to his feelings in a
letter dated the 13th of January, 1863, and, as the
following lines will show, did not confine himself to
a simple expression of feeling :—

" . . . . What will you think of my having turned
protector of monks and nuns ?   Yet such is the fact.
I have been so disgusted with the harsh proceedings of
the President of the Commission appointed to take
possession of the property of religious corporations
that I could not help doing my best to get the fellow
removed from his office ; and I am glad to say he has
been recalled to Turin by telegraph, and another
person appointed, of whom everybody speaks well.
The illegalities which are committed are innumer-
able. . . ."

Similar sentiments are expressed in another letter to Mr. Gladstone, from which the following is an extract :

"Naples, January 18, 1863.

" . . . . So soon as I arrived here I found that the person who was at the head of the Commission for the suppression of convents, monasteries, &c., behaved with unjustifiable harshness and rudeness : the dissatisfaction and discontent his conduct caused cannot be exaggerated.   I backed the representations made to the Ministers to put an end to this abuse of authority, and the fellow was recalled by telegraph."

These honourable protests against oppression, and possibly others more openly made in language equally forcible, caused an abundance of silly surmises and talk of the conversion of Panizzi, and of his having become an adherent of the Pope and of the Bourbons, &c., &c.

Utterly unworthy as were these of being repeated, we should leave the subject unmentioned, did it not afford the opportunity of introducing a letter, dated Turin, the 2nd of April, 1863, too important to be omitted, from that distinguished diplomatist and most amiable of men, Sir James Hudson:—

"This is the first quiet moment I have had since I received yours of the 25th.

"How can you seriously pay attention to the chatterboxes of Naples, who had written here that you had gone over to the enemy? But, my dear friend, you don't suppose that in Upper Italy anybody would believe such ridiculous gossip !

R2

"I knew very well that you would have come here at once had I asked you to do so. But the necessity, the strait we were in, was not sufficiently great to require that sacrifice. I will tell you what it is when we meet.

"And now about meeting. I still say, 'Don't put yourself out,' don't come to Genoa merely to see Giacomino. If you come to Genoa, you *must* come here. It's all very well to say, 'I don't want to see anybody but you.' Well, that's like *you;* but it won't do. *You* cannot come so near Turin, and not come to Turin. You occupy too large a space in the Italian and European eye. Many people want to see you, especially Minghetti and Amari, and doubtless Peruzzi.

"The journey is nothing now over the Mont Cenis. If you say positively you won't, why I can't help it; but I repeat, don't come to Genoa if you won't come to Turin. But if you do come to Genoa I will meet you there. We shall meet in July at all events, for I am quite serious in declaring my intention of residing with you at the British Museum, and am very grateful for the kind reception you have given to my proposition.

"I have read your letter *three times,* which is what I never did for a Foreign Office instruction.

"I have not a word of news to send you.

"God bless you!

"GIACOMINO."

On the 1st of May, 1863, Panizzi returned to his duties at the Museum; and with melancholy reflections we must here record that his life of action had practically reached its limits; not, however, that the patriot's zeal had in any way decayed, nor had the politician's interest in public affairs relaxed one iota.

To this point we have endeavoured briefly to follow up the fortunes of Italy from the year 1820. How much energy had been expended, how many lives of her truest sons had been devoted to the achievement of her liberty and union, and how far England had lent her powerful aid towards the accomplishment of the dearest wishes of patriotic Italians, it is beyond our province to discuss, and we leave such questions to be answered in the sterner pages of history.

Though natural decay crept on Panizzi, and though he felt his powers decreasing, he still continued his activity of body and mind, not resigning himself, as many men would have done, to indolence and absolute rest, but still taking an interest in all that was occurring around him, proffering aid and counsel where it was required or willingly received, and turning a stern countenance to everything approaching injustice.

Returning to his official duties in England, he cheerfully resigned the beauties of his native Italy, although to him they must have had an especial charm, and doubtless he coincided with the patriotic Neapolitan who exclaimed :—

"Vedi Napoli e poi muori!"

Yet not in this balmy air, nor within the influences of that sea whose azure tint delights the eye did he linger; duty called him thence, and at the post of duty was Panizzi ever to be found.

CHAPTER XXVI.

DEATH OF MR. ELLICE—GARIBALDI IN LONDON—
MASSIMO D'AZEGLIO—FOSCOLO'S REMAINS RE-
MOVED TO FLORENCE — PANIZZI'S DESIRE TO
RETIRE—CORRESPONDENCE—DEATH OF LORD PAL-
MERSTON — SUPERANNUATION ALLOWANCE — POR-
TRAIT—MUSEUM STAFF—PRIVATE RESIDENCE.

DURING the year 1863 Panizzi repeated his visit to
Biarritz, and his Italian friends urged him to see the
Emperor Napoleon, and to cultivate, so far as possible, that potentate's friendship. With reference to
their persuasive arguments, he thus wrote to Mr.
Ellice:—"I am urged by Lacaita and Pasolini to go,
who think I may do some good, *which I do not hope
in the least.*" However, he went ; but, on October
15th, 1863, addressed Mrs. Haywood in these
terms :—"I have been abroad on a visit to the Emperor and the Empress of the French, with whom I
spent four weeks. I might have remained a little
longer, but on receiving the news of the death of
Mr. Ellice,* the greatest friend I had lost since I
lost one ** still more dear to me, and to whom I owed
more, I hasten back to England. . . . My rheumatic
pains have become more violent, and curiously, or
rather unfortunately enough, my right wrist is more

---

* 17th of September, 1863.
** Mr. Haywood, 31st of May, 1858.

affected than my other joints, which renders my
writing always difficult and painful—at times impossible. As you may conceive, as writing is what I
must do, this distresses me greatly. At night, too, I
suffer particularly, and am kept from sleeping, so
that in the daytime I cannot work as energetically as
I used to do, and as is required of one who fills my
place. I have often thought of resigning, but the
Trustees won't hear of it, and flatter me by saying I
am absolutely necessary to the Museum, which I do
not think!"

In fact Panizzi, with all his conscientious care of
himself, that he might still be fit for office, had never
succeeded in rooting out the seeds of that illness
from which he suffered so much in 1862. The same
exhausting sleeplessness at night wore him out, and
every symptom of disease seemed aggravated. How
acute were his sufferings the biographer well remembers, and how, notwithstanding all, he never relaxed
the undeviating regularity of his attendance to official
duties.

His health was in the very
worst state when he received
from General Garibaldi a letter
—very brief—announcing an
intention of visiting London.
This news, which, under other
circumstances, might have been
a source of unalloyed gratification, was not altogether welcome, as it foreboded extra work
in Panizzi's then condition, and

he well knew that on him would devolve much extra
care and supervision on behalf of the great patriot.
The entry of this illustrious hero into the metropolis,
the manner of his reception by the people, and the
acclamations with which so popular a stranger was
greeted, will not have faded from the recollection of
the majority of our readers. On the 15th of April,
1864, Garibaldi dined with Panizzi. The guests entertained at the banquet were the Duke of Sutherland, the Earl of Shaftesbury, Lord Wodehouse, Lord
Frederick Cavendish, Mr. Gladstone, Lord Granville,
Sir John, now Lord Acton, and the present writer.
At the end of dinner the General addressed his host,
expressing a strong and sincere desire to visit the
tomb of Ugo Foscolo, whose friendship for the subject of the memoir has been mentioned in a former
chapter, and who was buried, it will be remembered,
at Chiswick.

In accordance with this wish, at the early hour of
five o'clock on the morning of the 20th of April, Panizzi
and the present writer started from the Museum to
call on the General. They found him in bed, half
asleep; but, in compliance with their summons, he
arose, and in somewhat less than ten minutes came
downstairs, having thus promptly prepared himself,
as became a soldier.

A brougham was ready to convey the three to their
destination at Chiswick; and it was on this occasion
that, for the first time, was suggested the advisability
of Garibaldi's departure from London. Arrived at
Foscolo's tomb, the General requested his friend to
address the crowd which their appearance had col-

lected from all sides; the latter did not, however, hesitate to declare frankly that such a course would be contrary to the customs of this country. Not far from these two distinguished personages stood, towering above those surrounding him, a brewer's man, of gigantic proportions, who delivered himself in the following words:—*Gentlemen, the man who is buried there has done with the pen what Garibaldi has accomplished with the sword!* Nothing in the way of a speech could have been more appropriate, and so thought all present.

Panizzi had written to Massimo d'Azeglio on the subject of Garibaldi's visit to London and his reception there. Azeglio's most interesting reply will be found at page 478 of the *Lettere ad Antonio Panizzi*, &c., *Firenze*, 1880, and will repay perusal. It is dated the 25th of July, 1864, and occupies six pages, but space will only allow us to give some extracts in a free translation :—

" I have always admired Garibaldi. When he was beaten at Cesenatico I treated for peace with Austria, and endeavoured to save him. Then I got him a pension which he accepted for his mother and refused for himself. I think with you that he is one of the choicest natures created by the Almighty—a lover of his country, enterprising, substantially humane and generous, averse to cupidity, and he has rendered eminent services . . . but, after all, let me add that no deserts, no extent of service, entitle a citizen to set himself above the laws of his country and to violate them. No one is allowed to create *imperium in imperio*, to treat with his sovereign as an equal, to outrage and ignore the constituted authorities, or to assume the permanent decision of peace and war. . . Garibaldi, by instinct shy and mild, has been thrust forward by scamps for their own purposes, and they have intoxicated him with flattery that would have turned the brain of the hardest head, much more his. . . . " You say that we are behindhand in respect for the laws, and that we ought to follow the example of the English. Let us see :—

" After Aspromonte I was a member of the Council of Ministers which was to decide the fate of Garibaldi. I said : *Bring him to trial like any other citizen, and after sentence let him be immediately pardoned by the King.* . . . But it was thought better to grant him amnesty, which he refused, saying that he had only done his duty. . . . Many of the Council were of my opinion, and so were most of the people in the country. . . . Before Aspromonte Garibaldi was elected by acclamation in thirty districts; after Aspromonte by *ballot* in two. The Italians said, we don't want prophets above the laws; one said even, we don't want him to come as a second Redeemer.

"Do you think we are so very much behindhand?

"Let us now turn to the English people. Garibaldi went to them with the harbinger of a fantastic legend such as no one ever had before. I should have thought it natural for him to be received, applauded, exalted, *clubbefied*, and *dinnered* by the whole population, including the Italians in London. But that a man who boasted of superiority to the laws, a man still reeking with the blood of Italian soldiers whom he had slain, should be officially received by the State, by Parliament, by the Ministers, by the heir of the English throne, with honours never accorded to any sovereign . . . and this while he who was receiving them was the declared friend of Mazzini, who, could he have got the chance, would have had all such personages hanged, that this should have happened amongst a people that thinks it has a mission to preserve intact the idea of truth, of justice, and of honour, must be bitterly deplored by every one of sound common sense, and I cannot persuade myself that you think differently."

To this we will append a translation of another letter from the same writer, which will speak for itself.

" Cannero, May 26, 1865.

"Dear Panizzi,

You will understand that' I adopt Galileo's experimental method, not the doctrine of one of the Aristotelians.   . . .

I had heard a worthy person speak of Spiritualism, and I said to myself, *Let us see,* then I will believe.

I have made a series of experiments *at home* with three or four safe people, so as to be sure there should be no charlatanism. Here is the result, which for me is definitively demonstrated.

1st.—The experiments have produced phenomena absolutely inexplicable by the ordinary laws which govern matter.

2nd.—We put ourselves in communication with an intelligence, to the exclusion of any explanation purely material.

3rd.—It is impossible to establish either the personality or the truthfulness of the said intelligence, hence the final result is but of slight importance for any one who is not a Materialist. I am not so and never have been ; so the only benefit that I derived from the experiments was to witness phenomena which before I should have thought impossible.

Those who are Materialists in good earnest ought necessarily to accept Spiritualism.

If you should have the same curiosity as I had, and would like to make experiments, you ought to read the *Doctrine Spirite*, a very common book. It is not right to judge any doctrine until you are acquainted with it, and have tested it.

It was bound to be acceptable to me, because it harmonises with many of my old ideas on the origin of evil, so I found myself at home. I do not say that it absolutely explains the mystery, but it affords a glimpse of a solution much less illogical than that of original sin, much more consistent with divine perfection, and of far greater comfort in the uncertainties to which we are condemned.

* It has often been said that D'Azeglio was a believer in Spiritualism ; this letter is, therefore, of importance as a confession of faith on the subject.

Now you know as much about it as I do. If at any time you should make up your mind to come to my place, we can make experiments to your heart's content.

Take care of yourself and of your friendship for me, and wish me well.

Sincerely yours,

MASSIMO D'AZEGLIO."

In April, 1871, Panizzi received a semi-official letter from General Menabrea, announcing the proposed removal to Florence of Foscolo's remains. We are bound to say that the recipient did not much approve of this step. He was of opinion that in Santa Croce, where are the tombs of Dante, Michael Angelo, Galileo, Macchiavelli, Alfieri, &c., &c., the exiled patriot would be out of place. However, the following inscription will tell the tale of the interment, removal, and final deposition :—

On the East end of tomb :—

UGO FOSCOLO,

DIED SEPTEMBER 10, 1827, AGED 50.

On the South side :—

FROM THE SACRED GUARDIANSHIP OF CHISWICK,

TO THE HONOURS OF SANTA CROCE, IN FLORENCE,

THE GOVERNMENT AND PEOPLE OF ITALY

HAVE TRANSPORTED

THE REMAINS OF THE WEARIED CITIZEN POET,

7TH OF JUNE, 1871.

On the North side :—

THIS SPOT WHERE, FOR 44 YEARS,

THE RELICS OF

UGO FOSCOLO

REPOSED IN HONOURED CUSTODY,

WILL BE FOR EVER HELD IN GRATEFUL REMEMBRANCE

BY THE ITALIAN NATION.

256 LIFE OF SIR ANTHONY PANIZZI.

In speaking of Mazzini, mention has been made how the biographer undertook the delivery of a message which resulted in the departure of Garibaldi.

The reader's forbearance must be solicited for the abruptness with which one subject succeeds another, but at present we are relating a succession of occurrences, not deeply important, yet too interesting and too deeply connected with our narrative to be altogether omitted before entering upon sterner topics. The following note of invitation to Mr. Gladstone is of an amusing character :—

"B. M., January 11th, 1865.

"My dear Sir,

'*Like a good fellow*,' I will certainly dine with you on Tuesday, the 25th instant.

There is an Italian opera buffa, in which a gentleman who wants to become a poet, and takes lessons as to the mechanism of verse from a poet, wishing to ask his master to dine with him, tries to convey his invitation in an hendecasyllable, and begins, *Volete pranzare meco oggi?* (Will you dine with me to-day?) but it would not do, so he changed, *Volete pranzare meco domani?* (Will you dine with me to-morrow?) it would not do either, and the poet suggested at once, *Volete pranzare meco oggi e domani?* (Will you dine with me to-day and to-morrow) a very good line, and so it was settled. Now I have made a line for our dinner here, of which you must approve. *Pranzate meco il ventitre e quattro* (Dine with me the 23rd and 24th.) The poetry is not good ; have patience, and, '*like a good fellow*,' come both days.

Yours ever,

A. PANIZZI."

Such was the natural humour of the man that, as in this instance, he seldom forebore from giving a jocose turn to his subject when opportunity afforded.

The first written intimation of Panizzi's serious wish to resign his high office is to be found in a letter to Mr. Gladstone, dated May 25th, 1865.

"British Museum.

" My dear Sir,

On seeing Lacaita yesterday I learnt from him, as I expected, he had communicated to you my intention of retiring from an office which I cannot any longer fill with advantage to the public or satisfaction to myself. I am sorry that you have learnt this intention of mine from a third party and not from me, but if I have abstained from speaking of it to you myself, it has been from motives of delicacy, and not to seem to presume on the kindness you have uniformly shown to me.

My first impulse, indeed, was to speak to you, and to avow how deeply I should feel to separate myself from an Institution to which I owe so much, and in which I take, and shall ever take, more interest than in anything else in the world; but circumstances have arisen that, I fear, render it impossible it can be otherwise.

I do not mean to resign till after the discussion (whatever be its fate) has taken place in the House of Commons; and I then mean to offer to the Trustees my poor services for a limited time and gratis, if they will condescend to accept them, and should they consider them of any use till my successor has got in harness, or any other arrangement is come to which may be considered best for the Museum. I told this to Lacaita yesterday, and you may have already heard it from him.

Yours ever,

A. PANIZZI."

This letter shows how deeply the thought of separation from his beloved Institution, on which he had centered all his energies and aspirations, affected him, and how cogent must have been the reasons which impelled him to meditate such a step.

Mr. Gladstone's reply was most complimentary, but showed little inclination to fall in with the contemplated scheme; it consisted of original Italian verses, and admirable Italian too, a fine specimen of the abilities of the great statesman in a language not his own.

On the 24th of June, 1865, however, Panizzi informed the Committee of the Trustees that, in justice to the Museum, as well as to himself, the state of his health compelled him, much against his will, to tender to Her Majesty the resignation of his appointment as Principal Librarian. The Report in which he made this communication ran as follows:—

"Mr. Panizzi respectfully represents that he is reluctantly compelled, humbly to beg of the Queen to accept his resignation of the place of Principal Librarian, to which Her Majesty was graciously pleased to appoint him. Mr. Panizzi regrets being obliged, after long hesitation, to take this step; but he finds that neither in justice to this great Institution nor to himself, he ought to continue to hold a place, the duties of which, to be efficiently performed, require a vigour, not only of mind but of body, which Mr. Panizzi is conscious that he no longer possesses.

"Mr. Panizzi hopes that the Trustees will add to the many acts of kindness with which they have been pleased to honour him, that of submitting to Her Majesty's Treasury the accompanying statement of Mr. Panizzi's services, and of recommending their Lordships to award him such a superannuation allowance as they may consider just, under the circumstances, in conformity with the Superannuation Act, 1859, sections 2 and 9, with the Treasury letter of the 7th of June, 1860, and with the Treasury Minute of the 24th of August of the same year.

"Should the Trustees do Mr. Panizzi the honour of considering that, on his resignation being accepted by Her Majesty, his knowledge of Museum affairs might be of use to the Trustees for a limited period, to be fixed by themselves, Mr. Panizzi will feel proud if his humble gratuitous services be accepted, until his successor can enter on his duties and become familiar with them.

" As a mark of respect to the Trustees, Mr. Panizzi begs to submit to them his letter of resignation, previously to transmitting it to the Secretary of State to be laid before Her Majesty."

In consequence of this the subjoined resolutions were passed:—

"Saturday, June 24th, 1865.
" Resolved :—

" 1.—The Trustees having heard that Mr. Panizzi proposes to resign his office of Principal Librarian, desire to record their deep sense of the ability, zeal, and unwearied assiduity with which he has discharged the many arduous and responsible duties which from time to time have been committed to him."

" 2.—That, in the opinion of the Trustees, the resignation of Mr. Panizzi, at a period when great changes are contemplated in the administration of the British Museum, is to be peculiarly regretted." *

" 3.—The Trustees desire to state that the special services of Mr. Panizzi, over and above his ordinary

---

* This resolution was added on the special suggestion of Mr. Disraeli.

S

duties, have been of such a nature as to entitle him to a special reward under the provisions of the 9th Section of the Superannuation Act, 1859. They would therefore urge that Mr. Panizzi possesses a just claim to a retiring allowance equal to the full amount of his salary and emoluments."

" 4.—That the Chairman of this meeting is requested to transmit the foregoing resolutions, together with Mr. Panizzi's report and its accompanying enclosure, to the Lords Commissioners of Her Majesty's Treasury."

The Trustees present on the occasion were :—The Speaker, in the Chair, the Duke of Somerset, Lord Eversley, Lord Taunton, The Right Hon. S. H. Walpole, The Right Hon. B. Disraeli, The Right Hon. R. Lowe, Sir P. de M. Grey Egerton, Bart., Sir R. I. Murchison, Dr. Milman, Major-General Sabine, C. Towneley, Esq., and G. Grote, Esq.

On the 7th of July following, Sir George Grey wrote in answer :—

" . . . . It is with sincere regret that I have learnt that you no longer feel yourself fully equal to the duties of an office which you have so long filled in a manner entirely satisfactory to the Trustees, and eminently conducive to the interests of the Museum."

He then refers to the resolutions of the Trustees, and continues :—

" Under these circumstances it would afford H.M.'s Government much satisfaction if, without risk of injury to your health, you could continue your valuable services to the Museum, at least until early in the next year. I shall be obliged by your informing me

whether you can concur in this arrangement, before
I lay the tender of your resignation before Her
Majesty."

The amount of the retiring allowance was £1,400
per annum, a goodly solace for old age and infirmities,
yet none too much for the unremitting zeal Panizzi
had evinced in the exercise of his important duties.

On the 8th of July he reported to the Trustees his
willingness to place himself entirely in their hands,
and to continue, should they desire it, his services for
a while, an offer of which the Standing Committee
gladly availed themselves, expressing a hope that he
would continue his valuable exertions until the following year.

Let us, however, leave the Museum, for a few
minutes whilst we draw attention to that which, at
the time, assumed the proportions of a national
calamity.

On the 18th of October, 1865, Lord Palmerston
departed this life. How severe a blow this was to
Panizzi may be judged from our frequent allusions to
the veneration in which he held the distinguished
statesman; and that Mr. Gladstone thoroughly
understood, and entered into his feelings, the letter
now quoted will show :—

"Clumber,
October 18, 1865.

"My dear Panizzi,

*Ei fu !** Death has indeed laid low the most
towering antlers in all the forest. No man in England will
more sincerely mourn Lord Palmerston than you. Your warm

---

* Manzoni thus begins his famous "Cinque Maggio," or his Ode on the
Death of Napoleon, which has been translated by Mr. Gladstone.

s2

heart, your long and close friendship with him, and your senso of all he had said and done for Italy, all so bound you to him that you will deeply feel this loss. As for myself, I am stunned. It was plain that this would come; but sufficient unto the day is the evil thereof, and there is no surplus stock of energy in the mind to face, far less to anticipate, fresh contingencies. But I need not speak of this great event. To-morrow all England will be ringing of it, and the world will echo England. I cannot forecast the changes which will follow; but it is easy to see what the first step should be.

I cannot write on any other subject.

Yours ever, and most warmly,

W. E. GLADSTONE."

Another year was entered upon, and the Principal Librarian yearned for rest. On the 5th of June, 1866, he addressed a letter to Sir George Grey, earnestly requesting that he might be released from his official duties, and on the 18th of the same month received an answer from the Treasury informing him that immediate steps would be taken to appoint a successor. Eight days afterwards, on the 26th of June, Mr. John Winter Jones was selected as the new Principal Librarian. On finally relinquishing his post, Panizzi addressed the following circular letter to the heads of Departments :—

" British Museum, July 16th, 1866.

" I cannot leave the Museum, and close my official connexion with those with whom I have had the honour and pleasure of serving the Trustees for so many years, without returning to all and each of them individually my warmest thanks for the efficient help which I have received from them in the discharge of my duties. Although conscious of having at all times acted to the best of my ability, and only for the advantage of the Museum and of those connected with it, I wish to add that, if I have ever given unnecessary pain to any one, I regret it most sincerely, and trust that credit will be given to me for having been uniformly influenced solely by a sense of duty.

" Allow me to request that you will bring this communication to the individual knowledge of every person in your Department. I shall always take the warmest interest in their future happiness, and shall never cease to feel the sincerest regard for them."

Numerous and hearty were the responses, and it must have been highly gratifying to their recipient to know that his endeavours had gained the approval of all, and that, now that the battle was over, so far as he was concerned, he could rest satisfied with his own share in the struggle which had ended so triumphantly for himself. It will be unnecessary to quote more than one of the replies, that from his successor :—

" British Museum, July 18th, 1866.

"I have communicated to all persons in this Department the kind and generous letter you have been so good as to address to me on the subject of your retirement from the post of Principal Librarian. On this event there is but one feeling throughout the Department—that of deep regret that we are about to lose one who has the strongest claims upon us all, not only for acts of personal kindness, but for substantial benefits.

" It is no secret throughout the House that whatever improvement has taken place in the condition of

those employed in it has originated with yourself and
been won by your exertions. They are indebted to
you for increased pay and extended vacations. They
are indebted to you for the abolition of the system of
payment by the day, which was injurious to the service
and painful to the feelings of the gentlemen employed.
Your exertions procured for the Library those increased
grants which have rendered possible its vast growth
and the high position it at present occupies. In short,
we feel, and are proud to feel, that all the important
improvements in the Institution had their origin in
this Department while you were its Chief Officer, and
that the very great development of the Museum
generally commenced at the period when you became
Principal Librarian.

" For myself, I shall always feel most grateful for
the unvarying kindness with which you have treated
me during the long period of nearly thirty years that
I have acted more or less immediately under your
superintendence. Your advice, support, and encouragement have never been wanting to me in all cases of
difficulty ; and if the present state of the Library deserves commendation, it is to you that the praise is
mainly due.

" While speaking thus in my own name, I am in
fact speaking in the name of all, and only expressing
the sentiments which have been conveyed to me by
those in the Department. Although officially separ-
ated from us, your name must always be inseparably
connected with this great Institution ; and be assured,
my dear sir, that you carry with you into your retirement not only the best wishes, but the warm and
affectionate feelings of us all."

Shortly after he left his post a subscription was set on foot throughout the Museum to present him with a fitting testimonial; this ultimately took the form of a portrait painted by Mr. George Frederick Watts, R.A. It is now hung in, and forms one of the chief ornaments of the Trustees' Committee-Room. As a likeness it is perfect, by far the most successful example of the kind; as a picture it is one of the finest works of the painter, the modern Tintoretto. Produced in a low and yet powerful key of colour, the whole work exhibits a potent combination of ruddy-brown carnations, with black broken into deep greys—tints which are admirably harmonized with each other, and so happily toned as to produce just and broad chiaro-oscuro. The figure is life-size, three-quarters length, seated in three-quarters view to our right, and easily, as well as sedately, posed in a large chair; the head is slightly bent forward, and the eyes, although directed *towards* the spectator, are not directed *at* him; they have an expression of habitual thoughtfulness which is very striking when its influence is felt by the observer, and this is not the less effective because it is undemonstrative. Owing to the position of the eyes themselves, no reflections of the light appear on their surfaces, which by no means common circumstance adds to the gravity, and even to the dignity of the picture, and is perfectly faithful to nature. It increases the repose of the work, and excludes that which is often a disturbing element in designs of equal simplicity and breadth of motive. The steadfast expression of the features, and the restful attitudes of the body and hands, are valuable elements of this very important and impressive master-piece of painting.

We have given an exact and faithful account of the causes which led to Panizzi's resignation of the office which he had held with honour for so many years, of the manner in which it was carried out, and of the testimonials which it evoked. We have now merely to mention that in the House of Lords a scene was enacted similar to that which took place in the House of Commons on the 21st of April, 1856. Whoever is anxious and willing to enter more fully into that controversy, unpleasant as it was, need only examine Hansard's Parliamentary Debates, House of Lords, Monday, February the 12th, 1866.

Let us give Panizzi's own words to prove whether or not he was pleased and satisfied with the treatment he received at the hands of the Trustees. He thus wrote to Mrs. Haywood, on the 15th of July, 1866:—

"The Trustees have behaved most handsomely, and so has the Government, both in words and deeds. First of all ample justice, and perhaps some may say more than justice, was rendered to my long and many services. I shall certainly remain in London, the pension I am to get being ample for my wants ; and now, my dear Mrs. Haywood, let me add a few words from my heart. The first feeling, when my future was settled, was one of deep grief, that the friend who would have so heartily rejoiced at the close of my honourable career, who cheered me when lonely and unknown, who thought of my welfare as much as he did of his own, that he was no longer here. This feeling overwhelmed me for a moment, and even now I can hardly master it."

It was a common remark of Panizzi's that during his long official career he had never, with very few exceptions, (and even then he felt he had acted for the best) shown favour to any one employed in the British Museum who had not afterwards become an honour to the Institution, and of this we have ample documentary evidence, dating so far back as the year 1837.

In the month of June, 1855, requiring the services of a Hebrew scholar, he applied to the firm of Asher, of Berlin, to recommend such a gentleman. Accordingly *a certain young man of 23, and a Jew, endowed with natural ability, who understood Latin, Greek, and French, of strict moral integrity, and of faultless character, and thoroughly respectable*, was introduced to the Keeper of the Printed Books; this was Emanuel Deutsch, afterwards well-known as the writer of several letters to *The Times* respecting the discovery and reading of the Moabite Stone, and the article in the *Quarterly Review* on the Talmud. This *Assistant* was one whose talents his superior officer did not fail to recognise. Unfortunately death claimed him at an early age on the 14th of May, 1873.

It is a somewhat delicate subject to touch upon, but, as we are discussing these matters, we feel bound to mention by name others who were, in a manner of speaking, Panizzi's children; and let us hope we are not exaggerating or exceeding our proper limits by remarking that they looked up to him as their protector and adviser. For example, Mr. E. Maunde Thompson, the present Keeper of MSS., was ever held by him in high estimation, and also, in an equal degree, were Mr. John T. Taylor, Mr. John Cleave, and Mr. Richard Garnett.

The first of these became his intimate friend, and it was also through his intervention that Mr. Taylor gave such valuable literary aid to the late Princess Mary Liechtenstein, in the compilation of the interesting volumes entitled "Holland House." Mr. Cleave, then, as now, the Accountant of the Museum, had, as we know, many lengthy discussions with Panizzi on financial matters, and, indeed, the opinions of the latter on these points were always regarded as decisive. Greatly esteemed also was Mr. Garnett, whose appointment as Superintendent of the Reading-Room rejoiced the ex-Librarian extremely. Nor, although he has left the Museum, should the name of Mr. W. R. S. Ralston remain unmentioned.

Many more names might be enumerated ; one, however, we will not omit— that of the clever mechanician and metal-worker, Mr. Sparrow, who, by his ingenuity, contrived or carried out many appliances for the comfort of the aged Librarian. All were labouring in unison as Panizzi's barque was nearing the harbour, after its eventful voyage ; and truly reciprocal were the feelings of friendship and respect which had grown up between Panizzi and his fellow-workers—friendship in full stream, flowing from the purest sources.

In this manner, applauded on all sides, beloved and respected, did the Principal Librarian retire from the position he had gained step by step by hard and uninterrupted labour. Still the memory of the past clung to him—still he would have devoted, had it

been possible, his waning physical and mental strength
to the internal and external workings of that Institution upon which he had so persistently set his heart.
His own words bear witness to the affection he
retained for the vicinity of his past efforts :—" I have
got," wrote he, " a house. It is in a very unfashion-
able quarter, though very respectable, near here, being
31, Bloomsbury Square." So it was that he still
desired to linger with his memories and experiences
within sight of the building which had cost him so
much in brain and body, and those who read these
pages may easily conceive how far his thoughts were
interwoven with his expressions.

We have endeavoured faithfully to detail the circumstances of this eventful life, until the time arrived
when, succumbing to the stern dictates of nature,
Panizzi was compelled to retire behind those scenes
which his presence had so long graced.

When the actor or the author departs from the
boards where his production or his acting has
delighted audiences, how acute is the grief of parting
with his admirers ! Who does not remember the
almost ominous words of the late Charles Dickens,
when, at the last of his readings, he made use of the
remarkable expression, *From these garish lights I
vanish now for evermore, with a heartfelt, grateful,
respectful, and affectionate farewell?* These words—
though, of course, not exactly applicable to the present
case—may be strained so far as to indicate the deep
feeling with which a different, but not less successful, contributor to public requirements was
severing himself from labours which had been

to him pre-eminently a "labour of love," and may justly be cited as implying the same affectionate remembrance of his fellow-workers and those who appreciated his undoubtedly great abilities. In addition to a faithful recital of facts and an unprejudiced view of the career of the chosen subject of any memoir, a biographer owes somewhat more to his readers. No life is worth recounting unless it affords an example worth following, or unless it is acknowledged at the first to have been set forth for some other specific purpose, either as mere matter for history, or as the life of one whose errors were so great that it is thought advisable to reproduce them as a warning to future would-be evil-doers.

Nothing appertains to the present biography but an intent to put before the world a man who, under the most adverse circumstances and with the most beneficial intentions, by sheer perseverance and by unflinching energy, attained the object of his heart's desire—a desire that has redounded to his lasting praise.

No words of our own shall be used. Let those of Dean Milman be quoted as our justification for what has been already said of the subject of our memoir. On the 5th of February, 1866, writing from the " Deanery of St. Paul's," he used these words :—" As to his (Panizzi's) public services, his long and most careful connection with the British Museum cannot be more fully or justly appreciated than by yourself" (this letter was addressed to Sir R. I. Murchison), " and I am sure that we should entirely agree on this subject. Above all, the great national gift of the Reading-Room, the envy and admiration of Europe, is, as you well know, almost his entire creation, from the original design to the most minute detail—from the dome to the inkstands and bookshelves."

Those who knew Dean Milman will acknowledge the worth of a testimonial thus given by such a man to the value of Panizzi's labours.

Yet it is not here that we must stop short; an unbiassed account has been rendered of his difficulties at the outset of his career, never resting he persevered in his onward journey where ordinary men would have resigned the effort. His own national misfortunes were enough to occupy his time and thoughts; yet he found opportunities to attend to all business that pressed upon his attention.

These are the facts and uncontrovertible facts; and the details upon which we have fully entered must excite admiration for the man who could thus concentrate his mind upon duties of the most onerous description, and yet, when occasion required, be found able and willing to befriend a cause which was unquestionably as dear to his heart as any other— viz., the liberty, freedom, and happiness of his own beloved Italy.

No undue exaltation of Panizzi is intended on the part of the biographer; wherever such may seem to be attributed, it is from no personal panegyric of his own.

Numerous letters might be adduced corroborative of the estimation in which the deceased was held— letters whose signature place their contents beyond suspicion; but they are withheld lest a charge of adulation should be laid at the author's door, that charge he has studiously endeavoured to avoid.

At this important point in the narrative it has been thought nothing but reasonable to pause, before entering upon topics connected with the last years of this eminent man.

CHAPTER XXVII.

PROSPER MERIMEE—EMPRESS EUGENIE—PRINCE IMPERIAL.

IT would appear to be taking a liberty with the reader—or, indeed, what is far worse, to savour somewhat of bookmaking—to engraft a biography on a biography. At a former period of our work we promised to give some account of the relations subsisting

between Panizzi and Prosper Mérimée, the well-known writer and statesman, which account would be incomplete were we to omit some special mention of Mérimée himself. By way of justification, it may be asserted that such a personage as Mérimée deserves, not only for his connection with Panizzi, but for his own intrinsic merit, a place in the memoir of our proper subject. Happily it has been our pleasing task of late to edit the whole of the letters which, during the long friendship of the two, passed between Mérimée and Panizzi; and as nothing affords a better insight into the true character of a man than his familiar epistles to his friends, we shall make so bold as to use these letters as freely as

may appear desirable in this short notice of the writer
of them. It is much to be regretted that Panizzi's
letters to Mérimée have all been destroyed, with the
exception of the very few already quoted, copies of
which have been found amongst his papers. In the
time of the unhappy Commune, on the 23rd of May,
1871, amongst other and more important buildings,
Mérimée's house was burnt down, and with it much
which would have been most valuable for our present
purpose. *What has distressed me most,* wrote a friend
to Panizzi on this calamity, *was to see the place where
poor Mérimée's house had been!   It is a total wreck!
All his furniture, his fine library, his manuscripts, his
letters, and the thousand souvenirs of a long and intellectual lifetime all reduced to ashes.* In conversation
one day, Mons. Du Sommerard, of the Hotel Cluny,
whose name is frequently mentioned in Mérimée's
letters, informed the present writer how he went to
the spot shortly after the fire, in the hope of saving a
few little things as souvenirs. But, alas! nothing
was left as a relic of Prosper Mérimée except an old
pipe.

Happy indeed had he only succeeded in rescuing a
picture of Mérimée at five years old, painted by his
mother, and another by Alexander Colin, painted
about 1865.

The biographer knew the house well, Number 52,
Rue de Lille (Paris), and remembers the room hung
round with pictures of the Spanish School and English
line-engravings. In September, 1869, he stayed with
Mérimée. May his vanity in inserting the following
record of that visit be pardoned by the reader!

" Paris, 15th September, 1869.

" Mon cher Sir Anthony, *alias* Pan,

" J'ai eu la visite de Fagan, qui a diné avec moi Dimanche. Il m'a paru grandi et développé de toutes les manières, toujours très bon garçon, conservant malgré toutes les nationalités par où il a passé l'air de *l'English boy.*"

At what time and in what manner the acquaintance between Panizzi and Mérimée began, we are unable to determine. It would be passing strange, considering the position of the two men and their frequent opportunities of meeting, the similarity of their tastes and opinions, and the numerous attractions which the character of each must have had for the other, if such acquaintance had never been formed, and stranger still if it had failed to ripen into that intimate and lasting friendship which afterwards subsisted between them. Panizzi's affection for his friend was intense, and he used often to say (though we do not allege this as any proof of the intensity of his friendship) that he was the best Frenchman for whom he had ever formed a liking. Mérimée, who was a master of the English language, an accomplishment which in his country ought to be less remarkable than it is, was in the habit of spending a month or so yearly in London. On these visits he always stayed at Panizzi's house. As regards his external characteristics, he was tall of stature, upright in figure, and his eyes shone with remarkable brilliancy; in manner the most pleasing of men. One of his minor peculiarities was an extreme nicety in the matter of dress, which, though not an unfailing sign of genius and culture, may

T

be put down to the credit of his good taste. And,
indeed, what more can be said in laudation of a
finished gentleman's taste than that he had all his
clothes made in London, and not only in London, but
at Poole's, of which great artist Mérimée was the
constant patron. This fastidiousness of his was the
cause of much facetiousness on the part of Panizzi,
to which, however, the other seems to have been not
altogether without means and opportunity of retort,
that is to say, if we rightly construe the following
passage in one of his letters containing a reflection
on an article of Panizzi's ordinary costume, Mérimée
in asking some information as to a picture of Lord
Spencer's, says :—

" Cannes, 5, Décembre 1857.

" 1°· Dans le tableau que possède Lord Spencer,
Julie d'Angennes, Duchesse de Montausier, est-elle en
buste ou jusqu'à la ceinture ?

" 2°· Est-elle maigre, ou a-t-elle de l'embonpoint?

" 3°· A-t-elle les cheveux noirs ou blonds, les yeux
noirs ou bleus ?

" 4°· Peut-on discerner si elle a une belle taille et
si elle est grande ?

" Si vous pouvez obtenir ce signalement avec l'exactitude d'un gendarme Autrichien (dont vous avez la
robe de chambre), vous m'obligerez infiniment de me
l'envoyer ici où je pense que M. Cousin ne tardera pas
à venir."

But in this friendly contest, if contest it may be
called, Mérimée had to deal with a less exquisitely
polished wit than his own, a wit which occasionally
when Panizzi was, or pretended to be, more than

ordinarily annoyed by his friend's extreme attention to his attire, was developed in practical joking. One of Panizzi's especial dislikes, and for this he had sound patriotic grounds of justification, was a peculiar cap, much of the kind worn by officers of the Austrian army, which Mérimée persisted in wearing both in the house and in the garden, known as the *Principal Librarian's.* This was so peculiarly an object of annoyance to the *Principal Librarian* that he once went so far as to purloin the cap and lock it up, adding to the peculation the sin of denying to its owner that he knew anything whatever about it. Nor, though the treachery was discovered, is it on record that the rightful owner ever recovered possession of his property. He had his revenge, however. That the ghost of the victim should haunt the criminal, Mérimée made a drawing of the cap, which he placed every morning at breakfast, and every evening at dinner, in Panizzi's napkin. The kind of footing on which Mérimée was at the British Museum may be gathered from the following self-invitation to Panizzi's:—

" Paris, 14 Avril, 1858.

" Vous recevrez de toute façon un mot de moi, qui vous marquera précisément le jour de mon entrée dans la ville de Londres. D'autre part, il se trouve que ma cousine est un peu malade, en sorte que son mari reste à Paris.

J'irai donc, si vous voulez le permettre, droit au British Museum à mon arrivée.—Cependant il faut que nous fassions nos conditions.— La première, c'est que vous ne vous dérangerez absolument en rien pour moi ; que vous irez dîner en ville et passer vos soirées

T2

comme vous en avez l'habitude, sans vous inquiéter en rien de ce que deviendra votre serviteur, qui est assez pratique de Londres pour n'y pas mourir de faim ni même d'ennui."

At the Museum Mérimée was well known and a great favourite with the whole staff.   In this he took just pride:—

"Londres, Mardi, 7 Août, 1860.

"Je reviens du British Museum qui m'a paru tout sombre depuis votre absence.   M. Bond m'a montré un très beau manuscript qu'on vient d'acheter pour soixante livres sterling.   Les *messengers* et les *attendants* m'ont reconnu et ont été aussi aimables pour moi qu'à l'ordinaire."

Prosper Mérimée was born at Paris on the 28th of September, 1803.   His father, Jean François Léonore, was a painter of some eminence.   Prosper was educated at the Collège Charlemagne, whence he passed the course of *Ecole de Droit*, and in after years as is well-known took an honourable position in political life.   It is not, however, our office here to enter on a history of Mérimée's career, which, as well as his published works, has been too long before the world to demand particular notice at our hands.   Seeing that we have been simply the mechanical means of introducing to the public his letters to Panizzi, we hold it to be no transgression of the limits of modesty most heartily to commend these as among the best specimens of the art of letter writing that can well be found in any language.   Upon them we shall principally rely for our information about Mérimée; nor, indeed, seeing that we have treated of him mainly in

his character of Panizzi's friend, should we think ourselves justified in travelling very far beyond their contents. Unstudied and unartificial, unrevised after
being written, as is plain from the careless repetition
that abounds in them, and written with no purpose of
meeting any eye but their recipient's, they present a
clearer reflection of the writer's mind than could be
obtained from more elaborate compositions.

Moreover, the multitude of interesting subjects
treated in them gives them a value for general history
as well as an insight into the disposition and actions
of their author.

In politics, Mérimée was of the school commonly
known as Liberal-Conservative. He seems to have
been singularly free from the gregarious instinct of
his race and countrymen, who, to genuine liberty, are
apt to prefer enforced equality, which, from the insupportable tyranny of the mob, leads, in nine cases
out of ten, to the Despotism of the Dictator. Of the
great political principle of vesting the Sovereign power
in that quarter where the greatest number of noses
are to be counted, he had the most genuine horror, as
also of the instrument towards that end, universal
suffrage, to which he expressed fears lest the reforms at
that time projected in England should cause the nation
to drift. It is natural that he should couple the expression of his fears with the praise of one, the moderation of whose opinions on this point he must heartily
have approved :—

"Cannes, 10 Mars, 1867.
"En ce qui concerne la réforme, il me semble
toujours que le beau rôle est à notre ami M. Lowe.

Lui seul est dans le vrai et a le courage de son opinion. Ménager la chèvre et le chou est chose bien difficile, et je ne crois pas possible de faire une réforme définitive. Autant vaut prétendre s'arrêter au milieu d'une glissade que de fixer les conditions du droit électoral pour toujours ou même pour longtemps. Si on détruit ce qui existe, on ne retardera guère le suffrage universel."

Happily we have not arrived as yet quite so far as that, although could Mérimée now see us, he might possibly be disturbed at finding that his forebodings of evil were not wholly without foundation, and that he was justified in predicting that tendency on our part towards the American system of politics which he so much disliked. Altogether he views England and its institutions from a strong Conservative standpoint, which position, however, enables him to be a good deal more complimentary to us than to his own countrymen :—

"Cannes, 2 Avril, 1866.

"Tout le monde devient-il fou? .C'est ce que je me demande souvent en lisant les journaux. Je ne parle pas seulement des Allemands dont c'est l'état habituel, mais des gens que je suis habitué à considérer comme possesseurs de la plus haute dose de raison qui ait été accordée à la nature humaine. Cette affaire du 'Reform Bill' chez vous me semble de plus en plus incompréhensible et je suis désolé que Mr. Gladstone y ait mis les mains. Que cela réussisse cette fois ou non, je ne crois pas que le vieux prestige de l'Angleterre survive à cette épreuve. Elle est comme un vieux bâtiment encore très solide, mais

qui menace de s'écrouler dès qu'on y fait des répara-
tions maladroites. Ce qui me frappe surtout, c'est
l'imprévoyance ou plutôt l'insouciance de l'avenir de
la part de vos hommes d'Etat. C'est tout à fait le
'furia francese' qui cherche en tout la satisfaction
du moment. Vous paraissez croire que le ministère
se trouvera en minorité, mais on dit qu'il fera une
dissolution dans l'espoir que les élections faites sous
la pression démocratique lui seront favorables. A en
juger par le ton du *Times* qui semble désespérer, je
serais tenté de croire que, dans ce Parlement même,
la majorité est fort incertaine et que les Ministres
actuels ont d'assez grandes chances de succès. Vous
me parlez de Lord Stanley comme " Premier " probable, et en même temps de M. Lowe comme devant
occuper une place importante dans un nouveau
Cabinet."

The most old-fashioned politicians amongst us,
however they might regret the decadence of old
systems and deplore those changes which time and
necessity have forced upon us, would probably hardly
have the courage to utter such words as these:—

"Dimanche, 13 Mai, 1866.

"Je ne comprends pas grand'chose au second ' Bill'
de réforme. Il me semble seulement que c'est un
grand coup de marteau dans le vieil édifice. Le
résultat sera de diminuer la 'qualité' des membres du
Parlement, laquelle n'est pas déjà si brillante. Je
vois dans les journaux qu'on se félicite de voir ôter
aux fils de grandes maisons, des bourgs qui étaient à
leur dévotion. A mon sens, c'était un des beaux côtés
de l'Angleterre que cette initiation de jeunes aristo-

crates à la vie politique dès leur sortie de l'Université.
C'est ainsi que Fox, Pitt et Lord Palmerston sont
devenus de bonne heure des hommes d'Etat. Vous
aurez en place des industriels et des négociants, c'est-
à-dire des niais et des esprits étroits, excluant systéma-
tiquement toute grandeur de la politique. On fera
ainsi une Angleterre semi-démocratique inférieure à
beaucoup d'égards à la vraie et terrible démocratie des
Etats-Unis."

Some of his compatriots, while admitting the *good
sense* and *experience* shown in the general proposition
contained in the following passage may not be quite
so ready to admit its application to their own particular notions :—

" Cannes, 22 Février, 1866.

" Nous avons nos Fenians cent fois plus dangereux
et plus nombreux qu'ils ne le sont en Irlande. Donnez
à ces gens là les libertés qu'ils réclament et que M.
Thiers dit être nécessaires à tous les peuples, vous aurez
en trois mois une révolution. Le plus grand malheur
qui puisse arriver à un peuple est, je crois, d'avoir
des institutions plus avancées que son intelligence.
Lorsqu'on demande pour la France les institutions des
Anglais, il faudrait pouvoir leur donner d'abord le
bon sens et l'expérience qui les rendent praticables."

It remains a question yet to be decided how far
this people, which imitates English institutions before
it understands them, will be competent to manage a
Republic of their own. His praise of the decision
and energy of our colonial authorities in the celebrated Eyre and Gordon case is not unalloyed with a
dash of sarcasm, but here also there is no reason to

doubt that what he says of his own country is meant in earnest :—

"Cannes, 18 Décembre, 1865.

"J'admire beaucoup l'affaire de la Jamaïque. L'Angleterre trouve toujours des hommes énergiques à la hauteur des plus graves circonstances, et non seulement énergiques, mais assez dévoués pour risquer les plus grandes énormités, si elles sont nécessaires. Il me semble qu'on a pendu beaucoup plus qu'il ne fallait, peut-être même les gens qu'il ne fallait pas ; mais l'insurrection a été arrêtée net, et l'exemple durera, même si l'on désavoue le gouverneur. Voilà la véritable politique, malheureusement impratiquée et peut-être impraticable dans ce pays-ci."

He is not, however, it pains us to record, so lenient a judge of English foreign policy, under Lord Russell and Lord Palmerston, as he is a fervent admirer of the energy of our Colonial Governors, and of the beauties of our constitution in general. Indeed he seems occasionally a little unnecessarily severe, as, for instance, when he says :—

"Paris, 14 Mars, 1865.

"Est-ce la vieillesse qui règne dans le Cabinet Britannique, ou bien est-ce calcul de gens qui ont fait un bon coup à la Bourse et qui ne veulent plus se risquer ? Quoi qu'il en soit, vos Ministres affichent la poltronnerie avec trop d'éclat. Rien n'est plus bête que d'être fanfaron, mais il est dangereux, outre ridicule, de se poser en poltron. C'est le moyen d'avoir tous les faux braves à ses trousses."

And in the following extracts, in reference to Lord Palmerston, he shows himself scarcely so far-sighted as might be expected of him :—

"24 Octobre, 1865.

"Reste à savoir ce que dira la postérité. Pour. moi, je crois qu'elle aura un terrible blâme pour sa conduite dans les affaires d'Amérique ; s'il eût fait avec la France le traité qu'on lui proposait, il aurait sauvé la vie à quelques centaines de mille yankees (ce qui n'est pas très à regretter); mais il aurait encore détourné de l'Europe une abominable influence qui pourra bien un jour devenir une intervention active."

"Paris, 25 Juillet, 1870.

"L'Angleterre a perdu son prestige en Europe. Il y a quelques années elle aurait pu empêcher la guerre. En s'unissant à la France, elle aurait pu diviser à jamais l'Amérique en deux états rivaux ; elle aurait pu prévenir la scandaleuse invasion du Danemark, et aujourd'hui nous serions probablement tranquilles."

On the case of Denmark we refrain from remarking, but the policy recommended towards America might have been hard for that country, and assuredly would have been worse for England, however much some amongst us may have admired the chivalry of the South, and mistrusted the declared motives of those who (there never could have been much doubt at the time) would in the long run have come victorious out of the struggle. Few could seriously suppose that the power of England, even had there been a means of exercising it, would have been of much avail to prevent the ill-feeling which Mérimée admits to have been long smouldering between France and Germany from breaking out into war. After this criticism of our own, it is but fair to record a tribute to Lord Palmerston's worth in another letter :—

"Paris, 24 Octobre, 1865.

"La mort de Lord Palmerston est une belle mort, telle que je la voudrais pour moi et pour mes amis. Il a été l'homme le plus heureux de ce siècle. Il a fait presque toujours tout ce qu'il a voulu, et il a voulu de bonnes et belles choses. Il a eu beaucoup d'amis. Il laisse un grand nom et un souvenir ineffaçable chez ceux qui l'ont connu. Si vous trouvez moyen de me nommer à Lady Palmerston quand vous la verrez, vous m'obligerez. Vous pouvez lui dire qu'ici la presse a été unanime dans ses éloges. On a fait, bien entendu, force *blunders* historiques et autres, à cette occasion, entre autres de dire que Lady Palmerston était morte, etc., etc., mais il n'y a pas eu de méchancetés d'aucune part, et dans tous les partis on a été respectueux ; c'est un hommage bien rare en France, comme vous savez. L'Empereur et l'Impératrice ont montré beaucoup de regret en petit comité ; je crois qu'ils ont écrit à Milady."

De omnibus rebus et quibusdam aliis might be the collective title, and may be truly called the proper text of Mérimée's letters to Panizzi. But it would be as hopeless to attempt to follow the critic *omnium rerum, et quarundam aliarum*, through all the variations of English politics that happened in his time, as to review the numerous works with which he has amused and instructed mankind, or to recount the offices he filled, from his place in the Senate of France and his membership of the "Académie Française" to his office of Commissioner at the London Exhibition of 1862, or the several ways in which he did good service to art and to the State. One subject, then, only shall be 'added on what may be called public politics, viz., an opinion on the Eastern question, which, even if Mérimée's prophecy has not been actually fulfilled according to the very letter, shows, at least, a pretty sound notion of the stability of the Turkish Empire :—

" Paris, 3 Septembre, 1861.

" J'ai eu des nouvelles de Constantinople, où l'on se moque beaucoup des histoires qu'on a faites de la chasteté du Sultan, et de son goût pour l'eau pure. L'un est aussi vrai que l'autre ; mais son grand goût pour le moment, c'est pour les poules. Il vient de commander un poulailler de cinq cent mille francs pour élever ses volailles. Voilà comme il entend l'économie ! Croyez que nous aurons, d'ici à peu de temps, des choses sérieuses en Orient, qui donneront un cruel démenti à Lord Palmerston, lequel veut absolument que l'Empire Turc se tienne debout tant qu'il vivra. Je crois la Porte beaucoup plus près de sa fin que Mylord."

Mérimée was an author before he attained his twenty-second year. He wrote a collection of plays, published under the pseudonym of Clara Gazul, a Spanish authoress, and alleged to be translated by Joseph L'Estrange, an equally fictitious personage. Concerning this book and its originator, we quote the words of a writer of the time :—

" Ceux qui n'étaient pas dans le secret auraient difficilement reconnu un jeune homme à ces caractères dessinés avec tant de précision et de relief, à cette absence de déclamation, à ce style correct, ferme et nerveux, qui ne trahissait nulle part l'hésitation d'un débutant."

One of the best imaginary plays was entitled " Les Espagnols en Danemark," and was a satire directed by Mérimée against the extravagant laudation bestowed by certain people from hatred to the restoration on the régime of the first Napoleon. Whatever Mérimée may have thought of the First, he was on the best of terms with the ruler of the Second Empire. It would perhaps be a little rash as yet to assert positively that the last of the dynasty who had the slightest chance of attaining to future eminence has passed away, but it is a truism that requires no apology that it will be long ere the past fortunes of the house lose their interest for the reader of history, and some of the many anecdotes and other matters related in his letters to Panizzi by Mérimée, who was a constant guest of the Emperor and Empress, wherein he describes the inner life of the family, may be profitably reproduced. Here is an account of an innocent practical joke played on an enthusiastic German lady, which must have afforded some amusement to the perpetrators of it :—

"Paris, 13 Octobre, 1865.

"Madame de L * * * en sa qualité d'Allemande admirait fort M. de Bismark, et nous la tourmentions en la menaçant des hardiesses de ce grand homme qu'elle semblait encourager. Il y a quelques jours j'ai peint et découpé la tête de M. de Bismark très ressemblante, et le soir Leurs Majestés et moi nous sommes entrés dans la chambre de Madame de L *.* *

Nous avons mis la tête sur le lit, un traversin sous les draps pour représenter la bosse formée par un corps humain, puis l'Impératrice a mis sur le front un mouchoir arrangé comme bonnet de nuit. Dans le demi-jour de la chambre, l'illusion était complète. Quand Leurs Majestés se sont retirées, nous avons retenu quelque temps Madame de L * * * pour que l'Empereur et l'Impératrice allassent se poster au bout du corridor, puis chacun a fait mine d'entrer dans sa chambre. Madame de L * * * est entrée dans la sienne, y est restée, puis en est sortie précipitamment et est venue frapper à la porte de Madame de X * * *, en lui disant d'une voix lamentable: "Il y a un homme dans mon lit!" Malheureusement Madame de X * * *. n'a pas gardé son sérieux, et à l'autre bout du corridor, les rires de l'Impératrice ont tout gâté. Le bon est ce que nous avons appris plus tard. Un des valets de pied de l'Empereur était entré dans la chambre de Madame de L * * * et apercevant la tête s'était retiré avec de grandes excuses. Puis il était allé dire qu'il y avait un homme dans le lit. Quelques uns avaient émis l'opinion que c'était M. de L * * * qui venait pour coucher avec sa femme, mais cette hypothèse avait été rejetée comme improbable. Eugène qui m'avait vu fabriquer le portrait a empêché qu'on n'allat vérifier l'affaire."

Another great source of amusement must have been the Turkish Ambassador of the period,—of whom we read :—

"Château de Compiégne,
"16 Novembre, 1865.
"Nous avons ici l'Ambassadeur de Turquie, Safvet-

Pacha, qui parle bien Français pour un Turc. Il est assis à la droite de l'Impératrice, et hier, pendant le dîner, il lui dit: *Il y a une bien ridicule lettre sur l'Algérie dans le journal.*—Vous savez que tous les journaux ont répété la lettre de l'Empereur au Maréchal Mac-Mahon.—Voilà l'Impératrice qui rougit et, inquiète pour le pauvre Turc, elle lui dit: *Vous connaissez l'auteur de la lettre?*—Non; *mais je sais bien que c'est un imbécile!* Tous ceux qui écoutaient étaient prêts à crever de rire. *Mais c'est de l'Empereur!* s'é cria l'Impératrice. *Pas du tout,* répond l'Ambassadeur; *c'est d'un abbé qui veut convertir les Mussulmans.* Effectivement, je ne sais quel prêtre avait mis ce jour là une tartine que personne n'avait remarquée. Vous qui connaissez l'Impératrice et la mobilité de son expression, vous pouvez vous représenter la scène au naturel."

"Paris, 22 Novembre, 1865.

"J'ai trouvé à Compiègne Leurs Majestés en très bonne santé, ainsi que le Prince Impérial. On a passé le temps assez gravement sans charades ni facéties semblables. Il n'y a eu qu'une lanterne chinoise dont M. Leverrier, l'astronome, était le montreur. Il nous a fait voir des photographies de la lune et des planètes comme on montre à la foire les sept merveilles du monde. L'Ambassadeur Turc, qui, probablement, s'attendait à voir Caragneux ou quelque autre spectacle aussi anacréontique, a presque protesté, et a déclaré qu'il ne croyait pas un mot de tout ce qu'on venait de lui dire du soleil."

Nor must a notice of the visit of the Emperor to Algeria in this year be omitted:—

"23 Juin, 1865.

"L'Empereur nous a conté son voyage dont il paraît enchanté. Ne trouvez vous pas extraordinaire qu'après avoir eu quatre ou cinq cents mille hommes tués par les chrétiens, après avoir eu beaucoup de leurs femmes violées, après avoir perdu leur autonomie et je ne sais combiens d'*items*, les arabes aient reçu si admirablement le chef des gens qui ont fait tout cela. Sa Majesté est allée dans le grand désert avec une vingtaine de Français, tout au plus et est restée quarante-huit heures au milieu de quinze à vingt mille Sahariens qui lui ont tiré des coups de fusil aux oreilles (c'est la manière de saluer du pays) et ont nettoyé ses bottes avec leurs barbes. Pas un seul n'a montré la moindre revanche. On lui a donné des bœufs entiers rôtis, on lui a fait manger des autruches et je ne sais quelles autres bêtes impossibles, mais partout il a été reçu comme un souverain aimé. Il en est très fier et très content. Il m'a demandé de vos nouvelles. Je n'ai pas dit un mot de vos projets."

To enter now on more serious matters. The Nemesis of France governed for so many years on the *panem* and *circenses* system, and corrupted to the core, must have been hard to face, when the day of trial came for Napoleon III.

"Paris, 11 Août, 1870.

"J'ai vu avant-hier l'Impératrice. Elle est ferme comme un roc, bien qu'elle ne se dissimule pas toute l'horreur de sa situation. Je ne doute pas que l'Empereur ne se fasse tuer, car il ne peut rentrer ici que vainqueur et une victoire est impossible. Rien de prêt chez nous. Tout manque à la fois. Partout, du désordre. Si nous avions des généraux et des ministres rien ne serait perdu, car il y a certainement beaucoup d'enthousiasme et de patriotisme dans le pays. Mais avec l'anarchie, les meilleurs éléments ne servent de rien. Paris est tranquille, mais si on distribue des armes aux faubourgs comme le demande Jules Favre, c'est une nouvelle armée prussienne que nous avons sur les bras."

Concerning the unfortunate Prince Imperial, Mérimée's letters contain a good deal of matter which in these days assumes a very melancholy complexion, more especially in adverting to that fair promise of success, both in arts and arms, which his early life indicated :—

"Paris, 23 Juin, 1865.

"Votre favori le Prince, que vous ne reconnaîtriez plus, tant il est grandi et formé, a les dispositions les plus extraordinaires pour la sculpture. Un artiste nommé Carpeaux,* qui a beaucoup de talent, a fait son portrait ; lorsqu'il l'a vu pétrir de la terre glaise, il a naturellement eu envie de mettre la main à la pâte et a fait un portrait de son père, qui est atrocement ressemblant ; mais bien que ce soit

* Jean Baptiste Carpeaux, born at Valenciennes (1827—1875). Studied under Rude, Duret, and Abel de Pujol. In 1854 he took the *prix de Rome*. In 1865 he was commissioned to decorate the Pavilion of Flora in the Louvre; he there executed one of his larger works, called "Imperial France bringing Light to the World, and protecting Agriculture and Science." In 1869 his group of "Dancers" was placed on the façade of the New Opera at Paris. It will be remembered that in the night of August 27, 1869, the work was disfigured by having a corrosive ink thrown over it. The spots were removed.

U

gâché comme un bon homme de mie de pain, l'observation des proportions est extraordinaire.   Il a fait
encore un combat d'un cavalier contre un fantassin
plein de mouvement.   On voit qu'il sait manier un
cheval et qu'il a appris l'escrime à la bayonnette.
Mais le plus extraordinaire c'est le portrait de son
précepteur, M. Mounier, que vous aimez tant.   Je
vous jure que vous le reconnaîtriez d'un bout de la
court du British Museum à l'autre.   Ce ne sont pas
seulement ses traits, mais son expression.   Tout le
génie de l'homme se révèle dans ses yeux, son nez, et
ses moustaches.   Je suis sûr qu'il y a peu de sculp-
teurs de profession qui pourraient en faire autant."

"Biarritz, Villa Eugénie,
21 Septembre, 1865.

"L'Empereur et le Prince Impérial sont parfaite-
ment bien.   Le Prince est grandi; sa figure est un
peu allongée.   Il est toujours aussi actif et aussi
gentil que vous l'avez connu.   Il m'a demandé de vos
nouvelles ainsi que leurs Majestés, et cent cinquante
pourquoi? à l'occasion de votre retraite.   J'ai dit que
vous étiez devenu philosophe et paresseux, mais que
cela ne vous empêcherait pas de venir faire votre cour
quand vous passeriez par la France."

The lad seems to have had his full allowance of
courage, and to have been thoroughly imbued with a
knowledge of his own position and dignity :—

"Paris, 15 Octobre, 1867.

"Vous ai-je dit le mot du Prince à Saint-Jean de
Luz?   Leur canot par une nuit très obscure (N.B.
un prêtre était à bord) a donné contre un rocher.
La nuit était si noire que personne n'a vu le pilote

qui était à l'avant tomber et se fracasser la tête et se
noyer. Les matelots se sont jetés à la mer ayant de
l'eau jusqu'aux aiselles et par dessus la tête quand la
vague déferlait. Ils ont porté ainsi le Prince sur le
rocher trempé jusqu'aux os. L'Impératrice lui
criait: ' N'aie pas peur Louis.' Il à répondu: ' Je
m'appelle Napoléon.' Cela m'a été conté par deux
témoins, Brissac et M. de Lavallette."

At a very early age he appears to have entered
with ardour into his future profession :—

"26 Août, 1869.

"Le Prince Impérial a eu beaucoup de succès au
camp de Châlons. Il avait tant d'aplomb, et tenait
son rang si bien, qu'on croyait voir le père rajeuni.
Bachon son écuyer, que vous connaissez, me dit qu'il
n'y a pas un Prince pour passer une revue comme lui,
sur un grand cheval, qui piaffe de côté, du pas le
plus égal tout le long d'une ligne d'infanterie, sans
que la musique ou les éclairs des reflets du soleil sur
les fusils lui fassent perdre la piste."

To one of Mérimée's letters the Empress herself
adds the conclusion and signature. Her words in the
following extracts are in italics.

"Biarritz, 27 Septembre, 1863.

"Nous avons eu un très agréable voyage de Tarbes
à Pau et à Biarritz. Vos commissions ont été fidèle-
ment remplies et aussitôt que possible. Je suis
chargé pour vous de tous les compliments et tendresses
des dames et des messieurs à commencer par deux
augustes personnages. Adieu et portez-vous bien.

*Je veux vous dire, mon cher M. Panizzi, tout le
regret que j'ai de ne plus vous avoir parmi nous. Je*

u2

vous demande de vouloir bien me conserver un de vos
bons et meilleurs souvenirs.

Votre alliée politique,

EUGÉNIE."

These letters to Panizzi must not, however, cause
us to lose ourselves in a labyrinth of quotations and
remarks.

It is to be feared that enough has already been
placed before the reader to spoil his enjoyment of the
collection itself, and more than enough to fulfil our
own purpose of throwing light on Mérimée's life and
opinions from the letters themselves. By no means
always, but certainly sometimes, it has happened that
absolute dependence on some more solid reward than
popular applause has tended to fetter the pen of a
brilliant writer. It is equally true that what is done
by men for their diversion is frequently of superior
merit to that which is the product of sheer necessity,
and we have often thought, though this, we admit,
may be but fancy, that the peculiar facility conspicuous throughout Mérimée's works might be traced
to the fact that, being placed by fortune above necessity, he wrote as one in no way enforced, and as much
for his own pleasure as for the amusement of his
readers. The style of some of his lighter works, it
may be remarked *en passant*, reminds one strongly of
some of Voltaire's *Romans*, than which there can
assuredly be no higher praise.

Of artist blood on the side both of his father and
mother, he inherited much of his parents' ability,
and has left behind a goodly stock of productions, of
which (*Exceptis Excipiendis* for one, at least, might

be objected to on the ground of propriety) it is much to be wished that a collection could be made.

Readers of these letters to Panizzi, and, indeed, of other of Mérimée's works, can hardly fail to notice how greatly he, in common with his friend and correspondent, was affected by a malady, and that no imaginary one, common enough amongst the Roman Catholic nations, but little known in this country—the hatred of priests.

Nor is it much to be wondered at that, in countries where the Church seems to exist for itself alone, and not for that purpose for which it is supposed to have been founded—the benefit of mankind—where it dwells as a foreign authority, ever busied in jealously watching the temporal power, and opposing all that may be done for the cause of civilization and political advancement, simply because done by the State—the well-drilled officials of such a system should be viewed by the patriot and statesman, by a Panizzi, a Mérimée, or a Cavour, with mistrust and dislike. The letter to Panizzi, however, announcing the death and burial of Mérimée, with which this chapter concludes, shows a result not always brought about by this feeling of hatred of priests; yet we cannot but think that Mérimée had ceased to be a Roman Catholic in the strict sense of the term, rather than become a Protestant of any kind, and that his express desire for the place and manner of his burial is to be taken more as a protest against the creed of his birth than as a sign of his acceptance of any other. However this may be, it is hard to acquit the priests of the charge of

alienating yet another eminent man from that com-
munion.

Mérimée suffered greatly during the last years of
his life, and for a long time before his death was, according to his letters to Panizzi, in something like a
moribund state, enduring, in fact, a living death :—

" Cannes,

24th of September, 1870.

" My dear Sir,
          You loved my dear Prosper well—he loved you.
I know you will be grieved to hear he is gone. He died last
night without a struggle. All that devoted affection and care
could do was done for him. This is a consolation for me to
reflect on. The horrid political events have certainly shortened
his days. I need not say how miserable I am. We are at
Cannes without a friend, for Dr. Maure is at Grasse, and none
of our acquaintances have come yet. Dear Prosper often wondered and regretted that you did not write to him since he
left Paris.

Yours, &c., &c.,

J. LAGDEN."

And from another friend Panizzi received the
following :—

" Our poor friend is no more. He passed away in his sleep
so tranquilly they thought he was sleeping. He was buried,
by his express desire, in our Protestant Cemetery, as a Protestant. I always thought that he would direct this to be
done, if he died at Cannes."

CHAPTER XXVIII

SENATOR OF ITALY — CORRESPONDENCE — ILLNESS— "PRIESTS"—ATHENÆUM CLUB—KNIGHTHOOD— FRIENDS—DEATH—ETCHING—THE END.

THE end of our book approaches. Such materials as we have deemed it expedient to use in recording the events of a laborious life are almost exhausted, and it is necessary to look around and see that nothing has been omitted which may tend to illustrate Panizzi's unaspiring yet truly estimable character. Had he sought worldly distinctions he might have had more than his share of such unenduring and too often un-merited tokens of flattery. Those that he did accept were for the most part received with extreme shyness, if not with genuine reluctance, and—it would scarcely be using language too strong to say—were actually forced upon him, nor did he assume them until he was out of office.

In the autumn of 1865, Panizzi received a letter from Signor Nicomede Bianchi, announcing that the King of Italy desired to create him a Senator of the Kingdom. Conscious of his official position, he felt great difficulty and delicacy in accepting the high honour intended to be conferred upon him, and applied to Mr. Gladstone, as was his almost invariable

custom, for guidance and advice. He received the
following answer·—

"September 30,
1865.

"Upon reading your very interesting letter, I, like
you, feel myself in a strait. I am loth to say anything that may tend to even your partial removal
from among us; yet I cannot doubt that if a fair
regard to your health and personal comfort will permit, you should accept the offer of the King of Italy.
I know not what will be the precise effect on the con-
venience of the existing Administration, or even on
the Museum. But without stopping—for I must not
stop—to ask, I think that, considering the difficulty and
importance of constituting a Second Chamber or Senate
and of doing it in the best manner, and the advantage
to it of your character, prowess, long English experience, and thorough knowledge of our constitution,
I feel that you have before you a door opened for
rendering great services to your *other* country in the
hour of her need, and that such an opportunity cannot be generously refused, though I hope acceptance
will not practically remove you from us. I rather
blush while writing thus. Perhaps you will consult
some other friend. On my own responsibility I mentioned the matter recently to my host. He agrees
with me.

"The great Italian question needs all the strength
that can be applied to it. . . . I must not omit
to say that while I have written the first part of this
letter with very mixed feelings, I dwell with unmingled
pleasure on the high and honourable and most just

tribute which this offer pays to your character, abilities, and distinctions.

"Believe me ever

"Your attached friend,

"W. E. GLADSTONE."

Three years afterwards—on the 12th of March, 1868—Victor Emmanuel confirmed the proposed appointment, and on the 22nd of April following made Panizzi a Commander of the Order of the Crown of Italy. A letter, dated April 15th, to Mrs. Haywood, refers to this subject :—

"It is more than three years that I am offered to be made a Senator in Italy, it is a great honour. I begged to be excused, and I only accepted it when it was offered by the present Minister Menabrea, a man of honour and character. The offer came after the Mentana affair, that is at the time that poor Italy was most unfairly run down by everybody. I did not think I ought to shrink from doing what I could for my native country at such a moment, and had I not been taken ill as I was, I should have gone at once to take my seat."

The last words refer to an attack which, in January, 1868, reached a climax so severe that his life was despaired of by his medical advisers. His friends were unremitting in their attentions; amongst them may be specially named Mr. Winter Jones, Mr. Newton, Sir James Lacaita, and Mr. C. Cannon. The sufferer rallied, and when he had attained sufficient strength went for a short time to Hastings, the air of which watering-place greatly benefited him.

This illness must not be dismissed from notice

without placing before our readers a most characteristic extract from a "Memorandum" which speaks
for itself:—

"31, Bloomsbury Square,

April 14, 1868.

"It having come to my knowledge that during my
last illness a *priest*, who had never been called in by
me or by my orders, pushed himself into my
house, when he was with great difficulty hindered
from forcing himself into my bedroom, where I was
lying very ill, he alleging that he had been sent by
some nameless or unknown person; in order to prevent so vile and so impudent an attempt from being
successful if repeated, I warmly beseech my medical
attendants, as well as my true friends, and I order
my servants to forbid by all means in their power any
person not sent for by me, or not known as one whose
visit I should like to receive, from having access to
my presence, were he unfortunately admitted into the
house."

It may seem strange to some that Panizzi thus
strongly and decidedly expressed himself in regard to
a priest of his own Church: it can scarcely appear,
however, in this light to any one who has attentively
studied his character, as pourtrayed in these pages.
However disinterested might be the zeal of the Roman
clergy—and even of this the sick man seems to have
had some little doubt—the officious importunity of
this particular ecclesiastic was hardly fitted to commend him to the patient, whom an assumption of
spiritual authority would have disgusted at all times ;
it was, therefore, but natural that he should resent

the attempted intrusion of a stranger on his presumed helplessness.

He knew all the insidious arts of the Church to which he nominally belonged, and of the religion which he always professed; at the same time he was perfectly aware of the character of the doctrines which, even with the best intentions, the most worthy of the Romish priesthood are bound to inculcate. Knowing all this, he avoided controversy on the subject: if it were introduced in conversation, he would say, *I am a Roman Catholic*, and there was an end. Such being his ordinary frame of mind, his indignation was aroused at any attempt to pester him on analogous themes in his state of prostration.

No more need be said here to account for the peremptoriness of the "Memorandum."

About this period Panizzi wrote from Montpellier to the biographer, then travelling in South America: —"As you know, I have been very ill, and I really thought I should not see you again. I hear you are likely to come back. My expenses are frightful, or I should offer to pay your voyage. This climate, or rather Italy, would suit me very well; I could not live in France. The French, and especially the Emperor, have behaved very ill, perhaps cruelly to Italy. On the other hand, the Italians have acted like idiots. I should pass my time arguing and getting angry: so, if I can succeed, I shall return to England; but probably I shall die on the road."

The present writer returned in June, 1869, and with great regret clearly perceived the ravages in his friend's appearance caused by the late severe illness.

Many attempts had been made by friends to induce Panizzi to allow his name to be proposed to the committee of the Athenæum Club for election as a member. Sir Roderick Murchison wrote to him " that he would really be much gratified in seeing those services recognised in the manner he proposed by his (Panizzi's) contemporaries in science, art, and letters." To this proposal, honourable as it was, he did not accede. Sir Roderick did not allow the matter to drop, but, in the beginning of 1866, wrote again pressing the subject on his consideration thus : " The moment has arrived when the men of letters, science, and art, who constitute the committee of the Athenæum Club, *ought* to recognise your merit by electing you as a member on our list of *eminently distinguished* candidates."

Hereupon Panizzi overcame his scruples, and acquiesced in the proposal. Sir Roderick was very much gratified, a feeling shared by the Dean of St. Paul's, as the words of the former show. He said he " was so fortunate as to meet the Dean of St. Paul's, who joyfully became the seconder, saying that he never signed any document whatever with greater satisfaction."

An unforeseen difficulty, however, arose, which Sir Roderick thus communicated :—

" February 6th, 1866.

"My dear Panizzi,

" My efforts have been frustrated, to my deep regret, and that of all those men of eminence in science, letters, and art, whose opinion you value. After I saw you, accident placed me in the position to ascertain that *no arguments* of mine would or could change the resolve of one of the

Committee to *veto* your election, in case you obtained a majority of votes; and therefore, after giving the strongest reasons I could for thinking that you were singularly and highly qualified to be selected as one of our eminent nine, I withdrew your name.

The reason assigned for this opposition was, that as you were unpopular with a certain number of men in the Club *at large*, the Committee ought not to go against their feelings.

I protested against this doctrine on my own part; the more so as the gentleman, who acted in a frank and honourable manner in letting me know his resolve, had assured me that he had a high opinion of your capacity, acquirements, and character.

The result has given me great pain; for though your selection as a member of the Athenæum could be of no real value to you, and could not have added an iota to your well-earned and high reputation, it would have been a true gratification to myself to have had the opportunity of meeting you more frequently, now that you have retired from the office in which you have so distinguished yourself.

I may add that Sir Stafford Northcote and Lord Stanhope both expressed their regret that the step I took was rendered imperative, and many others have since spoken to me in the same sense.

I enclose the letters of the Dean of St. Paul's and Mr. Grote, whose sentiments I expressed to the meeting; assuring my auditors that the Trustees of the British Museum would endorse those sentiments. Not a word was said by anyone against you, or against the terms in which I proposed you.

Ever yours sincerely,

Rod. I. Murchison."

Already Dean Milman had written the following letter, a short sentence from which has been quoted in a former chapter, and is now reproduced for the sake of the context :—

" Deanery, St. Paul's,
February 5th, 1866.

" My dear Sir Roderick,

I greatly rejoice that you are about to propose our friend Panizzi for election at the Athenæum.

I know few persons for whom, if on the Committee, I should have voted with a more clear conscience, or with more earnest desire for success.

As a man of letters I know few persons with a more extensive knowledge of literature; as an author, his introduction to the edition of Bojardo and Ariosto, containing a most masterly view of Italian poetry, is, I believe, his chief claim. But I have read other scattered works, perhaps less generally known, which I hold in high estimation. As to his public services, his long and most useful connection with the British Museum, cannot be more justly or fully appreciated than by yourself, and I am sure that we should entirely agree on this subject; above all, the great national gift of the Reading-Room, the envy and admiration of Europe, is, as you well know, almost his entire creation, from the original design to the most minute detail, from the dome to the inkstands and book-shelves.

I most heartily, my dear Murchison, wish you success, and remain ever most truly yours,

H. H. MILMAN."

The answer to Sir Roderick's letter was this:—

" 31, Bloomsbury Square,
February 6, 1866.

" My dear Murchison,

Many thanks for the trouble you have taken in my behalf. The result is what I expected, and I am not in the least affected by it. I am only sorry for the pain that I know it must have given you.

I am proud of having received on this occasion additional proofs of regard and friendship from you, from the Dean of St. Paul's, and from Mr. Grote. This outweighs the unpopularity to which your colleague in the Committee says I am obnoxious on the part of some unknown members of the Athenæum, who certainly do not know me as well as you and the other Trustees of the British Museum do.

Believe me, &c.,

A. PANIZZI."

In the summer of 1861, Sir G. Cornewall Lewis, then Home Secretary, sought to confer another honour on Panizzi in offering him knighthood, which, however, he declined in these terms (July 23rd, 1861):—

"I can hardly find words to acknowledge as I ought your unexpected communication of to-day. Her Majesty's approbation of my humble services at the Museum is the highest reward I ever desired to receive for them. I can only regret my inability adequately to express my dutiful gratitude for Her Majesty's condescension.

"Permit me, however, to represent most respectfully that, occupying as I do, through Her Majesty's goodness, the honourable position I now fill, I feel great unwillingness to be the object of a further mark of Royal favour which may attract too much public attention to one like myself, a foreigner by birth, who will be considered by many to have already received too high a reward for his exertions.

"If, therefore, I may be allowed to give utterance to my feelings on the subject, I humbly but earnestly beg to be excused from having an honour bestowed on me, the value of which I fully appreciate and unfeignedly regard as far beyond my deserts. Apart from all other considerations, I feel an instinctive shrinking from all distinctions of this nature.

"With the utmost thankfulness to you for having advised Her Majesty to acknowledge in so gracious a manner the public services which you are pleased to state I have rendered at the Museum, I remain, &c."

Still the Government cherished the idea of conferring on him some title of honour; for, on the 27th of June, 1866, Lord Russell informed him that Her Majesty had offered a *C.B.*, as *a recognition, though slight, of his services to one of our great public Institutions.* With many thanks Panizzi reminded his Lordship of what had taken place several years before, and again declined the proferred distinction. However, in 1869, the Queen conferred on him the distinction of K.C.B. In addition to this he was, in the month of August of the same year, unanimously elected member of Parliament for the place of his birth. This onerous position he, however, found it out of his power to accept.

Here we will pause for a few minutes, as we have now arrived at the beginning, as it were, of the end of this remarkable career. As strength failed, and Panizzi no longer possessed his pristine powers of body, his life became more retired; indeed, from the year 1870 up to the time of his death it may be said that he remained in strict privacy. It is true that his friends, his intimates, continued as of old to visit him, nor did they omit to do so to the last; but his facility for correspondence had failed. The old pain in his hand had increased, until it was only with extreme difficulty that he could use his pen; and, for the last few years, he could do no more than append an almost illegible signature to what was written for him.

During this time his only occupation in the day-time was reading ; Dante, Virgil, and Scott's novels were his chief favourites. In the evening he was glad to see around his table those who still clung to him. Such as had been most in his confidence at the Museum were always welcome, and other old friends occasionally joined them. Then there was the whist party, with a very moderate stake to encourage attention to the game, and the company dispersed with pleasant recollections.

Amongst those who did not forget Panizzi in his latter days was the late Emperor of the French ; he paid him several visits, as did other foreign Princes when in London.

Not the least distinguished of the number was King Humbert, then Prince of Savoy, and lastly, his old and constant friend, Mr. Gladstone, who, when in town, never failed to pay his afternoon visit, fre-quently stopping to dinner, and cheering him with his intellectual conversation.

Nor were his declining days uncheered by sym-pathisers and comforters of the gentler sex, whose consciences still bear the impress of their good deeds. One only will we mention here—Lady Holland, whose innate gentleness and kindness of heart prompted her to anticipate and administer in many ways to wants and wishes that only a long and intimate acquaintance could have enabled her to understand. Having watched him throughout his arduous journey in life, who could have been better fitted to solace him, and how could she fail to be greatly attached to one whose character she had studied and knew so well?

x

On the Friday previous to Panizzi's death, Mr. Gladstone called for the last time. A sudden change for the worse was too marked to escape observation, and from that evening it was certain that the weary traveller was nearing his rest. He lay in a state of perfect composure, and in the afternoon of the next Tuesday, the 8th of April, 1879, his spirit passed from the scene of his long unceasing labours. His body remains for the present under a marble tomb in St. Mary's Catholic Cemetery at Kensal Green, where it was deposited on Saturday, the 12th of April, 1879, in the presence of many friends and admirers besides the recognized mourners.

So died Sir Anthony Panizzi, mourned for by all who knew him, and by men of genius especially; no one, in discussing his merits or demerits, can ascribe to him a spark of selfishness. The best part of his life had been devoted to one great object; that object he had attained and enjoyed. He had been rewarded by the appreciation of thinking men, and by the comforts that should accompany old age, *love, honour, and troops of friends.*

His death was the loss of a staunch friend to the biographer, who etched the portrait prefixed to this life, and on presenting Mr. Gladstone with the identical proof which he had before given to Panizzi, received from the eminent Statesman this gratifying note :—

" 73, Harley-street, May 10th, 1879.

" I thank you very sincerely for favouring me with a copy of your etching of Sir A. Panizzi. It carries us back considerably, I think, in our recollections of his general appearance from the sad wreck we lately saw, but it is a most interesting record of one whose image none of his friends who truly appreciated his fine manful character would be content to part with."

In conclusion the author cannot more faithfully indicate the scene which terminated the labours, the hopes, the fears, and the aspirations of his revered friend than by quoting these memorable lines in the language he loved so well and so keenly appreciated :—

" Non come fiamma che per forza è spenta,
Ma che per se medesma si consume,
Se n'andò in pace l'anima contenta :
A guisa d'un soave e chiaro lume,
Cui nutrimento a poco a poco manca,
Tenendo al fin il suo usato costume.—*Petrarch.*

x2

APPENDIX.

APPENDIX.

It is thought that the following document, written in Count Cavour's own hand, may interest the reader. It is well known that the Italian Statesman was in the habit of supplying Panizzi from time to time with information, for the purpose of publication in the English newspapers.

_____

(1852 ?)

"Peu de pays se sont trouvés placés dans une situation financière plus difficile que ne l'a été la Sardaigne après la désastreuse campagne du printemps 1849. Avec un trésor vide, le Gouvernement avait à songer à faire face aux frais de l'occupation étrangère qui dura plusieurs mois, à liquider les frais de deux guerres malheureuses, à fournir des secours aux nombreux infortunés qui venaient chercher en Piémont un refuge contre les atteintes de la réaction, partout ailleurs triomphante en Italie.

Plus tard il eut à pourvoir au payement de l'énorme indemnité de guerre stipulée en faveur de l'Autriche par la paix de Milan, et il dut songer à poursuivre les grands travaux publics entrepris par Charles-Albert qu'on n'eût pu interrompre sans éprouver d'immenses dommages.

Quand on songe que toutes ces difficultés étaient aggravées encore par l'existence d'un papier ayant cours forcé, on sera forcé de convenir que M. d'Azeglio et ses collègues, en acceptant le pouvoir le lendemain de la bataille de Novara, firent preuve d'un grand courage et d'un dévouement sans bornes à leur Roi et à leur pays.

Le nouveau Ministre des Finances, M. Nigra, pourvit aux premiers besoins par un emprunt volontaire ; par la vente de quelques rentes, anciennes propriétés des finances, et l'émission de bons du trésor, qui, sans avoir cours forcé, furent acceptés sans murmures par les employés du Gouvernement et les fournisseurs de l'armée.

Quelques mois plus tard, le calme et la confiance étant rétablis, toute crainte de réaction ayant disparu, grâce à la loyauté du jeune Roi, le Ministre jugea le moment venu pour contracter un emprunt à l'étranger.

Il parvint à le faire, à des conditions, qui eu égard aux circonstances financières et économiques de l'Europe, peuvent être considérées comme avantageuses,

Ce premier emprunt, négocié en Octobre, 1849, avec Mess. de Rothschild, fut suivi de deux emprunts contractés également avec cette maison l'année suivante. Avec les ressources qu'ils procurèrent au trésor, il fut possible de solder avec exactitude l'indemnité de guerre due à l'Autriche ; de liquider les dépenses arriérées des deux campagnes de 1848 et 1849, et enfin de pousser avec vigueur les travaux des deux grandes lignes de chemin de fer qui coupent le pays en forme de croix ; celle de Turin à Gênes, et de Gênes au Lac Majeur.

Mais ce n'était pas tout que de pourvoir aux besoins extraordinaires par des ressources extraordinaires, comme les emprunts et les bons du trésor ; le Gouvernement devait songer à augmenter d'une manière permanente les recettes du trésor, afin de faire face aux charges que les nouveaux emprunts imposeraient dorénavant à l'Etat. Pour cela il fallait se résoudre à établir de nouveaux impôts.

Le Ministère ne recula pas devant cette tâche ingrate ; rendue extrèmement difficile par la nécessité d'obtenir le concours franc et décidé d'une Chambre des Deputés jeune et sans expérience ; qui devait nécessairement éprouver la plus vive répugnance à débuter dans ses travaux parlementaires, en imposant de nouvelles charges à ses commettants.

Dans la session de 1850, le Ministre des Finances obtint une augmentation sur les droits d'enrégistre-

ment, et une extension des droits de timbre.
La session suivante, le Parlement vota une nouvelle
taxe sur les maisons; une taxe sur le commerce et
l'industrie; un impôt sur les revenus possédés par des
corps moraux; enfin une augmentation considérable
dans les droits de succession tant en ligne directe que
collatérale.   Enfin dans la session actuelle, le succes-
seur de M. Nigra, le Comte de Cavour, a proposé un
nouvel impôt personnel et mobilier ; l'augmentation
d'un quart de l'impôt foncier ; l'extension à toutes les
provinces de l'Etat des droits de consommation sur le
vin, et enfin plusieurs modifications aux lois sur l'en-
régistrement et le timbre, destinées à rendre plus pro-
ductives ces deux branches importantes du revenu de
l'Etat.

Les lois d'impôt votées en 1850 et 1851 ont déjà
augmenté de 10 millions les ressources de l'Etat :
celles que le Parlement discute dans ce moment
doivent produire une somme de 10 autres millions
encore.

Le budget des recettes de 1847 s'élevait à la somme
de 87,000,000.   Celui de l'année courante, calculé à
102,000,000 à raison de l'augmentation de la consommation du tabac sur 1847, et du nouveau produit pour
le chemin de fer de Turin à Arquata, atteindra en définitive le chiffre de 104,000,000 à cause du majeur
produit des impôts indirectes.   Celui de l'année pro-
chaine s'élévera probablement à 114,000.   Et celui

de 1854, époque à laquelle le grand réseau de chemins de fer entrepris par le Gouvernement sera achevé, il atteindra certainement le chiffre de 117,000,000.

Malgré ces augmentations successives de recettes, on ne peut pas dire que le budget de 1854 présentera un parfait équilibre ; car, sans se faire illusion, on ne saurait calculer les dépenses de cette année à moins de 120,000,000. Bien entendu que dans cette somme les dépenses des grands travaux publics ne sont pas comprises. Mais par contre dans le 120,000,000 se trouvent comprises les dépenses pour une armée de terre de 40 et plus mille hommes, et pour une augmentation de celle de mer, ainsi que pour autres dépenses improductives, qui ne pesaient pas en 1847. Toutefois lorsque le déficit apparent sera réduit à 3 ou 4 millions, on pourra dire qu'en réalité il n'existe pas. En effet la somme portée au budget de l'année courante pour fond d'amortissement s'élève à 7 millions ; en 1854 elle sera plus considérable encore, et il s'en suit que si en 1854 le déficit ne dépasse pas 6 millions, il sera inférieur à la somme consacrée à l'extinction de nos anciennes dettes.

Dans cet état de choses, il suffirait pour présenter un budget en parfait équilibre, d'adopter le système que l'Angleterre pratique depuis plus de trente ans, en ne consacrant à l'amortissement que le surplus constaté des recettes sur les dépenses.

Pour arriver à ce résultat de grands sacrifices étaient et seront encore nécessaires. Il a fallu se résigner à augmenter les charges qui pesaient sur les contribuables avant les derniers événements de plus du 30%. Les impôts en 1847 étaient de entre 78 et 80 millions ; ils seraient portés entre 108 et 110 millions. Les nouveaux impôts ont été votés et sont discutés par le Parlement avec un admirable patriotisme. Le pays les supporte avec une rare résignation ; cela est dû à ce que le Piémont payait fort peu d'impôts en égard aux autres nations d'Europe, et que même avec tous les impôts susénoncés il payera toujours moins qu'en France, ayant égard à la population et à la richesse territoriale.

Cependant devant faire cette augmentation d'impôts aussi rapidement en peu d'années, il était à craindre qu'ils ne tarissent les sources de la richesse publique et qu'ils apportassent une crise, si l'on laissait subsister l'ancien système économique, fondé sur les principes de l'école protectioniste. C'est ce que le Ministère Sarde a senti. Aussi s'est-il décidé à mener de front et les lois de finance et les lois de réforme économique. Dès l'année 1840 il proclame résolument son intentention d'appliquer le système du libre échange, en modifiant successivement toutes les lois qui avaient été faites dans le seul but de protéger quelques industries privilégiées.

Le Ministère débuta par l'abolition des droits différentiels de navigation. L'honneur de cette première mais décisive mesure appartient à un homme qui par le sublime courage déployé à son lit de mort a prouvé comment on pouvait allier, au sein du Catholicisme, les sentiments religieux les plus vrai et les plus purs, avec une indépendance complète de la Cour de Rome; au noble et généreux Sainte Rose,* dont le Piémont, après deux ans, pleure encore la perte.

Dans la même session le Ministre Azeglio faisait sanctionner la réforme du tarif postal, au moyen de laquelle le système de la taxe unique a été substitué en Piémont, comme il l'avait été en Angleterre, aux droits progressifs en raison de la distance. . . .

Aucune des industries qu'on disait devoir être frappées de mort par la concurrence étrangère n'a succombé. Quelques unes ont éprouvé un peu de gêne, des difficultés plus ou moins grandes dans leurs opérations. D'autres au contraire n'ont jamais été dans un état plus prospère que depuis qu'elles ont cessé d'être énormément protégées.

Nous citerons surtout les filatures et les manufactures de coton. Les fileurs, qui un moment s'étaient crûs ruinés, ayant repris courage améliorèrent leurs modes de fabrication, perfectionnèrent leurs machines, et par là ils réussirent non seulement à soutenir sur nos propres marchés la concurrence anglaise, mais encore à la faire aux produits étrangers sur les

* Count Pietro di Santa Rosa, Statesman.

marchés des pays voisins et notamment ceux des Duchés de Parme et de Modène.

L'état des importations des cotons en laine prouve que cette assertion est loin d'être exagérée :—

En effet dans le dernier semestre de l'année 1851
nous avons importé, quintaux métriques de coton 66,000

Nous en avions importés dans les six mois correspondants de 1850 17,000

Augmentation ... ... Q. m. 49,000

Dans le premier trimestre de cette année l'importation a été de... ... ... Q. m. 26,000

Elle avait été en 1851 9,000

Augmentation ... ... Q. m. 17,000

Ces chiffres nous paraissent d'une éloquence irrésistible. Ces résultats d'ailleurs n'ont rien d'étonnant, si l'on réfléchit que nos industriels tirant la matière première directement de l'Amérique, elle ne leur revient pas plus chère qu'aux Anglais, grâce aux bas prix auxquels naviguent les marins Sardes ; que la main d'œuvre est meilleur marché qu'à Manchester, et enfin que la force motrice qu'ils employent leur est fournie gratuitement par la nature. Avec ces éléments de prospérité, il n'est pas douteux que l'industrie du coton est appelée à prendre en Sardaigne un immense développement, et à être une des sources principales de la richesse du pays.

L'industrie des laines a été plus ébranlée que celle du coton. Peut-être parce qu'ayant été plus protégée, elle était relativement à celle-ci dans un état plus arriéré. Cependant elle ne présente aucun signe de décadence : au contraire, à en juger par le nombre et la perfection des machines que depuis quelques mois les principaux fabricants tirent de l'étranger, il est à croire que bientôt elle sera en mesure de lutter à l'intérieur et à l'extérieur avec les tissus de la France et de la Belgique.

L'industrie des fers n'a pas ralenti sa production ; ayant amélioré ses produits, elle n'a pas dû consentir à une grande baisse de prix. Nous ne pouvons pas nous dissimuler toutefois qu'étant forcée à employer pour la production du fer le charbon de bois, cette industrie n'est pas susceptible de grands développements ; mais qu'au contraire elle est condamnée à se restreindre à la production des fers de qualités supérieures à laquelle les minerais des Alpes sont singulièrement aptes.

Quant aux industries secondaires plus ou moins atteintes par la réforme, elles n'ont pas souffert notablement, et aucune d'elle n'a succombé jusqu'ici dans la lutte.

Les résultats financiers du nouveau système sont également satisfaisants. Il suffit pour s'en convaincre de comparer le produit des douanes avant et après l'application du nouveau trarif :—

Les douanes avaient donné dans les derniers six mois de 1850 un produit de ... ... Fr. 9,965,000

Dans les six mois correspondants de 1851 ...		9,485,00 0
Diminution ... ... Fr.		480,000

Pendant les quatre premiers mois de cette année
les douanes ont produit ... ... Fr. 6,355,00 0

Pendant les quatre mois correspondants de l'année
dernière... 5,450,000

Augmentation ... ... Fr. 905,000

Si on objectait que les produits de l'année dernière avaient été affectés par la perturbation causée par la discussion des traités et de la réforme douanière ; la comparaison de 1852 avec les années 1850 et celles antécédentes, confirmerait nos assertions : en effet le produit des quatre premiers mois de 1852 dans les provinces continentales a donné   Fr. 6,355,280

Des quatre premiers de 1850 a donné ...		...		6,274,687
„	1849	„	... ...	5,733,361
„	1848	„	... ...	4,603,929
„	1847	„	... ...	5,932,835
Augmentation de 1852 comparé à 1850		... Fr.		80,593
„	„	1849	...	621,919
„	„	1848	...	1,751,351
„	„	1847	...	422,445

Ces chiffres prouvent à l'évidence que la réforme radicale opérée dans le tarif, loin de causer un pré-judice au trésor, lui a été singulièrement avantageuse ; qu'en définitive elle a augmenté les recettes de l'Etat, tout en procurant un énorme soulagement aux contribuables.

Ce que les contribuables ont gagné ne peut pas être évalué à moins de 7 ou 8 millions par an.   En effet si les anciens tarifs étaient encore en vigueur, les importations effectuées dans les derniers 12 mois, auraient dû supporter une surtaxe équivalente à la somme susindiquée.

Si le trésor malgré ce bénéfice réalisé par les contribuables n'a pas perdu, c'est que la quantité des objets soumis aux droits a énormément augmenté.

Il ne faut pas croire toutefois que la consommation se soit accrue dans la proportion des chiffres que nous venons de citer. L'augmentation des recettes de la douane est due en grande partie à la diminution de la contrebande qui a presque entièrement cessé, tandis que par le passé elle s'opérait sur une immense échelle.

L'étendue des frontières des Etats Sardes par rapport à la surface de son territoire ; la facilité qu'offre au commerce illicite la plupart des lignes qui les séparent des pays étrangers, faisaient que sous l'appât de droits très élevés, la contrebande avait pris un énorme développement. Le Ministre des Finances dans la discussion des traités avait évalué l'importance des marchandises importées en fraude au tiers des importations totales ; l'expérience est venue confirmer cette assertion qui ne reposait que sur des données approximatives.

La cessation presque complète de la contrebande ne sera certainement pas estimée par tous les hommes qui pensent que les intérêts moraux des populations

Y

ne sont pas moins sacrés que leurs intérêts matériels, comme un des moindres bienfaits de la grande réforme que le Piémont a accomplie à l'instar de la Grande Bretagne.

Encouragé par le succès qui avait couronné ses premières mesures, le Gouvernement Sarde s'est décidé à étendre aux produits du sol les principes qu'il avait appliqués aux produits de l'industrie, et à réduire les droits sur les denrées alimentaires étrangères.

Le pays produisant beaucoup de vins, les producteurs parvinrent sous le dernier régime à faire frapper les liquides étrangers de droits énormes.   Avant 1847 les vins étaient soumis :

S'ils étaient d'une valeur de 20 fr. et au dessous, au droit de 16 par hect. ;

S'ils étaient de valeur supérieure, au droit de 10 par hect., plus le 30 % sur la valeur ;

et les eaux-de-vie de 22 degrés et au dessous, au droit de 22 par hect. ;

de degré supérieur, au droit de 40 par hect.

En 1850 un traité stipulé avec la France réduisit les droits

à 14 pour les vins au dessus de 20 fr. par hect. ;

à 10   „   au dessous de cette valeur.

et pour les eaux-de-vie

à 18 par hect., celles de 22 degrés et au dessous ;

à 30   „   celles de degré supérieur.

Malgré ces réductions, les droits étaient encore hautement protecteurs, surtout par rapport aux vins

communs. En effet les vins du Languedoc ne pouvant
être évalués à plus de 10 francs l'hectolitre, il s'en
suit qu'ils avaient à payer, pour pénétrer en Piémont,
un droit du cent pour cent sur la valeur.

La réduction du droit sur les vins présentait toutefois de sérieuses difficultés. La plupart des provinces
du Continent et de la Sardaigne étant couvertes de
vignobles, il était à craindre qu'une réforme un peu
hardie ne soulevat parmi les producteurs et par
contre-coup dans le Parlement, une opposition difficile
à vaincre.

Pour arriver plus facilement à son but, le Ministère
se décida à faire de la réduction des droits sur les
vins et les eaux-de-vie l'objet de négociations avec la
France, afin d'en obtenir en retour une diminution
des droits qui pèsent sur deux de nos principaux
articles d'exportation—les huiles et les bestiaux.
Dans ce but un nouveau traité fut signé avec la
France, qui parmi les concessions réciproques qu'il
stipulait, réduisait les divers droits sur les vins au
droit uniforme de 3, 30 par hectolitre ; et ceux sur
les eaux-de-vie

à 5, 50 de 22 degrés et au dessous,

à 10 — de degré supérieur.

Lorsque le traité fut connu, une vive émotion se
manifesta parmi les propriétaires de vignobles.
Toutefois cette émotion n'eut pas de suite dans les
provinces du Piémont ; elle ne prit pas de couleur

Y2

politique et elle ne tarda pas à se calmer. Le parti
libéral avait trop ouvertement prôné les théories du
libre échange, pour pouvoir embrasser la cause des
producteurs de vins : et quant au parti rétrograde, il
est trop faible pour exercer une influence sérieuse sur
le public ou sur les masses.

Il n'en fut pas de même en Savoie. Quoique prise
dans son ensemble, cette partie des Etats Sardes ne
produise pas le vin qui est nécessaire à sa consommation, la province de Chambéry possède une grande
quantité de vignobles, et les propriétaires de vignes y
exercent une influence considérable. Il était naturel
par conséquent qu'il ne fissent créer dans la capitale
de la Savoie une agitation très-vive. Le parti rétrograde, qui est beaucoup plus nombreux et puissant
dans cette ville que partout ailleurs, sut en profiter
avec une extrême habilité il parvint à donner, à une
question purement locale, le caractère d'une question
nationale pour la Savoie.

La Savoie compte bien plusieurs députés libéraux ;
mais malheureusement ils étaient en congé lorsque le
traité fut présenté à la Chambre ; de sorte qu'au premier abord la Députation Savoisienne parut unanime
pour repousser le traité.

Plus tard, il est vrai, cet état fâcheux se modifia.
Plusieurs Députés s'empressèrent de quitter leurs
montagnes pour venir protester contre les doctrines
illibérales de leurs collègues. Néanmoins ils ne par-

vinrent pas à détruire l'impression produite par ceux-ci, et il était facile à reconnaître que le principal obstacle que rencontrerait le traité dans les Chambres, viendrait de l'opinion que la Savoie lui était en grande majorité hostile.

C'est pourquoi, le Ministre des Finances, dans le discours prononcé a cette occasion, s'est attaché à traiter la question spécialement du point de vue savoyard.

Malgré cette tendance spéciale, ce discours contient une exposition exacte et consciencieuse des principes économiques et politiques qui guident depuis trois ans le Cabinet dont M. d'Azeglio est le chef. C'est pourquoi nous avons pensé qu'il pouvait présenter quelque intérêt pour le public anglais, que nous savons animé d'une si vive sympathie pour une nation généreuse qui, au milieu des plus graves difficultés et des obstacles de tous genres, a su demeurer fidèle à la cause de l'ordre et de la liberté ; tout en accomplissant une réforme économique non moins étendue, non moins considérable, toute proportion d'ailleurs gardée, que celle qu'une suite d'hommes d'Etat célèbres a opéré en Angleterre avec un si éclatant succès.

The following are the originals of which translations have been given at pages 156 and 193 of Volume II.

"27 Agosto, 1856,
14, Cambridge Terrace, Hyde Park.

"Pregiatissimo Signor Mio,

Ho esaminato il Catalogo della Biblioteca per ciò che risguarda l'arte e la scienza militare : è assai sprovvista delle opere più istruttive, e che sono uscite a luce durante e dopo le guerre di Napoleone. Così è pure dell' *United Service Institution*, a cui sono stato ammesso per consultare le opere che mi abbisognano pel componimento del lavoro militare che ho tra mano.   In seguito di ciò ne ho fatte venire parecchie dalla Francia a mie spese ; ma in appresso avrei d'uopo di consultare l'opera, di cui le accludo il titolo, e *La grande Tactique du Marquis de Ternay, Colonel d'Etat Major*.   Quelle opere, in ispecie quella di Martray, non mi è dato procurarle perchè troppo dispendiose.   Se ella credesse di proporre alla Biblioteca di farle venire, sarebbe per me una grande utilità. L'opera di Ternay, edizione di Parigi, non deve costare più di franchi 25 ; quella di Bruxelles assai meno.

L'opera che sto compiendo sarà in Inglese, e conterrà tutto che deve sapersi in campagna dal sottotenente delle tre armi onde si compone un esercito, fino allo Stato Maggior Generale inclusivamente.   E un peso assai grave, molto più che deve essere ristretto in un volume tascabile, e riunire *concisione*, *chiarezza*, e utto lo *scibile militare*.   Io mi riprometto tuttavia di, riuscire sia pei buoni studi che feci fino da giovane come per l'assiduità e diligenza che vi metterò. E tuttavia un lavoro che non posso recare a termine prima di sei o otto mesi.

Mentre sto scrivendo, posso però disporre di alcune ore al giorno per altre occupazioni; ed amerei, se fosse possibile, di dare alcune lezioni di lingua e letteratura italiana, e di arte e scienza militare. Per questa seconda parte io già fui Maggiore di Stato Maggiore, e posso dare lezioni assai estese: per la prima pure sono alquanto innanzi.

Sino ad ora io condussi una vita oltremodo agitata e di mezzo sempre ai pericoli: fui per conseguenza a carico della famiglia, che soffrì non lievi perdite a mia cagione. Ed ora mettendomi un po' più tranquillo ho in animo di trar profitto delle mie cognizioni, mentre sto aspettando il desiderato momento in cui possa di nuovo battermi per la nostra indipendenza. Per far conoscere che sarei pronto a dar lezioni mi si consiglia di mettere un avviso nel *Times*. Io non vorrei far ciò. Sembrerebbe che volessi profittare del buon nome che ho, benchè immeritamente. Credo invece che, ove la S. V. volesse, potrebbe assai giovarmi col mezzo delle sue relazioni. Comunque sia, io me ne starò pien a mente ai consigli di lei.

Ella però non conosce la mia privata vita: su ciò le do ampie facoltà, e può indirizzarsi agli stessi miei nemici o di opinioni, o di partiti, o di altra specie, chè tutti ne abbiamo. Quanto alle lingue conosco benis-

simo la francese, e mi disimpegno quanto all' inglese
per lezioni private.

Le ho scritto la presente, perchè temeva di recarle
disturbo; se avrà la cortesia la S. V. di darmi un
cenno, potrò recarmi da lei quando le piacerà, onde
prender su quanto le ho scritto miglior consiglio.

Venendo ora alle cose politiche, io non so nulla di
positivo: mi tengo, siccome le dissi, indipendente da
ognuno : e se il Governo sardo stimasse di potersi
valere di quel poco ch'io valgo in qualunque impresa
per quanto audace potesse essere, io sono sempre
pronto. Beninteso per la indipendenza della mia
patria : per la quale fin da che conobbi non ebbi mai
quiete, e sagrificai *tutto*. Nel dire di essere pronto a
dar mano al Governo sardo non sono influenzato che
dall' amore del mio paese, e dalla convinzione che
oggi, se egli vuole, è il solo Governo che possa fare
l'Italia indipendente, una e grande : ed io mi reputerò
felice se in un fatto d'*importanza* e di *gravi conseguenze*
per gli oppressori dell' Italia potrò adoperarmi con
tutte le forze, e finire anche una vita che non fu per
me fino ad ora che triste, passionata e melanconica.
Mi perdoni questa espansione d'animo.

Da quanto sento, pare che il mio libretto abbia
avuto qualche incontro anche in Piemonte presso
qualunque partito: certo che io nulla esagerai; mi
studiai per anco di far conoscere che debbesi sagrificare
qualunque principio politico alla indipendenza nazio-

nale; ed io così feci fino dalla mia prima prigionía del 1844.

Non mi occorrendo altro significarle, la supplico di avermi per iscusato, e rispettosamente me le offro

Di Vostra Signoria

Umilissimo e devotissimo servitore

"FELICE ORSINI."

"Leri, 24 Ottobre (1859).

" Carissimo Panizzi,

La vostra lettera del 17 andante mi fu consegnata solo ieri, troppo tardi per potere rispondervi lo stesso giorno. Mi affretto a farlo questa mattina, benchè io stimi che questa risposta debba giungere a Londra quando la questione del Congresso sarà stata decisa.

Che allo stato delle cose, a fronte degl' impegni assunti a Villafranca e sino ad un certo punto confermati a Zurigo dall' Imperatore, un Congresso europeo sia una necessità, parmi cosa evidente. Ove il Congresso non si riunisse, e la Francia impedisse l'Italia centrale dall' uscire del provvisorio col contrastare le decretate fusioni, quei paesi sarebbero esposti a gravi pericoli. Nelle Romagne gli uomini superlativi, e colà ve ne son molti, potrebbero spingere Garibaldi a tentare un' impresa nelle Marche e fors' anche negli Abruzzi ; a Modena l' occupazione per parte dell' Austria dell' Oltrepò Mantovano, conseguenza inevitabile del trattato, potrebbe far nascere collisioni dannose ; la Toscana forse potrebbe sopportare più a lungo una condizione incerta, ma anche colà le mène dei retrivi secondate dai preti produrrebbero forse gravi perturbazioni. Il Congresso adunque è richiesto dagli stessi interessi dell' Italia. Ciò ammesso, l' Inghilterra deve parteciparvi e per decoro suo e pel bene nostro.   L' Austria non contrasterà il suo intervento, e ammetterà le sue riserve, quando si stabilisca che nel medesimo non abbia a farsi parola delle provincie sulle quali conserva il suo impero.   E duro l' avere a rinunziare ad alzare la voce a favore dell' infelice Venezia ; eppure è forza il far tacere le più vive simpatie per non sacrificare il possibile al desiderabile.

L' Austria, rassicurata sul Veneto, dovrà acconsentire alla massima inglese, che si abbia a rispettare i voti degl' Italiani.   Per dare a questa forma più diplomatica, basterebbe il dire che le Potenze s' impegnano a non imporre colle armi una forma qualunque di governo ai popoli dell' Italia centrale. Questo è il principio di non intervento già proclamato dall' Imperatore nei suoi scritti e nei suoi discorsi.   Propugnato dalla Francia e dall' Inghilterra e fors' anche dalla Russia, sarà subito dall' Austria ed accettato dalla Prussia.

Passando quindi alla costituzione del Congresso, non esito a pronunziarmi per l'esclusione delle

Potenze minori. Se si trattasse solo dei Ducati e della Toscana, il loro intervento sarebbe giovevole; ma siccome la questione la più ardua e dirò pure la più importante è quella delle Romagne, temerei che il Papa avesse a trovare nella Spagna e nel Portogallo ardenti difensori.

Il Congresso riunito, la condotta dell' Inghilterra non può essere dubbia. Proporrebbe dapprima che i voti dei popoli legalmente espressi ricevessero la sanzione dell' Europa. Questa proposta essendo rigettata, proporrebbe che i popoli venissero interrogati pel mezzo del suffragio universale, da constatarsi dai rappresentanti del Congresso. Questa proposta troverebbe appoggio nella Francia, e sarebbe probabilmente accettata.

Quando nol fosse, l' Inghilterra dovrebbe entrare in una fase negativa e contrastare le proposte dell' Austria ed anche quelle della Francia. Il Duca di Modena essendo da tutti, non esclusi i suoi congiunti, abbandonato, non si avrà a combattere che la ristaurazione della Casa di Lorena in Toscana, l' installazione della Duchessa di Parma a Modena, ed il ristabilimento del dominio papale nelle Romagne.

Queste determinazioni si possono combattere non solo in virtù dei diritti dei popoli, ma altresì e più efficacemente ancora nell' interesse del principio monarchico, e delle idee d'ordine e di conservazione. Se si vuole che la rivoluzione ora schiacciata non

ritorni minacciosa e potente, non bisogna porla a
fronte di Governi deboli, senza radici, senza forze nè
fisiche nè morali; se si vuole che i troni sieno
rispettati, conviene non farvi sedere Principi disprez-
zati e disprezzabili, il di cui solo nome è in contrasto
irritante col sentimento ora dominante in Italia, il
sentimento nazionale. Ritorni il Granduca o suo
figlio a Firenze; ed in men di un mese la Toscana
sarà il quartier generale di Mazzini e della rivoluzione
militante. Forse si dirà che la Duchessa di Parma è
donna forte e non disprezzata. Quando ciò fosse
vero, non si potrebbero cancellare le memorie del
padre cotanto odiose, ed ispirare fiducia nel figlio.
D'altronde quel sistema dei compensi che se vorrebbe
applicare a favore di questo ramo borbonico, è in
urto diretto coi sentimenti e le idee che dominano ora
in Europa. I Modanesi sarebbero feriti nella loro
dignità, quando si vedessero assegnare in guisa di
douaire alla vedova dello scellerato Duchino di
Parma. Meglio per loro la ristaurazione dell' antico
sovrano. In quel caso sarebbero vittima di un falso
principio; ma non sarebbero trattati come un branco
di pecore, di cui si dispone per fare accetare da una
delle parti contraenti condizioni da lei riputate
onerose.

Il Trattato di Vienna ha molte parti odiose; pure
è men odiabile di quel di Campoformio.

Rispetto alle Romagne sarà facile all' Inghilterra il

far respingere l'idea delle riforme papali. Accettandola, si fa peggio che una cosa odiosa, si fa una cosa ridicola. Non è necessario di essere un gran statista nè gran teologo per rimanere convinti che il Papa non solo non vuole, ma non può acconsentire a serie riforme. Finchè sarà Papa e Re, dovrà in coscienza impiegare le forze del Re per fare rispettare i decreti del Pontefice. La separazione dei due poteri non è possibile. Il Papa non può acconsentire nè alla libertà dell' insegnamento, nè alla libertà dei culti, nè alla libertà della stampa. Non può tollerare le libertà municipali, salvochè per queste s'intenda la facoltà di regolare a beneplacito dei Municipi le strade consortili ed i lastricati delle strade. Il Papa, come Papa, subirà più facilmente la perdita di una provincia, che non la promulgazione nei suoi Stati del Codice civile napoleonico. La ristaurazione papale deve impedirsi ad ogni costo; è questione non solo italiana, ma d'interesse europeo. Importa a noi, ma importa pure all' Inghilterra, alla Prussia, alla Russia stessa, a tutti i paesi ove si vuole lo sviluppo della civiltà, il quale richiede come condizione essenziale la separazione assoluta dei due poteri. Se il Papa conseguisse una vittoria in Italia, la tracotanza e l'orgoglio dei Cullen e dei McHale crescerebbe a dismisura, e l'Europa sarebbe minacciata in non lontano avvenire dal pericolo di lotte religiose analoghe a quelle dei secoli scorsi. Si ceda su tutto anzichè sacrificare le

Romagne.   La lor causa, lo ripeto, è la causa della civiltà.

Quando l'Inghilterra riesca ad allontanare le proposte austro-franche, torni a mettere in campo le primitive sue, ed ove non prevalgano, proponga l'unione immediata di Parma e Carrara al Piemonte e lo stabilimento di un Governo provvisorio, ma fortemente costituito, che riunisca sotto di sè Firenze, Modena e Bologna.

Ecco il mio parere, ve lo do per quel che vale. Lontano dagli affari, con poche relazioni coi Ministri, ignoro forse molte cose che modificare potrebbero la mia opinione.   Tuttavia giudicando la questione dell'Italia centrale dai dati che sono in certo modo acquistati alla storia, porto ferma opinione che, ove l'Inghilterra seguisse la via de me tracciata, riuscirebbe nell'intento di assicurare le sorti dell'Italia centrale con utile nostro e gloria sua.

Addio, carissimo amico; proseguite a perorare la nostra causa presso la nobile nazione inglese, ed i vostri sforzi non rimarranno sterili.   Ripeto ora quel che dicevo in febbraio alla Camera ed all'Italia: Gli uomini di Stato, che hanno onorata la loro carriera col compiere l'emancipazione dei neri, non vorranno condannare l'Italia ad eterno servaggio.

Vostro affezionatissimo amico

" C. Cavour."

THE END.

INDEX.

z

z2

16